IN THE SHADOW OF THE
PYRENEES
THE FREEDOM TRAIL TO SPAIN

A compelling portrait of life, love, courage, and retribution.

Inspired by true events in WWII France

KATHRYN GAUCI

First published in 2023 by Ebony Publishing

ISBN: 9798863436289

This book is dedicated to the villagers of the Donezan region
in the department of Ariège, in south-western France,
and to the bravery of all those men and women who risked
their lives during World War II helping escapees cross
the Pyrenees into Spain in pursuit of freedom.

To this day, many remain nameless,
but their courage and selflessness lives on.

"A man of character finds a special attractiveness in difficulty, since it is only by coming to grips with difficulty that he can realise his potentialities."

—Charles de Gaulle

CONTENTS

MAJOR ESCAPE ROUTES
THROUGH OCCUPIED FRANCE

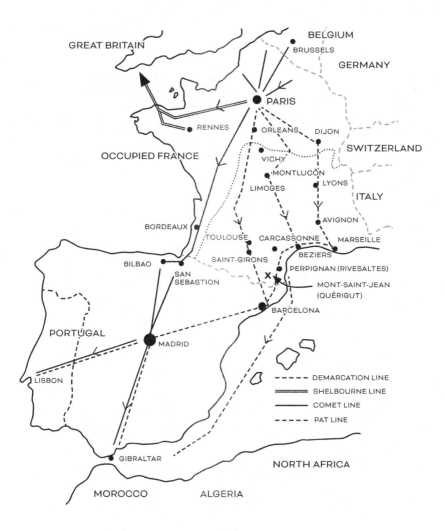

CHAPTER 1

The Schoolteacher, Armand Joubert, Remembers

I LEFT MONT-SAINT-JEAN forty years ago and never expected to return. The war had finally ended, the Germans had been defeated, and we basked in glory for a while, but the war had left a wound on our hearts that would take years to fade. For me, that wound was still there, as large and as painful as it ever was, and despite being treated by the best physicians and psychoanalysts in Paris, I could not rid myself of it. As the years passed, I learned to live with it. Some days, I hardly noticed it and got on with my life as best as I could. On other days, it consumed me and I took to my bed with the heavy curtains drawn, plunging the room into almost total darkness. On those days, I refused to eat and had no desire to see friends. Not that I had many friends anyway. Most had drifted away over the years, finding me too hard to be with.

The journey from Paris to the Ariège region bordering the Pyrenees had filled me with utter dread, and I found myself making numerous stops for a coffee or something stronger in one of those non-descript roadside cafés along the main highways to the south. Each time I stopped, I reread the letter sent to me by the estate agent and wondered if I was doing the right thing.

At one point, somewhere near Carcassonne, I noticed a winery that had a large sign at the entrance reading *OUVERT*. I made a sharp turn through a decorative set of wrought-iron gates, each displaying a golden bunch of grapes and trailing vines in the centre, drove along the driveway bordered by rosebushes, and pulled up outside an elegant winery with a fine restaurant. I sat at a table overlooking the peaceful, undulating vineyards, perused the menu, and ordered a fish dish accompanied by a local wine. While I waited for the food, I asked the waiter if I could use the telephone. He pointed to a glass booth next to a display of white wine. I took out the estate agent's card and started to dial his number. I had decided I was not going to go through with the sale after all. It had been a silly idea to put the house on the market in the first place and he should remove it immediately. I would pay him for his time and that would be that. When I died, it could go to one of those distant cousins I hadn't heard from in years. What did I care? I didn't need the money anyway.

The telephone rang and a woman's voice answered. *'Bonjour.* This is Monsieur Clement's secretary. He is out of the office at the moment, but if you'd like to give me your details, he will return your call as soon as possible.' I slammed the phone back down on the receiver. Something stopped me. I don't know what it was. Nerves — or fate perhaps. That same fate I felt when I decided to put house on the market in the first place just over three years ago.

I can't remember where the idea to sell the house came from. Maybe it was the psychiatrist; he was always telling me to move on with my life. Yes, that's right; now that I think about it, it *was* his idea. He knew the village held too many bad memories and suggested that, as I would never return, I should sell it, invest some of the money, and probably take a holiday where I could meet people and enjoy myself. He even suggested I might meet a "nice" woman and fall in love again. What a fool I had been to listen to him. If only things were that simple.

I returned to my seat and thought about my predicament while feasting on my fish and salad. It would be quite late when I reached the village. I'd pre-booked a room at the only *hôtel* there, but as it was out of season, it was doubtful that the restaurant would be open in the evening, which was why I was going to enjoy this meal while I could. I cut a sliver of fish and popped it into my mouth. The flavour of the fish, together with the delicate sauce of capers and roasted peppers topped with toasted pinenuts, exploded in my mouth. This might have been a small vineyard, but it was in the region of Languedoc-Roussillon and Midi-Pyrénées — a land well-known for its unique cuisine, a land where France and Spain had merged over the centuries in more ways than one — and the food was exceptional.

I closed my eyes and savoured the taste. The waiter noted my closed eyes and came to see if everything was alright.

'Is everything to your satisfaction, monsieur?' he asked.

'*Parfait,*' I replied. 'The fish is delicious.'

He looked quite relieved. 'It was caught this morning — fresh from Collioure.'

At the mention of Collioure, I thought of Colette. It was where we'd spent our honeymoon. A surge of emotions ran through my body. I was raking up the past once more.

The waiter took my plate away and brought me a dessert of *crème catalane.* When I tapped my spoon on the burnt topping, it released a subtle aroma of cinnamon and lemon zest. That too stirred up emotions. Colette used to prepare it on special feast days. In my mind, I saw her presenting it to us as if it was the grandest desert cooked by Escoffier himself. My dearest, sweet Colette, the love of my life, until — until... My head started to ache and I looked towards the telephone booth again, urged on by fear to make that call.

Before I knew it, the waiter was back again. 'Monsieur, are you quite sure you're alright? You look pale. Can I get you a drink? A muscat perhaps — on the house.'

'I'm fine, thank you. It's been a long day. Please give me the bill and I will be on my way. I still have quite a way to go and I'm late enough as it is.'

As I paid my bill, the waiter asked where I was headed.

'Mont-Saint-Jean. It's a small village in the Donezan, not too far from the Spanish border. You probably don't know it. It's a rather isolated little village — off the beaten track.'

The waiter smiled. 'Isn't it one of those places where people go hiking and skiing?'

'That's right. Have you been?'

'No. I'm afraid not. I've been to Andorra and Barcelona, but always via the main highway. I can't ski and I'm certainly not a hiker so it doesn't hold any appeal for me.' I paid my bill and turned to leave. 'Ah, I remember where I heard the name of the village before,' the waiter continued. 'There was a rumour about the place after the war. Weren't there a few villagers who were executed by the Germans?'

His words caught me off guard. 'I don't know what you mean.'

'Something took place — something unsavoury — to do with the Germans — and the villagers kept quiet.' He gave a shrug. 'It was such a long time ago. I can't recall anything else, and besides, you know what people are like. They love to gossip.'

'Where did you hear this story?' I asked. I realised my voice sounded sharp.

'Steady on,' the waiter said, his palms upwards towards me in a calming gesture. 'I wasn't even born then. From what my father told me, after the Germans left, there were lots of rumours about everyone; it was hard to tell truth from fiction. Maybe I got the wrong village.'

'Who was your father?' I asked. 'Was he from the area?' Again, I knew I sounded more interested than I should and apologised. 'I'm sorry. As I said, it's been a long day. I will bid you a good evening and thank you once again for the wonderful food. *Bonsoir.*'

The man watched me leave. Just as I was about to walk out of the door, he called out. 'My father belonged to the maquis. He hid in those mountains. Whether the story was true or not, I don't know. He died several years ago.'

I stopped in my tracks and spun around. 'I'm sorry for your loss. What was his name?'

'Garcia Mendez. He was a refugee — from Madrid. He came here during the days of the Retirada.'

My heart skipped a beat. Garcia Mendez, the right-hand man of don Manuel de Caballero, head of one of the most important Spanish maquis groups in the Pyrenees. I bid the man a good evening and left. I should have listened to my heart. It had been a bad idea to come back.

4

I felt rather light-headed, but somehow managed to pull myself together and drive on, following the River Aude through the town of Quillan towards the mountains. From there, the road narrowed and it wasn't long before I reached the Gorges de Saint-Georges, a torturous drive that meandered through the bottom of a steep canyon formed by the river. On a good day, the views are stunning: massive, sheer rocky walls that appear to rise out of the earth, trapping pockets of sunlight that highlight the granite rocks in dramatic textural variations of colours from the palest greys to molten red and gold. Now the light was fading fast, throwing up long, dark shadows which concealed an abundance of caves and narrow fissures that overflowed with water in the spring from the melting snow. Thankfully, I encountered few vehicles, which was a good job as the road was barely wide enough for more than one vehicle at a time. On two occasions, I was forced to squeeze alongside a ridge while a tractor and a truck carrying logs passed by, narrowly missing my car by a few centimetres. Falling rocks were a constant hazard too, especially after heavy rain and snowfall.

A few kilometres past the gorge, the road started to climb upwards into the mountains and the landscape changed again, this time becoming more expansive and densely forested. I spotted a few deer grazing in the bushes at the side of the road. They pricked up their ears when they heard the car but made no attempt to run away. At one time, the sight of a deer would have filled me with delight and I would have raised my hunting rifle in readiness for a kill. Those were the days when a deer meant the difference between hunger and a good meal. Thankfully those days were long gone.

Ten minutes later, I passed the remains of the eleventh-century Château d'Usson, once an impregnable fortress and the property of the Marquis d'Usson until the French Revolution, and I knew I'd almost reached my destination. At this point, the road became much steeper until it reached the nearby village of Rouze. After a few more villages and hamlets, I finally reached my destination — Mont-Saint-Jean. It was the largest village in the area and stood at the top of a hill dominated by the ruins of another eleventh-century. Around the base of the château were a cluster of stone houses, some of which had wonderful views of the valley below and a vast mountain range that divided the Donezan — the eastern part of the department of Ariège — from the Pyrénées-Orientales.

My heart pounded in my chest and my throat constricted as I rounded the last bend into the village. In fact my throat constricted so much that I found it hard to breathe and wound down the window to get some air. I always knew returning would not be easy for a multitude of reasons, but this part was the worst. For it was here, in the cemetery at the bend that leads to the village, that Colette was buried. My eyes filled with tears. I would give anything to undo the past, to right my wrongs, but we humans are not infallible — least of all me, the schoolmaster of Mont-Saint-Jean — the man everyone looked up to.

It turned out that I was the only guest that night at the Hôtel Bellevue. The new owners, a middle-aged man and his wife from Normandy, had bought the hôtel three years earlier. The man's wife had retired to bed early, leaving her husband to look after me. He took my details and noted down my Parisian address. He had no idea I was from the area and most likely knew the village better than I did now, and I chose to leave it that way.

'How long will you be with us, monsieur?' he asked. 'I have you down for two nights. Maybe you might decide to stay longer — explore the region perhaps. There are some interesting places around here, you know.'

He then went on to tell me that a family would be arriving in the morning. Apart from that, he gave me the impression that business was slow. One look around the place and I could see why. The dark brown paint was flaking in places, and for the most part had lost its gloss, the chairs, tables and lighting were rather shabby and dated, and the floor, mostly wooden but with an occasional carpet to add a touch of warmth, was uneven and creaky, as if it would give way at any moment. It certainly had none of the elegance and sparkle that the original owners had endeavoured to give it when they built it in the early 1930s. I recalled the day it opened. What a fanfare! The sight of such a beautiful hôtel in a village like this was a rarity at the time. We all thought the owners, Madame and Monsieur Frenay, were slightly mad. Surely they would go broke after the first year? After all, Mont-Saint-Jean was an agricultural village, like all the others in the Donezan. The villagers were poor and much of their lives were spent in the fields. What they didn't produce, they swapped at the markets as far away as Quillan, Foix, or Formiguères. The roads were unpaved and the streets churned into mud by carts pulled by muscular oxen, and by sheep and milking cattle which were herded through the streets on a daily basis. One got used to the smell of animal excreta, which was worse during the long hot summers.

None of this bothered Madam and Monsieur Frenay. They were visionaries. They could see the area would expand due to the sporting lives of the young set with money from towns and cities further afield and began catering for skiers in the winter and hikers in the summer. The grand opening was the most anticipated event on the local calendar. Two bands were hired to play: a jazz band from Toulouse for the townspeople and a local band from Axat with violinists and accordions favoured by the villagers. It was advertised in all the newspapers from Perpignan to Toulouse and Ax-les-Thermes, and without a doubt, it was a resounding success and put Mont-Saint-Jean on the map.

As the hôtel manager showed me to my room, all that seemed a distant memory — the laughter, the hopes and dreams — all gone. Relegated to another age, the one before the world came crashing down on us.

I woke up early the next day and mentally prepared myself as best as I could for the task of meeting the estate agent at the house. After a breakfast of crusty fresh bread, a croissant, and a bowl of fresh fruit, I left the hôtel and headed in the direction of the old house. It was the moment I dreaded. It was also highly likely that someone would recognise me, and I didn't know how I would cope if that happened. I glanced up and down the street. A few people were going about their business and as I didn't recognise them, I left for my rendezvous, which took me past the church and the village fountain, towards a country lane at the edge of the village. I passed a couple of old houses with large vegetable gardens and orchards, and two or three new houses that had obviously been built in the last few years. From the look of their closed shutters and locked gates, I assumed they were owned by people from out of the area.

My footsteps crunched loudly on the stony pathway and my heart beat wildly. With each breath, I inhaled the fragrance of the late autumn flowers, the resin of the pine trees, and the earth itself, filled with the richness of fallen leaves. From somewhere in the dark recesses of my mind, I heard familiar voices and my eyes welled up with tears. They laughed and called out to me in the respectful manner I was used to as a schoolteacher, especially the voices of the children: Michel, who excelled at algebra; Antoine, who loved Napoleon; Jean-Louis, whose father was the grocer and who brought us toffees and nougat; Marcel, who loved to play pranks on everyone and was made to stand in the corner for being a chatterbox or for being naughty. One of the saddest, yet smartest boys was Arnold, who was born with a deformity. His spine was bent and his spindly legs wouldn't carry him, but he wanted to study so badly that the villagers all collected money and we bought him a brand spanking new wheelchair which he was immensely proud of. And there were the girls too. Aimee, a quiet girl with long dark curls who brought her doll to school with her; Alice, a pretty girl who had a pleasant and flirtatious nature that would one day get her into trouble; and sweet Marie, who was so shy she stuttered every time she had to recite something.

I was soon brought back to reality when I rounded the corner and saw the old house nestled among an overgrown garden. I stood by the wooden gate where the estate agent had erected a large sign saying "FOR SALE" and stared at it for a few minutes, fighting back a surge of emotions that threatened to unnerve me again. After all this time, I wasn't sure what to expect. It had crossed my mind that it would be in such bad condition that it needed to be demolished, but that was not so. It was as I remembered it when I left: a two-story house with three bedrooms on the upper floor, considered to be quite bourgeoise for a farming village at the time it was built, and with picturesque views of the valley and the forest from every window. The once bright blue shutters were still in place, except that now there was hardly any colour at all, just a few patches of drab, pale grey-blue on the otherwise exposed wood that had darkened over the years. Thankfully the grey slate roof was mostly intact, and any loose slates could be fixed quite easily.

I pushed the gate open and walked along the garden path, overgrown with long grass speckled with delicate white and pink wildflowers. The outside wall at the front of the house was completely covered by a rambling red rose that was clearly in need of a good pruning, as was everything else in the garden, the fruit trees especially. My hand shook as I fumbled to unlock the door. It was several minutes until I finally plucked up the courage to enter. Inside, it was dark with a powerful odour of damp through years of neglect. I walked from one empty room to another, reliving the place as I had once known it: the kitchen, where we once entertained so many friends; the parlour, which had held my library of books; the bedroom, where Colette and I made love and where she'd given birth to our only child, Justine; and underneath the stairs, the secret hiding space where we'd hidden so many people fleeing across the Pyrenees. To those who didn't know, it looked just like a timber wall with old coat hooks. Even to this day, I doubt anyone would know the real purpose it served.

I opened the shutters and windows to let in the light and fresh air, hoping to alleviate the musty odour. In the late autumn light, I realised how dated the decor now looked. Each wall was partially clad in vertical wooden boards which had been stained a dark mahogany, and the rest of the wall was covered in pin-striped wallpaper in shades of green, cream, and white. At the time Colette and I thought it tasteful, but by today's standards, it looked ghastly. The new owners would certainly need to renovate and that would be costly. I hoped they weren't the type to hassle about the price because I was in far too much of a delicate mood to argue. The enormity of what I was doing was sinking in and I had heart palpitations. I needed some fresh air before Monsieur Clement arrived. I looked at my watch. He was due here in fifteen minutes, but these estate agents can often be eager, annoying people and I didn't want

9

him to catch me feeling like this. I went outside and sat on old garden seat to calm myself.

As I sat there, it struck me just how much the terrain had changed. This region had always been poor, and for generations the villagers eked out a living through agriculture. Large tracts of the countryside, particularly the mountainsides, were tiered with low stone walls that allowed for the planting of vegetables, keeping beehives, or rearing chickens and the occasional pig. Larger animals like sheep, cows and horses usually grazed higher up in the mountain pastures and were only brought back to their stables during the late autumn and winter. Now, it was clear that nature had reclaimed the land. Where once I'd had a perfect vista of La Pla or Mijanès, all I could see now were fields interspersed with swathes of woodland. Even behind the house — where my own garden had once been tiered to grow potatoes, cabbages, beans, and beets — trees and shrubs had taken over and the property appeared in danger of being swallowed up by the forest. Life on the land was difficult, and the younger generation no longer wanted such hardships. They preferred to find work in the bigger towns and cities. It saddened me deeply to think that these villages were slowly becoming a shell of their former selves. The old life had gone. I too was part of that exodus, but for other reasons.

I listened to the twitter of birds for a while — finches that darted in and out of the shrubs towards the mountain ash covered with clusters of showy, bright orange berries — and savoured the warmth of the sun on my cheeks. A gentle breeze blowing from the south rustled the leaves in the apple trees. The ground surrounding them appeared to have recently been churned up and fallen apples lay scattered here and there. Wild boar! They were just as prevalent today as they were when I lived there. How this new terrain suited them. They could disappear into the woods and reappear when no one was about. Only a hunter would be able to locate them easily. I had never been a hunter, until my good friend Théo taught me. We often went hunting together. At first I recoiled at the thought of harming an innocent animal, but as the war dragged on and food became scare, I grew to appreciate a hunter's skill and I took pride at putting food on the table. It always cheered Colette up, especially when we had more and more mouths to feed.

Dr Théo Berdu lived in the village, not far from the once massive château, of which only part of the tower that used to be a dungeon now remains. The château, a brooding mass of crumbling rocks, served to remind us of just how bloody the region once was. From the upper bedroom, I could still catch a glimpse of the few remaining walls of the tower. At the thought of Dr Berdu, I became overwhelmed with such great sadness that I broke out in a sweat and wiped my brow with my handkerchief. He had been my greatest friend, a man I trusted like a brother. That was a long time ago, and yet it felt like yesterday. How complicated the human brain is. We want to remember the good times and not the bad, but life isn't like that. After the war, there were many like me whose brains became scrambled: reality and imagination jumbled together. Trauma they called it. All I know is that there were many days when I wished I was dead. Now I am here again, slap bang in the middle of where my "trauma" began.

I saw a neatly dressed man in a dark suit striding jauntily towards the house. It was the estate agent. When he reached the gate he waved and called out. 'Monsieur Joubert, bonjour — I am so pleased that you could make it after all.' He shook my hand firmly and gave me a warm smile.

'Where are the clients?' I asked. 'The potential buyers — I thought they'd be with you.'

'They're running a little late. It will give us time to go through a few things before they arrive.'

We went into the house and discussed a few problems that he thought might be an issue, but he told me the buyers seemed like nice people and he was sure any problems could be dealt with without much fuss. When I asked why it had taken so long to find a buyer, he replied that the area was only just being discovered by outsiders and the locals wanted to keep their own houses in the family. 'The buyers are foreigners,' he said.

I was someone taken aback that he hadn't mentioned this before.

11

'Yes. They live in New York. They've been to the area a couple of times and fell in love with it. They have three young children so could not afford to buy before.'

'I see,' I replied rather dumbly. 'But the place is in need of modernizing, and there's the matter of the damp walls. That won't be cheap to fix. Have they actually seen the place?'

'They've seen the brochure so they have a good idea of what they're buying.'

My heart sank. I wasn't as optimistic as the estate agent. He saw my face and gave me one of his reassuring smiles. 'Don't worry. Just leave it to me.'

At that moment we heard the voices of children and a woman's voice call out. 'Be careful. You might fall and hurt yourself.'

We peered out of a bedroom window on the first floor and saw a couple enter through the gate. Ahead of them, running towards the house and laughing merrily, were three children: a boy in his early teens, a girl who looked about ten or eleven, and a smaller girl who appeared not much older than six or seven.

'They're here,' the estate agent said. 'We'd better go and greet them.'

The man shook hands. 'I am Michael Goldman,' he said, in English, and then introduced his first two children, the older boy, David, and the middle daughter, Rachel. His wife came up behind him holding their youngest daughter's hand. 'This is my wife, Sarah.'

Sarah extended her hand and quickly turned to her small daughter, who was hiding her face in her mother's dress. 'And this little one is Ellie,' she said in perfect French while gently stroking her daughter's head. 'Say hello to the gentlemen, Ellie.'

The young girl coyly said bonjour. At that moment, I felt a lump rise in my throat and was so overcome with emotion, I couldn't speak. I looked from mother to daughter and thought I was imagining things. The striking dark-haired woman who stood in front of me looked exactly like a woman I had known all those years ago — Hélène, the beautiful Jewish lady who had arrived one day out of the blue; Hélène, the woman who still haunted my dreams all these years later; Hélène, the woman

12

who had destroyed my life. The young girl, Ellie, was much fairer, but there was no getting away from it, she too reminded me of the Hélène I once knew. The same features, the same dark brown eyes.

I felt my legs give way and would have collapsed if Michael Goldman had not caught me in time. They sat me on the seat where I had previously sat, causing me great embarrassment.

'Are you alright, monsieur?' Sarah asked. 'You look quite pale.'

There it was again — that same voice — *my* Hélène's voice. The Goldman children had suddenly gone very quiet and were staring at me with quizzical faces. 'Old age catching up with me I'm afraid.' I forced a smile. 'Tell me, Madame Goldman, where did you learn to speak French?'

Sarah laughed. 'Oh, that's a long story. I won't bore you with that now.' She turned to the estate agent and said that they could come back again when I felt better.

'I'll be fine,' I replied. 'Please don't fuss. Let's proceed with the inspection, shall we?'

CHAPTER 2

Mont-Saint-Jean, Autumn 1940

ARMAND JOUBERT WAS teaching a class when he caught a glimpse of a young man in his early twenties approaching the school on a bicycle. He propped it against the wall and hurriedly entered the building. Minutes later, Maria, the only other teacher in the school, who taught the girls in the room on the opposite side of the hallway, entered his classroom, handed him a note without uttering a word, and walked out again, closing the door quietly behind her. The boys momentarily looked up from their school work, curious to see what it was. Armand nonchalantly slipped the note in his pocket, looked at them sternly over the top of his glasses, and told them to get on with their work.

'Hurry up,' he said to them. 'Anyone who doesn't finish will have to stay behind, and you don't want that, do you?'

'No, Monsieur Joubert,' they called out in unison, a few sniggering and cheekily exchanging glances with each other.

He watched the man cycle away towards the village and then glanced at the large round clock on the wall. Classes finished in ten minutes. He would wait until the boys had gone before he looked at the note, but already he had an idea of what it would contain. At four o'clock, the bell rang, and the boys, eager to leave, closed their exercise books and handed them to him for marking. Minutes later, the boys and girls could be seen heading towards the village square, where they congregated in groups for a while, laughing and chatting with each other before going home. The weather was too cold for them to stay outdoors and play, and a snowstorm was predicted that night. Only Arnold, the boy who had been born with a deformity and who came to school in his wheelchair

14

was left behind, but it wasn't for long. His mother came to pick him up, pulled up the collar of his heavy coat, wrapped a thick warm scarf round his neck, and gave him a kiss on the cheek as she did every day without fail when she dropped him off and picked him up.

Armand stood by the wood heater and took the note out of his pocket. In code, it read — *another parcel will arrive at midnight.* He opened the door of the heater, threw it inside, and watched it burn. Maria knocked on the door before entering.

'Everything alright, Armand?' she asked. 'Henri seemed anxious that you got the message straight away.'

'Everything's fine,' he replied.

Maria had a good idea what was going on, but she was a loyal woman, especially to Armand, who was not only her friend and fellow teacher, but the headmaster of the school too, and she was sensible enough never to pry. Nor did she want to. She was a spinster in her late forties and she had a soft spot for Armand. Whatever he was up to, she knew it was for a good reason. She bid him a good evening and departed, leaving him to contemplate Henri's message.

The weather was worsening; a reef of rolling dark clouds were approaching over the mountaintops and it wouldn't be long before the countryside would be cloaked in a deep layer of snow making their work a lot harder. He put another log on the fire and settled back down at his desk to mark the boys' exercise books. It had been a history lesson, but as all classes were in French, some of the students were still not up to scratch and he had to make a special effort with them. Most of them went back to a home where the main language was still Occitan, especially if there were grandparents living in the house. In some cases it was Catalan too. Now the French government decreed that only French would be used in schools. The country must remain united if it was to become a modern nation. As far as they were concerned, all these local languages were a problem and should not to be encouraged.

Armand didn't have a problem with French being spoken at school. After all, it was essential for everyone to learn the French language if they wanted to get on, especially if they moved away to the bigger towns and cities, but he was sensitive enough not to want the local language and dialects to die out altogether. To his way of thinking, all these languages made for a rich heritage which the people should be proud of. The problem became worse with the German occupation. Vichy-appointed inspectors kept a close eye on the schools to make sure everyone conformed, and occasionally he had to resort to giving a few boys a whack with his cane if he heard them speaking in Occitan. The last thing he wanted was to be reported to the officials for not following rules. That would see both him and Maria lose their jobs, and it would also mean he was not as free to move about doing his "secret" work, which occupied his time and thoughts far more than teaching children.

While he marked the boys' work, he put on the radio and tuned it to a classical music station rather than listen to Vichy propaganda. A learned man, fluent in English, Spanish, Catalan, and Occitan, he loved nothing better to read or listen to classical music. Besides the French composers, his favourites happened to be Beethoven and Bach, although he did enjoy Chopin and Tchaikovsky. He also enjoyed Mendelssohn and Mahler too. Mahler's Fifth Symphony, in particular, often reduced him to tears. Mahler was Jewish — as was Mendelssohn — and it was rare to hear them on the radio these days. Instead, Colette, who was an excellent pianist, played those for him at home.

His thoughts drifted to what would take place later on this evening. Another parcel would be arriving. A parcel, or package, another term he and his associates used, meant a person — someone in hiding — most likely heading to Spain, although it could be someone coming *from* Spain. Who would it be this time? How many? Where had they come from? He wondered what state of mind and physical condition they would be in. Each parcel presented a problem. He prayed it wouldn't be a woman with a small child. They were always the most difficult. How life had changed in the past few years. Those carefree days dancing to jazz and swing bands and the music of Trenet at the Hôtel Bellevue on a Saturday night were now replaced by songs deemed politically correct by the Germans and their Vichy collaborators. He realised just how much he too had changed.

Armand had always taken an interest in politics but was never fuelled with the same fervour and energy as some of his friends. As long as things didn't affect him adversely, he was content to sit on the sideline and listen to their heated debates with interest. As schoolteacher and headmaster of the largest village school in the Donezan, even if the students did not number more than forty, he was aware that he should appear neutral in the interests of his profession. A schoolteacher who subscribes to certain ideologies, especially Communism or radical socialism, was not a good idea. It was better to keep his thoughts to himself and let others argue their points. Sometimes he was criticised for this.

'Speak your mind, Joubert,' someone would say.

'Tell us what you really think,' another said.

That all changed one day when his friend Dr Berdu arrived at his house early one morning and asked if he would accompany him to the small frontier town of Le Perthus. He recalled the date as if it was yesterday — the first week in February, 1939. The weather was terrible. All week there had been violent storms and the roads were treacherous.

Colette answered the door. 'Théo! What brings you here so early in the morning? Come in quickly before you catch your death of cold.'

'I need to speak with Armand. It's urgent.'

'He's still in bed. Go into the kitchen and pour yourself some coffee while I fetch him.'

Armand was fast asleep when Colette shook him and said they had a visitor. He looked at the clock. It was six o'clock. 'What on earth does he want at this time of the morning? Tell him I'll be down in a minute.'

Colette returned to the kitchen, aware that the doctor was far away in his thoughts. When Armand entered the room, he knew something serious had taken place and wondered if a close relative had died.

'I want you to pack a bag and come away with me for a few days. I need your help,' Dr Berdu said.

'But the school, I have classes.'

'Joubert, this is serious. I wouldn't be here if it wasn't. You can get Maria to teach your class.'

17

Dr Berdu rarely called Armand by his surname, so whatever it was, it had to be bad. 'Théo, at least tell me what this all about.'

'You have a basic knowledge of biology and the human body. I need you to help me.'

Colette looked from one to another. 'He isn't a doctor, Théo.'

Théo Berdu let out a deep sigh. 'If there was anyone else I could call on, I would. The truth is, I need all the help I can get — reliable help.' He paused for a moment. 'I'm going to help the Republicans, who, at this very minute, are trying to cross the frontier into France and desperately need our help. They are dying in their hundreds as we speak — men, women, and children — the young, the old, and the wounded. As my aide, I will tell you what to do; you'll be fine.'

Colette looked alarmed. 'There's a difference between studying human biology in books and medically treating someone. What if you make a mistake and someone dies? Can't you take Babette? At least she knows more about medical procedures.'

Armand saw the look of desperation on his friend's face.

'No. Babette will stay here in case there's an emergency. The truth is, Armand, I want you to see for yourself what's taking place. I can assure you that after this, you will no longer be a fence-sitter.'

Armand's face reddened. 'Théo's right, Colette. I must go and help. Please let Maria know I'll be gone for...'

'A few days at least,' Dr Berdu said. 'Maybe a week.'

There was little more to be said. Armand packed a bag, kissed his wife goodbye, and drove away with the doctor.

The car headed south out of Mont-Saint-Jean through the snow-laden Col des Hares with its hairpin bends, across the plateau of Capcir, towards Formiguères and the citadel of Mont-Louis. Capcir is on a plateau, averaging 1,500 metres above sea level, and on a good day, the views towards the Pyrenees were spectacular, but on that particular morning, the blizzard was so bad, they could barely see the road. Capcir was certainly living up to its nickname of little Siberia.

As they drove, Dr Berdu filled Armand in on the situation at the frontier. It was common knowledge that the Spanish Civil War was reaching an end. People had been fleeing across the border into France for a while, but since the fall of Barcelona, it had worsened. He'd read about it in the newspapers and listened to it on the news, and his heart went out to all those who were forced to flee. In the name of freedom, for the Republicans, it had become a matter of life and death. Théo told Armand it was far worse than anyone could imagine, but he could tell Armand still thought he was being rather dramatic. He brought the car to a skidding halt and looked him straight in the eyes.

'Armand, if you took your nose out of your books for a while, you might understand what is *really* going on around you. What is taking place on our doorstep is inhumane.' His eyes were moist with tears. 'What you are about to see, you will not read in the newspapers. You are about to witness the end of democracy as we know it. You don't have to be a Communist to have empathy with the Republicans, you know. After all, not every Republican is a Communist. These people just wanted a better life — like you and I.'

Théo Berdu was not the kind of man to exaggerate. He was usually a quiet, kind, controlled sort of person and now he was angry — very angry. Most of all, he was disillusioned. Armand said nothing, allowing his friend to let off steam. Dr Berdu started the car and they continued on again. He'd made his point. As they skirted the roads towards Le Perthus, French military vehicles and ambulances passed by, all driving at a terrifying speed through snowdrifts and thick mists of sleet and snow that blocked out everything. Twice, they almost plummeted to their deaths when the car swerved around a hairpin bend to miss an ambulance or a vehicle that had got stuck in the snow. Nearing Le Perthus, the roads became jammed with trucks, cars, and carts pulled by horses, oxen, and donkeys. People wearing heavy coats or wrapped in sodden blankets dragging battered suitcases and bundles filled with whatever possessions they could carry huddled together to protect themselves from the harsh weather. Many carried children, old people, and the wounded, slipping and slithering on the terrible roads. In some cases, they emerged out of the mountains along donkey tracks — places where it was impossible for vehicles of any sort to go. Only animals could traverse such terrain filled with forests and dense undergrowth, but these people were desperate and there was no other option available to them.

Armand was dumbstruck. Where once the frontier with Spain had been a quiet, picturesque area, now all he could see was a seething mass of humanity unlike anything he had seen in his life. It was as if the mountains were disgorging people from the very earth. Soup kitchens were everywhere and long lines of hungry people shuffled forward hoping to get a bowl of hot soup to warm their half-frozen bodies. Everywhere, nurses and doctors could be seen doing their best against difficult odds. Dr Berdu recognized a nurse from the Red Cross in Perpignan standing near an ambulance attending a wounded man. The woman looked worn out.

'We can't manage,' she said, wiping her brow. 'I've just had to prise a dead baby from a woman's arms. God help us.' She peered into the car and saw Armand. 'Have you both come to help?'

Dr Berdu said they had and she told him they might be better off if he went to the Fortress of Bellegarde just above the town. 'We've had to put many of the wounded there. 'Berdu got back in the car. 'Don't bother going to Perpignan,' she shouted out. 'The city is full of spectators. This is where you're needed.'

They drove upwards towards the fortress, a drive that took forever due to the clogged roads and bad weather. Armand made a comment that there seemed to be more women and children in the town.

'That's because the French government has issued a decree that only women and children are allowed to stay. Franco wants us to send the men back, even the wounded — to a certain death. It seems that the government has agreed because they've started pushing men back over the border, clubbing them and hitting them with batons to make a point.' Dr Berdu glanced towards his friend. 'It's shocked you, hasn't it?' Armand couldn't speak.

At the fortress, Dr Berdu located the surgeon in charge and introduced Armand as his aide. 'Where do you want us to go?' he asked.

The wounded were lying on makeshift straw beds on the floor, and everywhere, stretcher-bearers were moving people away and replacing them with others. The place smelt of decay — a cloying mixture of blood, urine, gangrene, and fear. Armand had to fight hard not to throw up. They found a long table in the middle of the room filled with medical equipment and bowls of water that were constantly being replenished by nurses' aides. Dr Berdu opened his bag, put on a white jacket, and gave another to Armand. 'Here,' he said, 'put this on.'

They washed their hands thoroughly and a nurse led them to a man who was in enormous pain. 'Take a look at this leg and see what you think?' she said. A section of the man's trousers had already been ripped open and Dr Berdu could tell by the stench how bad his situation was. 'I'll leave him in your capable hands.' She pressed the man's arm reassuringly, and with a warm smile, told him he would be alright.

'Good God,' Armand thought to himself. He dared not say it aloud. From now on, he had to remain strong. That's what his friend wanted and he would rise to the occasion.

Dr Berdu handed Armand surgical gloves and a mask, opened his medical bag, and took out all the necessary instruments, in particular a knife and saw. He asked Armand to fetch a large bowl of boiling water. Armand rushed off and soon returned with a few other things he'd also been asked to get, including a large number of bandages.

Even though the man was in great pain, he somehow managed a smile. 'After what I've seen, what you are about to do is nothing, so let's get it over with, shall we?'

Berdu dabbed chloroform onto a cloth and handed it to Armand, telling him to make sure the man was "looked after" while he performed the operation. Within minutes, Dr Berdu was sawing the man's leg off at the thigh. Blood splattered everywhere. To Armand, the sound of the saw cutting through bone seemed horrific. Here was a human being, not a sheep or cow being killed for the village fête.

'Good,' said Berdu, after the leg was off. 'His blood pressure is fine. He'll live.' He inserted an intravenous drip into the man's arm and told Armand to hold it while he cauterized the wound. The same nurse came by and picked up the gangrenous leg to dispose of it — her fortieth amputation for the day.

When they'd cleaned up, the man was taken by stretcher-bearers to the recuperating room where he would lie on fresh linen on a straw bed and be given a bowl of soup when he came round.

Armand excused himself, went outside, and retched. Five minutes later he was back. 'What's next?' he said to his friend.

They stayed for over a week, occasionally making trips to Prades or Perpignan for medical supplies. Shortly after they returned to Mont-Saint-Jean, the French government closed the border and enforced harsh asylum laws which meant that families would still be separated. The women and children, the elderly, and the wounded would now be sent to internment camps throughout France. An order was issued by the government for the border guards to confiscate all weapons and vehicles and offer the men the chance to join the French Foreign Legion. Those soldiers and able-bodied men who refused this offer and who would not go back to Spain were herded behind hastily prepared barbed-wire camps on the beaches in the south-eastern towns of Argelès-sur-Mer and Saint-Cyprien. In such conditions, many perished.

Colette couldn't believe her eyes when her husband walked through the door. In the space of a week, he had lost weight and looked drawn. When she asked what was happening, he didn't want to talk about it. After she heard him sobbing like a child during the night, she went to see Dr Berdu. He came over straight away and told Armand that Colette was a wise woman and he owed it to her to tell he what was going on.

'Besides, it's not healthy to bottle up your emotions.' He said he was leaving for Prades that day and left a bottle of sleeping tablets for him.

Armand took his friend's advice. Colette was indeed shocked and tried to assure him things would all work out in the end. 'At least the government has allowed them to stay,' she said.

Armand was no longer convinced about the government's reasons. 'It was their response that hit me hard. It's inhumane and the mortality rate is high,' he replied. 'They have nowhere to sleep and no fresh drinking water. Look how we welcomed the Belgians in the Great War. I now know what Théo meant when he said we are witnessing the end of democracy as we know it.' He shook his head sadly. 'Where were we when the Germans and Italians were aiding Franco? Where was Britain too? We sat back and let thousands die. What is that telling Nazi Germany?'

Over the next few months, refugees continued to pour into France. Most were not aware of the French government's policies. Many were peasants, barely able to read or write. No matter how difficult the terrain, there was not one area of the Pyrenees, from the Mediterranean to the Atlantic, that didn't see refugees attempting to flee. They even started arriving in Mont-Saint-Jean. Some found a way through Puigcerdà or Bourg-Madame, ending up in Capcir and Cerdagne and the Ariège. Many avoided the gendarmes and border guards by living in rudimentary huts that inevitably became so unsanitary they died from an array of diseases. Dr Berdu's patients in these areas alerted him to this fact. In turn, he alerted Armand, who by now had accumulated a lot of first aid knowledge and was able to deal with quite a few cases. Théo Berdu was proud of his friend.

With Colette's support, Armand now had two jobs — one official, the other unofficial — and he gleaned much about the dire situation from the people he helped. This only resolved to make him take more than a passing interest in politics. The internment camps were emptied out in the spring of 1939, but detention was unbearable for many of the men and with limited options, many committed suicide. By this time, Armand had gathered a few friends together who were willing to help. Colette, Babette Berdu, Théo's wife, and Maria the schoolteacher became a part of their organisation. They asked around the villages and many farmers were only too happy to have an extra pair of hands. Some of the skilled refugees found jobs in factories. They certainly achieved a lot in a few months.

On September 1, 1939, Germany invaded Poland. On September 3, France and Britain issued an ultimatum to Germany. The Germans took no notice and officially France was at war. Throughout the country men of fighting age were called up and sent to the border. Officially France entered a period which they called the drôle de guerre, or the Phoney War, but in reality, they were preparing for war.

By April 1940, there were around 100,000 Spaniards working in the war economy. It was a good job because the inevitable happened. Germany attacked in the west on May 10, 1940. Initially, British and French commanders had believed that German forces would attack through central Belgium as they had in World War I, and rushed forces to the Franco-Belgian border to meet the German attack. The main German attack, however, went through the Ardennes Forest in south-eastern Belgium and northern Luxembourg. German tanks and infantry quickly broke through the French defensive lines and advanced towards the coast. By the time this happened, Armand Joubert was no longer a political novice. He and his close associates had expected it. But were they prepared for the consequences? That was the question. As events spiralled out of control, it would soon test their resolve.

Armand poked at the embers of the fire in the classroom and then put on his jacket. It was time to go. The route to the meeting place took him by his home. Colette was in bed reading a book when he entered the bedroom. He told her where he was going and not to worry about him.

'There's bread and cheese and a string of blood sausage on the table for you. Take it with you.' She closed her book and held out her arms towards him. He sat on the bed and caressed her. 'I love you,' she whispered in his ear. 'Please take care.'

'I love you too,' Armand said. His kiss lingered on her soft lips for a while, then he got up to leave. 'Get some sleep and don't worry about me.'

She heard him moving about in the kitchen for a few minutes, and then heard the front door close. She got out of bed and peeked through the curtains, watching him walk down the path. There was hardly any moon and the snow was falling softly. Within minutes he was gone, heading towards the steep mountain that they called La Madrès. 'God be with you,' she whispered to herself as he disappeared into the darkness.

She took one of his sleeping tablets and got back into bed. However much he and Dr Berdu tried to persuade her all was well, Colette still worried. The Vichy government had decreed it was forbidden to aid foreign soldiers or French deserters. What he was doing was illegal and highly dangerous, not just for Armand, but for her, their daughter, and the other villagers.

CHAPTER 3

The Refuge at La Madrès

AFTER A STEEP, winding climb through the forest, Armand finally reached the refuge situated in a small clearing in the nearby mountain, La Madrès. He never knew why it had that name — the mother. On a clear day, its peak dominated the landscape and could be seen from several other villages in the area. This was the terrain of wolves and wild boar, the occasional bear, and an array of different types of deer. Sheep and cows rarely grazed here, but the shepherds and cowherds did sometimes use the pathways towards the pastures further out on the high plateaus of Capcir and Cerdagne during spring and summer, rather than take the winding route through the Col des Hares. The altitude was high and the air thin. Armand was a fit man, but this steep, stony route, covered with thick bushes, tired him out so he knew how difficult it would be for those city types.

Nearing the stone dwelling, he stopped to assess the lay of the land. A wooden stick was propped up against the outside wall near the door, a sign that all was well, and he could smell smoke from a wood fire. He stood behind a tree and whistled. A man inside wiped away the condensation from the windowpane to double-check who it was, then opened the door and gestured to Armand.

Armand stepped inside the cabin to find a man wrapped in a thick grey blanket warming himself beside the hot stove and drinking a glass of red wine. His wet clothes hung from a clothesline strung near the fire. He stood up to shake Armand's hand.

'Billy,' the man said, 'Billy McGregor.'

Armand introduced himself as "Alain". His friend Lucien — "Luc", went back to stirring his potato and cabbage soup, noting how each man viewed the other with slight suspicion until he made it clear to Armand, via a coded sentence, that Billy's reason for being there was above board. Lucien refilled Billy's glass and poured one for himself.

'What happened to your clothes?' Armand asked.

'I had to cross a stream and slipped on the stones. After several days hiding to get here, I'm ashamed to say my strength ran out.'

'No need to apologise,' Armand replied, waving his arm through the air. 'At least you're safe.'

The man lowered his blanket to prove he really did fall. His buttocks were badly bruised and his elbow grazed.

'Well, Billy, what's your story? Where did you come from and how did you find us?'

'I served with the 51st Infantry Division — the Highlanders. On June 12, about 10,000 men, including many French soldiers, were captured at Saint-Valery-en-Caux after we surrendered to Major General Erwin Rommel. We'd been fighting further along the coast from Dunkirk. It was hell.' The more he talked, the more his Scottish accent became apparent — and his almost complete lack of French. 'I was left behind, so you could say I was one of the lucky ones. I never thought I'd make it. I hid when the Germans arrived and saw most members from my regiment, along with French troops, marched away. I escaped to a farm where I found a few other soldiers who'd been left behind at Dunkirk talk about the horrors they saw. They witnessed men who had just surrendered being taken to a farm, where it was rumoured they were murdered — machine-gunned in cold blood, the poor sods. Anyway, after a few days, we parted ways and I was spotted stealing food in a market. Fortunately, the stall owner who saw me felt sorry for me and took me home, where his family hid me. There were three of us in his cellar for a week, all from different regiments and with similar stories of German atrocities. There, we were questioned by two Frenchmen who checked we really were Allied soldiers. One night, they appeared and told us to hide in the back of a van, where we learned that we were being taken to a forest somewhere north of Paris. At first we thought it was a trap and we were done for. When the van stopped, the driver opened the back door, and one of the men told us to wait there.

'"You'll be looked after," he said, "but don't do anything stupid." He got back in the van and drove away.' Billy rubbed his temple with the tips of his fingers. It was a few minutes before he continued. 'It was pitch black and we had no idea where we were, but did as we were told. After about ten minutes, three men carrying guns appeared and told us they were taking us somewhere safe. We were blindfolded and put into another truck and driven for miles. We must have been driving all night. Finally, we came to a farm and were told to stay in the barn. We were also assured the farmer and his wife would look after us, but we were not to put them at risk or we'd be shot.'

Lucien ladled out a huge bowl of soup for each of them while Billy continued. 'We stayed there for days and were eventually picked up by a woman who gave us new identity cards and a change of civilian clothes. By the time we moved further south, we knew the French government had left Paris and Pétain had called for an end to the fighting. The farmer's daughter spoke English and kept us up to date with the news. We were on the move for three weeks! A lot can happen in three weeks.' He let out a deep sigh.

'Then what?' Armand asked. 'What did you do next?'

'The woman who picked us up appeared very young. She reminded me of my sister — couldn't have been more than twenty. Eventually we found ourselves in Toulouse and were given another identity card.'

Armand picked up the French ID. 'Is that where you got this?'

'Yes.'

'What happened to your other friends?'

'We parted ways there. I was placed in the care of another young woman. They said it was safer if we broke up as the Germans and Vichy police were stepping up their efforts to catch Allied soldiers and airmen, and as none of us had good French, it was better if we did not continue on together. I was to stay with the woman and pretend I was her boyfriend.' He blushed at the thought of it and then quickly pulled himself together. 'None of us liked the idea of being separated. We had come so far and looked out for each other, but we were assured that if we wanted to leave France without getting caught, it was better to take different routes. "From here on this is where it really gets difficult," the woman told us. "Border guards are being strengthened. You can catch up again in London."'

'What was the name of the young woman who looked after you in Toulouse?' Armand asked.

'Jacqueline.'

Armand exchanged looks with Lucien. They gave a faint smile. "Jacqueline" was none other than Justine, Armand's daughter, who was living in Toulouse.

'A pretty girl who spoke excellent English,' Billy added. 'She couldn't have been much older than twenty-one. Slim, with delicate features and determined eyes. The men never said who they were. I was just told that I was to do exactly as Jacqueline said.'

'And what was that?' Armand asked.

'Stay out of sight until she was ready to move me on. She also said my French was atrocious and taught me a few basic phrases in case I got caught.' He laughed when he thought about it. 'In the end, she said, I was the worst student she'd had and it was better to act like a mute if I didn't want to get caught. When the time came for me to leave, she escorted me to Quillan. From there I was on my own. I was given a map and I still had my compass, which she sewed into the collar of my jacket. I was told to make my way from Quillan to here — Mont-Saint-Jean. When I neared the Château d'Usson, I would need to cross the stream — where I fell — and walk about three hundred metres up through the woods until I came to a stone house with blue shutters. I hid there until Luc collected me the next day.'

Armand wiped his mouth and pushed his empty bowl away. 'You can stay here and rest for a couple of days. Get your strength back and then we will take you to the border. Rest assured, if you don't venture too far from this cabin, you will be safe. The Germans don't come here, but you have to watch out for the gendarmes.' He offered Billy a cigarette and they sat in silence for a while, pondering the situation.

29

'I want to thank you for everything you are doing for us — for us soldiers and airmen, I mean,' Billy said. 'I was told Britain has destroyed the French fleet just off North Africa. I'm sorry. It won't exactly endear the French to us.' He shook his head sadly as if it was all too confusing to contemplate.

Armand said he was right, the French were angry, but he himself agreed with Churchill. 'He wouldn't have taken that decision lightly. If the navy fell into German hands, especially after Pétain has given in to the Boche then it would have been used against Britain. One day, the people will understand that.'

This fact still did not make Billy feel any better. He felt the French would see Britain as acting treacherously. Armand told him Pétain was the one who was treacherous, not Churchill. 'He gave in without a fight. He is the one who should be ashamed.'

Billy stared into the fire. 'Who'd have thought it would end like this?'

'It hasn't ended yet,' Lucien said. 'It's only just started. We haven't forgiven them for the last war. Regardless of what is to come, we *will* win this war against tyranny.'

'But with Pétain calling for an end to the war and telling the people to lay down their arms — how?'

Armand shared out the food that Colette had left for them. 'Haven't you heard? De Gaulle has been making broadcasts over the BBC. He wants France to continue the fight.'

'I've been told. Do you think the people will rise up?'

Armand laughed. 'You are not the first person to want to cross the border, you know. Some men have already left to join the Free French Forces in North Africa. What does that tell you?'

By this time, Billy could barely keep his eyes open and Lucien prepared a bed for him. Minutes later, he was fast asleep, snoring loudly. The snow had stopped, and Lucien and Armand went outside the refuge to have a smoke and talk about what they would do next.

'Let him stay here for a day or two before he heads to the border. Poor man is exhausted and he will need all the strength he can muster. In the meantime, I'll get a message to Pablo to prepare himself for another border crossing.'

It was three thirty in the morning when Armand returned home. He quietly undressed and slipped into bed, taking care not to wake up Colette, who was facing away from him. She did not let him know that she was awake, unable to sleep as usual until she felt him by her side again.

A gentle smile eased her tenseness. 'Now I can finally sleep,' she thought to herself.

CHAPTER 4

Justine, Code Name "Jacqueline", Remembers

WHEN THE GERMANS invaded Poland on September 1, 1939, I was preparing to go for an interview for a new job in Toulouse. I distinctly recall a deep mixture of fear and shock, although, following the rise of Hitler as I had, it wasn't altogether unexpected. All the same, when the reality hits, it really hits hard. My interview was a short one as everyone's minds were on Poland and how Britain and France would react. I was told to come back for a second interview in a few days' time. On September 3, Britain and France issued an ultimatum to Germany which was ignored and we were at war.

On my way to the second interview, I bought a newspaper and scanned through it while waiting to be called into the meeting. There were several people going in and out of the reception room and the atmosphere was tense. Everyone had a sombre look on their faces. I had just turned the page to the part where it said young men of serviceable age should report for duty to be sent to guard the border with Germany, which was now closed, when Monsieur Cassou's secretary said he was ready to see me. I closed the newspaper, put it in my bag, and entered the large, elegant room, where Monsieur Paul Cassou, owner of the Ariège Charcoal Company, stood to greet me.

'Take a seat, Mademoiselle Joubert.' He noticed the newspaper sticking out of my bag and gestured to it. 'What do you think about all this?' he asked.

'Excuse me?' His question caught me off guard.

'The fact that we are now at war.'

'The Germans can't possibly win,' I blurted out. 'If they invade, others will unite against them. Herr Hitler is obsessed. He wants to gain *Lebensraum* and he's a raging anti-Semite. Look at the influx of Jewish and political refugees who fled here since 1933. I've read *Mein Kampf* and I think he's a madman. So for everyone's sake, let's hope the Germans back down, although I doubt they will.' I realised I had said too much and felt my cheeks redden. I had probably botched my chances at the job now.

Monsieur Cassou smiled. 'Did you really read *Mein Kampf* — in German?'

'Of course.'

'I'm impressed.'

'I apologise, monsieur. I didn't mean to talk like that. You must think me rude.'

'I like a spirited woman,' he replied. He looked at my file and proceeded with the interview. 'I see that you speak several languages fluently — Spanish, English, German — no Italian.'

'I'm afraid not. I do speak Catalan and Occitan though.'

Cassou commented that Catalan could be useful. 'Tell me something — I know you are a friend of my son, Jules, and that you studied at Toulouse University together, so what makes you want this job as a secretary with this company? After all, you have the qualifications to teach at a university. Wouldn't that bring you more prestige?'

I had anticipated this question. 'It says in the advertisement that the successful occupant would occasionally be required to travel. That appealed to me. If I am honest, the pay also appealed as I would like to purchase my own apartment and that would not be so easy if I were to become a professor. Besides, in my spare time, I aim to give private language classes.'

'You stated that your father is headmaster of the school in Mont-Saint-Jean and your main interest is literature. You are an academic, mademoiselle. This is not really the sort of work for an academic.'

I knew he was testing me. 'I admit I love literature, most of all the classics. I get that from my father. But I love the outdoors just as much. If you notice, further on' — my eyes indicated to the file in front of him

–'you will see that I also said I enjoyed hiking and skiing. Being brought up in an agricultural area in the mountains, I love the outdoors. Being cooped up in a classroom all day would drive me crazy after a while. In that sense, I do not want to follow in my father's footsteps.'

'Much of a secretary's work can be tedious, you know.'

'The position stated that the successful applicant would need to drive a car and occasionally accompany yourself and other members of the board to your other headquarters, which, if I am correct, are in Paris, Lyon, and Marseille. I can drive, monsieur, so that wouldn't be a problem.'

'What do your parents think about this?' He looked over his glasses at me. 'I'm assuming you *have* discussed it with them?'

'No, monsieur. My parents brought me up to make my own decisions and do what I think is right for me. If I am happy, they will be happy.'

'That is what I and my wife and I want for Jules. Now I am afraid his future is dashed for the moment. He will be called up.'

I didn't know what to say. I was aware of this as I'd seen Jules the night before and I knew his parents would be worried.

Paul Cassou closed the file. 'I will admit, I hadn't expected to hire someone so young. Do you mind me asking if there is a man in your life? He may not agree with your being away on behalf of the company.'

'There is no one, monsieur. I am answerable only to myself, and I certainly wouldn't want to be with a man who didn't count me as his equal in every way.'

Paul Cassou grinned. He stood up and offered me his hand. 'Congratulations. The job's yours. You can start in a week. Madame Pignon, the secretary who showed you in, leaves in two weeks' time. You can spend a week with her and she will show you the ropes.'

After the matter of salary was discussed, which was a substantial amount for a woman who had never held a secretarial position before, I thanked him and assured him he wouldn't regret hiring me.

Cassou gave a warm smile. 'I think we'll get on just fine.'

I returned to my apartment in high spirits and called Jules. 'Guess what? Your father gave me the job. We must celebrate.'

Jules said he was happy for me. With extra money from paying students, I now stood to make quite a lot of money. 'My father likes you,' he said. 'He called you a feisty little thing with determined eyes.' We laughed, but the laughter quickly faded when he told me he couldn't catch up as he had been called up to go to the front line. 'I have to report to the police station in the morning. Failure to do so means I would go to prison.' There was a moment of silence. 'Don't worry, Justine. I will be fine. We'll celebrate when I get back. Take care of yourself.'

There was a click and the line went dead. 'Jules! Jules!' I called, but there was no reply. My moment of happiness waned. Jules and I held the same views about politics, but he was a pacifist and I knew the thought of having to use a weapon would sicken him.

The following day, I decided to go to the Donezan to visit my parents for a few days and give them the news about my new job. I hoped they'd be excited for me. I took the train to Carcassonne and then the bus to Quillan. From there it was a three-hour wait for the bus to Mont-Saint-Jean. While I waited, I had a light meal in a restaurant, noting that most of the patrons appeared to think that a real war with Germany would not eventuate. We *were* at war, yet it all seemed strange. A war without fighting; what sort of war was that? From what I could gather, hardly anyone understood the extent of what Hitler was capable of. In their minds, the French government would rise to the occasion and save the day.

When it was time to leave, I headed to the bus station, where the bus driver was loading cases and bags onto the roof. The bus soon filled with an assortment of people, from agricultural workers carrying their tools of the trade to women who had purchased new clothes and who jostled for a seat with older villagers carrying cages of live hens and baskets of food. I just managed to get the last seat next to a woman who only wanted to talk about her new clothes purchases. She never mentioned the declaration of war at all. The trip was long and tedious as the bus meandered through all the villages in the Donezan before it reached its final destination, Mont-Saint-Jean, a few hours later. It was dark when the bus stopped in the main square, just below the looming walls of the old château. There, the last half dozen passengers got off. Only three were from the village. The rest still had long walks through the mountain before they reached home. After Toulouse, the isolation of the village seemed strange.

Papa was already there to greet me, sitting on the low wall next to the Monument to the Fallen in the Great War, and we hugged each other affectionately.

'Welcome home, my little one. You are just in time. Théo and Babette are coming over for dinner. They will be so happy to see you. We are all eager to hear about your adventures.'

I smiled at the way Papa still called me "his little one". I knew that's what I would always be to him, even in old age. It was only a short walk to the house, yet neither of us wanted to break the spell of being together again by talking about the war. That would come later. Maman had just finished setting the dining table when we arrived. She wrapped her arms around me and shed a tear of happiness.

'How we've missed you.' She stood back to admire me. 'Let me look at you. My, you look beautiful,' She turned to Papa. 'Doesn't she, darling?'

Of course, Papa agreed. He took my coat and suitcase upstairs to my old room while Maman fussed over me. 'Just look at your hair — so stylish, and your dress is wonderful.'

At that moment, the Berdus arrived. They too fussed over me. I was surprised and pleased to see that Babette Berdu was pregnant. 'Seven months,' Babette said. 'We kept it quiet for a long time just in case...' The "just in case" was because she had already had two miscarriages during the early stages of pregnancy.

I congratulated them on the good news. 'You look radiant,' I said to her.

Papa opened a bottle of Blanquette de Limoux and we toasted the happy occasion. It was good to be home. How different the atmosphere was in Mont-Saint-Jean to Toulouse. We sat down to a tasty meal of rabbit in mustard sauce, which Maman knew was one of my favourite dishes. That was followed by a delicious apple croustade made with apples from our own garden. Over dinner I told them about the new job. At first Maman and Papa were shocked. They'd always thought I would be a professor of classics at a good university, but when I explained the conditions of the job, the pay, and who I would be working for, they warmed to the idea. Dr Berdu, in particular, congratulated me.

'A distinguished gentleman,' he said. 'I've met him on several occasions, especially when he became president of the Ariège General Council.'

I was relieved that my news was well-received. When the meal was over and coffee and chocolates were being served, it was then that the subject of the war was brought up. I knew Théo Berdu had strong political feelings similar to myself, and wasn't surprised when he expressed his thoughts. It was Papa who puzzled me. He had always been completely ambivalent about politics — as if any troubles would all go away and things would be fine. All of a sudden, he'd changed. I was astounded when he began voicing deep feelings, not just about the Germans, but about the situation in Europe in general too. What had happened while I'd been away that Papa could change so much? When I told him that Jules and others like him had been called up, the discussions became heated. No one there that night believed the war would go away and we all feared the Germans would invade. Thankfully, we shared the same thoughts, unlike many families who were already being torn apart over what was happening in Europe.

After a pleasant weekend, I returned to Toulouse and my new job, which soon became extremely time-consuming. However, I enjoyed it. It distracted me from politics. Monsieur Cassou was a delight to work for. Within a few months, I had the use of a company car whenever I wanted and on several occasions, was even allowed to use it to visit my parents. I travelled once with Monsieur Cassou to Marseille and Bordeaux and managed to get in a little sight-seeing. Then the Phoney War abruptly ended and the real war began. Germany invaded France and my life changed forever. At the time I had no idea just how much, but it soon became apparent that I would need to muster all the strength I could: strength I never thought I had.

After the Germans occupied Paris on June 14 and Philippe Pétain became premier of France upon the resignation of Reynaud's government, I overheard Monsieur Cassou talk with several of his closest associates about the dire situation. He was disgusted and vowed retribution for such a humiliating defeat. After the armistice was signed, he became much quieter and disappeared from the office for days at a time without telling us where he was going. It was the first time I'd ever seen him like this. One day he asked me to drive him home to his villa for the weekend. He told me I could keep the car as his wife would take him back to Toulouse. They lived in a beautiful villa on the edge of a village just outside Saint-Girons in the Ariège, so after I'd dropped him off, I took the opportunity to visit my parents. I travelled across the Col de Pailhères, a mountainous region reaching almost two thousand metres, with winding roads and stunning views of the surrounding mountains. Along the way, I passed cattle and horses grazing on the high pastures, but hardly any vehicles. The isolation was a welcome relief as it gave me time to think. The inhabitants of Toulouse were panic-stricken and I wondered how news of the German occupation had gone down in the Donezan.

When I arrived, Papa had gone to Perpignan with Dr Berdu. Maman said he wouldn't be back until Sunday evening, which meant that I would miss him. She told me he'd been away a few times since the Germans arrived and that he rarely discussed his reasons for his absence. All he would say was "Trust me". I told her Monsieur Cassou was the same.

'Your father told me he won't recognize the new government,' she said. 'He has heard that de Gaulle has broadcast over the BBC for France to continue fighting. At least here in these villages, we will be far away from the troubles. The new demarcation line means we should be fine.'

'Is that what the villagers really believe?' I asked.

Maman nodded. 'It is. What would the Germans do here in this quiet backwater? There is nothing for them here except agriculture, and with many men killed or sent to German labour camps, they need all the agricultural workers they can get.'

I returned to Toulouse without seeing Papa, but in the pit of my stomach I had a sinking feeling that the future looked bleak. When I returned to work, Monsieur Cassou called me into the office. He was a tall, handsome man with a calm demeanour who seemed to take things in his stride, but that day he looked tired.

'We've heard that Jules has been sent to a labour camp in Germany.' He stared out of the window, deep in thought for a few seconds. 'I suppose we should be thankful he is alive.'

I bit my lip and tried to be stoic. 'He'll be fine, you'll see.'

It was then that he opened up to me. 'Can I trust you, Justine?'

'Of course, monsieur. You know you can.' I found it an odd thing to say until he continued. 'I am going to try and help those whose lives are now in danger. There are many who are trying to flee while they still can — I think you know what I mean?'

'Do you mean Jews?'

'I am talking about others too. People who pose a problem because of their political beliefs, and Allied soldiers who managed to evade the Germans. They need help too.'

The fact that he had spoken so openly filled me with honour, but it also frightened me. 'Monsieur, we are talking about hundreds, if not thousands, of people. It's not possible to help everyone.'

'If I can save even one life from the Nazis and these collaborators now in power, then I will be happy, but I aim to save as many as I can.' He gave me a penetrating look, as if he could read my thoughts. He knew I was not the sort of person to sit back and do nothing. 'You are a clever girl,' he said. 'I would like you to join us.'

'Us! How many people are we talking about?'

He leaned forward with his elbows on his desk and folded his hands together. 'That is not something I can tell you. You must trust me on that.'

I did not hesitate. 'Count me in.'

The meeting was brought to a close with a handshake. A few days later, he asked if I could stay behind for a chat when the rest of the office staff had gone home. He said he had a job for me. Was I willing to do it as it could be dangerous? I told him yes.

'I want you to go to the train station and pick up a middle-aged couple. You will pose as their niece, and tell them it's good to see them again. Make a show of affection.'

'How will we recognize each other?' I asked.

'Carry a bunch of flowers as a welcome gift. Make sure they are red. In addition, carry a book with you, one of your favourite classics. Just in case there are other people at the station with similar flowers. What do you have?'

'What about *The Count of Monte Cristo*?'

'Excellent. There is also something else I must ask of you.'

I wondered what on earth he was going to say and was relieved when he told me I must use a code name. He asked what I wanted it to be as that would be the name I would use for all future assignments.

'What about "Jacqueline"?'

'Excellent. I like it. The couple will call you that. Do not answer to any other name.'

'What are their names?' I asked.

'Madame and Monsieur Elise and Henri Sadrin. They are Jews who have escaped from Belgium and are travelling with forged documents. If you think you are being watched, or anyone apprehends them and takes them away, don't interfere. We must hope that doesn't happen.'

It sounded as though he expected there might be a problem. 'We are in the non-occupied zone. People are allowed to travel freely.'

'It may seem that way to most people, but the Abwehr, Gestapo, and Vichy officials are still monitoring what goes on here, so don't be fooled. It's important to keep a low profile.' He saw a flicker of panic in my eyes and asked if I wanted to back out. He said he would not hold it against me if I did, and would never ask me again.

I nodded that I was fine.

'Good. When you have established all is well, I want you to take them to an apartment at 201 rue Voltaire — apartment three. It's a safe house. Leave the couple with the man who lives there. His name is Robert.'

I knew Robert was probably a code name too, so didn't bother asking his surname. 'Then what?'

'That's it. Your assignment is done.'

'That's all?' It didn't seem much of a problem, but he stressed I must be cautious and never discuss this with anyone. He also told me that for this work, I should refer to him as "X".

And that's how it all began. The meeting with the Sadrins went according to plan and a week later, I was called to take someone else to a safe house. Each time, it was Robert who took care of my "parcels" as he called these people. After two months, Monsieur Cassou realised I was completely trustworthy and asked me if I knew anyone in the Donezan who might help in arranging escape routes. I immediately thought of Papa and Dr Berdu. He asked me to check them out and, if they were agreeable, we would have a meeting.

I returned to Mont-Saint-Jean and cautiously broached the subject of an escape route with Papa. To my great surprise, he told me he and Dr Berdu had already helped half a dozen people.

'Papa, what we are doing is dangerous. We know what the Nazis are capable of.' I asked him how he had become so political and defiant against the government when he had always been so conservative and afraid to step out of line. When he said it was Théo who opened his eyes, I wasn't surprised.

'Then Dr Berdu will help us too?' I asked eagerly.

'I suggest we have a have a little chat with him, but I know he will say yes. Besides, he respects Cassou.'

I couldn't help smiling. I had not mentioned who I was working for in this clandestine group, but he'd guessed right away.

The following week, Dr Berdu and Papa met with Monsieur Cassou at a restaurant in Foix. I went with them. It was there that they agreed to find safe houses and hideouts for escape routes through the Donezan and along the nearby Spanish border. Cassou was pleased to hear there were people who would be prepared to work as "helpers" but the real difficulty was in getting trusted *passeurs* who knew the border well.

Dr Berdu assured Cassou that was not a problem. 'Price may be an issue, but I am sure we can manage that,' he said. 'I already know of a couple of loyal smugglers who know the area like the back of their hand. They have contacts on the Spanish side who are willing to help.'

I hadn't realised until that moment that Monsieur Cassou had already established an escape route through Andorra, but we all knew that the Donezan would be easier to work in as it was more remote. While at one time, I had seen that as a problem in my life, I now realised it was an advantage.

By the autumn of 1940, we had managed to help a few dozen people cross into Spain. The network was still in its infancy, and at the time we had no idea just how well established and far-reaching it would become.

CHAPTER 5

Pablo and Mercedes

ALTHOUGH THERE WAS a dividing line between the occupied and non-occupied zones, listening to the BBC was strictly forbidden and the Vichy government was continuously warning of the consequences to those caught. Yet there were still many who listened in secret, risking imprisonment or being sent to a labour camp in Germany. At the time, many Frenchmen were angry with Britain after their fleet was destroyed at Mers-el-Kébir. They couldn't understand why and this anger only served to fuel Vichy propaganda. Already people were being denounced by friends and family. There were also many who believed that de Gaulle was destabilizing the Vichy government and making things worse; therefore, he was not to be trusted. After all, what did a general who had fled his country know about what was truly happening in France now? The only people who didn't listen to propaganda were people like the Jouberts, the Berdus, and the Cassous, who took great risks listening to the BBC, but it was a risk they were prepared to take.

De Gaulle had not given up the good fight. He consistently urged the French people to resist, and this is what Justine and her father were doing. Théo Berdu had lived in Marseille for a few years before moving to Mont-Saint-Jean, and he was familiar with influential, like-minded people there. Paul Cassou's business contacts were even wider. Between them, they soon established a network across the south of France from the Atlantic to the Mediterranean. As yet, the network was fragmented, which was a worry as the Gestapo, who worked hand in hand with the Vichy government, already had their spies in the unoccupied zone, particularly around Marseille. In fact, the whole coastline was monitored.

43

At first, getting people out of France on fishing boats moored away from the coastline was not too difficult if those fleeing had the right papers and could pay off a few coastguards and officials, but after a while, that became highly dangerous.

The worst area for undercover work was in was the occupied zone itself, where they liaised with a network based in Paris. The other area of concern was near the Pyrenees. A ten-to-fifteen-kilometre zone along the frontier with Spain was now sectioned off as part of the forbidden zone and administered by the Germans. Special documentation was needed to travel in that area. To aid the Germans, the government recruited more men for the border police, or Guarde Mobile, as they were known. Despite this, the main train line from Perpignan to Spain was still open, as were others across the length of the Pyrenees, but false IDs had to be perfect and connections in customs, trustworthy. In the first few months, many evaders were detained and imprisoned for days and weeks at a time in terrible conditions. Some were even shot or deported to Germany. Jews and Allied soldiers were high on the list, as were their helpers.

After the meeting with Billy McGregor, Armand contacted Dr Berdu. Which route and helpers would they use this time? Using the same one was not wise. If they were caught, it could take weeks to find someone else. Between them, they decided to move Billy to a farmhouse just outside Matemale, between Puyvalador and Mont-Louis. Puyvalador, although not far from Mont-Saint-Jean, was in the canton of the Pyrénées catalanes, and after the German occupation was one of the few places in the area the Germans kept an eye on. Puyvalador itself was a small village, but strategically it was important as it had a large dam which needed to be well-guarded at all times. In fact, all the dams and hydroelectric plants were now monitored by the Germans, even in the unoccupied zone. Should anything go wrong, the Germans could always call for back-up from the border guards.

Nearby Matemale was barely more than a hamlet, a haphazard cluster of stone and timber houses and a church surrounded by a few farms owned by agricultural families, cowherds, and shepherds. Pablo and his wife Mercedes were two of them. Their farm was on the edge of the village and they kept about a hundred sheep, a considerable amount as many shepherds owned little more than a few dozen.

The couple fled Spain towards the end of the Spanish Civil War when Barcelona fell to the Nationalists on January 1939, and met in France sometime later. Pablo, a man in his mid-forties, lost his wife and twelve-year-old daughter when they were spotted by German planes as they fled across the mountains with hundreds of other Spaniards. Many were killed that day, but with the planes about to target them again, there was no time to bury the dead. It was to be one of the many nightmarish scenarios Pablo would endure. He finally ended up at a camp in Argelès-sur-Mer, fenced in by barbed wire, beaten by guards, and surrounded by disease and the dying. It was a stroke of luck that he was taken out of the camp one day to be checked by a doctor, then put on a list of men able to help with agricultural work. That doctor was Théo Berdu.

Mercedes's story was equally harrowing. A beautiful woman in her early twenties, she managed to reach France unscathed, but was raped by a Senegalese French guard in one of the women's camps. A few weeks later, she escaped and made her way to Quillan in the Haute-Vallée de l'Aude with another group of evaders, a woman and two men. There, they were picked up by the gendarmes. The men were returned to a camp, and the two women were given shelter at the nearby hat factory of MontCapel in Montazels. At first, Mercedes thought she would be able to work, but it was not to be. The hat factory housed more than six hundred Spanish women and about fifty children, and they spent most of the time lying on their straw beds wedged between the machinery. The only work they were allowed to do was sweep the floor and fetch and carry for the hat workers. There was no pay, but at least they were safe and well-fed. It was then that Mercedes realised she was pregnant. In May, the women were told to leave and offered work throughout the area, mostly working on the land or menial jobs for a subsistence pay. Mercedes went to a farm at Réal, the village next to Matemale, with half a dozen other women. She toiled in the fields for hours every day and was allowed Sunday off to go to church.

Fearing she would lose her job, she kept the pregnancy to herself until it was no longer possible to hide it. When the farm owner questioned her, she told them her husband had died soon after reaching the border. Her answer seemed plausible and, as she was a good worker, they offered to help her when the time came to give birth. The problem arose when the child was born — a boy with distinct African features. It was a terrible shock, not only to the farm owner and her co-workers, but to Mercedes herself. When she first realised she was pregnant, she'd tried to abort the child. When that didn't work, she prayed night and day that the child would at least look Spanish.

Gossip and ill will ran rampant through the villages when they realised Mercedes had given birth to *un enfant noir*. Had she given favours to the guards for food when others starved? Despite their animosity and gossip, she refused to say that she had been raped as it was her word against a member of the French guards — a soldier who would deny everything, a soldier who had probably been sent to the German border to defend France when war was declared, a patriot. Rather than leave and find herself out of work, Mercedes decided to ignore the laughs and jibes and stoically went about her work, carrying the baby on her back while she toiled in the fields. It was at this time that she met Pablo.

Pablo had been a shepherd in Spain and, through Dr Berdu, was given employment with an elderly shepherd in Matemale who was suffering from severe arthritis and finding it hard to take his stock out to pasture. Pablo and the shepherd struck up a close friendship and when the old man became too ill to work, he decided to leave the farm with all its contents to Pablo as he had no heirs.

In the early days, before the old man died, Pablo happened to go to a village fête in Formiguères, the nearest large village to Matemale and Réal. It was there that he first laid eyes on Mercedes, dressed in a red and white floral dress and wearing a red rose in her long, thick mane of glossy black hair. With her olive complexion, large dark eyes, and haughty manner, he knew immediately that she was also Spanish. He also noticed she carried a baby on her back.

The old shepherd saw the look in Pablo's eyes. 'She has cast a spell on you,' he said with a laugh. Pablo did not reply.

The fête lasted well into the evening, with lots of feasting and drinking and musicians playing a variety of French, Catalan, and Occitan songs. That day, the villagers forgot their hard work and drowned their sorrows, dancing and singing to the guitar and accordion. Pablo noticed that Mercedes sat apart from the other women, occasionally rocking her child, which was wrapped in a blanket. She saw him staring at her, blushed, and turned away. He thought about asking her to dance, but what would she do with the child?

The farmer leaned closer and whispered in his ear. 'She's not married and the baby is black.' Pablo looked at him in surprise. 'She says she was married and that the father died, but others say she gave favours to a Senegalese guard at Argelès-sur-Mer and that's how she got pregnant. Best you don't go there, son.'

Remembering his own treatment at the hands of the guards, Pablo's emotions oscillated from hatred to sadness and then disbelief. He had seen women give themselves to men for a slice of bread. At the time he pitied them, but understood that's what starvation did to people. This woman didn't seem like those. He was sure there was more to her story than met the eye. The next week, he was herding the sheep across the grassy plain when he saw her again. She was walking along the road carrying the child on her back. He bid her good day but she ignored him and walked on.

'You don't have to be afraid of me,' he called out. 'I won't hurt you.' Still, she ignored him, yet there was something in his voice that made her think he wasn't like the others.

Pablo herded the sheep along this same stretch of land for a few weeks until they needed to roam in another pasture. During that time, he passed her twice and always said hello. One day he prepared a bunch of wildflowers and handed them to her. At first she refused, but he insisted. 'I picked these for you. It would please me if you accepted them as a token of my friendship.'

In the end she took them, but kept on walking. Inside, her heart raced. Here was a man who wanted to be friends, even though she knew he would be aware she had a black baby. The next time, she vowed to speak to him. It was some weeks later when she saw him again. She was buying ribbons and buttons at a stall in the market in Formiguères. He approached her and asked if he could buy her a drink. She nodded. 'I'd like that,' she replied shyly.

Not wanting her to feel uncomfortable in the midst of so many prying eyes, he took her to a bar tucked away in a side street where there were few people.

'What will you have?' he asked. 'Wine?'

'Thank you.' She took the child from the sling on her back and held him, still careful to hide his face from view.

Pablo ordered two glasses of red wine and a charcuterie platter. Mercedes's eyes widened when the waiter placed it on the table. Was he doing this just for her?

'My name is Pablo — what's yours?'

'Mercedes.'

Pablo's eyes rested on the child. 'A boy or girl?'

'A boy.'

'Is he still breast-feeding? If not, maybe I can get him some milk or yogurt?'

'He's breast-fed. He'll be due for a feed soon, so I can't stay long.'

Pablo sensed her nervousness. 'I couldn't help noticing that you always keep him covered.'

Mercedes became anxious and stood up to leave until Pablo reached out to stop her. 'It's alright. Please don't be afraid.' She sat down again but could barely look Pablo in the eyes. 'I heard the story,' he continued. 'You have *un enfant noir*. I don't care what people say. I've never been one for gossip. I am my own judge of character.'

Mercedes slowly pulled the cover away from the child's head to show him. The African features were indeed strong. 'Satisfied?' she asked, expecting a rebuke.

'He's beautiful.' Pablo moved closer to stroke his cheek. He thought of his own daughter — one minute alive; the next minute dead. 'What's his name?'

'Louis. I decided to give him a French name.' Tears welled up in her eyes. 'Do you know, you are the first person to touch him — apart from the midwife that is.'

'Can I hold him?' Pablo asked.

Mercedes handed him over. Louis awoke from his sleep and stared at Pablo with his large dark eyes. He gurgled and kicked his tiny legs happily. Pablo kissed the child's forehead and handed him back. 'Don't hide him away. He's too precious.'

Tears streamed down Mercedes's face. It was a long time since she had heard such kind words.

'Wipe away those tears,' Pablo said, handing her a handkerchief, 'so that I can see the depth of your beautiful eyes.' She straightened her back in an attempt to pull herself together. 'We share much in common, dear lady. I also suffered coming here.' He told her about his wife and daughter. 'I see them in my dreams and sometimes feel like killing myself. So you see, life has been cruel to us both, but we are still here, so we must give thanks to God for that.'

Mercedes was so moved by Pablo's sincerity and kindness that she couldn't find words to answer him. He eased the tension by telling her he worked for a very kind shepherd who had more or less adopted him as the son he never had. 'I must count my blessings,' he said. 'Now, Mercedes, let me see you smile.'

At first she gave a shy smile, but with a little more coaxing, she laughed more.

'Can I see you again?' Pablo asked. 'Maybe we can meet here next weekend?' Mercedes nodded. 'Good. Now drink your wine and eat the food.' He raised his glass. 'I feel reborn.'

Mercedes felt the same, but she wasn't about to tell him that. She didn't want any more disappointments in life. Later that evening, she left the child in her room and walked along the quiet lane to the Chapel of Notre Dame de Villeneuve to give thanks to the Virgin for her good fortune in meeting Pablo. She cut a lock of her hair, put it in a box along with the bunch of wildflowers he'd given her, which she'd kept as a memento even though they were now dry and brittle, and offered them to the Virgin as a thank you. She placed the box on a narrow shelf on the wall alongside other votive offerings left there by so many other believers over the years, said a prayer, and left. Her heart felt lighter than it had been in a long time.

Some weeks later, Pablo declared his love to her. 'Let me take you in my arms and make you feel safe. Let me love you. Let me be a father to Louis too.'

How could Mercedes resist? He was much older than she, but he was a good man and she loved him too. They were married soon after Germany attacked Poland. As a Spaniard, Pablo was not called up to go to the front, and he and Mercedes lived with the old shepherd, who took a liking to this strong, beautiful woman who cooked and cleaned for them all. He even took a liking to little Louis and defended them against village gossip. After the shepherd died, Pablo inherited the farm and livestock, and except for the dark clouds of war on the horizon, they were happy.

When the Germans attacked France, Pablo told Dr Berdu he would do all he could to resist. 'I've seen what fascism can do,' he said. 'We must never give in.'

Dr Berdu shook his hand. 'Pablo, we may need your fighting spirit soon.'

Thus it was that Pablo and Mercedes opened their home to escapees from the very beginning, and like everyone else, they had no idea how it would end.

CHAPTER 6

1940–41

BILLY ENDED UP staying with Mercedes and Pablo for several weeks until Pablo decided the time was right to cross the border. When the snow was thick on the ground, he took him to a refuge above the town of Osséja, a few kilometres from the Spanish border. By car the drive would have taken under an hour; by foot through the snow, it took five hours. Once they reached the refuge, they rested for a while and ate the food Mercedes had prepared for them. Billy was already exhausted but Pablo insisted they continue. When they left Matemale, the snow was falling steadily; now there was a snowstorm — just the right conditions to cross the frontier without attracting attention. Billy had no idea where he was. Only Pablo knew they'd bypassed one of the barracks used by the border guards at Osséja by two kilometres. Any closer and the dogs would have picked up their scent.

They reached the frontier an hour later. 'This is it,' Pablo said, 'but we are not out of danger yet. Stay here while I find your guide. Don't move or I'll lose you.'

Pablo crossed into Spain and returned a short time later with the Spanish guide. Billy, who by now was shivering with cold and continuously stamping his feet to stop frostbite, looked at the short, shabbily dressed Spaniard carrying a rifle and wondered if he had been deceived. The man looked like a bandit. He did not smile or utter a single word.

'This is where you and I part ways,' Pablo said. 'Do not ask questions. Our friend doesn't want to draw attention to himself, and he's liable to kill you if you make trouble. Besides, he wouldn't understand you anyway. I can assure you that you're in safe hands so don't worry. From here you will be taken to the coast and from there to Gibraltar. God be with you.'

The pair disappeared into the ghostly whiteness of the snowstorm and Pablo returned to the refuge, where he slept until morning. The next day, he arrived back at Matemale and was greeted with a kiss from Mercedes.

'It went well,' he said, warming his hands in front of the fire. 'All being well, he will be back in Britain in a week's time.'

'Good,' Mercedes replied, 'because I had a visit from Dr Berdu. There's another parcel on the way.'

Pablo sat in his favourite chair by the fire, pulled some tobacco from his pouch, and filled his pipe. 'All I want now is some of your succulent *boules de picolat*.'

He picked Louis up, sat him on his lap, and gave him a big kiss. '*Mis dos queridas* — my two darlings who make me so happy despite this war.'

*

Throughout winter and spring, Justine worked with a small group of forgers on identity cards and travel documents in Toulouse. Baptism certificates were also provided for the Jews. In France, the Jewish problem grew even more desperate after news leaked out that Warsaw's Jews were being moved into the ghetto. It meant more safe houses needed to be found, and that was not an easy task. Plus, there was a new problem. Many of the helpers were young and enthusiastic, but they also had Communist leanings. When news leaked out that Hitler and Ribbentrop had met Molotov in Berlin, they were angry and disillusioned. Was it really possible that the Soviets would side with the Germans, especially after they'd supported the Communists in Spain? Surely not, yet it certainly appeared that way. They always thought the Soviets would help them. Now they were on their own, except for Britain who was still in danger of being invaded any day now. Paul Cassou suggested they focus their attention on North Africa as he suspected the great Rommel might not be so successful there. The BBC was constantly reporting the events there and, for many wanting to leave France, North Africa seemed the best option.

It was during one of these meetings that a helper, code-named "Jacques", brought up the fact that a man of similar age to him — early twenties — had been following him for a few weeks.

Everyone looked at each other. 'A few weeks! Does that mean he followed you here too?' Robert said, angrily.

Jacques was offended. 'Of course not, what do you take me for? I noticed him in one of the bars I frequent. There was something odd about him and I suspected he was watching me. When I left, he left too, but I gave him the run-around and haven't seen him for the past week. I'm particularly cautious. I just thought I'd mention it because the same might have been happening to some of you.'

'Anyone noticed anything unusual?' Robert asked, looking at everyone. They shook their heads. 'What does he look like?'

'Medium height, slim with mousy hair. No particular distinguishing features. Oh, and he wore a dark brown coat.'

Robert sighed. 'That's not much to go on, is it? Did he wear glasses?'

'No. Sorry, I can't tell you anymore. He just seemed — well — quite ordinary.'

'Why don't we set a trap?' Justine said. 'Then follow him. He could be a spy, maybe with the Abwehr or Gestapo.'

They all agreed. When Jacques was asked where he first noticed the man, he said at a bar near the corner of Quai de Tounis and Rue de Metz. 'Near the bridge.'

Everyone knew it.

A plan was hatched for Jacques to go there each evening and someone would watch. One of the girls, Mimi, a university student, would also be there and if the same person came, she would signal another of the group waiting on the quayside.

'Putain!' Robert said. 'As if we don't have enough to do.'

Justine agreed, but they all thought it was better to sort it out now before it was too late. '"X" would not like it at all if we put the network at risk.'

'Anyway,' said Justine, 'it's probably nothing — just Jacques being paranoid.' He gave her a dirty look and she threw him a kiss. After that everyone lightened up.

The group arranged their plan for the following evening and decided against telling "X" as they didn't want to worry him unnecessarily. Jacques went to the bar and passed the time drinking and reading a newspaper. Mimi sat on the other side of the room. Justine and Robert, pretending to be a couple, sat outside on a bench overlooking the River Garonne. From there they had a good view of the bar. After two hours, the stranger didn't turn up and they decided to go home, but not before a heated discussion about whether to do it again.

'Alright,' Justine said. 'Let's give it a week. If he doesn't turn up, we will conclude it was nothing.'

The next night, they repeated the exercise — and the night after — and the night after that. Still nothing happened. Then he appeared. Jacques looked at Mimi, who went outside to tell the others. Jacques stayed in the bar for another fifteen minutes then left. As agreed, he didn't look at the others, but walked across the bridge to the other side of the river. The man came out, got on a bicycle, and followed him. Mimi also had her bicycle and took off after them. At the other side of the river, Jacques stopped and sat on a bench. The stranger rode by, took a good look at him, and continued. Then Mimi appeared. Jacques indicated for her to follow him. The man turned down a narrow street and stopped at an apartment block where he went inside, taking his bicycle inside with him. Mimi returned to Jacques and the others.

'He went into an apartment block — 20 rue du Pont Vieux,' she said.

'Did he recognise you from the bar?' Robert asked.

'I don't think he saw me. There were other people in the street too.'

'Do we inform "X"?' Robert asked.

Justine suggested they tail him for a few days first. Everyone agreed and Mimi suggested she would be the one to do it as she'd had a good look at him. The problem was, it was impossible to stake out the area twenty-four hours a day as they all had work to do. They just hoped the man would appear again soon. He did. The next night, he stepped out of his apartment block, and rather than cycle, walked some distance to a bistro. There he met with a middle-aged couple. Mimi pulled a dark brown scarf over her hair, put on a pair of plain-looking glasses, and sat at a table as she had done in the bar, watching them. The couple appeared frightened. She couldn't hear what they were saying, but they seemed to be having a heated argument. They stopped talking when the waiter placed their food on the table. Mimi ordered a meal and quietly asked the same waiter if he knew who they were, saying she was looking for a friend.

The waiter narrowed his eyes. 'The man comes here regularly. As for the couple, I've never seen them before.' He moved closer to whisper in her ear as he placed a bread basket and cutlery on the table. 'I wouldn't ask too many questions if I were you.'

Mimi was stunned. When the waiter brought her meal, he made it obvious he wasn't going to say anything else. After the man and the couple had finished eating, their conversation started again, this time less heated. Ten minutes later, the man called the waiter over and paid the bill. The three got up and left. Mimi noticed that the couple were carrying a small suitcase each. She also observed that they were well-dressed, the man in a well-tailored suit with a smart overcoat, and the woman in a light brown cashmere coat with fur collar and cuffs. Everything about them told her they were a couple with money.

Mimi quickly paid her bill and left the premises. The three made their way back to the man's apartment. Mimi cycled all the way to Justine's apartment, and also notified Jacques and Robert.

'The couple gave me the impression they were on the run,' Mimi said. 'They had that same fear we've become used to seeing with the people we've helped.' Justine asked if they might be Jews. Mimi shrugged. 'Who knows, but I think that man was trying to help them.'

'Then why were they arguing, and why did the waiter warn you off?' Robert was puzzled.

'The poor things looked really scared,' Mimi replied. 'Maybe the man is doing the same as us — trying to help people on the run. Goodness knows, we've seen quite a few people show distress due to fear.'

Justine turned to Jacques. 'Maybe that's why he followed you. He suspected you were doing the same thing and thought you might help.'

'It all sounds too fishy to me,' Robert replied. 'I feel sorry for the couple if they are on the run, but we can't jeopardise ourselves. Let's leave it at that and just be careful. We've too much to do to go chasing people we barely know.'

Two weeks passed before Paul Cassou asked Justine to meet a man at the station again. 'He's an RAF pilot. His plane crashed near the Belgian border and our contacts in Paris have asked us to help him. Unfortunately, he's another who barely speaks French. You know the ropes. Take a bunch of red flowers, pretend he's your boyfriend, and take him to the safe house.'

Justine wondered if she should tell him about the stranger, but decided against it as no one had seen him since the episode with the couple in the bistro. When the time came to pick up the man, she arrived at the train station as usual with a bunch of red carnations and her book tucked under her arm. The platform was teeming with people and an announcement was made that the train was running late by half an hour. She went to the café on the platform, ordered a coffee, and pretended to read her book. At one point, she glanced up and saw the suspicious man they had followed a few weeks ago walk past the window. She strained to watch him and saw him stop and look at his watch. Was he waiting for someone on that train too?

A voice over the loudspeaker announced the arrival of the train and she went outside, careful to make sure the man wouldn't notice her. When the train arrived, it was full and she was in danger of losing him as she had to keep a lookout for her parcel. The passengers got off, filling the platform even more. Justine held the red flowers and book prominently in front of her and watched for someone to recognise her. A young man approached her. He was about to say something when the other man approached him and shook his hand effusively.

'Welcome to Toulouse,' the man said. 'It's good to see you again.' His face bore a beaming smile.

Justine's parcel appeared confused. Evidently, he hadn't been expecting someone else to turn up, especially a man. Justine immediately realised the man had walked into a trap and hurried away as fast as she could without attracting attention. She didn't dare look back at her parcel in case the other one recognised her. As soon as she was out of the station, she threw the flowers in a bin and put her book in her bag. A man called out to her.

'Hey, mademoiselle, why did you do that?' He fished them out of the bin. 'I can give these to my wife.'

Justine ignored him and walked away to hide behind a kiosk. From there, she glimpsed her parcel being escorted to a black car, which drove him away. She felt weak at the knees. Until now, everything had gone well. The kiosk owner asked if she wanted to buy something or was she going to stand there all day? She bought a magazine and glumly walked to Cassou's car, which she had been allowed to use, and headed home.

In the safety of her apartment, she burst into tears for the first time since she'd been involved with the network. Now she had to tell Paul Cassou what had taken place and she feared he would think her incompetent and a danger to them and ask her to leave. She picked up the phone.

'Cassou here,' the voice at the other end of the phone said. There was a moment's silence. Given that he was involved in secretive work, he immediately became suspicious. 'Hello, who's speaking, please?'

'Monsieur Cassou...' Justine's voice wavered. 'I am not feeling well today. If you don't mind, I will take the day off and try and get some sleep.'

'Justine!' Cassou instinctively knew something had gone wrong. He chose his words carefully. 'Of course, thank you for letting me know. I hope you feel well soon.'

He put the receiver down, picked up his hat and coat, and drove himself to her apartment. When she opened the door, he knew from the look on her face it was bad news. She told him the whole story, from the moment Jacques had seen a man he felt was suspicious, Mimi seeing the same man with a frightened couple, and now this.

Cassou considered the situation carefully before replying. 'I'm going to get you a camera,' he said.

Justine looked surprised. 'What does a camera have to do with what I've just told you?' she asked.

'If possible, we need a picture of anyone we think is suspicious — man or woman. This man is obviously some sort of spy, but without a picture, I can't go to my sources to see if they recognise him. In fact, I think both you and Robert need a camera. Naturally, it's impossible to give one to everyone.'

'I told you where he lived. Maybe I or Robert can hang around and get a picture.'

'Good idea. I'll get you one straight way.'

'I already have one — for my holiday snapshots. I never thought to use it. I would have thought it could draw attention to me.'

'Not if you're careful. You can assess the situation. If it's too risky, don't do it. But photographs can help us, especially in a case like this.'

The mood remained sombre as neither had any idea what happened to the airman she was supposed to pick up.

'If his French is not good...' Justine was stopped mid-sentence.

'*If*, and I stress *if*, something has gone wrong, it won't be the first time and it certainly won't be the last, so you must snap out of this way of thinking. It will bring us all undone.'

She apologised.

'I have to leave now,' Cassou said. 'I have an important meeting, but first I will call on Robert and inform him about our discussion. I don't want to appear harsh, but there will be no more assignments for you or Robert until this situation is sorted out.'

Justine felt as though she'd just blown her chances with the network. What would her father and Dr Berdu think? She had to find out who the man was.

Alone in her room, she went over the situation again and again. There was only one thing to do. She looked for her own camera and put it in her bag. The last time she'd used it was when she'd visited her parents. She recalled stopping to take photographs of the mountains at the Col de Pailhères. It was a place where she'd hiked and skied many times.

The next day, she met up with Robert and they agreed to stake out the man's apartment. Pretending to be a couple, they hung around, hoping the man would come out. After an hour or so, they realised if they stayed any longer, they would look suspicious themselves. Robert came up with another plan. He told Justine to be ready with the camera, walked to the apartment, and pressed one of the bells. An elderly man opened the door.

Robert flashed a card in front of the man, and then quickly put it back in his pocket. 'I've been sent out from the gas company. Someone has reported a leak in one of these apartments. I need to inspect the premises.'

The man looked at him. 'I'm the concierge. No one mentioned a leak to me.'

'Monsieur, there are leaks all the time and often people don't notice until it's too late. Can you please notify the occupants and I will make a quick inspection?'

The startled man told Robert to step inside. 'I'll wait by your desk while you get everyone out. It shouldn't take long. Oh, and please advise everyone not to light a cigarette.'

There were only four apartments and it didn't take long for the concierge to notify everyone. One by one, they all assembled into the hallway. An elderly couple, a single man, and the man they had been looking for.

'Please stay outside while I inspect your gas connections,' Robert said with an air of authority. 'The concierge will accompany me while I take a look.'

The disgruntled occupants went outside, complaining and asking each other who had reported a problem. In the meantime, Robert and the concierge went into each room. 'I can't smell anything,' the concierge said.

Robert looked thoughtful as he sniffed the air. 'There's certainly no distinctive odour of gas, no smell of rotten eggs.' He located the gas pipes easily. 'There's no hissing sound of leaking gas either' — he looked around the rooms — 'or dead or dying plants. I am satisfied the leak is not from coming from this building, but I would advise leaving the windows open for a while until we've located it. I think we can call everyone back inside. Do you mind if I use your telephone to call the gas company?'

'Go ahead,' the man replied.

They returned downstairs and while the concierge called the occupants back in and told them all was well, Robert picked up the phone and made a fake call in a louder than normal voice to the non-existent gas company. 'Yes, monsieur, I am quite satisfied there is no leak here.' A pause, while the men passed by. Then he raised his voice a little louder. 'Yes, monsieur, I will try that address next.'

Robert put the phone down, took a notebook from his pocket, and scribbled down some notes. 'Sorry to inconvenience you all,' he shouted out after them, thanked the concierge, and left.

In the street he saw Justine putting her camera away in her bag. 'Did you get him?' Robert asked, as they hurried away.

'I got them all, but how on earth did you manage that?'

When he told her, her eyes widened. '*Mon Dieu!* What an actor. Tell me, what *was* the card you showed the concierge?'

He pulled it out of his pocket and she burst out laughing. 'Toulouse Gas Company!' It was a card for a showroom selling household gas appliances. 'You're crazy,' she said.

'It worked, didn't it?' he replied with a grin. 'Now let's get the photos to "X".'

CHAPTER 7

Lies and Deception

PAUL CASSOU TOOK the roll of photographs from Justine and gave both her and Robert a lecture on letting their guard down and not letting him know of their suspicions in the first place.

'If you'd told me this when Jacques first noticed the man, maybe we could have done something. As it is now, it's highly likely we've lost a parcel.' Cassou tapped his pen on the desk while looking at Justine. 'If this man is a spy, I am surprised he didn't wait until you'd made contact. Then he would have had you both. Let's hope it means he didn't dig up anything on us.'

Justine could not bear to look Cassou in the face. She felt responsible.

'As soon as I get this roll developed, I will see if my sources can identify him,' Cassou continued. 'Until then, I don't want any of you meeting up — and, Robert, I want you to vacate your apartment immediately, just in case you've been watched. The same goes for Jacques. Notify him immediately.' Cassou wrote an address on a piece of paper and handed it to Robert. 'You and Jacques can both stay here for the moment. It's an apartment owned by the company. Don't invite anyone there though.'

Robert took the note and apologised again for the situation they'd found themselves in. Cassou ignored the apology and told him he could leave, but Justine would need to stay as he had urgent work for her to do on behalf of the company. When they were alone, Cassou handed her a file of documents.

'I'm sorry we didn't let you know at the beginning,' she said, noting the cool look on his face.

'What's done is done. I'll leave you to get on with your work while

61

I get this film developed.'

After he left, she sat at her desk and let out a deep sigh. It had been a stupid thing not to tell him. She realised she still had a lot to learn. As she did her work, her mind kept wandering back to the man on the platform. How on earth had he known there was a parcel to be picked up? She hoped there would be a good reason for this and that the man was still alive.

The work Cassou had given Justine was time-consuming: New contracts to be drawn up for charcoal deliveries all over France, particularly Vichy. She noted that many addresses in the occupied zone were for German companies which had once belonged to someone else. She had learned from Cassou that one of the conditions of the armistice was to pay the costs of the occupying German army, which amounted to millions of Reichsmark per day. Because the artificial currency was arranged in favour of the Germans, they were able to requisition many French companies. A closer look indicated that many of the previous owners were probably Jews. None of this was reported in the news. 'Bastards,' she said aloud to herself. 'They are plundering the country.'

Justine couldn't stop thinking about the Jews. They had helped quite a few flee to Spain so far, and she had little doubt that Cassou had helped others and not told her. He was always so secretive. Anti-Semitism was particularly virulent in Vichy France. She'd learned of the drastic measures imposed on Jews through newspapers and business contacts, but the real hardships she'd learned of from those they'd helped flee the country. She had even seen propaganda notices on "who is a Jew", which disgusted her. Many businesses and professions were now closed to Jews; the Germans confiscated all their radios, then their telephones, and they were forbidden to use public telephones. They could not change their address or leave their homes between 8:00 p.m. and 5:00 a.m., and all public places, parks, and certain shops were now closed to them. The Germans issued new restrictions and decrees by the week. Jews were barred from public swimming pools, restaurants, cafés, cinemas, and concerts, etc. Their cars and bicycles had been confiscated during the first weeks of the Occupation and they were only allowed to ride in the last carriage on the metro. Foreign Jews in the non-occupied zone were particularly vulnerable and being rounded up.

With all this, Justine wondered why any Jew would want to stay in France. The problem was, it had all happened so fast and if they hadn't fled before the Occupation, it was almost impossible to flee now without help. Many simply did not have the know-how or the means to pay people to help them.

By nine o'clock, she could barely keep her eyes open. Just a few more documents to type and she would go home. She heard heavy footsteps approaching in the hallway and Paul Cassou entered. The look on his face told her all was not well.

He put four photographs in front of her. The rest — her holiday snapshots — he put aside.

'Point him out to me,' Cassou said, matter-of-factly.

She tapped her index finger on one man in the small group outside the house they had watched. 'That's him.'

Cassou shook his head. 'My source told me they have it on good authority he works for the Abwehr.'

'Is he French?' Justine asked.

'Yes, he's French alright. His name is Gabriel Martin. He's an engineer and works in the civil service. It seems he lived in Berlin for a while and was recruited there. He's probably been spying for them for a while now, we believe before the German Occupation. He reports to someone here in Toulouse by the name of Monsieur Guy Vigneau, a German posing as a Frenchman originally living in Brussels until the Belgians surrendered. He, in turn, reports to his superiors in Paris and Berlin. I don't need to tell you the Abwehr's network of spies is far-reaching.' Cassou scooped up the four photographs and slipped them into the inside pocket of his jacket. 'I have no idea what he told them about us — if anything. For all our sakes, we'd better hope he knows nothing. As for the poor airman... well, best not to think about it. He's either dead or been sent to Germany by now.' Justine winced.

'I haven't heard anything negative from our contacts in Paris,' Cassou continued, 'so I am presuming he may have come under suspicion whilst travelling here. If he was tortured, all he would have been able to say was that he was to meet a woman in Toulouse. He wasn't given your name — only that you would be carrying flowers and a book, *The Count of Monte Cristo*. You'd better get rid of that now and we'll use another one.'

Justine had a hard time absorbing it all. 'We are in the free zone,' she declared, and then realised that sounded quite naïve.

'Only until they find an excuse to occupy the whole of France,' Cassou said. 'That's why we're helping so many to flee. De Gaulle knows this. Winston Churchill and the rest of the free world know it too. Even Pétain must know it, although he will never admit it. I'll drop you home, and then call round to tell Robert and Jacques. We'll lie low for a while.' He picked up her coat and held it open while she slipped into it. They drove to her apartment in silence.

'Get a good night's sleep,' he said, as she got out of the car. 'You'll feel better in the morning.' He kept the engine running and watched her until he was sure she was safely in her apartment. After scanning the road to make they weren't being watched, he drove away.

When she arrived at work the following day, Justine was told Cassou was away on business and was expected to be gone for a week. They were to carry on as normal. Ten days later, Cassou returned and informed her in his office that on May 14, almost four thousand foreign Jews had been arrested by French police. They were interned in Pithiviers and Beaune-la-Rolande. Justine had heard these rumours, but was not sure what to believe.

'It's worse than we thought in the occupied zone,' Cassou said, 'particularly for the Jews. My contacts have over two hundred Jews hiding out in safe houses in Paris alone, plus there are Allied soldiers as well. I really don't know how we'll cope. It's not just more trusted people along the escape line that we need; we need money to pay people too. And then there's the issue of food, which is becoming more difficult to get by the day.' The list of problems went on and on: trusted forgers, paper, ink...

Paul Cassou was usually calm and emotionally controlled, but Justine had never seen him look so downcast. He pulled a bottle of whisky and two glasses from out of his desk cupboard. 'Would you like one?' He'd already poured it before she could answer.

Justine hated the stuff but didn't want to offend him.

'So,' he said, after a few large sips, 'the bad news for us is that one of our groups in Paris was infiltrated by a collaborator working for the Vichy government. According to the agreed rules set out in the armistice, which we already know, the French authorities have been working with the Sicherheitsdienst — the intelligence service of the SS — and their security police to round up not only Jews, but also anti-fascists and other dissidents.'

'What exactly do you mean?' Justine already thought the Jews would be deported as had happened in Germany and Austria, but she wasn't sure what he meant about the others. 'If they have to deport the Communists or any other anti-fascists, we're talking about thousands of people. These people will resist.'

A half-smile crossed Cassou's smooth, sun-burnt face as he shook his head. 'Justine. Do you have any idea how many people belong to the French Popular Party and the National Popular Rally? They each have twenty to thirty thousand members, and there's talk about developing a special militia group which will be given unprecedented powers. What happened to resisters in Germany will happen here. People will vanish without a trace.'

Somehow, she managed to finish the whisky, which had the effect of numbing her slightly, and Cassou continued with the story of the collaborator. 'Apparently this man spoke perfect English and said he'd been left behind at Dunkirk. He pretended to know little French. A couple took him in for a few days and he maintained his facade very well. He said little, asked few questions, and altogether was a charming man. When asked about his civilian clothes, he said he stole them from a tailors' shop one night. He evidently knew his military stuff because when he was later asked about his regiment and his life in England, it all seemed to stack up. He was given the green light and, on the day before he was due to leave Paris, was given a new ID as were two others, one of them being our parcel who, it seems, showed him his ID and said he was going to Toulouse.'

Cassou went on to tell Justine that the other parcel was to be picked up elsewhere and it seems that he had the good sense not to show anyone his ID or discuss his travel plans. 'The two men — the collaborator and our man — travelled together. At some point, near Toulouse, the train stopped and the collaborator got off without our man seeing him. He immediately telephoned his contact in Toulouse and described the man on the run: his name and address on the false ID, the exact clothes he was wearing, the colour of his hair. He was most observant.'

'How do you know that?' Justine asked.

'Because it was a small station, and the station master, who works with us, overheard his call. He tried to communicate this to one of our contacts at the station in Toulouse, but unfortunately it was his day off. Bad luck.'

Justine's jaw dropped. 'Bad luck! I'll say it was.' She pushed her glass towards him and he refilled it.

'You don't really like whisky, do you?' he said with a half-smile.

'No, but right this moment I need something strong.'

'We've had a near miss, Justine. I believe the man who was watching you may have suspected you, but as far as we know, he had nothing on you. All the same, it's a lesson to be learnt that we are being watched. Do I make myself clear?'

Justine nodded. 'Absolutely. There's something else though. What about Monsieur Vigneau, or whatever his real name is?'

'His real name is Gerhard Krauss and he spends much of his time living in the Hôtel Lutetia in Paris.'

'I know it. It was a frequent gathering place for the anti-Nazi German exiles. Heinrich Mann was one of them.'

'The hôtel now houses a different type of clientele — the Abwehr. However, I have been informed that he comes here every week but rarely ventures out, which is why no one ever sees him. Obviously, he is collecting information from his informers. I do know that he drives here rather than take the train.' Cassou didn't say any more, but Justine felt he knew much more than he was going to say. He was up to something and she was itching to know what it was, but refrained from asking.

'Thank you for filling me in,' she said. 'I think I'd better get going now. I promised a friend I would go with her to the cinema.'

Paul Cassou watched her leave. He had come to like and respect her. To him, she was the daughter he never had, but one thing worried him. She was fine now, but how would she be if the Germans moved into the free zone? Cassou knew it was only a matter of time before an opportunity presented itself for them to occupy the whole of France. He switched on the radio to listen to the BBC. De Gaulle, the man who had been sentenced to death in absentia, was about to speak. Both England and Germany were being heavily bombed, and de Gaulle was still urging the French to resist. Already many Frenchmen had gone to join the Free French in North Africa, which pleased Cassou enormously. He felt a surge of pride when he thought of the men his network had already helped to get there, but the situation was still far from good. Greece too had just fallen. How he wished America would not be so obstinate and come to the aid of Britain. Without the Americans, he felt the free world would collapse.

On June 22, Justine learned from the BBC that the Germans had invaded the Soviet Union. She was alone in her apartment and shouted out in glee. '*Dieu merci,* this will be their undoing. If Napoleon couldn't conquer Russia, the Nazis won't.' She couldn't wait to see what the others had to say.

She was one of the first to arrive at work the next day where employees were poring over the newspaper. If she had hoped for a splashy headline from the French denouncing it, she was wrong. The Vichy propaganda machine was working overtime. Jacques Doriot, the leader of the fascist French Popular Party, commented, "This war is our war, we will see it through to the end, to victory" and called for French troops to be sent the Eastern Front.

Justine quickly understood that sending a military unit of French volunteers to the Soviet–German front would be considered a good propaganda move. The others in the room understood that too. Paul

Cassou was careful of the people he employed, even though they may have not actively been helping his escape network, and they were all voicing their disgust with Jacques Doriot. While they were in discussions about how this would affect the French people, she noticed a smaller headline: *Man killed when his car was struck by a train at a crossing just outside Toulouse. The dead man was identified as Guy Vigneau, a Parisian who rented a property in Toulouse.* The article said little more except that the car appeared to have stalled on the tracks and the incident was deemed an accident.

A huge smile crossed her face. She knew this was no accident. One of the secretaries noticed and made a comment. 'What have you got to smile about, Justine? This war just got bigger.'

She blushed. 'I was thinking about something else, not the war,' she replied.

Another employee, a male filing clerk, made a comment in jest. 'Maybe our Justine has a boyfriend and she's not telling us.'

She poked her tongue out at him. 'If I have, you will be the last to know.' They all laughed. At that moment, Paul Cassou entered the room. 'Look, monsieur,' someone said, waving the newspaper in the air. 'What do you think of it? Now the Soviets will change sides and we'll have another ally.'

Cassou went into his office and turned to face them. 'Be careful who you share this good news with. Not everyone will agree with you.' He closed the door behind him and the room went silent.

'He's right,' Justine said. 'Best keep our thoughts to ourselves. We don't want Doriot's thugs bashing us up, do we?'

They all agreed.

Later that day, Cassou called Justine into his office. 'I presume you saw the other article in the newspaper?' he said.

'I did, monsieur. Well done.'

He looked at her, but did not smile. 'I have no idea how it happened, if that's what you're thinking.'

'Of course not. I understand.'

He eyed her carefully. 'Good. Now that we've got that straight, I have some jobs for you. So, "Jacqueline", it's back to work again.' Justine was relieved. She was getting bored doing nothing. He took his wallet out and handed her some money. 'A little something for you to celebrate with Robert, Jacques, Mimi, and the others, but a note of caution, make it look like a birthday celebration. Do *not* mention the recent events.'

'Thank you, monsieur. It will be wonderful to catch up with them again.' She tucked the money in her pocket. 'And the other work — what assignment do you have for me?'

'Take a week off. I want you to go back home to the Donezan. Judge the political situation there. Speak with your father and the doctor and find out what's going on. We need more safe houses and helpers.' He stopped and studied her for a moment. 'I don't have to tell you what we need. You know.'

Justine felt honoured that he still had faith in her after the incident with the stranger. 'May I ask something, monsieur?' Her voice was almost timid. 'The man we photographed — the collaborator — what happened to him?'

Cassou grinned. 'You don't have to worry about him any longer.'

She knew from his short reply and his grin, this meant that he had "disposed" of him, but he would never tell her.

She left the room and returned to her desk. Her heart was beating wildly. The others saw the look on her face — a look that was different, a look they couldn't quite fathom.

'You were in there a long time,' one of them said. 'You didn't get the sack, did you?'

His comment broke the ice and they all burst out laughing.

That evening, Robert, Jacques, Mimi, and two others, joined her in a little celebratory drink. They were all relieved to be back together again. No one mentioned the invasion of the Soviet Union, the car accident, or the stranger. Justine was sure they too had been warned against it.

She went home that night feeling happier than she had in a long time, although the man she was supposed to have picked up still plagued her thoughts.

CHAPTER 8

Keep Your Friends Close and Your Enemies Closer

IF THERE WAS one time of the day Justine loved the most in the Donezan, it was dusk. Soft, silent shadows crept across the landscape, transforming the contours of the mountains and valleys from a palette of variegated greens into shades of rose and purples, then to inky blue-black, until eventually there were no contours left — only the darkness of the earth and a night sky lit by the moon and countless twinkling stars. It was at times like this that she felt at peace. There was a comforting silence, yet if one listened carefully, it was not silent at all. Somewhere within those shadows was an orchestra of wildlife. The hoot of an owl, the rustle of a bird settling down for the night, the croak of a frog, a babbling brook, the creak of a branch when there was a soft breeze. It was the sound of peace, and just as each season nurtured the next, this glorious quiet nurtured her soul.

Looking out from her bedroom, she understood she'd missed it more than she realised. Living in Toulouse, life had been so hectic, particularly over the past few years, that she'd had no time to reflect. 'Reflection is good for you,' her father once told her, and she certainly had a lot to reflect on.

There was a soft knock on the bedroom door and her mother entered. 'I've brought you a cup of hot milk and a biscuit.'

Justine smiled. 'Maman, do you realise you have been doing this since as long as I can remember?'

'Doing what?'

'Giving me hot milk and a biscuit at bedtime.'

Colette put the small tray on the bedside table. 'Just because you have grown up and live in a big city does not mean I cannot care for you as I always have. You are still my little Justine, you know.'

Justine wrapped her arms around her mother. 'I didn't mean to be ungrateful. You know I love you.'

'And I you, my sweet, but I think you are taking on too much. You have a good job — you must be careful.'

'What does Papa think? Does he agree with you?'

'You are the light of his life and he thinks you're a smart girl, but we can't help worrying. If anything happened to you, I don't—'

Justine cut her short. '*Nothing* is going to happen to me. You worry for nothing.' She patted the side of the bed. 'Now come and sit on the bed with me and tell me how *you* are. You look a little drawn these days. Are you ill and you're not telling me?'

'It's true, I've not been feeling quite myself, but Théo says I'm fine. I just need a rest.'

'There you are.' Justine squeezed her mother's hand affectionately. 'You worry about me, but you don't look after yourself.' Colette stared ahead for a few moments in reflection. 'What's wrong, Maman?'

'It's your father. I worry about him too. He disappears for days on end. He's changed, you know. He used to be so quiet and — well, predictable — always with his head in his books. Now he disappears for days and never tells me what he's doing. "Trust me," he says. I'm not sure that I know him anymore.'

'Maman, you have always been a worrier. We *all* change — even you. He hasn't got another woman, has he?' It was meant as a joke, but her mother didn't smile.

'I wouldn't know.'

'You're being quite silly, you know,' Justine replied, light-heartedly. 'If he is with an upstanding man like Dr Berdu, then I doubt it.' She sighed. 'You know we have problems because of the Germans. If Papa is quiet, it's because he loves you and is protecting you, that's all.'

'Maybe you're right. Anyway, I'm glad you're home. That will cheer me up.'

Colette kissed her goodnight and went into her bedroom. Her father was out and wasn't expected back until the early hours of the morning. It wasn't hard to guess where he'd gone. Her mother was worrying unnecessarily. She took a sip of the hot milk and put on the radio and listened to some music. Lucienne Boyer was singing *"Parlez-moi d'amour"*, one of her favourites. She hummed to the music and swirled round the room. It was such a beautiful love song and it occurred to her that she had never been in love — not even a teenage fantasy. Finding love would be even harder now; you couldn't trust anyone.

The song finished and she flopped on the bed, watching the crescent moon in the night sky. No time for love — not until the Germans had left French soil. She didn't want to end up like her mother, worrying every time her father left the house.

Justine never heard her father return that night. She was fast asleep in her feather bed. When she went downstairs for breakfast, he was sitting at the table eating a hearty breakfast. She put her arms around him and kissed the top of his head as he continued to eat.

'Your mother says you are staying for a week this time,' he said, wiping his mouth with a large chequered serviette.

'That's right. Monsieur Cassou gave me some time off so I thought we could go hiking like old times.'

'Good idea, but it will have to wait until tomorrow as I have some things to do at the school.'

'I'll walk there with you. I may even go and visit the château. It's been years since I climbed to the top. I wonder if it's still safe to climb.'

'I don't think that's a good idea,' her mother said. 'Occasionally rocks tumble down, especially after a heavy snowstorm.'

Armand interrupted. '*Chérie*, you know she's as sure-footed as a mountain goat. She'll be fine.'

Colette picked up his empty plate and mug, and frowned. 'Like father, like daughter,' she replied. 'Obstinate. Just be careful.'

It was another beautiful day in the Donezan when Justine and her father walked into the village. The fields were a mass of blue, white, and yellow wildflowers and the scent filled her nostrils. She let out a deep sigh.

'All this beauty reminds me of you and Maman and the first notebook you gave me for pressed flowers. I still keep a botanical notebook. In fact, I've brought one with me. Who knows, I might even find a rare orchid.'

They parted ways at the school. The approach to the château was across the road and she knew her father would be keeping an eye out for her. Justine climbed to the top in no time at all. She knew it so well she could have done it blindfolded. When she reached the only remaining room in the château, the roof long gone and the remains of the thick walls stubbornly defying the elements through the centuries, she took her camera out of her bag and looked for the best spots to take photographs. Luckily there were a couple of deep, arched windows on which she could sit, which gave her an excellent view towards the Massif du Madrès to the south. For other photographs of the area, she had to venture outside the walls and perch carefully on the steep, almost vertical granite slope on which the castle was built. She took a few more photographs towards the south, where the land stretched out in a series of cultivated terraces interspersed with orchards and woods, and then retraced her steps back down the winding path. This gave her a good vantage point of the other side of the castle, past the schoolhouse towards Carcanières, Le Puch, La Pla, Artigues, Rouze, and Mijanès. Beyond these villages were lakes and more mountains: the pic de Ginebre, and the steep and dangerous pic de la Camisette, which she passed coming over the Col de Pailhères. When she was satisfied she'd photographed the entire area around Mont-Saint-Jean, she headed back to the village and noticed a dark-haired young man standing by the Memorial to the Fallen during the Great War. He was holding his bicycle and watching her.

'I thought it was you,' the man said. 'I haven't seen you for ages. Welcome home.'

'Claude Durand! What a lovely surprise.'

'How long has it been?' Claude asked. 'Quite a while. Each time I heard you were home I missed you.' He looked her up and down. 'You are no longer the Justine I remember — the girl with the long plaits and colourful ribbons. You have blossomed into a beautiful woman. City life certainly agrees with you.'

Justine smiled. 'You don't look so bad yourself — quite dashing, in fact. What are you doing with yourself these days?'

'Didn't your father tell you? I'm a gendarme now. Here in the village.'

Justine raised her eyebrows in surprise. 'You — a gendarme! You were one of the naughtiest boys in the class.'

They both laughed. The two had known each other all their lives. They had played together as children and gone to the same school. Justine's father had taught him, while she was taught by Maria in the girls' class. The laughter gave way to sadness when Claude told her his father had died and his mother had suffered a stroke and was now bedridden.

'I had to grow up quickly,' he said, 'get a job and look after her. There's no one else. It was your father's idea for me to take this job. I'm surprised he never told you. They were recruiting more gendarmes in the area and he thought I would make a good candidate. I did my apprenticeship in Perpignan.'

'But you always wanted to go to university and become a teacher.'

'We all have dreams, Justine, but not all of us are lucky enough to achieve them. Fate had a different plan for me.'

'Are you happy?'

'As happy as I ever will be, I suppose. Monsieur le Commissioner Godard, my boss, is a bit old-fashioned — a stickler for doing things by the book, if you know what I mean — but he's a good man and I have a fellow companion from Mijanès. We get on well.' He sighed. 'I suppose I must count my blessings. There's not much else to do around here and I certainly wasn't cut out to be an agricultural worker like Papa — or a shepherd. I was also lucky this job meant I wasn't sent to the front when war was declared. I might have been killed or ended up in a German camp.'

Justine thought of Jules Cassou and wondered how he was coping.

'Anyway, enough about me. What about you? I heard you passed all your exams at university and now have a good job.' He grinned. 'You must have to be driving a car like that. What is it — a Citroën 7C — a Traction Avant? Very smart.'

Justine laughed. 'I certainly couldn't afford a car like that. It belongs

74

to my boss and he occasionally lets me use it to come here.'

'He must like you a lot to do that.'

'It's not what you think. You may be a gendarme, but you're still cheeky. My boss is a happily married man, and besides, he's old enough to be my father. I often use the car for work.' Justine playfully wagged her finger at him. 'So don't go spreading rumours — or...'

'Or what?'

'Or — I'll have you charged.'

They both burst out laughing.

'Do you have a "friend"?' Claude asked.

'If you mean a boyfriend, the answer is no.'

'I'm surprised. You've blossomed into a rose. I'd have thought you'd have plenty of admirers chasing after you.'

'Maybe I do. If I did, I wouldn't tell you. What about you? I see you're not wearing a ring.'

'I did have a girl, but someone stole her from me — someone with better prospects.' He gave a bittersweet laugh and there were a few seconds of awkward silence before Claude changed the subject. 'Are you still an amateur botanist? I recall you used to keep a book and were always pressing wildflowers.'

'You have a good memory. Yes, in fact I often carry it with me.'

'Did you know the Corona del Rey is in bloom at the moment?'

Justine's face lit up. 'Really! Where? I've been trying to see it in flower for years.'

'About an hour from here, halfway between Puyvalador and Usson.'

Justine shot him an enquiring glance. 'Where exactly?'

'In the gorge. It just happens to be my day off so I could show you if you like?'

'Would you?' She was beside herself at the thought of seeing this beautiful slow-growing plant that only flowered once in its lifetime.

'Do you still have your bicycle? Going by car would be difficult and I don't think your boss would appreciate it if it rolled down the cliff.' Knowing the terrain, Justine agreed. 'Meet me back here after lunch — two thirty sharp — and wear sturdy walking shoes.'

Justine was so thrilled at the thought of seeing this plant that she was at their meeting place ten minutes early. They cycled for about forty minutes and left their bicycles in the bushes at a certain point where the terrain rose sharply towards a granite cliff face. From there they clambered through ferns and over fallen rocks, several of which were covered in velvet-like moss due to the dampness from a narrow waterfall that thundered through a nearby narrow fissure in the rockface. Claude led the way, clawing onto rocks and bushes until they reached a ledge, barely wide enough to stand on. He took Justine's hand and pulled her up.

'Now comes the hard part,' he warned her. 'We have to get around this ledge.'

The sun was beating down and sweat was pouring off them both, but the view across the gorge was stunning and dramatic. Not a building in sight. Justine was thankful she didn't suffer from vertigo. One slip and she would go hurtling to her death. She pressed her back against the rock and cautiously inched herself another few metres until the ridge widened and levelled out onto a stony outcrop. She looked ahead and gasped out loud. There ahead, clinging to the cliff face, were at least ten Corona del Reys in full bloom, each one suddenly sprouting a central flower stalk almost sixty centimetres in length and covered with a mass of up to five hundred small white flowers.

'Mon Dieu! They are stunning,' Justine exclaimed and took her camera out of her bag. 'To think it takes each one five years to bloom.' Claude watched while she snapped shot after shot. 'Why don't you sit here?' she called out to him. 'Let me take a photograph of you with this magnificent specimen.'

Claude was only too happy to oblige. What he didn't realise was that Justine had spotted caves further up the rock face and wanted to photograph them too. After a few more photographs of the gorge itself, they headed back, spotting several curious isards with their ruddy brown summer coat, graceful long legs, and backward-hooked horns watching down on them from the higher peaks.

'I can't thank you enough,' Justine said. 'You have no idea how thrilled I am.'

'You can repay me by accompanying me to the fête at Formiguères on Saturday. That is if you are still here.' He gave her a cheeky wink. 'You won't be disappointed. I believe there's going to be a few bands there. Lots of entertainment — just like old times.'

'All right, you win. It's the least I can do. But won't you be working?'

'I'll do a swap with my partner.'

They parted ways outside the church in Mont-Saint-Jean. Her father just happened to be heading home at the same time and she told him all about their afternoon.

'He told me what happened to his parents and that it was you who advised him to become a gendarme. Is that right?' she asked.

'Yes. I knew he wanted to go on and study, but his mother needed him. He seems to be enjoying his work. Let's face it, there's not that much for him to do around here, is there? Hardly any murders, the occasional cow or sheep theft, and that's about it.'

'Until now,' Justine replied. Her father knew she was referring to the evaders.

'Claude doesn't venture too far past Formiguères. His area is the Donezan.'

'Do you trust him, Papa?'

Armand stopped in his tracks and looked at her. 'Yes, I trust him, but I don't know about the commissioner. He keeps his thoughts close to his chest. All our evaders have reached Spain, and several Frenchmen and Allied friends have come back into France. Were you suggesting we bring him into our network?'

'Not exactly, but if things get worse, we will be in need of more helpers. Maybe he's worth keeping an eye on.'

'I'm already doing that,' Armand replied. 'I might add that I think I know the inhabitants of Mont-Saint-Jean better than you do.' There was a note of annoyance in her father's voice. 'I'm as aware as you that we need more helpers, but we have to be careful.'

They arrived home to find Théo and Babette Berdu at the house. Babette looked very happy and was clearly enjoying motherhood. They had been blessed with a healthy girl — Marie, who Babette referred to as their *petit ange*. "Little Angel" had auburn hair, blue eyes, and her mother's fine features, and was now walking and getting into mischief. She constantly needed attention, which both her mother and Colette provided joyfully. After dinner, Justine accompanied her father and Dr Berdu into the sitting room, where they discussed the situation of the evaders and the worsening situation in the occupied zone. Her father produced a small notebook in which he'd made a note of everyone they'd helped. Not all the evaders were sent from Paul Cassou's network in Toulouse; some came through Dr Berdu's contacts in Marseille and Perpignan. Over the past year there was a noticeable rise in Jews fleeing the occupied zone, and since the first roundup of foreign Jews in Paris, that number was growing at an alarming rate.

Justine voiced her concern about her father keeping a notebook. He showed it to her and she could barely decipher it. He had used his own code to remember each one — names that he gave people from books he'd read. Billy McGregor was there as Billy the Kid, as was an Australian soldier called Richard who he'd named Moby Dick. There was another British airman by the name of Tommy who he'd called Tom Sawyer, and on it went. Only the Jews were identified with their real names. Against each name was a date and a small tick.

'Why are you doing this, Papa?' Justine asked. 'You know they travel on false IDs. Cassou would be angry if he knew. It could compromise us if you were caught.' She looked at Dr Berdu and asked if he knew about the book.

'Of course. We discussed it the first time we helped someone. We need to account for all those we help and where they go after they leave us. Each helper and smuggler must assure us that our parcels are safe. When we know they have reached Spain, we try to find out if they safely reached the embassies in Barcelona, Madrid, or arrived in Gibraltar, North Africa, and England. Then we tick each one. From the moment you or any of my contacts elsewhere send someone here, we are responsible for these people. Their life is in our hands. With more and more people needing help, we not only must account for them, but know what it's costing us — and that, Justine, is a lot of money, which we are quickly running out of.'

He could tell she was still concerned. 'Don't worry. Your father keeps this book safely hidden. Even your mother doesn't know it exists. I also have my own book.' Justine raised her eyebrows in surprise. 'Remember,' Berdu continued, 'we don't always operate together. Your father might take someone to a safe house while I might be meeting up with another contact or trying to find a smuggler when I'm doing my medical rounds in the border towns.' He paused for a moment. 'One day the Germans will leave France and we will want to know how many of our parcels survived. There is also another reason we need this information. If something goes wrong and someone is betrayed, we need to find out who that person is. The notebooks help us retrace our steps.'

'I understand,' Justine replied.

'We are in the unoccupied zone, but we are still monitored,' Armand added. 'How Cassou operates, especially within the occupied zone, is entirely his business, which I am sure he would never discuss with you. We are showing you this because of our family bond. So let's keep this between the three of us, shall we?'

Justine nodded. 'You have my word.' She wondered if Cassou did keep a little book of names too. Her father was right, he would never tell her. It occurred to her that, in all likelihood, he did, especially knowing that he had connections throughout the whole of France. Without a record, it would be impossible to remember everyone.

'Now, Armand,' Berdu said, looking at the clock on the mantelpiece, 'it's almost time for de Gaulle's speech. Maybe we can enjoy a little cognac while we listen?'

Justine took three glasses from the drinks cabinet and poured them all a drink. Without uttering a word, they listened to de Gaulle still urging resistance. Justine wanted to tell them about Gabriel Martin and the "accident" concerning Monsieur Vigneau, but she was sworn to secrecy. Knowing how close she was to her father and Dr Berdu, not being able to discuss this or any of her work in Toulouse was hard for her, but she knew it was in all their best interests. If Cassou wanted them to know, he would tell her.

During the next few days, Justine hiked around the countryside with her father. The weather was warm, the air fresh, and the dense forest that held so many secrets was green and verdant, interspersed with patches of colourful wildflowers. It made one feel good to be alive. Throughout these walks, she took lots of photographs: mountains, plateaus, villages, lakes, and dams. She never told him, but her father knew exactly why she was doing it. She also picked the occasional wildflower and pressed them into her book, writing the common name and the Latin name underneath. Armand asked if he could take a look. He studied it carefully, looking at her drawings and tiny notes.

When he handed it back, he made a comment. 'I see Théo and I are not the only ones to keep a notebook. You also keep your own little book.'

Justine looked at him. 'I don't know what you mean?'

Her father burst out laughing. She knew perfectly well what he meant.

The week flew by quickly. Every day they talked about the situation in the unoccupied zone, particularly the plight of the undesirables — mainly Communists and foreign Jews, many of whom had been in France speaking out against fascism since Hitler's rise to power. In theory, the unoccupied zone was under French administration, but due to increased German pressure, in March 1941, the Vichy government created a central agency and the General Commissariat for Jewish Affairs now coordinated anti-Jewish legislation and policy throughout the whole of France. In an effort to ensure that material goods and assets confiscated from the Jewish population would not fall into German hands, the government instituted an extensive program of "Aryanization", appropriating Jewish-owned property for the French state. Such a move left most Jews in France destitute. It particularly affected foreign Jews. Now the French authorities interned thousands of them under deplorable conditions in French-administered detention camps such as Gurs, Saint-Cyprien, Rivesaltes, Le Vernet, and Les Milles, all of which had once housed the Spanish refugees. With a stroke of the pen, the hated camps, filled with disease and hunger which carried off the weak and vulnerable like the plague, were once again put to use.

Knowing the dire situation in these camps, Dr Berdu, aided by his associates, did what they could to rescue as many Jews as possible, but the need for more safe houses, helpers, and smugglers was indeed dire. To anyone passing through the Donezan, the region still appeared as peaceful as ever, but in reality, things were becoming desperate. Justine's father said that if they were to continue, they would need more funds. Somehow this fact had to be relayed to de Gaulle, who could put pressure on Churchill. Cassou thought the same thing.

On the day of the fête in Formiguères, Justine's parents decided they too wanted to join them, so rather than take the bus, she drove them there in her car. With most people making their way on foot, bicycle, or cart, the arrival of such a beautiful car attracted a lot of attention, and a small crowd gathered around to look at it. Most locals already knew the Joubert family and congratulated Justine on finding a good job in Toulouse. However, there were a few who displayed a touch of envy. While the band in the square played jaunty music and the smiles of people having a good time provided an uplifting mood to the day, one man in particular watched them with a cold look.

'Who's that?' Justine asked in a low voice. 'That,' whispered Claude, 'is the new commissioner of Formiguères — Monsieur Rossignol.'

'What happened to the other commissioner?'

'He was getting ready to retire, but we think he was removed before his tenure was up to make way for this man, who by all accounts is pro-German and pro-Vichy, so we must be on our best behaviour.'

'*Mon ami*, Claude, I am *always* on my best behaviour.' She gave him a cheeky smile and they headed towards the square to find a table. They were lucky — a family were just leaving and offered them theirs. While they waited for drinks, Claude excused himself to go and say hello to a gendarme from another village.

Justine moved closer to her father and whispered, 'Papa, did you know this new commissioner was pro-Vichy and pro-German?'

'I did hear something of the sort, but I've never seen him until today.' They gave each other a knowing look. 'Let's just try and enjoy ourselves, shall we?'

With the fête in full swing — couples dancing, people laughing as if they didn't have a care in the world — Justine eyed Claude, standing by the band, deep in conversation with the other gendarme, and wondered what they were talking about. They both wore a serious look. A couple with a small child came towards their table and greeted them. It was Pablo, Mercedes, and Louis. Armand asked them to join them. Noting the cool looks of several people nearby, they hesitated, but Armand insisted.

Colette knew them well as she often bought cheese and saucisson from them, a ruse she used when Armand wanted her to pass Pablo a message. She picked up Louis and gave him a hug. 'How are you, young man?' she asked. She stroked his glossy, dark curls affectionately.

Mercedes leaned closer to him. 'Aren't you going to give Tante Colette a kiss?'

Colette laughed. 'He's growing up to be a fine boy. Handsome too.'

Louis was a shy boy, but even at such a young age, he was aware of the cold way some of the country folk still treated both he and his mother. He had no playmates and the only real love he had was from his parents, although he had warmed to the Jouberts and the Berdus. Justine shook his little hand and said hello. He quickly pulled it away.

'He'll be fine when he gets to know you better,' Mercedes said.

'My name is Justine,' she said to him. 'What's yours?'

'Louis.'

'Well, Louis, I want you to know that I'm your friend — okay?' Louis nodded shyly.

At that moment, Claude returned. 'That was quite a long conversation you were having with your friend?' Justine said.

'I haven't seen him for a while. He's being posted to Font Romeu in a week's time to work with the border police.' Justine glanced at her father. Claude noticed and told them that his friend was an honest man. His comment was made to put them at ease. Did he suspect them of helping evaders cross into Spain, but tactfully ignored it? As a gendarme, Claude was already familiar with Pablo and Mercedes, and also purchased food from them. 'Their cheese is the best in the area,' he said, acknowledging them with a smile. 'In fact, it's excellent. My mother, in particular, loves it.' Mercedes thanked him.

Claude turned to Justine and asked her if she would like to dance.

'I was wondering when you'd ask me,' she replied.

Pablo asked Mercedes and she too was happy to join the dance group. Louis was sitting on Colette's knee and felt perfectly safe. The square was filled to capacity, with everyone jostling against each other or twirling to the lively Occitan music from the band from Axat, all of them wearing their distinctive black berets. Trumpets blared; an accordionist moved around, encouraging the onlookers to get up and dance; and a portly woman in a colourful striped skirt and white blouse, over which she wore a partially embroidered bolero, beat her tambourine in time with the tune, adding a rhythmic element that contributed to the overall effect of the song. Every now and again, the trumpets stopped to allow the haunting sound of the double-reed oboe-like graile to drift through the air, reminding Justine of the gentle breezes that rustled through the trees around Mont-Saint-Jean.

'Don't you miss these fêtes in Toulouse?' Claude asked as they danced, narrowly avoiding bumping into other couples.

'There are other things there to enjoy, you know, like the cinema, opera, the theatre, and countless bars and restaurants.'

'Quite a lot of night life, then? You're making me regret my decision to stay here. Maybe I should ask for a transfer.'

'Somehow, I don't think you'd like it?'

'Why not? Am I so much of a peasant that I can't appreciate the finer things in life?'

'I didn't say that; don't twist things. It's just that with the Germans and Vichy government creating the demarcation line, it's not a safe place to be at the moment.'

'It's not in the occupied zone?'

'Claude, for goodness sake, stop pretending to be naïve. You know full well what I mean. There's a lot of distrust. The atmosphere is filled with fear. Anyway, you're happy here.'

The song ended and the accordionist announced there would be one more number before they took a break. 'Another dance?' Claude asked. 'It's the *jota.*'

Justine wiped the sweat from her brow. 'I think I'll sit this one out. It's getting hot and I see Papa has ordered food.' The smell of roast meat from the spits set up around the square, filled the air. 'Let's eat. I'm famished.'

As they made their way to the table, Commissioner Rossignol bumped into them. It seemed to Justine he'd done it on purpose.

'Durand,' he said, 'aren't you going to introduce me to your friend?'

Claude looked embarrassed. 'This is Justine Joubert.' He then turned to Justine. 'Justine, this is Monsieur Rossignol, the new commissioner of Formiguères.'

Justine appeared delighted to meet him. 'Welcome, Monsieur le Commissioner. I do hope you will enjoy your stay here. I think you'll find the people exceptionally friendly.'

He smiled courteously. 'Joubert — so you must the daughter of Mont-Saint-Jean's school teacher?'

'That's right. Have you met my father?'

'I'm afraid not, but I do make it my business to know everyone around here.'

Justine responded with a courteous invitation for Rossignol to join them. 'Please come and eat with us,' she said, cheerfully, 'and meet both my parents. It will be an honour. I'm sure my father would like to meet you too.'

She put her hand on his arm in a warm encouragement of hospitality and guided him to their table, where everyone was helping themselves to roast pork, lamb, and local sausages from a huge wooden platter in the middle of the table. Everyone looked rather surprised to see Rossignol, but Armand smoothed over the awkward moment by standing up to welcome him. 'Please do join us. As you see, there is more than enough food for us all.' Claude hurriedly found him a seat while Armand poured the commissioner a glass of wine, and the group feasted as if they were all good friends, when in reality nothing could be farther from the truth. The only exception to this good humour was that Rossignol occasionally glanced towards Louis with more than a hint of curiosity.

Rossignol said he'd heard that Armand was a good teacher and well respected in the area. They talked about a variety of subjects, from books and literature to regional foods and wines, and even the Occitan music the Axat band played — anything but the German occupation. None of them asked anything about the commissioner, except for Justine. She wanted to know where he was from, and, seeing that he was wearing a wedding ring, asked if his family was here too. That is when they found out that he was from Amiens and was married to a woman from Alsace. He informed them that she and their four children would be joining him soon.

Given the awkward circumstances, everything was as pleasant as could be until Mercedes and Pablo returned to the table. More introductions by Armand in which the commissioner said he'd already met Pablo, but had not met his wife. Mercedes was a striking woman and it was evident Rossignol was struck by her beauty, but when she picked up Louis and thanked Colette for taking care of him, his eyes widened. He had not known Pablo had a black son. It was a tense moment which eased when Justine asked the commissioner if he had a photo of his wife and children. Rossignol was only too delighted to show her. He reached for his wallet and showed her a photograph of his four children and elegant blonde wife. In the background were snow-capped mountains.

'Such beautiful children,' Justine said. 'You must be very proud of them. Your wife is also beautiful, monsieur. You are a lucky man.' Justine's easy-going charm was working. 'I see you like mountains too. They don't seem to be around here though. Are they the Alps?'

Armand threw her a sideways glance, hoping she wouldn't push things too far.

'No. This picture was taken in Bavaria.'

The conversation stopped abruptly and Justine handed back the photograph. Thankfully the music started up again. This time it was a group from Perpignan playing Catalan music. A few of the Spanish got up from their tables and began to dance the *sardana*. Mercedes started to clap in time with the rhythm. It was evident that she was happy to hear this music. One of the musicians motioned to her to come and dance. She glanced at Pablo, who gave her his approval. She strode into the square, planting herself next to another Spanish friend. The men and women joined hands alternately in a closed circle. The music started off slowly and then picked up speed as they danced in a series of long and short steps. All the time, their faces remained solemn and dignified. Mercedes loved this music, which was intimately bound up with Catalan national consciousness.

For the onlookers, the greatest joy was watching the excellent footwork of the dancers. They were mesmerized, particularly by Mercedes dancing with such grace. Most of the villagers there that day knew Mercedes, even if they had not spoken to her — the dark-haired beauty with the black child — but today they could not fail to ignore her. Pablo stood up and clapped loudly, saying to Armand, 'She feels drawn to her homeland when she hears this music. It climbs up inside you, from the soles of the feet. As Lorca said about flamenco, "Everything that has black sounds in it has *duende*." This mysterious power which everyone senses and no philosopher can explain. For us, the sardana is the same.'

Armand stood up and clapped too. To him, the music was different to flamenco, yet it still held the same duende that had scorched the heart of Nietzsche, who searched in vain for its external forms on the Rialto Bridge and in the music of Bizet.

When the dance finished, the dancers and musicians thanked each other. Mercedes, her head held high after everything she had suffered, returned to the table amid chants of *'Bien fait. C'était magnifique, señora'*. She sat down and picked up her son. With tears streaking her face, she whispered that she loved him –*'Te amo, mi hijo'*– and drank the glass of wine given to her by her proud husband.

Justine also congratulated her. 'Where did you learn to dance like that?' she asked.

Mercedes replied that she had taken dancing lessons before the war, and often danced while the bombs dropped. 'It was a way of blocking out the horrors we went through.'

Rossignol, who had been struck by Mercedes's beauty from the moment he laid eyes on her, took the back of her hand and kissed it, his lips lingering a fraction longer than was polite. He then turned to Pablo, and in an authoritarian voice tinged with envy, told him to take good care of her. He then thanked everyone for their hospitality, particularly Armand, and said he must take his leave as he had other things to attend to. When he'd gone, Mercedes breathed a sigh of relief and said something rude about him in Spanish. *'Que bastardo'.*

Claude apologised. 'I'm sorry about that. I feel as though it's my fault.'

Justine said she was the one who invited him to their table. She leaned over and whispered in her father's ear, 'Keep your friends close, but keep your enemies closer.'

Armand smiled at her, proud that he'd raised such a clever daughter.

That night when the family were alone, they spoke about Rossignol. 'As Claude said, he's pro-German,' Justine said. 'But who on earth would have the cheek to tell their fellow Frenchmen that they had been holidaying in Bavaria. That speaks volumes.'

'What does Claude think?' Armand asked.

'Not much, but it's obvious to us all that Rossignol has been sent here to keep an eye on things by the regime, otherwise they'd have appointed someone who knew the area — another local.'

Colette frowned. 'Did you see the salacious way he looked at Mercedes? She's beautiful, but unfortunately, that's the way most men view her, especially many of the locals. No wonder Pablo is so protective of her. And Louis — well, he stared at that poor child as if he wasn't human.'

'It's a timely warning,' Armand said. 'We must not let our guard down.'

CHAPTER 9

The Situation in the Occupied Zone Intensifies

PAUL CASSOU WAS pleased with the information Justine had picked up during her time in Mont-Saint-Jean. She showed him her photographs of the region, the roads, mountains and gorges, and the various caves she'd noticed. When she mentioned Rossignol, he asked why she hadn't taken a photograph.

'He's a sly one and I didn't want him to become suspicious of me,' she replied. 'Anyway, I thought you would be able to find out more about him from your "sources".'

Cassou was pleased with her answer. 'Given the circumstances, you did the right thing.' He noticed the man in the pictures in the gorge and asked who he was.

'A gendarme in the village — Claude. I've known him all my life.'

'What do you think about him? Would he be useful to us?'

'I think so, but my father wants to check him out a bit more — maybe put him to the test. Apparently, his boss is a bit of a dark horse. Quite conservative and keeps his thoughts close to his chest, so we'll have to be careful as far as he's concerned. One thing is for sure, Rossignol said he's making it his business to get to know everyone in the area. If he's pro-Vichy, no one will dare cross him.'

The subject of money to pay the helpers and smugglers came up again. Cassou told her he'd been in touch with an Englishman in Bilbao who was trying to get funds for them. That was heartening news amid more and more dismal news. As the summer wore on, Justine witnessed many fights involving the pro-Nazi forces in Toulouse when they plastered posters on the walls and wrote articles in newspapers asking Frenchmen to go and fight the Soviets alongside the Germans. Recruiting stations had opened where those wishing to "defend civilization against eastern barbarism" could sign up. It shocked her just how many people were prepared to fight for Germany. At one point, she almost had to tear Robert away from getting into a fight with a man in a bar distributing leaflets telling them all to join and fight the scourge of Communism. The barman kicked him out, aided by a few patrons, but later that week, someone set fire to his premises. It was sign of things to come.

Like many of his friends, Robert was a Communist and had felt let down by the non-aggression pact between Germany and the Soviet Union. Now he and his Communist friends were thrilled. 'Finally,' he said to Justine, 'the Soviets have realised what liars the Germans are.' He spat on the ground. 'Why can't the Vichy collaborators see this? Bastards.'

On August 22, the German Occupation Authority announced that anyone found either working for, or aiding the Free French would be sentenced to death. This announcement was meant for everyone in France but it still didn't deter Cassou or any members of their network from continuing the work. It was hardly a surprise to anyone who followed events closely and only served to show them that the Vichy authorities were well and truly under the Germans' thumb.

Soon after, another roundup took place in the occupied zone, this time collecting *both* foreign Jews and those with French nationality, including lawyers and other professionals. They were sent to the Drancy internment camp and the other camps in France, which were now overflowing with the wretched and dispossessed who could not understand why this had happened to them.

Throughout this period, Cassou's network in Toulouse intensified. Justine, Robert, and the rest of the group followed the events daily and made a point to read the newspapers from cover to cover and listen to the radio. Anti-Semitic articles were frequently published in newspapers and the Germans organized anti-Semitic exhibitions to spread their propaganda. By this time, the music of Jewish composers was banned, as were works of art by Jewish artists. Only in the unoccupied zone did anyone dare to play Jewish music, but by the time of the roundups, that was becoming a rare event as every move they made was being watched.

On October 3, 1941, just one day after seven synagogues were bombed, Cassou asked a few members of the group to collect more parcels from Toulouse railway station. In total they were to pick up twenty-five people, including children. It had become a dangerous operation as almost all the main railway and bus stations were under surveillance by Germans working with the Vichy officials, who were already gathering names of people suspected of aiding "undesirables". Justine, Robert, Mimi, and Jacques were assigned to pick up their parcels and, as on previous occasions, were not to arrive together or make eye contact with each other, and were to greet their parcels as relatives. If they suspected they were being watched, they should leave quickly.

They arrived at the station as per their instructions and waited for the train to arrive. Each time a train pulled into the station, Justine's heart started to beat wildly. All of them were afraid, but trained not show it. The atmosphere that afternoon was particularly stifling and humid; thunder was in the air and the grey sky threatened to unleash a huge downpour. A few raindrops splattered on the platform, but thankfully, the thunderclouds rolled by.

At the allotted time, she heard the sound of another train approaching and readied herself with a new book — *The Hunchback of Notre Dame* — and a bunch of flowers. The train drew to a standstill and the platform filled with throngs of people, some of them running up and down, anxiously looking at the faces that peered from the windows. The doors opened and hundreds of people stepped onto the platform with their suitcases and bags. In the mayhem, she spotted Robert casting his eyes around in search of his parcel. As she looked around, a beautiful dark-haired woman dressed in the latest Parisian fashion stepped onto the platform. She was holding a small boy in one arm and her small suitcase and false documents in the other. A girl, about six years old, stood by her side clinging to her mother's skirt and clutching a doll with blonde curly hair. Justine felt a surge of pity. They didn't look strong enough for the journey ahead of them.

'"Jacqueline", how wonderful to see you again,' the woman said

Justine was surprised to see such young children. Cassou had not told her about them. She was also taken aback at the woman's elegance. She wore a chocolate-coloured velvet suit and matching hat with a narrow brim that was worn at the side of the head and kept in place with a gold hatpin. She looked as though she had just stepped out of a fashion magazine.

'You too, "Jeanne". You're looking so well.' Justine gave the woman a warm hug and kissed the children as though they were family. 'My, how the children have grown since I last saw you. Let's get you home — everyone is looking forward to seeing you again.'

Justine helped with the suitcase and they made their way out of the station, showing their papers and travel documents without incident, and walked a few streets to where the car was parked. Jeanne put the two children in the back and Justine covered them with a warm blanket while Jeanne got into the passenger seat next to Justine. 'Is it far?' she asked.

'About twenty minutes.' Justine noticed Jeanne was shaking like a leaf. Her friendly, composed demeanour on the platform had been well-rehearsed, when in reality, she was anxious and frightened. Justine assured her all would be fine. 'What are the children's names?' Justine asked.

'Their real names or their new ones?' Jeanne asked in a low voice so that the children couldn't hear, and then proceeded to tell Justine without even waiting for an answer. 'Their real names are David and Miriam Weiss. Their new papers have them as Albert and Fleur Dubois.' My name *was* Hélène Weiss. She pulled the new identification cards and travel passes out and waved them towards Justine, who could not look as she was driving. Jeanne's voice was tinged with anger and disgust. 'Miriam has practised answering to her new name. Fortunately, David is not yet two. Far too young to understand, so he will adapt.' She put the papers back in her bag. 'Do you mind if I smoke?'

91

'Go ahead. I'll have one too.'

Jeanne lit up two cigarettes and handed one to Justine. As she did, Justine noticed her beautifully manicured fingernails, painted with bright red nail polish that matched her red lipstick. In the confined space of the car, she couldn't help notice she wore perfume too — woody, with a hint of spice — sensual. Throughout the drive, neither woman spoke. It seemed to Justine that Jeanne was far away, probably wondering if she would ever see her home again, yet her face remained oddly stoic, almost devoid of emotion. It wasn't the first time Justine has seen this same expression on the faces of those she picked up. Maybe it was the best way to cope. If they dwelt too much on the situation, they would not be able to carry on. She looked at the rear view mirror and saw that the children were fast asleep, the girl still holding her doll, with one arm wrapped around her brother. It was a pitiful sight and Justine felt a lump rise in her throat.

The safe house was a two-room apartment in a busy street on the outskirts of Toulouse. It was quite small and cramped. Justine put their suitcase in the bedroom, where there were two beds. 'I'm sorry it's small, but it's quite safe, and there's food for a few days.'

By the look on Jeanne's face, Justine could tell the apartment was not what she was used to. 'How long will I be here?' she asked.

'I'm not sure. We'll move you on as soon as possible. I'll be back tomorrow evening. In the meantime, please make sure you stay inside, and don't open the door to anyone.'

The girl rubbed her eyes and lay on one of the beds. 'I'm tired, Maman.'

Jeanne put the sleeping boy on the other bed and then started to undress her daughter. 'It's alright, my sweet. You can rest now.' She opened her suitcase and took out two nightdresses, one for her daughter and one for herself. Justine caught a glimpse of the sort of clothes Jeanne had brought with her and was astonished. Here was a family on the run and yet she'd packed the most exquisite clothes. The girl's nightdress was white cotton with an embroidered edging around the neckline in pink and green rosettes, and her own was pale pink silk, edged with lace.

'How long have you been travelling?' Justine asked.

'Three days, so it will be wonderful to get a good night's sleep.' Justine wondered what their journey had entailed and she was amazed that the woman looked so smart after such a long ordeal.

At work the next day, Cassou called Justine into his office and asked her how it went. 'Any problems?'

'None at all, but this woman has two children and one is under two years old, so that safe house isn't really suitable for them. Children make too much noise. I think we should move them into the country as soon as possible.'

Cassou frowned. 'I was not told of the children.' He paced the room for a few minutes, deep in thought. 'This changes things. We can't get children across the border at this late stage. I'm going to have to think about this one.' He dismissed her and told her he'd speak more about it at the end of the day.

Justine returned to her desk, opened a file of contracts, and started to type, but it was hard to concentrate. These were the first children she'd helped and she knew it was unlikely they'd be the last. Cassou told her he had to leave Toulouse but would return the next day and they would speak further. He arranged to meet her at a restaurant by the river. She was to bring Robert along too.

That evening, Justine returned to the apartment to check on Jeanne and found her in tears. Finally, the horrors she'd endured and tried to keep at the back of her mind exploded. Tears streamed down her face and she kept apologising for being such a problem. The children sat in silence, evidently scared at seeing their mother in such a state. Justine put the kettle on and made them a hot drink. She could see that none of the food had been touched and prepared something for them. The children ate it hungrily while Jeanne wouldn't touch hers. The girl whispered to Justine that her mother didn't know how to cook. 'In Paris we had a cook,' she said. Justine didn't know what to say. Life had certainly changed for them.

The children finished their food and Fleur asked for more. Justine took her into the kitchen and showed her where the food was, whispering that she was to make sure her maman ate something or she would get ill. The child nodded. 'I will, Mademoiselle Jacqueline.'

Justine sat with them, playing with the children until Jeanne told them it was time to go to bed. She sat listlessly in the chair while Fleur picked up her little brother, kissed her mother goodnight, and said she would tuck him in. Jeanne said nothing.

'Goodnight, mademoiselle,' Fleur said. 'Thank you for the food.'

The atmosphere was so sad that Justine thought she might break into tears. She made another cup of ersatz coffee for them both and asked Jeanne if she wanted to talk about anything with her. 'You'll feel better if you get it off your chest,' she said.

Jeanne shrugged. 'What can prepare you for what we went through? We survived the second roundup in Paris by minutes. A non-Jewish neighbour warned us Jewish houses were being searched and people were being forced into trucks and driven away. She had no idea where, but told me to pack a suitcase and she'd hide us. I took the children and we hid in her home for three days. During that time, she and her husband took it upon themselves to locate my husband, who had been her husband's close friend. They found out that he was last seen climbing into a truck at gunpoint along with other Jews. A day or so later, they put me in contact with a woman who was running an escape line to the free zone. I had no idea if the people helping were genuine or not. All I could do was go by my instincts. I offered them some money too.'

'Did these people take it?' Justine asked.

'They took a little "for expenses", and gave the rest back, telling me I had better hide it somewhere safe as I would need it. The day before we left Paris, I was informed that my husband had been sent to an internment camp. I'd always thought of myself as French, even though I am a Jew. I realised then that none of us were safe. We should have got out earlier, like other friends did. The moment I left Paris, I felt as though my life had ended. It took all my strength not to commit suicide. The only reason I didn't was because of them.' Jeanne glanced towards the bedroom.

Justine proffered a few words of hope, but was powerless to fill her empty heart. Jeanne's story was one of many that she'd heard, all distressingly similar.

The next evening at the restaurant in Toulouse, an upmarket establishment where waiters moved about refilling glasses and being attentive to their customers, Cassou introduced Justine and Robert to four more members of his network. Two were around twenty years old and the other two were middle-aged. Justine told them about Jeanne. They were unable to find the right words to ease the pain these people were suffering. Unfortunately, they had to put their emotions to one side for the time being, and concentrate on other more pressing matters.

'As you know,' Cassou began, 'we are in dire need of more good Samaritans and have now recruited quite a few more helpers who we believe to be reliable. While it may not appear like it, the situation with the roundups, worsening food rations, beatings, and our own Frenchmen being sent to Germany in the occupied zone, is slowly changing the tide of public opinion. The problem is that the smugglers refuse to take anyone who is not strong enough to make the journey. This includes children and the elderly or those too ill to walk. In fact, they are a danger to us all.'

'No children at all?' Justine asked, as if to clarify the situation.

Cassou gave a deep sigh. 'You know the Pyrenees well. It's a harsh landscape, especially in winter. Small children would not survive. Maybe if the child was over twelve and fit — it would depend on the person involved. Other groups try to escape to Switzerland. It might be easier through the Alps, but for us, that's not where we operate.'

'But the Alps are also in the forbidden zone,' Justine replied. 'They'll be shot, or at the very least imprisoned and sent to Germany.'

'And they won't through the Pyrenees?' Cassou's response was sharp. 'Don't let your parcel and her two children cloud your judgement. There's no easy answer.'

'Then people like Jeanne will have to go into hiding until the Germans have left?' Justine said. 'So let's pray they leave soon.'

They all looked at each other. 'All of us here feel as you do,' Cassou continued, 'but without our network, thousands risk being killed or imprisoned. We *must* think of the bigger picture.' There were a few minutes of silence. Justine suddenly had no appetite and pushed her plate away.

'The good news is,' Cassou continued, 'some of our new Samaritans are prepared to take people for as long as possible. That means your parcel can be moved to a safe house in the countryside.'

There was little more to be said on the subject of evaders, and the subject of the war in North Africa came up. They all agreed that the Germans had made a big mistake by opening up another front.

Cassou paid for their meal that night in appreciation of the work they were doing. He scribbled something on a paper serviette and gave it to Justine. 'Take the day off work and take your parcel to this address in the countryside. They will be better off there — away from prying eyes.'

Sometime around midday, Justine's car turned off the main road just before Saint-Lizier, south of Toulouse and not too far from Paul Cassou's home near Saint-Girons. From Toulouse, the drive through the countryside had taken them through pretty hamlets and rolling hills, and she sensed Jeanne was feeling much calmer. They drove along a narrow, rutted road for two kilometres until they came to a farmhouse with outbuildings and stables. All around them were fields and woods.

'We're here,' Justine said.

Fleur pointed to four horses standing in the shade of an oak tree. 'Look, Maman,' she cried out happily, and asked Justine if she would be able to ride one. Justine smiled. It was the first time she'd seen a glimmer of happiness in their eyes.

'I don't see why not.' She turned to Jeanne. 'I think you're going to like it here. Madame and Monsieur Tillot are good people, and they're only too happy to take care of you.'

The farmer and his wife, a couple in their later years, came out to greet them. Madame Tillot scooped Fleur up in her arms and gave her a kiss. 'You are just like my granddaughter,' she said. 'Just as pretty.'

'Does she like horses too?' Fleur asked.

Her mother chastised her. 'Darling, you mustn't be so rude.'

Justine explained that Fleur had expressed delight when she saw the horses and had asked if she could ride one. Monsieur Tillot said that would be fine. There were two ponies and she could take her pick. Fleur was thrilled.

'We want you to feel at home here,' Madame Tillot added.

After showing Jeanne and the children to their rooms — two small bedrooms close together at the back of the farmhouse next to the stables — Madame Tillot prepared lunch. When they'd finished the meal, there was much to be discussed and Justine asked Fleur if she would like to go outside and "explore" while the grownups could discuss certain things. Fleur did as she was asked. Already she understood their lives were in danger, though she couldn't understand why.

Madame and Monsieur Tillot had the demeanour of warm grandparents, but they were also direct and aware of the danger they were in by hiding "undesirables" and they wanted to straighten out a few things.

'We expect you to follow the rules,' Madame Tillot said. 'The first is that you don't venture towards the main road. You are not prisoners here, but make sure you stay within sight of the farmhouse at all times. It's because we don't want nosy neighbours asking awkward questions. I'm sorry if it sounds harsh, but I'm sure you understand.'

'We are indebted to you, madame,' Jeanne replied. 'You will not have a problem with us.'

Madame Tillot felt quite embarrassed at having to spell things out. 'My husband and I don't care who is Jewish or not. We care what is right, and have a moral duty to help anyone in need.' Jeanne nodded. 'We must refer to you at all times by your names on the new identification papers. If anyone comes here, you are our cousins from Paris.' At that point, Madame Tillot glanced at Jeanne's elegant clothes. The contrast between the two could not have been more striking. 'Maybe you should keep your beautiful clothes for a special occasion,' she said tactfully, 'and wear something more suitable to farm life — something a little more simple.'

There was no mistaking what Madame Tillot was saying — blend in.

'My daughter has a wardrobe full of clothes here. I think you're about the same size, so maybe you could choose a few items.'

'That's most kind of you,' Jeanne replied, 'but what about Fleur — and Albert?'

Madame Tillot waved her hand through the air. 'Oh, that's not a problem at all. I'll run something up for them on the sewing machine.' She reached out and patted Jeanne's hand. 'My dear, we will do our best to take care of you.' She asked if she could hold the baby for a while.

Albert had such a placid nature. He smiled and waved his chubby arms in the air when Madame Tillot pinched his little round cheeks. 'He's adorable,' she said. 'A little angel.'

'He looks like his father,' Jeanne replied, and then turned away to look outside at Fleur playing ball with one of the farm dogs.

To ease the tension, Monsieur Tillot went outside and called out to Fleur. 'Come on, young lady. Let me show you the pony.'

'Has she ridden before?' Justine asked.

Jeanne replied that she'd had a few lessons so it wouldn't be a problem. 'All the family rides. Hopefully we will do it again when the Germans have gone.' The other two women could see she didn't really believe it, but hope was a powerful thing, and at the moment everyone needed a good dose of it.

When it came time to leave, Justine said she wasn't sure when she'd be back but if she needed her, to let Madame Tillot know. 'In the meantime, look after yourselves and don't worry.' She gave her a hug.

Throughout the drive back to Toulouse, Justine couldn't get Jeanne and her children out of her mind. It had been impossible to tell her there was a problem getting to Spain with the children. For the moment they would let her settle in.

The situation didn't get any better. There were more and more parcels to be picked up and with them, more children, some of them orphans accompanied by one of the other networks. Safe houses for these children were even harder to find. Fortunately, Cassou's contacts with the Swiss Red Cross and children's organisations proved vital. In return for free charcoal supplied by the company, they each took a few children, trying hard to keep siblings together. In a radius of one hundred kilometres, they found several other homes, some of which were disused châteaux which were now put to a good use. Throughout this period, Cassou tried to find out what had happened to Jeanne's husband. It turned out that he was interned in the Gurs camp, less than fifty kilometres from the farmhouse. With the aid of camp guards, they managed to free half a dozen men, but unfortunately her husband was ill with typhoid when the escape happened and was caught. He died some days later. Cassou wanted to be the one to deliver the news to Jeanne personally as he felt it would be too emotional for Justine. After two weeks regaining their strength, the other men were deemed fit enough to join the escape line into Spain. From there they headed to Bilbao and on to Lisbon, where they would join the Free French in England or North Africa.

Jeanne's reaction to her husband's death was one of numbness. It was as if she'd expected she'd never see him again. The only thing she said was, 'Thank God he died before he suffered the humiliation of deportation.'

By now most of the population knew the Germans had begun deportations of Jews from France to the death camps in Eastern Europe. News travelled fast and it was no longer possible to ignore what was taking place. The first trains left on March 27, 1942.

On May 29, 1942, another law ordered all Jews to wear the yellow star. When Jeanne heard this, she lost her composure and burst into tears, taking to her bed for two days until Justine went to visit her and told her in no uncertain terms that she had to pull herself together. Almost six weeks later, another roundup occurred. This one was the worst to date. The papers called it the Vel'd'Hiv Roundup and there was no doubt that it required detailed planning and the use of the full resources of the French police to carry it out. Paul Cassou was at a meeting in Paris when it happened and reported back that it collected nearly thirteen thousand Jews, seven thousand of whom, including more than four thousand children, were interned and locked into the Vélodrome d'Hiver without adequate food or sanitation.

The situation had been dire for at least a year and Cassou's network was stretched to their limits, as was Dr Berdu and her father in the Donezan. There were endless meetings about the need for more good

Samaritans or everything would collapse. Where once they had taken a while to check someone out, they no longer had time and were often forced to trust their instincts. On the positive side, some Jews, like Jeanne and her children, or Allied airmen too ill to make the journey over the Pyrenees, found refuge in the peace and quiet of the beautiful countryside, particularly in the Ariège.

CHAPTER 10

The Germans Occupy the Free Zone

A BREATH OF cold air drifted through Mont-Saint-Jean as Justine and her father approached the village from a long walk to La Pla.

'It's going to snow tonight,' her father said.

She was about to answer when they heard a fearful rumble of motor vehicles approaching from the south. Within minutes, a convoy of German armoured vehicles — trucks and motorcycles with sidecars – roared into the village. It was the Feldgendarmerie, which operated under the direct control of the German High Command. A Wehrmacht major general, accompanied by his Feldgendarmerie subordinate in charge of all personnel, followed in a *Kübelwagen*. Everyone in the battalion was armed with pistols or machine guns. After her training with Cassou, she recognised some of them — the Walther PP, which was designed as a civilian police pistol, and the Luger P08, which this major general appeared to favour.

The major general ordered the soldiers to go through the village and inform everyone they were to assemble in the square near the church. The unbelievable had happened: the Germans had finally arrived in the Donezan. The villagers looked at each other with a fearful sense of foreboding. The peace and tranquillity of their lives was shattered. They had entered a new and darker phase of the war.

'Maman will be terrified,' Justine whispered. 'She'll think it has something to do with us.'

A soldier standing nearby called out to her. 'No talking!' His fierce tone frightened the children, who cowered behind their mothers. Within a short time, a nervous Colette arrived with Babette Berdu and her daughter and the rest of the villagers, except for those out in the pastures or woodcutters in the forests. They gathered outside the church, shivering with cold and filled with anxiety, waiting to see what was happening. The major general, dressed in a smart field-grey uniform and wearing the *Schirmmütze* — a peaked hat emblazoned with the insignia of an eagle with a small swastika, oak leaves, and a neat silver double braid, spoke to them in French over a loudspeaker. With a voice of authority, he told them in no uncertain terms that the free zone was now occupied and under German military control and officially known as the *zone sud* — the south zone. What they had previously known as the occupied zone was renamed *zone nord* — the north zone. While they were assured the French government was still in charge, few listening to his speech that day believed it.

The villagers were told that they must abide by the law, which included a host of things: supplying the German army with agricultural products and animals — in particular, horses; obtaining travel documents when moving from one area to another; and respecting the hours of curfew, which were now in place. He particularly asked that anyone who owned a vehicle report it to the gendarmerie. Unless they had a good reason for needing it — in which case they would have to show proof to obtain documents — it would be requisitioned. For those with an exemption, they would have to convert them to charcoal and wood burners as fuel was only to be used by the army. Most villagers did not own a car anyway, and those who did had already done this. Guns were also to be handed in. His final instructions sent a chill down their spines.

'Anyone caught hiding Jews, Communists, or other undesirables will be shot. You should also take note that a group has been temporarily assigned to special operations, such as anti-partisan duties. Partisans and anyone caught trying to flee the country will be severely dealt with.' He stressed that should anyone suspect their neighbours of doing so, they must report it immediately, or they too would be implicated. The Reich would look favourably on such people who abided by the law. 'Any questions?' he asked.

When no one answered, he thanked them for their time and told them that everyone must report to the gendarmerie the next day and fill out a form — their names and addresses, age and occupations, etc. Failure to do this would have consequences.

The officer got back into the *Kübelwagen* and drove away in the direction of the Col des Hares with the rest of the vehicles following. The villagers stared at each other in disbelief, too shocked to say anything. One by one, they returned to their homes and, for the first time in years, locked and bolted their doors. Neighbours they had known all their lives would now be looked upon with suspicion. Justine and her parents were no different. They, too, locked their doors and sat in front of the fire trying to take it all in.

'Did you see the look on Claude's face?' Justine said. 'He was so embarrassed.'

Her father told her that was to be expected. 'The villagers won't know whether to trust him or not if he has to answer to the military police.'

'Do *you* trust him?' she asked.

'Over the past few months, I've got to know him better. I wasn't sure about him at first, but now I think he's a good man. He's given me names of people he believes are sympathetic to those "in trouble", as he called them, and might be willing to help us. He may be a small-time village policeman, but at the moment, he is just the sort of person we need. He can play a vital role. He can inform us of the Germans' movements in the area. It's just what we need to stay one step ahead.'

'I hope you're right,' Colette replied.

The next morning, they went to the gendarmerie as requested and found it already packed with villagers. People wanted to get their paperwork over and done with and get on with their busy lives. During the night there had been a heavy snowstorm and those waiting outside huddled together, moving from one foot to another trying to keep warm. Those inside were lucky enough to get some warmth from a wood heater that stood in the centre of the waiting room. Every now and again, a gendarme told them to get into line and stop jumping the queue; they would all be dealt with in good time. 'Hurry up,' a man called out. 'I've got animals to feed.' Others called out similar things. Claude spotted them outside and called them into his office, a space so small it could barely hold more than a filing cabinet, wooden desk, and two old chairs. Colette sat down while Justine and her father stood.

'I'm so sorry,' Claude said. 'It was a quick "invasion". We only got wind of it at the last moment. Apparently, it is in response to the Allies attacking the Germans in North Africa.'

Armand didn't bother telling him they'd already heard that on the news. 'What is it we have to do?' he asked.

'Fill out these forms. They have to be handed to the Germans.' He gave them several sheets of paper. 'As head of the family, you can fill one out for Madame and Justine.'

Armand glanced through it first. Then he took out his fountain pen and ticked the boxes or made comments where appropriate. Most of the questions were basic: name, age, address, occupation, how many children, whether they possessed a car or radio, and a whole section on how much land and how many animals they owned. If they needed to travel, they should apply for permits immediately. This would be granted at the discretion of the gendarmerie or town hall, or other appropriate places depending on the size of the town.

There was another section, this one more intrusive — religion. Baptism papers needed to be checked.

Armand signed the form and pushed it across the desk to Claude. 'Is that it?'

Claude's face reddened and he tried to avoid Armand's eyes. 'I need to ask you if you know of any Jews in the area — French or foreign Jews?'

There was a few seconds of silence while Armand waited for Claude to look him in the eye. In a low whisper, Claude said he was obliged to ask this question.

'Not to my knowledge.' The tension in the room was palpable.

Claude scribbled something down in a book.

Justine glanced at her mother. Everyone in the area knew there was a Jewish family in Mijanès. They had been there since before the war. Even Claude knew that.

'Your boss? Monsieur le Commissioner Godard?' Armand said in a low voice. 'He's not from around these parts, is he?'

'No. He's from Limoux.'

Armand smiled. 'Claude, a word of advice from your old schoolteacher; we villagers will respect and work with you — if you respect and work with us. Remember, the Germans may be here today, but tomorrow... well, it would be nice for everyone if we could one day celebrate our freedom together. The villagers of the Donezan have a long memory.' Claude understood exactly what Armand was saying. He was testing him.

The men shook hands. 'Monsieur Joubert. You have my word. I will do my best by our people. Now I must give you your travel passes and ration cards. Come with me.'

They left the office and Claude led then to another desk in the main waiting area of the gendarmerie, where another gendarme from Formiguères had been sent to help. Everyone was still milling around getting more frustrated by the minute. Claude handed Armand the signed documents and told him that as he was the school headmaster, he was entitled to a travel pass for all the villages in the Donezan and Capcir. He also managed to get one for Colette too — as a teacher's aide.

'What about Mademoiselle Joubert?' the gendarme from Formiguères asked.

'She lives and works in Toulouse,' Claude said. 'Give her a pass to get back.'

Justine was handed her documents without any more questions being asked. Claude escorted them out of the building. Someone was heard muttering that the Jouberts had not had to queue because of who he was. Already disenchantment and resentment was setting in. Outside, well out of earshot of others, Claude told Justine that it was up to her to get any other passes she needed in Toulouse. It was out of his hands. He also whispered that he'd heard the Germans were securing all the dams and hydro plants in the area in case of sabotage and that would mean more battalions of Germans would be setting up camp in the area. Armand did not say anything, but his look was one of thanks.

They walked back into the village and headed to the Hôtel Bellevue for a drink. It was midday and the snow was steadily falling, covering the street in a ghostly sheet of whiteness, gathering here and there in glistening, white clumps on the rooftops and window ledges. The village, with its stone houses and slate roofs, looked sombre and desolate, as if wrapped in a blanket of despair. By now, the hôtel was steadily filling with those who had already filled out their papers. After the frosty atmosphere of the gendarmerie, it was cosy and homely, with a roaring log fire and the aroma of food.

'What will you have?' Madame Frenay asked Armand.

'Mulled wine. What's on the menu today? Something smells good.'

'Roast pork,' she answered, 'with baked vegetables.'

'We'll have that too,' he replied. 'After what we've just been through, we deserve a good meal.'

Madame Frenay laughed. 'Good idea; might as well make the most of it before the Germans steal our food and animals for themselves. I heard they're particularly fond of pork.'

The food was delicious, but the mood was as solemn as the weather. 'He knows what we're doing?' Justine said, referring to Claude. 'I wonder how?'

'I think he just put two and two together. He has no real proof. We're not the only ones around here to detest the Germans and help evaders. However, it was decent of him to stick his neck out and tell us about the dams and hydro plants. He didn't have to do that.'

'What about the Jewish family in Mijanès? He certainly knows about them.'

'He knows they've assimilated into the community. Let's hope for his sake, he keeps quiet. I think his official demeanour just now was for the sake of his boss and the other gendarmes. I'm sure he's trustworthy.'

The next day, Justine left for Toulouse. Due to the severity of the situation and the snow, which was steadily worsening, she decided against driving across the Col de Pailhères and took a longer, more circuitous route. She was stopped several times and her papers checked, but she was allowed on without any problems. She reached Toulouse before the curfew and found a coded message slipped under her door. Paul Cassou had arranged for an urgent meeting at a safe house. When she got there, the atmosphere was thick with tension combined with cigarette smoke. Two bottles of cognac stood on the table, one already half empty. She opened a window to let in some air while Robert poured her a drink.

'How was the Donezan?' Cassou asked.

'As to be expected. The villagers don't know what to make of it all. I think we can count on the local gendarme though. He respects my father. He told us that the Germans are setting up camps near all the dams and hydro plants in the area.'

'Well, things are not exactly the best here. The Germans have decided to settle some of their forces in Saint-Girons in order to control the entire Couseranais sector of the Franco-Spanish border. The *Zollgrenzschutz* and the *Verstärkter Grenzaufsichtsdienst* have been reinforced by the Sipo-SD German Customs who have established their headquarters at the Château de Beauregard. I have been told it now accommodates about three hundred men whose leader is a man called Commander Piersig.'

This was worrying news as Saint-Girons was not only important for one of their escape routes, it was not far from Cassou's home. Having the border and customs out of French hands and under the control of German Customs and militarized border guards was a disaster.

'I have some more bad news,' Cassou said. 'There's been an epidemic of diphtheria in the village where Jeanne and her children are staying.' Justine felt her throat tighten as she waited for his next words. 'The boy — Albert — we couldn't save him.'

Justine put her hands to her mouth to stop herself crying out. 'Jeanne — Fleur — Madame and Monsieur Tillot — what about them?'

'Fleur contracted it too. She was very ill, but thank God, has almost recovered. At the moment, she's being treated by one of our doctors. The others are fine too. The problem was that because they were in hiding, by the time we were alerted, it was hard to get the serum for the vaccine. Sadly the boy was too young to endure such an illness.'

The image of Albert's chubby cheeks and his beautiful, placid nature flashed through Justine's mind and she burst out crying, apologizing for not being stronger. 'I'm sorry, but I can't imagine how Jeanne is coping. First her husband, now Albert.'

Cassou handed her his handkerchief. 'It's alright to be upset. We're not made of stone. The day we can't lose our emotions is the day we lose everything.'

The rest of those assembled around the table sat quietly, allowing Justine her moment of grief. 'Now what?' she said after a while.

'We've already discussed the difficulty of children and the elderly crossing into Spain. There is no possibility of Fleur accompanying her mother. The only option is for her to go to an orphanage run by a group like the Red Cross. She cannot stay with Madame and Monsieur Tillot any longer. It's too risky now.'

'Jeanne will never agree to it,' Justine said.

Cassou's face showed little emotion. 'She has to, especially now that we have the Germans breathing down our necks.'

'And what happens to Jeanne?'

'We'll move her to another safe house, somewhere out of the way, and then try and get her into Spain. We can only pray that she will be reunited with her daughter after the Germans leave.'

As much as she hated the idea, Justine knew Cassou was right. She asked where he wanted to send her.

'There's a villa in Quercorbès in the area of Razès near the forest of Picaussel, not far from Quillan. To the south, via a series of winding roads through precipitous gorges, is Mont-Saint-Jean. It's the country home of Count Pierre de Crispin and his Belgian wife, Elsa, and was recommended by Dr Berdu, who has used it himself when moving Allied soldiers. He assured me that the owners will take as many people as they can and are only too glad to help.'

Justine said she knew the area.

'It's between the plateau of Sault and the hills of Razès and Piège. It's ideal as the area is sparsely populated and at the same time, not too far from Quillan and Limoux. Then we will arrange to get her out of France as soon as possible. You and I will go together tomorrow to give her this news. At the same time, I will arrange for someone from the orphanage to collect Fleur.'

'But if Fleur is still ill?' Justine looked worried.

'She will be fine. The people in charge of the orphanage know what they're doing.'

Justine brought up the matter of travel documents. Cassou had come prepared. He took a folder out of his briefcase and gave them new papers. 'The charcoal company is deemed essential to the economy of the country, so Justine, you have a travel pass because you work for me. This way, you are still able to drive a car. I am afraid your new car will be an older Citroën, as the other has been requisitioned. We will see to it that it gets refitted for burning charcoal and wood rather than petrol. Robert, the same goes for you. You are now part of my sales team. You are also registered to drive a truck *and* a car.' He turned to two other men and told them they too were to be employed by the company. Mimi was given a travel pass and her occupation was marked down as midwife. She protested that she hadn't the faintest idea about midwifery and the thought that some poor unfortunate mother and child might die if she was put to the test appalled her. Cassou simply told her to take first aid lessons and buy some books on the subject. He added that they should all to take first aid lessons. 'You never know when it will come in handy.'

The next subject on the agenda was cautionary measures. There was to be no use of the telephone as the Germans would be monitoring all calls. 'The only exception is if you are in dire trouble and there is no other way to communicate, and it should be done in such a way that it appears as if it's part of company business. Otherwise, we communicate by car, bicycle, on foot, or using trusted couriers.' They were handed a list with addresses.

'Each person is to be addressed by a code name only, and make any contact as short as possible, but for goodness' sake, be vigilant. If you get caught, and — God forbid — tortured, try and hang on for at least twenty-four hours.' There was a short pause. 'The next item on the agenda is arming yourself. I am sending you all to a farm where two

Allied soldiers are hiding out. They will give you a quick lesson on self-defence and you will also be issued with a pistol. It's vital that you learn how to use a gun.' He looked at each one and asked if they had any questions. 'Good, let's have another drink and then go home.'

CHAPTER 11

The Villa in the Forest

JEANNE WAS IN the bedroom with Fleur when Cassou and Justine arrived.

'She won't leave the child's side,' Madame Tillot said, despairingly.

She led them both into the bedroom, where Jeanne was sitting on the bed gently brushing her sleeping daughter's hair. Justine sat beside her and held her in her arms, feeling the shudder of Jeanne's body as she cried silently.

'They couldn't save him,' she whispered, barely able to get the words out. 'My boy, my darling boy — so good — so pure. Too good for this world.'

'I hear Fleur has almost recovered,' Justine said. 'We must at least be thankful for that miracle.'

Jeanne wiped her eyes and looked at her daughter's silken dark hair arranged neatly on the pillow. 'I don't believe in miracles anymore.'

Justine threw a quick glance towards Cassou standing in the doorway. This was not going to be easy.

'Jeanne,' Justine said in a soft voice. 'This gentleman has come all the way from Toulouse with me. We have something we'd like to discuss with you.'

Cassou introduced himself by one of his many aliases and offered her his condolences. He suggested it might be better if they went elsewhere as they didn't want to wake Fleur. Madame Tillot told them they could use the sitting room, where there was a warm fire. She brought them a tray of biscuits and a hot drink and left them alone to discuss the situation. Even though she was still numb with grief, Jeanne's instinct

111

told her something was wrong.

'What is it?' she asked. 'Is it the Germans? I heard what's happened. We are no longer safe, are we?'

'None of us are safe, Jeanne,' Cassou replied. 'Because of this, we have made a decision to move you away from here and try and get you out of France as soon as possible.'

Jeanne sighed. 'Well, I suppose it will be easier now without my darling boy, won't it?' She stared at the window, looking at the snowflakes softly collecting on the window ledge. Beyond, the picturesque fields had been transformed into an undulating sea of whiteness.

After a few minutes of silence, Cassou brought up the problem of Fleur. For Justine, those few minutes seemed an eternity. She was aware of everything around her — the crackle of the wood on the fire and the ticking clock on the mantelpiece.

'Jeanne,' Cassou said, 'unfortunately, it's not going to be as easy as you think. We have a problem. It was always going to be difficult getting children across the Pyrenees. The smugglers are reluctant to risk it. Now that the Germans have invaded the whole of France, they've redoubled their efforts to track down evaders.'

'What are you trying to tell me, monsieur?'

'We can help you escape, but not your daughter. We propose...'

Jeanne jumped up from her chair. 'I will not go anywhere without my daughter. Do you hear me? I would rather die.' Her body shook with anger and fear.

Justine asked her to hear what they had to say first and then make a decision. It was explained to her that she was not the only one in this position and that the safest option was to put Fleur into an orphanage for the time being. 'She will be with other children in a similar position. The people running the orphanages have experience in providing the best care and they already have Jewish children, including foreign Jews. More importantly, they are protected by the Secours Suisse aux Enfants, a sub-sector of the Red Cross of Switzerland.'

The idea of putting Fleur in an orphanage was more than she could bear and she collapsed into the chair. 'She is *not* an orphan!'

'Jeanne, these people are experienced with diplomatic issues,' Cassou said. 'They offer protection, *and* she will not be alone. She has the chance to make friends.'

There followed a long discussion in which Justine assured her she would try and keep her informed of Fleur's wellbeing. 'It may seem impossible to believe this at the moment, but we know the Germans will leave France one day soon, and then you will be reunited.'

Jeanne realised there was no other choice. Things had become too difficult now. She cursed herself for not leaving France when they had the chance.

'Alright. I have no other option, do I? When will this take place?'

Cassou told her someone would come for Fleur in two days' time. In the meantime, she was to assure her daughter all would be well. 'As for yourself, madame, Jacqueline will come for you that evening and move you to another safe place — somewhere a little more remote. Then we will get you closer to the Spanish border.'

Cassou went out to inform Monsieur and Madame Tissot what was happening while Justine tried to console a tearful Jeanne.

'It's for the best,' Monsieur Tissot said. 'The Germans have already been snooping around. The girl is still weak, but she's out of danger.'

Justine accompanied Jeanne to the bedroom to check on Fleur before she left. Choking back the tears, she gave the sleeping girl a peck on the cheek. 'God be with you,' she whispered.

After leaving the farm, it was a while before Cassou or Justine could speak. Both were profoundly affected by the situation. 'God help us,' Justine said. 'I don't know if I will be strong enough to endure all this.'

Cassou agreed. 'I wonder that myself sometimes. But what other option do we have?'

When the woman from the orphanage came to collect Fleur, she'd had the foresight to bring a fourteen-year-old girl with her. The girl had been with them for a couple of months and was able to help assure Fleur she would be happy and well-looked after in her new home. In the short time they'd been in hiding, Fleur had changed. Outwardly, she was still a child — small, pretty, and naïve — but inwardly she was a girl, wise beyond her years. Even at such a young age, she knew their lives hung in the balance.

Jeanne was still emotional, but the presence of a smiling young girl helped ease her fears a little. 'You will be a good girl for the lady, won't you, my darling?' she said, her voice breaking.

'I promise, Maman. Please don't worry about me.'

Allowing her only daughter to go with a stranger to an unknown destination, never knowing if she would see her again, was one of the hardest things Jeanne had ever had to do in her life. The sad sight of Fleur getting into the back seat of the car, still clutching her doll, and waving to them through the back window as the car drove out of the yard was difficult for Madame and Monsieur Tillot also, but they stood stoically next to Jeanne with smiles on their faces, watching until the car disappeared from sight. At that point, Jeanne, who had tried so hard to be strong, fainted.

When she came round, the thought of what had just taken place reduced her to tears again. No one uttered a word. She went to her room to pack her suitcase in readiness to depart herself and in that moment felt she'd lost everything that ever mattered to her. All she had to remind her of her family were a couple of photographs taken in their garden in Paris in happier times. Her husband had one arm wrapped around her as she held baby Albert, and the other around Fleur. All of them were smiling. How strange and unreal, and how distant it all seemed.

Later that evening, Justine arrived at the farmhouse in a truck belonging to Cassou's charcoal company driven by Robert. A space had been prepared at the back for Jeanne to hide in case they were stopped and searched. She handed Jeanne a thick blanket to cover herself as the temperature was plummeting again. Jeanne thanked Madame and Monsieur Tillot for their kindness, crawled into the dark, claustrophobic space, and covered herself completely with the blanket. It was a far cry from the days of elegant living in Paris, but at least she was safe.

Madame and Monsieur Tillot had grown fond of Jeanne and the children and the place seemed empty without them, but there was no time to dwell on the situation. Tomorrow they would be receiving another evader. This time, a young man, and if all went according to plan, he would be crossing the Pyrenees within a week. Madame Tillot went into Jeanne's room to change the sheets and prepare the young man's bed. When she pulled back the coverlet, she saw a note. It read: *"I will always remember your kindness. Please accept this gift as a token of my gratitude"*. It was signed *"J"*.

Next to the note was a small, folded piece of fabric, and in it was an exquisite emerald ring surrounded by small diamonds. Madame Tillot had never seen anything so beautiful in her life. She had never worn jewellery. There was never enough money for such luxuries. Even if there was, where would she wear it? She sat on the bed twirling it between her fingers in disbelief. What a dazzling thing of beauty. In the whole time Jeanne had been with them, Madame Tillot had never seen her wear any jewellery except for her wedding ring. She must have hidden it somewhere. She called out to her husband.

'What's wrong?' he asked. 'Has she left something behind?'

'You could say that.' She handed him the ring and note.

Monsieur Tillot's eyes widened. 'Mon Dieu, this must have cost a small fortune.'

Madame Tillot crossed herself. 'May God keep them safe.'

*

Jeanne was suffering from deep depression and slept for almost two whole days. When she woke, she entered a period of darkness that seemed to have no end. She refused to come out of her room and hardly touched her food. The count and his wife, who were used to people coming and going over the past two years, became extremely worried about her. They'd witnessed other evaders, especially the women who had left family behind, wallow in self-pity at their plight. Usually, the couple allowed them the luxury of doing so as they knew the next part of the journey would be even more difficult, physically and mentally. After a while of staying in such salubrious surroundings with cheerful company, they improved. Jeanne was different. She seemed vague and her thoughts became scrambled.

'Where am I?' she asked at least half a dozen times.

'You're in our home, safe from prying eyes.' Countess Elsa explained that this was their country home and that she and her husband also had a home in Paris, so they knew what she had gone through. They'd seen the way the Vichy government and the Germans acted. At the mention of Paris, Jeanne gave a little smile.

'We had a beautiful home, you know, with a large garden and servants.' The glazed look appeared again. 'I wonder who's living in it now.' Then she began to ramble about her husband, Fleur, and Albert. 'I'm all alone, you know.'

Countess Elsa didn't want to ask further questions and suggested a walk might do her good. 'It's stopped snowing and the air is lovely and crisp. I'll fetch you one of my warm coats. What do you think?'

Jeanne nodded.

The countess left the room and returned with a long sable coat and hat, a pair of leather gloves, and boots. Jeanne ran her hand over the fur. 'I have a coat just like this. My husband bought it for me — he was good like that.'

Countess Elsa could tell the melancholia was returning and hastily helped her into the coat. She walked with her to the terrace at the back of the house, where a young man was busily clearing snow from the pathway. He waved and called out. 'Bonjour, Countess Elsa. *C'est un jour glorieux.*' Jeanne shrunk back, wondering who he was. The countess explained that they had five other "guests" at the moment, all making the same journey as her. She did not want to use the word "evaders" for fear of adding to Jeanne's fragile state of mind. 'This young man is English and he's practising his French. Some of our guests like to help around the house as it passes the time. Now, I suggest you take a walk in that direction.' She pointed across the garden. 'When you come to the glasshouse, you'll see a narrow pathway. It will take you through the wood. At the end is a lake with a boathouse. The walk around the lake is pretty at this time of year. You'll be quite safe as it's private property, so no one will bother you. There are benches around the lake should you want to sit and enjoy the view.'

She watched Jeanne walk away. The airman bid her a good day as she passed. His friendly greeting seemed to warm her a little and she answered back, wishing him a good day too. The countess breathed a sigh of relief. Hopefully it was a sign she was recovering. All the same, she asked two other airmen who were playing cards in the library if they would follow her and keep an eye on her. 'Keep your distance,' Countess Elsa said. 'Don't let her know you're there. It will frighten her.' They were only too happy to oblige, grabbed their jackets, berets, and scarves, and headed towards the lake.

The two men soon caught sight of her and stood back, watching her walk around the lake. At one point she sat on a bench, staring out at the half-frozen water where two white swans were gliding through the broken ice. Several winter geese flew in and out of the reed beds. The men could see nothing unusual about her actions and thought the countess might be overreacting. They took their eyes off her for a few moments to look at a deer grazing amid the green firs and leafless deciduous trees decked with green tufts of mistletoe. Suddenly they heard a splash.

'Good heavens!' one of them shouted. 'She's jumped into the lake!'

While one man ran to save her, the other ran back to the villa. Within minutes, the man reached the spot where Jeanne had jumped. She had taken off the fur coat and hat and left it on the bench before jumping in. Without a second thought, he jumped into the freezing water and caught her only seconds before she disappeared from view. Luckily, he was fit and healthy, and managed to haul her unconscious body onto the bank. The man turned her head to one side to get rid of any water and then began to resuscitate her. Minutes later, everyone from the house arrived, some of them carrying blankets.

'She'll be fine,' the man said. 'She's suffering from hyperthermia, but she's breathing. It's a good job we were nearby.'

The count and countess wrapped her in blankets and the men carried her back to the house. 'She seemed to be fine,' the two men said. 'This was totally unexpected.'

'I blame myself,' Countess Elsa said. 'I shouldn't have let her out of my sight. It was too soon.'

Her husband tried to console her. 'You weren't to know this would happen.'

It wasn't long before Jeanne came round and realised what she'd done. 'I wanted to die,' she said. 'You should have let me go.'

Countess Elsa and her maid undressed her, gave her a warm bath, and put her to bed. 'Look, Jeanne. You almost died in that lake and the man who saved you could have died too. You have got to pull yourself together or you will put us all at risk. We have too much on our hands with the Germans and Vichy police breathing down our necks to put up with this sort of behaviour. You either change or I will have you sent elsewhere.' There was a pause while the maid brought her a cup of hot milk and honey. 'I will leave you to sleep now. At seven o'clock sharp, you will join us all for dinner in the dining room. Is that clear? The maid has left fresh clothes out for you.'

Leaving Jeanne in no doubt that she had run out of patience, the countess walked out of the room. Her stern words had the desired effect and later that evening, Jeanne, neatly dressed and with her hair beautifully swept back in a loose chignon, entered the dining room in a rather sheepish manner. Everyone seated at the table, including the five evaders, were well aware she was *extrêmement fragile*, and they welcomed her effusively. Embarrassed, she started to apologise for what she had done, but the countess cut her short. 'That's not necessary. We've all put it behind us. Please sit and enjoy your meal.'

The meal was an elegant affair. The table was set with a starched white tablecloth, the wine decanted and served in cut-glass crystal, and the food served on fine Limoges porcelain dinnerware edged with gilt and delicate hand-painted flowers. The food consisted of slow-cooked game casserole, creamed cabbage, and potatoes au gratin, all of which was from their land. There was even a desert — an orange cake studded with dried fruit. It was a far cry from Madame and Monsieur Tillot's basic food in their modest kitchen, although Jeanne did miss the homely atmosphere of the farm. The Tillots had little compared to the count and countess, but what they did have, they had shared from their heart, and for that she would always be grateful.

The young men were very chatty and she soon found herself at ease in their company. She discovered that the man who saved her was an American from Ohio who just happened to be a champion swimmer at university. The other four evaders were two Englishman, a Belgian, and an Australian who loved to tell jokes. After a while she was laughing — something she'd not done in a long time. They told her tales of being on the run and narrowly escaping the Germans as if it was all an adventure. After dinner, Countess Elsa suggested they play a few records while they sat near the fire sipping brandy. Jeanne had to pinch herself. This was not far from the life she had known in Paris, yet it would all be gone in a few days so she decided to make the most of it.

The American handed her a pile of records. 'Okay, what's first on tonight's hit parade?'

'This one,' Jeanne replied, handing him one by Léo Marjane — *'Seule ce soir.'*

'I was hoping you'd pick a Glenn Miller number,' the American said.

'For that you will have to listen to the BBC,' Count Pierre said. He looked at the grandfather clock and told them they could play two more and then they'd better get some sleep as they had a long day ahead of them tomorrow.

Jeanne looked at him, quizzically. 'Why, what's happening?' The count told her that two of them were moving on. 'Oh! What a shame — just when I was getting to know you.'

The men laughed. 'Maybe our paths will cross on the side of a mountain. Better still, maybe we will get to have a drink in a bar in London,' the Englishman said. 'Anything's possible these days.'

When Jeanne went into the dining room the next day, the two men had already left. 'I never got to say goodbye,' she said. The count explained that they'd had to leave while it was still dark. 'Where have they gone?' Jeanne asked.

'To another safe house. I can't tell you where.'

Jeanne sat down to eat her breakfast, but the countess could see a cloud of depression settling over her again. 'You can help me prepare tonight's meal, if you like?' she said. 'I could do with some help.'

That same evening they had another visitor. Jeanne was asked to set the table for an extra guest as he would be staying the night. It was dark when he arrived and Jeanne had just finished laying the table.

Count Pierre went outside to greet him. When the man entered the room, Jeanne was struck by his distinguished looks and friendly manner. He didn't look like someone on the run, so who was he?

'Allow me to introduce our good friend "Bertrand". Bertrand, this is Jeanne — she arrived a few days ago.'

Bertrand was none other than Dr Berdu. In the villages of the Donezan, where people knew him as their local doctor, he used his real name, but for the escape line, he was known by his alias "Bertrand". Unbeknown to Jeanne, the count and countess had been so worried about her that they'd sent an urgent message with a courier for him to come and check on her. It was only during the meal that she found out he was a doctor, but as the atmosphere was so convivial she hadn't realised he came specifically to see her. He wanted her to feel at ease before he broached the subject of her severe depression and attempted suicide.

The next day was another glorious day; it was cold but the sun was shining, tinting the snowdrifts a soft gold in the morning light. Dr Berdu asked Jeanne if she would care to accompany him on a short walk before lunch. She agreed. After ten minutes, he told her that her hosts were worried about her health, to which she replied she was fine. As he didn't press the matter, she decided to open up to him.

'I feel terrible for what I've put them through, but it's been hard since I left Paris. I've lost my husband and son, and I fear I'll never see my daughter again. When I attempted to drown myself, I really didn't want to live any more. I'm not even sure that I do now.'

Dr Berdu listened with the manner of a doctor used to someone with a fragile mind. He'd seen so much of it over the past few years, yet he'd never become hardened or lost his compassion. He let her talk some more. She spoke of Fleur and wondered whether she was happy at the orphanage.

'The people who advised you to allow Fleur to go there are responsible people. They did what was best for you both,' he replied.

'I know. "Jacqueline" said she would let me know how she was, but I haven't heard from her yet.' Jeanne looked at him. 'Do you know her?'

'I do. If she told you that, then she will keep her word. She is a woman of honour. Trust me when I say that.'

'Are you part of the escape network too?'

He didn't answer her question. She laughed, saying that it was hard to trust someone she didn't know.

'I understand, but that's how life has become. Use your intuition. What does that tell you about the people who have helped you so far?'

'They've been good to me. They've risked their lives for me too.'

Dr Berdu smiled. 'Jeanne, you *will* be fine, but as a doctor, I must be honest with you. At the moment, you are not in a fit state to cross the Pyrenees — mentally or physically. I don't think you know how hard it is, so you have to help yourself, and you have to start now. If you don't, no one will want to help you.' He paused for a while before adding the final truth. 'If you are alone, the Germans will certainly catch you, and when they do, they will want to know who helped you survive so far — and what happened to your daughter. They use harsh methods, my dear, so think carefully about it.'

They walked on in silence for a while, taking in the beauty of their surroundings.

Jeanne took a deep breath. 'You are absolutely right. What do I have to do to get fit?'

'Your words hearten me. Now I know you will be fine.' She looped her arm through his as they walked past the place where she'd jumped into the lake. 'What a fool, I was,' she said. 'It was sheer selfishness.'

During the rest of the walk, Dr Berdu told her what he wanted her to do. First, she was to walk, starting with one lap of the lake and build up daily, plus she was given a regime of exercises to strengthen her body. He also told her he would give her some sleeping tablets, but she must only take one at a time. 'If you follow this exercise regime and eat well, you won't need them. Write down everything you do in a diary and show it

121

to Countess Elsa. I also want you to write down your feelings for the day. Be honest with yourself. If you have a bad day, no one will hold it against you, but I must know. Otherwise, it's all for nothing.'

After lunch, Dr Berdu left the house, but before doing so, he discussed Jeanne's regime. 'I'll be back in ten days. If I find you have done everything you can and are fit and strong, you will continue on the next part of the journey. It's up to you.'

CHAPTER 12

The Safe House at Château d'Usson

It took almost six months before Jeanne was ready to move on — much longer than they'd planned due to several relapses, but at least she was now fit and mentally stable. In the meanwhile, Justine called by several times to report that Fleur had settled in well at the orphanage. This news gave Jeanne further impetus to get well. On the day she was to leave, Countess Elsa made sure she had a hearty meal. She would need it as part of the journey was to be on foot. At dusk, a car belonging to the resistance came to pick her up. She was hidden under a blanket and driven away, the car's headlights partially covered so as not to attract attention.

Jeanne was not told where she was going, but the men had orders to head towards the ruined château at Usson, located in the *commune* of Rouze, in the Ariège *département*. The castle was upstream from Axat, along the Aude river gorge, a dramatic landscape at the foothills of the Pyrenees. At 920 metres in altitude, it dominated the Aude valley. Although the castle was roughly thirty-five kilometres away, it took most of the night to get there as the mountainous road had many hairpin bends and was extremely dangerous. Falling rocks were a constant hazard and the car occasionally had to swerve at the last minute to miss them. After a few hours the car pulled off the road and Jeanne was asked to get out. Another two men carrying rifles were waiting for her. From this point, they would accompany her to her destination on foot.

It was now early summer. The days were warmer, but the dense forests were still carpeted in thick damp leaves which added a cool chill to the air. After giving her an extra warm coat with a hood and checking that she was wearing the right footwear, they set off, heading through woodland and bushes down the gorge on foot. One of the men carried Jeanne's few belongings on his back and gave her a walking stick, which certainly helped, but she still slipped and slithered constantly. It made her realise why Bertrand had ordered her to get fit. She would never have made it the way she was. There was not a full moon that night, but what little moonlight there was highlighted the landscape, which was simply magical. The trees were bursting with new leaves, and the ground looked like a glittering magical carpet, tinged with blue from the star-studded, indigo night sky. By the time they reached the bottom of the gorge, she was ready to collapse. She'd worn trousers and was well-clothed, yet her legs were full of scratches from thorny bushes and bruised from slipping on the rocks.

She was allowed to rest for a while. All around was a dense forest and she had no idea where she was, but she could hear the sound of rushing water tumbling over rocks. One of the men went ahead while the other stayed to keep an eye on her. He took out a flask attached to his belt, unscrewed the cap, and handed it to her. 'Have a sip,' he said. 'It will warm you up.'

Jeanne took one sip and screwed up her face. 'What is this stuff, pure alcohol?'

The man laughed. 'Only fifty percent, it's homemade.' He took a few more swigs and put it away.

They heard a sharp sound, like a bird call. Minutes later, the second man reappeared, this time with another man. The two resistants wished Jeanne a good journey and clambered back up the mountainside. Jeanne felt a chill run down her spine. Here she was, in the dead of night in the bottom of a gorge, where there were probably wolves and bears, with a stranger who could kill her in an instant and dispose of her body, knowing full well no one would ever find her. Her imagination was getting the better of her.

The man extended his hand. 'Bonjour, madame, my name is "Alain",' Armand said. 'I'll be looking after you from now on.'

The man was so friendly and disarming that Jeanne almost told him her real name. 'Jeanne,' she replied. 'Where are we?'

Armand would not divulge their whereabouts. All he would say was that she was a little closer to the Spanish border than before. 'I can see you're exhausted, but we only have another two kilometres to walk, then you can rest.'

At that moment another two kilometres seemed like ten. Armand picked up her bag, slung it over his back, and walked ahead. It was clear they were following the stream. 'Stay close,' he said, 'it's slippery.'

They'd only gone a few metres when she fell flat on her backside again. Armand pulled her up. 'You okay?'

'Sore, but I'll manage.'

She slipped twice more before they came to the remains of a wooden bridge which had collapsed in the middle. 'It's been like this for years,' Armand said. 'There's another bridge further upstream, but by the look of you, I don't think you'll make it. The only way to cross here is by a series of stepping stones.' They slithered down the embankment and Jeanne looked at the stream with dread. The fast-running water gushed down the hillside, splashing over the rocks in small foaming waves.

'I'll go first and you follow.' Armand deftly stepped onto the first rock and reached out for her hand. Then he moved to the second stone. 'Come on, a step at a time.' Jeanne did as she was told and wobbled precariously on the rock. 'It's alright. I've got you,' Armand said.

Step by step, they managed to cross the stream, avoiding the most slippery ones, until they came to the final one and she lost her balance and slipped on her backside again with her legs dangling in the icy water. Fortunately, Armand was still holding her tightly. With his free hand, he threw her bag onto the bank and pulled her out of the water, hauling her onto the bank. By this time, Jeanne was freezing and thoroughly drenched.

'Thank you. If it wasn't for you, I would never have made it. I apologise, but my legs are killing me.'

'We're almost there,' Armand said. Then he did something unexpected. He lifted her in his arms and carried her the rest of the way, only putting her down when they came to a stone house in the middle of the woods. 'This will be your home for a few days. It may not be the

Ritz, but at least you have a warm bed and a fire.'

The house belonged to a local forester in the network who lived in one of the nearby villages. It was comfortable even if it was basic. Most importantly, it was well hidden. Armand lit a fire and boiled hot milk for them. 'You can sleep here tonight — on this bed near the fire. There's another room upstairs which I will use.' He pointed to the sink, which had running water. 'You can wash here if you like and hang your wet clothes over the clothesline by the fire. They should be dry in the morning.' He opened the cupboard, where there was an assortment of tinned food, half a dried sausage, and hard biscuits. He put some on a plate and told her to help herself.

'I will bid you good night. Sleep as long as you want.'

When she was alone, Jeanne could hear him moving about in the room above her. She waited until it went quiet before deciding it was safe to undress. She added a few more logs to the fire, hung her clothes on the line, and slipped between the sheets, pulling a thick warm blanket over her. In the morning, she woke up with a start, wondering where she was. Alain was not there and she presumed he was still in bed. She took her now dry clothes from the line, dressed, and opened the shutters slightly to let in the daylight. It was then that she saw him in the distance bringing an armful of logs back to the house.

'Good morning. Did you sleep well?' he asked, as he placed the logs by the fireplace.

'I did, thank you. The bed is very comfortable.' This time, it was she who made him a drink. 'How long have you been up?' she asked.

'Since dawn; I'm an early riser. I didn't want to wake you, you looked so peaceful.'

Jeanne felt herself blush. She had not been wearing any clothes and hoped she was so well-covered, he hadn't noticed. If he had, he was far too much of a gentleman to admit it.

'So what happens now? Will I be here long?'

'A few days. It would be unwise to move you at the moment, especially after you fell in water. I don't want you catching pneumonia. You need to regain your strength. That's why I've prepared enough logs for a few

126

days. I'm afraid that I can't stay with you as I have other things to do, so keep the door locked. If you do venture outside, stay close to the house.'

Jeanne was scared. 'What if someone comes?'

'They won't, but if they do, only open the door if they call you "Jeanne". Only a handful of people know you are here. This house has been used by the resistance since the Germans occupied France. You would be surprised at the people who have passed through here — French, Belgians, Polish, Hungarians, British, Australians, New Zealanders, Americans — even Germans who hate Hitler.' He saw the look of surprise on her face. 'Yes, there are many who hate the Nazi regime and fled rather than be conscripted.'

'And quite a few Jews,' she added, dismally. 'Like me.'

'Quite a few.' He didn't want to tell her the number had grown over the past two years. If it wasn't for his little book, he would have lost count. He changed the subject. 'How are your cuts and bruises?'

She pulled up her trouser legs to her knees and showed him. She had quite a few, some of them raw and red. He pulled out a bottle of white lotion from a cupboard, shook it hard, and poured some onto a cloth. 'Here, let me rub this in for you. It's antiseptic but it won't sting.'

He knelt down on the old, worn rug in front of the fire, picked up one of her legs, and started to apply the white liquid. It had a soothing effect. She sat quietly watching him. His touch was gentle and caring, and she found she was enjoying it. It reminded her of the massages she'd had at the spa baths before the war. After five minutes he shook the bottle again and did the same with the other leg.

'How does that feel?' he asked.

'Much better.' She smiled. 'You have a soft touch; you're not a doctor, are you?'

'No, but I did learn first aid — and I've helped in hospitals.' Armand thought of the Spanish refugees. 'I'll leave you the bottle. Rub a little on before you go to bed — and anywhere else where you have a cut or bruise. They'll heal in no time.'

Armand left around midday and Jeanne suddenly realised she had no idea where she was, except that she was somewhere near the bottom of a gorge and there was a stream with a broken bridge nearby. She was completely alone and it was a frightening thought. At a loss what to do with herself, she took a five-minute walk around the house to see just what sort of place she was in. In the bright sunshine she saw the densely wooded gorge rising up around her. On one peak stood the remains of what she knew to be a Cathar château, although she had no idea which one. Apart from that, there wasn't a house in sight. She returned to the house and explored the two rooms upstairs. Both were exceptionally small. One had a bed, table, and chair, and the other had two mattresses on the floor with clean, folded sheets and blankets on top of them. Downstairs there was just the one room where she slept and ate. The toilet was an outside shed with a covered hole in the ground at the back of the house.

As promised, Armand returned two days later, bringing with him a bottle of wine, fresh bread, and cheese, which she was extremely grateful for after the tinned food. When he asked how she was and if everything was alright, she told him she would go mad if she stayed there alone much longer.

'I've decided to move you from here the day after tomorrow,' he said. 'I'm afraid things have become rather chaotic at the moment and I have much to do, so at this point, I can't promise when you will make your last leg of the journey.'

'Is there a problem?'

'I presume that you are aware that last year Laval asked for volunteers to go to Germany in exchange for the release of French prisoners of war?'

'Yes, of course.'

'Well, many young men refused to go and have been in hiding. The two men who brought you to me are just two of them. It seems that yet again the Germans have been putting pressure on the government for a larger quota. The German in charge of this appalling scheme, Fritz Sauckel, has been using intimidation tactics to secure more labour. Now the government has issued another law, the *Service du travail obligatoire* — the STO. All men between the ages of twenty and twenty-three must go to work in Germany as a substitute for military service. Previously suspensions were issued for students and farm workers but we expect this to change. Therefore, many men are joining the resistance or forming maquis groups everywhere throughout France. We are in dire need of money, food, and training to support them as no one knows how long this will go on. In the last few weeks alone, we have escorted many Frenchmen over the border to work with the Free French in North Africa.'

Jeanne looked downcast. 'Does that mean that I am now in a long queue — like buying bread? First come, first served.'

'It means that the Germans have stepped up their efforts to find *all* evaders.'

She noticed the way he stressed *all*. 'Do we Jews still stand a chance of escaping?' she asked. 'Tell me honestly.'

'Of course. I'm just telling you that the situation is difficult. I need you to understand that.'

'I do. Maybe I should join the maquis too. Do they take Jewish women?' She gave a sarcastic laugh.

'They take anyone willing to fight. Are you willing to learn how to use a gun? Do you think you could stand up to being hunted day and night, always on the move?'

She thought he was mocking her again and became angry. 'Don't underestimate me. What do you take me for? Do you know how many women I've come across working in clandestine ways — why, the one who helped me the most was just a girl — "Jacqueline".'

At the mention of Justine, Armand quickly turned away. Jeanne noticed. 'Don't tell me you know her.' Armand refused to say anything, but Jeanne wouldn't let up. 'You do, don't you? I can see it in your eyes.'

He changed the subject. 'How are your bruises and cuts?'

She sat on the bed and pulled up her trouser legs to show him. 'They're improving.'

'I'll massage some more lotion into them.'

Armand fetched the lotion, and at the same time poured them both a glass of wine. She noticed he could barely look at her. 'You *do* know that girl, don't you?'

'You're observant, so I will be honest. Yes, I do know her.' He continued massaging the lotion into her legs, but still didn't look up. 'She belongs to our escape network.'

'Well, well. So I *was* right after all.' She leaned back on the bed, propping herself up with her elbow and sipping her wine. 'I must say, she's a courageous young woman.'

He finished the massage and pulled down her trouser legs. As he was wiping his hands, he glanced up at her. She was looking at him in a strange manner with her large dark brown eyes. 'Kiss me,' she said softly. 'Please kiss me.' It was almost a plea.

Armand was taken aback, yet at the same time, he felt his heart race. It was so totally unexpected. It was as if she was begging him. Since he had joined the resistance and the escape network, he had moved quite a few women across the countryside. Some were alone and quite attractive, but none had ever been like Jeanne, and definitely not as forward as this.

He turned his back on her, took a sip of his wine, and stared thoughtfully into the fire. 'It's inappropriate.'

She leaned forward and kissed the top of his head. He didn't move and she didn't see his eyes close at her tender touch. Seeing that he hadn't moved away, she let her lips caress his head more, then his neck, and finally his earlobe. 'Kiss me,' she whispered again.

Armand had no idea what came over him, but this time, he turned round, looked into her eyes, and kissed her on the lips, a long lingering kiss that aroused him in a way he could not fight, nor did he want to. Still looking directly into his eyes, she lay back on the bed and started to unbutton her blouse. 'Make love to me.'

When she'd unbuttoned her blouse completely, she took one of his hands and pressed it against her breasts. 'Massage them like you massaged my legs. Kiss them, like you just kissed my lips.' Her voice was soft and sensuous — the voice of a siren beckoning him to a fate he could not resist.

His hands began to knead her supple breasts with her firm nipples thrusting towards him — softly at first, but as he became more aroused, his passions increased and he became less inhibited, less gentle. Hearing her soft moans of desire made him want her all the more. He lay on the

130

bed, pulling off her blouse and covering her in kisses until he could stand it no more. She took off his shirt and unbuttoned his trousers, putting her hand inside and feeling his hardness. In turn, he pulled down her silk panties and felt between her legs. She was moist with desire. Delirious with a sexual appetite he'd not known for years, he pulled off his trousers and mounted her. As he was about to climax, he rolled over and this time, Jeanne mounted him, rocking to and fro — gently at first and then faster and faster, her long dark hair like a wild horse's mane in the wind. Their sexual appetites satisfied, they lay in each other's arms, savouring the moment. After a while, she reached for the wine bottle and refilled their glasses. He studied her curvaceous body and her long, dark tousled hair glistening with sweat, like an artist studies a model. She was perfection. Aphrodite herself.

'*Santé.*' She grinned and kissed him on the navel. 'You are an excellent lover.'

Sometime later, they made love again, this time exploring each other's bodies more slowly. The scent of her body drove him wild. Every part of her was delicious. Afterwards he lay with his head resting on her stomach while she ran her hand through his hair. She watched him for a while in silence, wondering about his age. He must be in his late forties, quite a lot older than her. She had always like older men. Her husband was almost twenty years older. Somehow, older men gave her a sense of security, and security was what Jeanne really wanted now. That — and to be loved.

'You're wearing a wedding ring,' she said.

'So are you.'

This fact brought him back down to earth with a thud. He sat up and reached for his clothes. He was suddenly overcome with a terrible guilt and could barely look at her again. She smiled. 'Don't feel guilty. We enjoyed it, didn't we? This is war. I needed you — and if you are honest with yourself, I think you needed me.'

'What we have done is wrong,' Armand said. 'I don't do this sort of thing.'

Jeanne gave a little smile. 'Neither do I. It will be our secret. Nobody need ever know.' She started to dress, but Armand stopped her and held her tightly in his arms. Neither uttered a word. An hour later, he was gone. She crouched in front of the fire, poking the embers before adding more logs. When the fire was hot, she hung up a large pot of water on the chain, waited for it to get warm, and poured it into the washbasin. As she sponged herself, Armand remained on her mind. He seemed a quiet, conservative type and, up until that moment, she had been a loyal wife, but she didn't feel guilty as Armand did. She had no idea what made her do it, but she felt alive again. If that stolen moment of passion kept her alive, then it was worth it.

The next evening, Jeanne heard a sound near the house, like someone stepping on twigs. The shutters were closed, the door was locked, and the only light came from the fire and a small lantern. She thought it was Alain and waited for him to open the latch. Instead, someone knocked on the door. 'Open up! Please, open up.' Her heart was pounding wildly. Whoever it was sounded desperate, but they hadn't said her name. She quietly opened the drawer and pulled out a knife. The knocking continued and this time she heard whispers. There was more than one. Logic told her that it couldn't be the Germans or police. They would never act like that. After more banging, she went upstairs and peeked out of shutters. There were two figures at the door. From where she was, it was hard to make out how old they were as they were heavily dressed in thick overcoats and wearing scarves and caps.

She went back downstairs. 'Who are you? What do you want?'

'We're on the run from the authorities. Please let us in. We mean you no harm.'

Contrary to what she had been told, she slid back the bolt and unlocked the door to find two scruffy and dishevelled young men standing in front of her. 'We're evaders from the *Service du travail obligatoire*. If the Germans catch us, they'll either shoot us or send us to Germany.'

Jeanne slipped the knife back in her pocket, waved them inside, and locked the door again. 'How did you know about this place?' she asked. 'Has anyone followed you?'

'No one saw us. We didn't even know this house was here. We've been on the run all day and came across it by accident.'

'Where are you from?'

'Quillan.'

'Where's that?'

The young men looked at each other. 'You're here and you don't know where Quillan is?' They looked shocked.

'No. I'm on the run too — like you, but I've been moved around so many times, I haven't the slightest idea where I am. The people helping me don't want me to know.'

The young men introduced themselves as François and André, both of them workers in a hat factory not far from Quillan. 'A local who worked at the Town Hall sent us an urgent message that our names were on a list which was about to be circulated throughout the area. We had no option but to flee,' François said. 'Our work is not deemed important enough for an exemption. One day we are workers, the next, *réfractaires* — on the run.'

Jeanne felt sorry for them. They looked so young and innocent. 'Do your families know you've left?'

'We told them we were going to join the maquis. Naturally they are worried, but they understand. We couldn't tell them anything else, partly because the authorities will question them, and partly because we have no idea where we'll end up. All we know is that we will fight to our last breath.'

'What about you?' André asked. 'You have a Parisian accent.' He paused for a moment, surveying her looks — dark hair and eyes, and a light olive complexion. 'Are you Jewish?'

When she didn't answer, he apologised.

She took the pot of water from the fire and let them take a quick wash while she made them a drink of ersatz coffee made from acorns. André saw the empty wine bottle. 'No wine?'

'I'm afraid not. This is not a hôtel. You'll have to make do with this. There are a few tins of food though.' She opened up some lentils and gave them a spoon with which to eat it. After they'd finished, she found a scrap of paper and a pencil. 'Now your bellies are full, I want you to

133

draw a map for me. Tell me where I am.'

The young men looked at each other. 'If you weren't told, then there must be a good reason for it. Do you want us to betray those who are helping you?'

Jeanne sighed. 'Of course not, but I know these are dangerous times and if something were to happen and I found myself alone — really alone, I mean — then at least I would have some idea of where I was.'

André looked at François. 'Alright, but never say it was us who told you.'

'I promise — now, start drawing. Where are Toulouse, Quillan, and this place? Most importantly, where is the French–Spanish border?'

André started to draw the map, adding a few upturned Vs for mountain peaks. He also put in the river Aude. Jeanne looked on as he explained where there were densely wooded gorges and high plateaus. He drew seven villages, which he said were in the Donezan region of the Ariège and told her which was the furthest away — the one closest to the plateau and the Spanish border — Mont-Saint-Jean. She then asked how far to the border.

'Probably fifty kilometres.' Jeanne's eyes widened and a smile crossed her face. 'It doesn't sound far,' André said, 'but the terrain is hard going, and the Germans and French are carefully guarding the border — bastards.'

Jeanne would not be put off by his words. She studied the map closely. 'And where are we now?'

'When we left Quillan, we headed for the Château d'Usson, but because we got lost, we are not quite sure where we are.'

'I noticed the ruins of a château out there yesterday. That may be it.'

André and François looked delighted. 'We'll check it out in the morning.'

Jeanne took another good look at the map, memorized it, and threw it on the fire. 'For the moment you'd better go upstairs and get some sleep. I'm sure there will be a maquis group around here that will be only too happy to take you both. You are brave young men. That's what counts.'

It was dark when Armand arrived at the house the following evening. He heard voices as he approached and took a peek through a slit in the shutters to see who was inside before knocking. Seeing Jeanne at ease with two young men, he guessed why they were there. In the past twenty-four hours, he'd encountered six men on the run and helped them to safe houses. Like André and François, they didn't want to flee France either. Armand didn't know the young men, but after asking a few questions, ascertained that they were who they said they were.

'Can you help us, monsieur?' François asked.

'I will do my best. Tonight I have to take this lady away to another place of safety, and then I will look out for the best place for you to go. Things are not as safe as they were a year ago.' The men seemed happy with that.

Armand had brought another bottle of wine and more bread and cheese. He'd hoped to share it between the two of them, but instead, gave his portion of the wine to the men. After Jeanne had eaten, he told her to get her things. They had to get going as soon as possible. The two young men bid them goodbye and Jeanne wished them good luck.

'Where are we going?' she asked as they tramped through the damp undergrowth.

'You'll see,' Armand replied. They walked for about half an hour, this time in a different direction, and then crossed the stream again. Thankfully there was a large log placed across it, and although damp and slippery, it wasn't as bad as the rocks. From there, they walked to the village of Rouze, where they stayed the night with a Swiss engineer called "Henri" who was employed at the nearby Usson hydroelectric power plant. While holding such an important position, right under the noses of the Germans, he worked with the resistance in the Donezan and was a highly valued friend of Armand and Dr Berdu and participated actively in their operations. Having access to a travel pass to visit other dams and hydroelectric plants in the area allowed him to make contact with the resistance in Capcir and Cerdagne, helping to aid the network in their escape routes to Spain.

In the morning, a car arrived to collect them. Jeanne recognised the driver instantly.

'"Dr Bertrand"! This is quite a surprise.'

'I'm glad to see you've recovered and look fit and healthy,' Dr Berdu said. 'The mountain air agrees with you.'

'It's thanks to you that I'm alive.' She looked from Dr Berdu to Armand quizzically. 'It's certainly a small world. First, I find out that you know Jacqueline; now, I find that you also know Dr Bertrand.' She gave a little smile. 'You must be very important, Alain.'

Armand noticed Dr Berdu's face when he found out they had talked about Justine. He told her to get her things as there was no time to hang around. She went to her room to collect her bag and overheard the three men whispering. Armand was assuring Dr Berdu and Henri he hadn't said that Jacqueline was his daughter.

'I'm ready,' Jeanne said. 'Where to now?'

No one gave her an answer, and she didn't really expect one. She thanked Henri for allowing them to stay the night and Dr Berdu left a bottle of wine for his trouble.

This time they made their way to Mont-Saint-Jean. Throughout the drive, Jeanne tried to recall where she was from the map. Here the area was less wooded with more agricultural land. Just after the village of La Pla, they saw a convoy of German trucks in the distance and hastily turned into a dirt road lined with a dense hedgerow, keeping well out of sight until they passed. The presence of the Germans threw them off guard and they sat there for a while. Jeanne could tell something was wrong. When they started off again, they called into an old water-mill just before Mont-Saint-Jean. Jeanne was told to stay in the car while the two men went inside. They came out five minutes later with a look that told Jeanne something was seriously wrong.

'There's been a change of plan,' Armand said. 'I was going to take you to a safe house, but for the moment you will stay with me and my wife. If anyone asks, you are a relative who has come to visit for a while.' Jeanne was alarmed. 'Don't worry, the villagers keep to themselves, so we should be fine.'

All these moves and changes were starting to affect Jeanne again. What was going on that they weren't telling her?

CHAPTER 13

Colette Joubert Remembers: Summer 1943

I CAN REMEMBER the day I first met the woman known as "Jeanne" as if it was yesterday. There had just been a raid in Mont-Saint-Jean. The Germans were looking for evaders who, they were told, were hiding out in the area. We were all scared, as no house was spared from a thorough search, and I was alone as usual while Armand was away with his "other" work. Throughout the winter and early spring, I had barely seen him. If he wasn't at school, then he was away on some mission or other. Sometimes he told me where he was, but he always said that the less I knew, the better. Often, evaders stayed overnight with us, but never longer. I knew they were heading for Spain, but Armand told me that after the Compulsory Work Service laws were introduced, many young men did not want to flee; they wanted to stay and fight. When I asked how it was possible to fight without arms, he said that was being taken care of. They were trying to get them from the Allies.

I worried about him. I worried every time he stepped out of the house. Here in the Donezan, we were not bothered by the Germans as much as other places, and for that I thank God. We villagers were hardworking people and in general had a hatred for the Vichy government. After so many were killed during the Great War, we couldn't understand the Pétainists. They had let us down. We even helped the Spanish refugees when the government turned their back on them, but there *were* collaborators among us. Some people have no heart and will do anything out of jealousy or spite. I often confided in Babette about my loneliness and she said it was the same with her. Théo was always away, taking care of someone in another town or village. As a doctor, he

137

covered a wide area and was able to use the car too. Now that the zone sud was occupied, we also had a curfew, although few in Mont-Saint-Jean took any notice of it. No Germans were living in our village.

When I was introduced to Jeanne and was told she would be staying with us until they sorted something out for her, it worried me deeply. With more Germans in the area, it wasn't safe. Even though she affected a confident manner, I could tell that she was scared. After Armand showed her to her room, which was opposite our own bedroom, he took me aside and said she was in a fragile state of mind and had attempted suicide. I felt sorry for her. I've always tried to show compassion to anyone in trouble so naturally, I agreed to let her stay.

'How long are you expecting her to be here?' I asked. 'After all, there's just been a raid — what if there's another?'

'Théo thinks it highly unlikely, especially if they didn't catch anyone. They are looking for those hiding in the forests,' he said. 'The authorities want to round the young ones up and send them to Germany to prove they are on top of things.'

'What if they *do* come back?'

'Then we'll hide her,' Armand replied. 'In the cellar.'

I thought about it. Access to the cellar was through the door under the staircase. If anyone opened that door, all they would see was a set of shelves containing jars of pickles and dried foodstuff. Only if they moved the shelves would they see the set of steps leading to the cellar. It was dark and damp down there and the only light was from a kerosene lamp. We used it to store extra food to feed the evaders.

We'd just finished our conversation when Jeanne reappeared. She was keenly aware of the ramifications for us and apologised. We assured her it was fine and she was not to worry. Sometime later, Armand said he was going out and I didn't ask where. When Jeanne and I were alone, I made us both some food and tried to make her feel comfortable. We sat at the table looking at each other, both summing up the other. It was a strange feeling.

I was struck by her extraordinary beauty. It was a beauty combined with strength and fragility. She had thick, dark hair tied up in a loose chignon at the nape of her slender neck and wore a floral kerchief. It didn't take too much to see that she wasn't used to wearing such a thing. She must have been given it to blend in with country folk, yet there was nothing of the country about her. She was *une vraie Parisienne* through and through. She possessed such elegance that even if she were dressed as a shepherdess, one would pick her out. I noted her intense dark eyes framed with long lashes. They reminded me a little of Mercedes, except that Mercedes's eyes were defiant and determined. Jeanne's eyes were different — sensitive.

I wondered if she would ever make it out of France, but she told me she had been exercising and trying to get strong. I knew she had no idea what it took to cross those mountains. They were harsh. Our smugglers tried to find the best routes, but none were easy. They tested even the fittest.

Later that evening, when Armand and I were alone, he told me he'd been to see Claude at the gendarmerie to find out if he knew anything about the raid. He assured Armand that if he had known the Germans were coming, he would have put the word out. He said even Monsieur le Commissioner Godard had not been informed. It worried Armand as we were supposed to have lookouts in the mountains to warn us. He asked if Jeanne had confided in me. When I asked about what, he shrugged. 'I don't know — anything.'

'She told me very little,' I said. 'Only what you told me: that she lost her husband and son, and about her daughter being put in an orphanage.'

'Is that all?'

I asked what else he wanted to hear. Again he shrugged. 'I'm not sure that she's ready to make the crossing yet. She needs to get stronger.'

I agreed with him, but there was something in the way he said it. I knew my husband well and I had the distinct feeling that he cared about this woman more than any of the others.

Over the next few days, I watched him. Whenever she was in the room, he seemed different. I couldn't put my finger on it. Jeanne's presence certainly lit up the room. She helped me during the day, and in the evening we played the piano. She was an excellent pianist and we took it in turns to play — Chopin, Shubert, Mozart, and especially Mahler. She excelled when it came to playing Mahler. Much to Armand's delight, she was also an avid reader and loved to talk about books — Armand's favourite subject. Then one evening, I went outside to collect the washing. When I returned, I noticed them standing close together. Armand stepped back a little when he heard me enter. They weren't doing anything inappropriate. He was handing her a book, but something about it struck me as odd. Were they a little too close, or was it my imagination?

'I'm rather tired,' Jeanne said. 'Last night I didn't sleep well. If you don't mind, I will retire for the night.' She thanked Armand for the book.

When she'd gone, I asked what was wrong. He told me he'd given her the book to help her sleep. 'She is worried about Fleur and wants to know if she's alright. I said I would try to find out.'

'And will you?' I asked.

'I made a promise, Colette.'

I looked into his eyes and in that moment I could tell he was smitten by her.

CHAPTER 14

The Network Suffers its First Major Blow

In Toulouse, things were not going as planned. Even before the occupation of the free zone, those organising escape routes had to be careful. Although they were not directly under German rule, the Vichy government's Armistice Commission was vigilant in clamping down on smugglers and those helping evaders. They worked in conjunction with the secret police, now firmly under the direction of Admiral François Darlan, officially opposing Communist activities and resistance efforts under the terms of the armistice. This allowed the Gestapo to operate with them, especially in the bigger towns and cities. It was not always publicized in the censored newspapers, but imprisonment, torture, and deportation to internment camps throughout France was common. Everyone was under suspicion.

Apart from running a legitimate business, Paul Cassou and his network had so much to juggle it was hard to cope. Moving people from one safe house to another took time, just as it did for Armand and Dr Berdu in the Donezan. Those who wanted to help carefully put out the word, but trusting newcomers was fraught with danger and it took time and resources to check people's backgrounds and motives. No matter how many checks and safeguards were in place, one could never be quite sure if a spy had infiltrated the group.

The other problem was that the railway and bus stations were already monitored by the Germans and the Vichy government, albeit in a more covert manner. Now the Gestapo's presence intensified. Justine had to learn how to disguise herself each time she picked someone up and she started to wear various coloured wigs and different spectacles. Quite often, the clothes she wore belonged to Robert's aunt — homemade, dowdy, and practical, and devoid of any sense of fashion whatsoever. When she looked at herself in the mirror, she let out a gasp, saying that if this was old age, she had nothing to look forward to. Robert dressed as a middle-aged man, adding grey streaks to his dark hair. Occasionally he wore a false moustache, which made him the butt of jokes from the others. Mimi, the youngest of the group at twenty-one years old, made herself look younger by wearing a simple skirt paired with a pale pink ribbed pullover, and by separating her hair into two equal parts and weaving each section into braids which she neatly coiled up either side. Everyone laughed and told her she looked like a genuine "Gretchen". Fortunately, they had access to good forgers who always made sure their identification papers and permits were in order. In a short time, they had become consummate actors.

The laughing soon stopped when they left for the station. It was dangerous work and all of them knew their instructions by heart. Leave immediately if you sense trouble. A major help to Cassou's network, and indeed to other networks throughout France, were the railway workers. Many were extremely sympathetic to the evaders and the resistance, and put their own lives at risk by informing them where the exit doors in toilets and waiting rooms on the platforms were, if a train was delayed, or if anyone had been picked up. Because of Gestapo and militia activity at the railway stations, railway workers on the trains often sounded the whistle minutes before they approached a station. With the train travelling at a much slower pace, evaders were able to jump from the train and scramble down the embankments to waiting helpers who whisked them away to safety.

Throughout the following months, Justine was busy moving evaders from one safe house to another and the situation was becoming more and more difficult. Without help from the Allies, it was highly likely the network would collapse. Cassou told her that he had a vital mission for her and it would entail going back to the Donezan. When she asked what it was, he said he would tell her in due time. In the meantime, she was to help Robert pick up another two evaders at the railway station in Toulouse. Due to increased surveillance, it was agreed that he would wait outside the station, rather than on the platform, make contact with his parcel, and they would follow him down the street where Justine would be waiting with the car. A signal would be given at the appropriate time and she would step out of the car to pick them up, allowing Robert to walk away in a normal fashion. Toulouse station was always busy; Robert was to hold a small bunch of red flowers, and as usual, had taken great care to disguise himself.

The couple, a middle-aged Jewish lawyer and his wife, spotted him and approached. After giving a sign of recognition, Robert quickly turned around and walked away with the couple following at a safe distance. They turned a corner and Justine saw them heading towards her as planned. She waited until they neared the car and was just about to get out when two black cars suddenly pulled up beside them. Four men jumped out, aiming pistols at the couple and ordering them to stop. Justine had no doubt as to who they were — the Gestapo. The middle-aged couple froze. While one of the men picked up the couple's suitcases, another ordered them into one of the cars. Robert realised what was happening and made a run for it, with the other two Gestapo agents running after him and firing shots.

Justine's heart thudded wildly as he approached the car. She was praying he would jump in and they would drive away, but Robert knew he would never make it. Instead of going to the car, he jumped over a wall into a garden. The Gestapo followed, still firing their guns. Petrified, Justine slid down in the driver's seat, just enough that they couldn't see her but she could see them. A part of her wanted to drive away, but that would attract attention. To add to the situation, another Gestapo car arrived from the opposite direction. She stayed put, watching them join in the chase to find Robert. In the meantime, the car with the Jewish couple drove away and she could still hear shots from behind the garden wall.

Several minutes passed before she saw Robert being dragged out of the garden at gunpoint. He was handcuffed even though he was bleeding from what looked like a gunshot wound to the right arm. Without even as much as a glance in her direction, he was pushed into one of the cars and taken away. When all three cars had gone, she found herself alone in the street. Knowing that an incident with the Gestapo was taking place, no one wanted to be caught witnessing such a scene.

Justine felt a sinking feeling in the pit of her stomach. It was doubtful the couple would withstand interrogation, and they were bound to implicate Robert as their helper. How had the Gestapo known what was going on in the first place? There were plenty of people standing around waiting for friends and relatives, and Cassou was assured the couple's papers were foolproof. She also felt terrible for not opening the door and at least giving him the chance to get in, but his actions had purposely diverted him away from her. In all likelihood, he knew they'd never make it together, so it would be better that at least one of them got away. The thought that he had deliberately tried to save her was more than she could bear. *Oh God, please don't let them hurt you.*

After waiting a few minutes to be sure all was safe, she drove away, heading to the company offices in the hope that Cassou was still there. Unfortunately, he was out. One of the office workers asked if everything was alright.

'I need to speak with Monsieur Cassou immediately as a delivery of charcoal has not reached its destination.'

The man had a good idea what this meant but said unfortunately he wouldn't be back until the next day. She tried not to panic. There was only an hour before curfew and it wasn't long enough for her to drive to his villa. Besides, she didn't want to upset his wife. She returned to her apartment and, as sleep was impossible, stayed up all night wondering what to do. Calling from her apartment was out of the question. Cassou did not want them contacting him at home by telephone as his villa was probably tapped and he didn't want to involve his family. Neither could she take the risk and sneak out to tell one of the others what had happened. Alone and depressed, all she could think of was Robert and the couple being tortured at Gestapo HQ.

In the morning, she arrived at work early looking terrible from lack of sleep. One of the other secretaries brought her a drink. 'You look ill. Maybe you should go home,' she said.

'I think I ate something that didn't agree with me.'

When Cassou arrived, he told her to bring her pad into the office as he needed to dictate something to her. The others looked on, wondering what was going on.

'What in God's name happened?' he asked in a steely voice.

'So you've already heard they took Robert and the couple?'

'I was informed by an insider that he was taken to Gestapo HQ and later moved to Saint-Michel Prison.' He gave her a despairing look. 'I'm afraid the couple confessed that Robert was the man who was supposed to meet them at the station. They have already been sent to a camp and from there will go to Drancy to await the next transport to Poland.'

'Do you think Robert will talk?'

At that moment, there was a knock at on the door. 'Come in,' Cassou called out in a stern voice.

It was one of the other secretaries. Justine steadied her writing pad with her shaking hand, making out she was taking notes. The woman told him a customer was outside. 'He said something about an urgent truckload of charcoal.' She added that he seemed extremely agitated.

Cassou left the room immediately, telling Justine to stay where she was.

When the other secretary had gone, Justine went to the window. In the yard below, she saw him talking to a man wearing a dark overcoat and a beret. She didn't recognise him. They were together for only a few minutes before parting company. She hurried back to her chair.

When Cassou returned, she knew by the look on his face that something terrible had happened.

'It's bad news. Robert was executed by firing squad just over an hour ago.' Justine felt as though her world had collapsed. She always knew something would go wrong sooner or later, but when it happened, she wasn't ready for it. She wanted to scream, but instead she froze. 'I do believe Robert went to his death without telling them about us,' Cassou said. 'If he'd said anything, we'd have been rounded up by now.' He told her he was just as devastated as she was. He was even more shocked that it had all taken place so quickly, as if to set an example to others.

Gradually Justine's frozen state turned to anger and despair. 'Only a couple of people knew that we were meeting the couple, and they're trustworthy.' She thought of the man who had been following them near the river a while back, but that had been sorted out. Her eyes were now filled with tears.

'We can't always think there are traitors, Justine. Maybe it was the couple themselves. Perhaps the Gestapo thought them suspicious, smelt a rat, and pounced. It's not easy to act normal when you're on the run.' He leaned back in his chair and sighed heavily. 'Go back to your work and try and carry on as usual. Meet me tomorrow night at Bar Maurice. We'll discuss more then.'

Justine went back to her desk and, with shaking hands, placed a sheet of paper in her typewriter and started typing as if everything was fine, even though others were staring at her.

At Bar Maurice she was not surprised to find Mimi and Jacques there too. Robert's sudden death had affected them all but they had to carry on. Cassou said he had a special assignment for Justine and another person in the group who operated from Saint-Girons. He asked how their shooting and self-defence lessons with the two Allied soldiers were going, to which they replied, the instructors were happy with them.

'Excellent. This brings me to the point of this meeting. Now that you have received some basic training, I want you, Jacqueline, to cross the border into Spain and go to the British Consulate in Barcelona. Another man, who couldn't make it tonight, is doing the same, but he is going to Bilbao and then to Lisbon.'

Justine's eyes widened. 'You want *me* to cross the Pyrenees?'

'That's right. The mission is two-fold. I want you to judge for yourself how the escape route via the Donezan and Pyrénées-Orientales is going — how the smugglers operate; where the guards are, etc. When you do cross the frontier, I want details on the guides there too. Once you reach Barcelona, you will plead our case to the Consulate-General. I am told he is sympathetic to our cause and will help if he can. We need at least one radio operator but preferably two, as we operate in a wide area and need to communicate more efficiently. Up to now, I've been gathering arms via a few sources which are to be used later when the time comes to fight. For the moment they are well-hidden, but we need much more, and we need experienced men to train us in sabotage. Most importantly, we need money immediately to pay off the smugglers and helpers right now. Aiding evaders is an expensive exercise.'

Justine digested the request with a mixture of fear and excitement. 'What about getting back into France?'

'You have the contacts. They've already helped others return. Most likely you will make new contacts too. You are perceptive and resourceful, so I know you'll be good at evaluating people.'

'When do you want me to go?' she asked.

'Tomorrow.'

'What!'

'No time to waste. I want you there and back within two weeks at the latest. You are also going to have to make your own way to your home as I've been notified that your company car has been requisitioned. I am only allowed to keep three — my own and two for the salesmen.'

Mimi and Jacques were also given new tasks. Evaders would now be changing trains in Toulouse and heading straight to Saint-Girons, a distance of over seventy kilometres, which would take an extra two hours by train if there were no hold-ups. It was closer to the border and not far from the village where Cassou's family lived. It also marked the start of one of his escape routes into Andorra and Spain. When the train approached the town, the train driver would sound the train whistle just before they arrived at Saint-Girons station, and the train would slow down, allowing the evaders time to jump off before they crossed the bridge. Mimi and Jacques were to wait in the bushes for them and take them to safe houses.

It had been a long hot summer, making it easy for them to carry out their missions, but the weather was once again changing and the cold harsh winters had arrived. It was a blessing and a curse. The deep snow drifts were hard to navigate, yet at the same time offered protection. The snow made it harder for the Germans to move about, although the German border guards, mostly Austrian, were expert skiers. How

147

Justine longed for spring when the trees were bursting with fresh green leaves and the meadows were awash with wildflowers. Her journey would take her from Toulouse to Mont-Saint-Jean via Carcassonne and Quillan, but now she had to travel by bus and train. Cassou handed her a new travel pass. With her documents in order, her excuse for travelling was that she was taking some time from work to visit her parents. From Saint-Mont-Jean, she then had to make her own way to Spain and back.

Her mother was the first to spot her walking down the laneway. With no prior notice and seeing that she'd arrived by bus, rather than in the company car, Colette thought something terrible had happened. Had she lost her job? Was Toulouse no longer safe and she was coming home for good?

'Chérie.' Her mother gave her a big hug. 'What a lovely surprise, but is everything all right? What happened to the car? Why did you come by bus?'

Questions, questions. Her mother was a worrier.

'I'll tell you when we get inside. How have you been?'

'Fine.' Colette hugged her daughter again. 'Your papa will be so happy to see you. He's out at the moment.' Her mother's smile disappeared. 'I must warn you though, we have someone staying with us — an evader. She's going to Spain.'

Justine's first reaction was that they might even make the crossing together, but she sensed a note of concern in her mother's voice.

'Who is it?'

'A Parisienne — a Jewish lady they call "Jeanne".'

Justine couldn't believe her ears. Surely it couldn't be the same Jeanne, not after all this time, yet from the description, she knew there was only one Jeanne who fitted that description.

At that moment, Jeanne was watching from behind the lace curtain. She too couldn't believe it. If it had been anyone else, she would have gone to her room, but seeing it was the girl who had helped her, her face lit up. Had "Jacqueline" come all this way to give her news about Fleur?

As soon as Justine and her mother stepped inside the house, Jeanne was standing in the hallway, her arms outstretched to welcome her.

'Dear Jacqueline. I never expected to see you again. How did you know I was here? Do you have good news about Fleur?'

The shock of seeing Jeanne in her own home stunned Justine and she could barely find the words to answer. Her mother looked from one to another in surprise. The whole time Jeanne had been at the house, Colette had spoken about her daughter — Justine — and now she saw they already knew each other.

It was Jeanne's turn to look confused. 'What's going on?'

Justine knew this awkward situation had to be cleared up quickly. 'I think we need to have a little chat,' she said, 'and by the way, the last time I heard, Fleur was fine, so please don't worry.'

Colette made them a drink of real coffee given to them by one of Dr Berdu's German contacts. As she served it, she asked how they knew each other.

'I helped Jeanne in Toulouse. I was responsible for her going to the various safe houses and for what happened to her daughter. I knew she was heading this way, but never expected to find her here.' She turned to Jeanne. 'I thought you would be in Spain by now.'

At that moment her father entered the room. He was also surprised to see Justine, but even more surprised to see the three women sitting at the kitchen table with a serious look on their faces. Colette stood up to greet him. 'It seems we have a situation on our hands that needs to be cleared up immediately.' She didn't look at all happy.

Armand took off his hat and jacket and hung it up, deliberating on what to say. If he hadn't insisted on Jeanne staying at the house, Justine and Jeanne would never have met again.

First, he kissed his daughter and told her how happy he was to see her. The women all looked at him, expectantly, wondering what he was about to say.

'Jeanne,' he said, in a calm voice, careful to watch his words. 'The girl you came to know as "Jacqueline" is our daughter, Justine. We know of her work in Toulouse, but have no idea of all the people she deals with. Many people have passed through here — as you are doing now — while others go elsewhere. When you mentioned her name at the safe house, it was a surprise, but I couldn't tell you how I knew her. I hope you understand. Discretion is the key to our safety.' His face reddened as he tried to find an excuse as to why Jeanne was in their home. Colette saw it immediately and got up to replenish their drinks for fear she too showed her concern. Armand continued.

'Jeanne, now that I have told you "Jacqueline"– or Justine as she is to us — is our daughter, I beg you not to repeat this to anyone. Outside this house, she must still remain Jacqueline to you. Is that clear?'

Jeanne nodded. 'You have my word. I would never betray those who have been kind to me.'

Justine asked Jeanne if she would be good enough to leave them alone for a while. They had things to discuss. Jeanne's face reddened. She looked uncomfortable and wondered if they would now move her on. Waiting until she heard the door to Jeanne's bedroom close, Justine turned to her father and displaying more than a hint of despair, asked why she was still there, and worst of all, why was she in their home.

'You know we always move people on as quickly as possible. Not to mention the fact that she now knows our real names. What if she is caught?'

Colette, who had re-entered the room when Jeanne left, looked at him, wondering how he would answer this.

'Did you know she tried to drown herself?' he asked.

'No. I had no idea. Where and when did this happen?'

'After you left her at the villa, she went for a walk and tried to kill herself by jumping into the lake. If it hadn't been for two evaders keeping a watch on her, she wouldn't have made it.'

'I didn't know. If Cassou knew, he certainly didn't tell me.'

'That's when Théo got involved. The count and countess were so worried, they contacted him. Apparently, they know each other well. He laid it straight on the line with her. Either she tried to snap out of her depression and get strong, or they would let her go. Knowing she would never survive, she took his advice and made an effort to get fit. I met her when I picked her up at the stream below Château d'Usson. She told me about you helping her, but I never said you were my daughter. That's the truth.' Armand sighed. 'How was I to know you would meet up again?'

Justine was exasperated. Things were hard enough without this. 'She looks fine to me, Papa. Obviously Théo's pep talk and medical care worked, so why is she still here?'

Colette studied Armand's face. 'She's still fragile. I wanted to give her time to get strong. You know that crossing the border is hard.'

'Papa, it's been months! If anything, she looks better than when I last saw her.' Justine was exasperated. 'She's putting us all in danger by staying here. What does Théo think about this?'

'He's given her sleeping pills as she still finds it hard to sleep. She has nightmares.'

'What do you feel about all this, Maman?' Justine asked.

'If I am honest, I am not happy about it, but if your papa says she is not ready, then I must listen to him. He knows the situation better than I.'

Armand took Colette's hand and squeezed it affectionately. Justine detected something was not quite right but for the moment she didn't pursue it. Her father changed the subject and asked why she was here. When she told him she had been asked to cross into Spain herself *and* return, all within two weeks, he looked anxious.

'It's one thing to help people as we do, but entirely different when it's you making the crossing.'

She laughed. 'Why? Can we help others when we're not willing to risk it ourselves? This is a matter of urgency.'

Colette told her that she was proud to have raised such a brave daughter.

'I don't consider myself brave at all, Maman. I am as scared as everyone else, but I could not live with myself if I didn't do my duty by others.'

'You are like your father,' Colette said with a deep sigh. 'Stubborn. Do what you must. I cannot stop you.'

She told them she would leave the next day, but first she wanted a meeting with Théo Berdu. 'Is he at home?'

'He's just come back from Capcir,' Armand said. 'We could go over later when it's dark.'

Théo and Babette were in the pharmacy checking on the diminishing stock of medicines when Justine and her father arrived.

'What a lovely surprise,' Babette said.

'I have to cross into Spain as soon as possible,' she said. 'Cassou needs help from the Allies and has asked me go to the British Consulate in Barcelona.'

Realising it was of the utmost importance, Babette suggested they go upstairs and talk while she finished the inventory herself. Théo produced a bottle of wine and they settled down to talk.

'Cassou's not the only one who needs help. I am in dire need of medical supplies and have to make trips to Perpignan every week. Thankfully, the Germans supply me with a few basics, but that's only because I am called to treat some of their own.'

'Give me a list and I'll see what I can do,' Justine said. 'What else do you need?'

The reply was the same as Cassou's list — arms, and someone to train the maquis in sabotage, etc. 'A radio operator would be a godsend also. Then we can communicate better. I did ask someone the last time I was in Perpignan — an American crossing the border — but that was six months ago. I've not heard from him since. How are you intending to cross?'

'I was thinking about using Pablo.'

'You just missed him. He left a week ago.'

'Who else do you suggest?' Justine asked.

'Just lately we've been working with a few more maquis groups. Some of them have excellent spies and links to smugglers. It was a case of necessity because of the Germans pouring more resources into protecting the border. We needed to find alternatives in case something happens to Pablo. German repression is vigorous and several smugglers have been caught.'

Justine shuddered at the thought. If Pablo was caught, then Mercedes would be targeted too. 'Did you know, the Germans just executed someone very close to us at Saint-Michel Prison? It still weighs on my mind as we have no idea why he was arrested and we don't suspect a traitor among us.'

'Sometimes it's a matter of being in the wrong place at the wrong time. Luck — or, I should say, bad luck,' Théo said.

Thinking about Robert depressed her so she changed the subject. Her father and Dr Berdu started to tell her about the other groups they were in contact with. Because she'd taken Jeanne to the villa, she already knew Berdu had significant links with other maquis, particularly the fledgling Maquis de Picaussel between Foix and Carcassonne, plus, escape chains had been established on the Narbonnaise coasts. What she didn't know was just how many connections he and her father had established since the STO laws were enacted. Organisations now flourished throughout the Aude Pyrénées, the upper valley of the Aude, including the Ariège, Donezan, and the Pays de Sault. Spread over several villages, they took charge of the réfractaires from the STO, and wherever possible, gave them new identities to work in forestry or companies such as that of charcoal manufacturers similar to Paul Cassou. Aiding someone of military age was punishable by death and rewards were posted in every town and village.

Théo and Armand also developed contacts with Marcel Taillandier and the Morhange group, who were extremely active. Like Cassou, their network spread from Toulouse to the Pyrenees. Even though squabbles still existed inside most groups, the *armée secrete* was finally coming together, which made it easier for the leaders to co-ordinate with one another. One of the first maquis groups in the area was that of the Roc Blanc, where some of the resistance activities were linked to the Donezan via the two departments of the Aude and Pyrénées-Orientales rather than the Ariège. Some evaders used this as a starting point for the escape routes to Andorra, but Justine did not want to go via that route. She preferred to cross further east, in Cerdagne, as she knew that area well, as did Dr Berdu and her father. It was also closer to Barcelona.

After discussing the pros and cons of each group, Dr Berdu suggested the Spanish maquis. 'We got to know of them through Pablo,' he said. 'Their *chef* is don Manuel de Caballero, a man of action and one of the most daring and effective leaders on the border of the Pyrénées-Orientales. We call him *el intrépid* — the fearless one. He operates the *Lagartijo* Network. They are fierce Republicans and good fighters because they have seen first-hand what Fascism does, and because they want to go back, kill Franco, and live in a free Spain. They mainly work in small groups in the mountains between Villefranche-de-Conflent, Bourg-Madame, and Puigcerdà.'

'Will they take me?' Justine asked.

Armand said they'd taken quite a few French, foreign Jews, and Allied airmen, but don Manuel was adamant they all had to be strong enough to make the journey. 'He warned us that if there was any doubt someone couldn't make it or caused them trouble, they would be disposed of. By that, we took it to mean they would be shot or pushed off a mountain pass.'

Justine listened carefully. 'That's a harsh line to take. So many strong men and women find the crossing hard, especially in winter.'

'Is it?' Dr Berdu replied. 'If the border guards find someone left behind, they torture them until they find out who helped them. They can't take chances.'

'So will they take me — a slip of a girl?' she asked with a hint of sarcasm.

Berdu laughed. 'You can climb a mountain like an isard. I wish I was as fit as you. The thing is, we will have to make contact first so you might have to wait a couple of days. You need a pass to get past Puyvalador as there is a large German base there now because of the dam. Go and see Claude tomorrow. Tell him you are accompanying me as my nurse's aide because Babette is busy with the pharmacy. As soon as we hear something we will be on our way.'

Justine decided to voice her thoughts about Jeanne. She told them it worried her that an evader had stayed in their house so long. 'When do you think she will be fit enough to move on?' she asked Dr Berdu.

Berdu threw a quick glance at Armand. 'Hopefully in a couple of weeks when Pablo makes his next trip.'

'Good. I know she's a troubled woman and it's all very well saying she is a relative, but in all honesty, she is a true Parisian and if the Gestapo get wind of it, they will check us all out. Besides, if we leave her any longer it will be the middle of winter. The worst time to cross.'

Berdu sighed. 'Don't worry. We'll get her sorted out.'

Justine did worry. She wasn't quite sure what it was about Jeanne, but something was wrong, and she felt Berdu knew that too. 'Well let's hope she's on her way by the time I return.'

The next day, Justine went to the gendarmerie to get her travel pass. Claude was happy to see her as usual. She told him she was spending a few days with her parents but needed the pass to go with Dr Berdu and help him as Babette was busy.

Claude prepared the papers. 'Dr Berdu has already informed me you're joining him. I can get you a pass as far as Mont-Louis, just in case he needs to visit any other patients.' As he was typing and stamping the pass, he asked if she would have a drink with him at the Hôtel Bellevue. Thinking she might glean some information about what was going on in the area, she accepted.

'Excellent,' Claude replied. 'I'll meet you at six thirty.'

He handed her the travel pass just as another young women came into the building. It was Alice, one of her father's former pupils.

'Alice! I hardly recognised you,' Justine said. 'I think the last time I saw you was just before I moved to Toulouse.'

Alice was a couple of years younger than Justine. She had a pleasant and flirtatious nature, excelled in all her subjects, and like Claude, wanted to go to university until the Occupation put a stop to that. Now she worked with her parents on their farm, tending the animals or making saucisson and cold cuts to sell at the local markets. She was carrying a small package and put it on his desk. 'A little snack for you,' she said, flashing him a caring smile.

From the aroma, Justine could tell it was saucisson. Claude thanked her and put it in the drawer. By the twinkle in Alice's eyes, Justine realised she was keen on him and decided to leave. Claude was about to call out after her — *don't forget: six thirty* — but thought better of it.

Justine spent much of the rest of the day with Jeanne, quietly assessing her state of mind for herself. She asked if Jeanne had thought about where she intended to go once she reached Spain and freedom.

'I haven't thought about it too much. It's hard to think of leaving without Fleur. I suppose I will try and go to England and wait there. When the war is over, I hope we can return to our home in Paris. Who knows? I take things a day at a time at the moment.'

Justine told her the people at the orphanage had about fifty children and they were all well looked after.

'What about the Germans? Is Fleur safe from them? Tell me truthfully.'

Justine could not tell her that the Gestapo had started checking out all the orphanages. 'All I can tell you is that the authorities do their best to protect them. They have connections.'

Jeanne put her head in her hands. 'My darling girl — how scared she must be.'

'I hear Dr Berdu has given you a regime to help build your strength for the crossing. Do you feel confident that you are strong enough to make the journey?' Justine's questions were now becoming more pointed.

'I believe so. I hope to be leaving soon.' Jeanne looked at Colette, who was preparing vegetables at the kitchen sink and had her back to them, listening to every word. 'Everyone has been so good to me.'

At six thirty, Justine went to meet Claude. In the past, the hôtel would have been full, but since the Germans now occupied the southern zone, most villagers stayed at home. The menu was considerably diminished: extremely basic with none of the specialties it used to offer. Added to this, the prices had more than doubled and were well out of reach of Mont-Saint-Jean's poor agricultural farmers.

Over a glass of wine, Claude said he was happy to see her again, that she looked as attractive as ever. He also told her she'd lost weight, which, given the amount of work she was doing, the sleepless nights, and then the death of Robert, was hardly surprising. In a low voice he brought up the subject of her "relative from Paris". It wasn't a total surprise as news travelled fast in the villages of the Donezan.

'So you've met her then?' Justine asked.

'Not exactly. I happened to be passing your house one day as I was making my rounds and saw her in the garden. When I mentioned it to your father, he said she was a relative on your mother's side who'd come to stay due to the deteriorating situation in Paris.'

Justine listened, sipping her wine as if all was normal, until Claude's next words really made her sit up and take notice.

'Whatever you're hiding, your secret is safe with me, but I did advise your father to be careful. Her presence should have been reported to the gendarmerie and it wasn't. I let it go and have not registered her, but the Gestapo is constantly checking up and asking about new residents. Since you were last here, there have been a considerable number of battalions posted in the area, particularly near Capcir and further south towards the frontier.'

Justine said she'd already heard that, but thought they rarely came to the villages.

'That's true. The nearest place is Puyvalador, but it's only a twenty-minute drive away and they *do* come every now and again to check that everything is okay — and to take a poor unfortunate farmer's animal when they feel like it.' He sighed heavily. 'The real problem is not with them, it's the collaborators.'

Justine swallowed hard. 'Are you telling me we have collaborators in the village?'

'Not that I know of, but people are beginning to feel the hardships and there are posters everywhere reminding people to do their service by their country and report anything suspicious. It says they will be well rewarded. It's also in the newspapers.' He paused to let his words sink in. 'It doesn't take much for opportunists to rat on each other these days, either because they are hungry or because they dislike someone.' Justine couldn't imagine her parents having any enemies who would do such a thing. 'All I am saying is that your parents must be careful. If people get wind of a stranger in the village — and they haven't been introduced — they might start to wonder. Be careful.'

Claude was declaring his hand by telling her all this. If his conservative boss found out he hadn't yet registered Jeanne, the consequences for his actions would be dire.

'Thank you, Claude. I value our friendship, but, as I said, she is a relative and not well. That's why she doesn't go out. The country air has done wonders for her and she will go back to Paris soon.'

Claude leaned back in his chair and looked her straight in the eyes. 'As you wish, Justine, and now maybe we should change the subject.'

She smiled. 'I see you have an admirer.'

Claude glanced around the room. 'Who?'

'Alice. She has a crush on you.'

He waved his hand through the air and shrugged. 'Oh, her! She's certainly grown up to be a good-looking girl, but she's not my type.'

'Really! I got the distinct impression something was going on between you and that my presence had interrupted that.'

'She calls in occasionally with food from her parents' farm. It's always appreciated, but as for a love interest, you are wrong.'

Justine laughed cheekily. 'So, who is your type?'

Claude blushed, which made her laugh again. 'Stop teasing me. I only know it's not Alice.'

Justine changed the subject again and asked about the German presence in Capcir and Cerdagne. She slipped it in easily, catching him off guard.

'It's heavy, that's about all I can tell you.'

'Have they caught any smugglers?'

'Why do you ask?'

'Because it's common knowledge people have been trying to cross the Pyrenees from the first moment the Germans set foot on French soil. It's hardly a secret.'

'I've heard that people have been caught, yes, but didn't hear of anyone I knew. If they have, it hasn't reached my ears.'

Justine believed him. After another drink, she told him she had to leave as she needed to be up early.

'Can I walk you home?'

'You can walk me as far as the church. After that I will be fine.'

They left the hôtel and had almost reached the church when they spotted a figure wrapped in a warm woollen hat and coat standing near the village fountain. It was Alice.

Claude looked embarrassed. 'You'd better go to her,' Justine whispered. 'She doesn't look too happy and she'll catch her death of cold.' She bid him goodnight and continued home alone. At one point she glanced back and saw Claude chatting to Alice. Poor Claude, she thought to herself.

CHAPTER 15

Justine Remembers: Don Manuel de Caballero and the Spanish Maquisards

USING MY NEW travel pass, I accompanied Dr Berdu to the village of Puyvalador, where he was waved through the German encampment to attend to a German engineer who'd had an accident at the dam. The Germans at Puyvalador already had their own doctor, but he was away at one of the border towns. This particular doctor had taken a liking to Dr Berdu and always allowed him to replenish his medical supplies without reporting it as he knew access to medicine was scarce in the Donezan. As a result, Dr Berdu managed to use some of it to treat injured maquisards.

I pretended to know what I was doing as I prepared Dr Berdu's array of medical equipment while he set the man's broken leg and arm, and stitched deep cuts to parts of his face. The man grimaced as his bones were being set and I thought of Mimi pretending to be a midwife and how difficult it must be for her. For our troubles, the German engineer gave Dr Berdu a bottle of cognac. We then drove to Formiguères via the village of Réal to Pablo and Mercedes's farm. It had been a while since I'd been there and I was surprised to see how much Louis had grown. Though still a small child, he now spoke Catalan and French. I was impressed. His dark features and curly hair made him stand out from the other children, but he was a good child and everyone had grown to accept him. Mercedes, who still disliked the villagers for the way they had shunned her, preferred to keep to herself, rarely mixing with them unless she had to.

'Are you going to Formiguères, Théo?' she asked.

'Yes. I have to visit Commissioner Rossignol. He likes me to call in every now and again — for a little chat. You know what he's like. He asks about my visits, etc. I need to keep in his good books in order to reach the border towns.'

'What about Justine? Won't he wonder what she's doing here?'

'She's my helper for the day. Sometimes it pays to declare yourself up front, even if it is not warranted.'

Mercedes nodded. 'I know what you mean. He likes my cheese.' She gave us a wink. 'That's how I keep in his good books, so please take him a wheel and give him my regards.'

Commissioner Rossignol now worked out of the Hôtel de Ville, emblazoned outside with the Vichy and Nazi flags, and was surrounded by all the accoutrements of power. He was pleased to see us and remembered me from the fête; or rather I should say that he remembered my car. He asked if I still had it and didn't look surprised when I told him it had been requisitioned. Dr Berdu presented him with Mercedes's gift of cheese, which he smelt with great delight, and the commissioner asked how things were going. Dr Berdu told him all was well except that there had been an outbreak of diphtheria in one village, but it was now contained. He handed him a list of the places he'd been to, which the commissioner cast his eyes over, and we went on our way.

'That man has eyes in the back of his head,' Dr Berdu said as we drove away. 'It's best to stay friendly.'

One leaving the town, rather than return home, we headed to an inn on the outskirts of Formiguères run by Martial Derain and his wife, Brigitte. Martial was an enthusiastic anti-Pétainist who despised the Germans, especially after his brother, a soldier, was sent to the front lines and killed during the first few days of the invasion. Martial's inn housed many fugitives on their way to the Spanish border and his proximity to everything going on in Formiguères made him an ideal spy for the resistance. He and Brigitte made a note of how many trucks passed in out the town, when Commissioner Rossignol departed, etc. It was he who said we were to head towards a small farm at the base of the mountains. A farmer known by the code name of *le renard* — the fox

— would be waiting for me. It was the first time I'd been to this farm and I was introduced to the farmer by another code name — "Marie-France" — even though I was aware my father and Dr Berdu knew him. It was now becoming normal for us all to have more than one code name. Dr Berdu and I parted ways here.

Le renard said very little when we were alone. He didn't let on whether or not he knew I was the schoolteacher's daughter, but I could tell he knew I was someone vital to the network, and that the mission was important. I changed into my hiking clothes and donned a pair of skis le renard gave me. Aware not to take anything that would attract attention, I put a change of clothes in a slim backpack. As soon as it was dark it was time to make a move. We headed into the mountains running parallel with the border. Although I knew most of the mountains in the area, this was somewhere I was not familiar with. Heading towards the border would have been the most direct route, but he was leading me away, more in the direction of Villefranche-de-Conflent, rather than Bourg-Madame and Puigcerdà, which was the area Pablo used. We skied for several hours, up and down the mountainside, and headed towards a ravine. Throughout the whole journey, he never uttered a single word. He was an excellent skier and it was hard to keep up with him.

At a certain point we halted and he gave a shrill whistle. We waited for a few minutes, but there was no answer. He whistled again and this time received a reply — two whistles. Minutes later two men appeared. I was introduced as *Señorita* Marie-France and handed over into their care. One of the men introduced himself as Garcia Mendez, don Manuel's right-hand man, a small, swarthy-looking individual, with a solid build.

The farmer bid me farewell and returned home while I continued the rest of the way with the two men. There was a full moon that night and in between the cloud cover, I could just make out the snow-capped mountain ridges of the border in the distance. From where we were, they seemed almost unattainable. A wide valley lay below us with these mountains soaring up on the other side. By now, I had realised we were almost halfway between Mont-Louis and Villefranche-de-Conflent

— such an indirect route. At this rate, it would take longer to get to Spain than expected. Sometime later, we stopped again and Garcia Mendez gave another signal. A tall man wearing a beret and a bandolier filled with cartridges across his chest, and with a rifle in his hands, as well as a revolver and a knife in his belt, approached from behind the rocks to greet me. With him were half a dozen men, also armed to the teeth with rifles and guns. He introduced himself as don Manuel de Caballero, the leader of the group.

He welcomed me in Spanish and, throughout our time together, that would be the language we spoke. Don Manuel was in his late thirties or early forties; it was hard to tell as he had the rugged, olive complexion of a hunter — someone who had spent months in wilds of the mountains. He had black hair and a dark beard, but the most noticeable thing about him was his eyes — intensely dark and framed by thick eyebrows. He had a reputation for being ruthless and the looks to match. He also had a loud, booming laugh which seemed to sum up his character — fearless, a master of his own destiny, and, as I was later to find out, someone who took no prisoners. If people crossed him, their days were numbered. He was not a man not to be messed with, yet for all his ruthlessness, I could tell he was a man of his word and I took an instant liking to him.

Like most maquis groups, he and his men were constantly on the move, but this was his favourite spot. As soon as it grew light, I could see why. We were perched precariously on a rocky outcrop near a cave and well hidden. From here, we had an excellent view of the snow-covered valley and main road snaking through the pass. All vehicles travelling along this route were monitored day and night. His men knew every German division, every type of truck and tank, and whether it carried prisoners or not. His links in the area were so extensive, it didn't take him long to know what was happening. Directly across the gorge were the steep mountains — some of the most formidable in the area: the pic de la Dona, the pic du Géant, and the Puigmal de Segre, to name just a few.

'The border police always expect smugglers and evaders to take an easier route,' he said. 'But *that* road belongs to the devil.' He pointed to a particularly steep mountain.

Don Manuel's network stretched for about fifty kilometres along both sides of the border, with connections loyal to supporting his cause. Over a meal of lamb roasted over the coals in the nearby cave, he told me his feared reputation was more of a legend, when in fact he was a family man who just wanted to live in peace on a farm somewhere back in Spain and raise animals. As he ripped the meat off the bone with his teeth, wiped the fat from his beard, and swigged copious amounts of wine, I found that hard to believe. Some people have the devil inside them — like the mountains we had to cross — but after I heard his story, I understood what had tipped him over the edge into this life of exile.

It was Garcia who told me the story. Don Manuel's family had been killed after the Fascists took Barcelona. He lost his parents, his only child, and other friends and relatives when the Italian planes strafed the area as they were fleeing. When he and his wife reached France, they were parted in Prades by the authorities. She was put into the women's section at Rivesaltes internment camp, but he was luckier. As other men were rounded up, he managed to escape and flee west where he found work as a farm labourer. The farmer was desperate and didn't care if he was on the run from the authorities. He worked day and night to save money, and as soon as he had enough to secure his wife's release, he went to the Rivesaltes camp to try and get her out, but it was too late. She had died of an illness a few weeks after being transferred there.

'When he learnt of this, he didn't want to live,' Garcia said. 'He took to drink, but with the help of friends, eventually snapped out of it, more determined than ever to defeat Fascism. Then the Germans invaded and we made the decision to organize anti-fascist actions in France against the Vichy government. In October 1940 the Vichy regime began permitting other prisoners to leave the camps, if they would go to work in factories. Many fled into the mountains and countryside, finding work as agricultural workers. That's when our numbers expanded.'

He told me that the earlier French evaders crossing into Spain were mainly civilians, but a few were remnants of the defeated French army. 'Since the STO law for French citizens was announced, those who escaped to the forests and mountains joined up with us rather than leave. We had already been fighting Franco and knew how to fight,' he said proudly. 'The young Frenchmen learned a thing or two from us.' He paused for a moment and I saw the sadness in his eyes. 'We want France to be free again, but our real aim is to go back to Spain and bring down Franco.'

I learned that to do that, don Manuel needed guns. That was the real reason he and his maquisards helped evaders — they didn't do it for money, although money was needed to pay off helpers and smugglers.

I asked about the route we would take into Spain, stating that it appeared extremely steep. Don Manuel smiled. '*Si*, Señorita Marie-France, there are easier routes, but I know these mountains like I know a woman's body.' His men laughed. 'Judging from your apparent fitness, you won't have any difficulty crossing them. From what I hear, you are as sure-footed as an isard so you're used to the mountains anyway.'

All this talk about being compared to a Pyrenean chamois and his comment about knowing the mountains like a woman made me blush. There was no point asking any more questions as he wouldn't tell me anyway. He was already aware I needed to reach Barcelona as quickly as possible and assured me I would be there in a few days. After our enormous meal he indicated to a pile of blankets. 'Get some sleep. You'll need it.'

I woke up to the aroma of more cooking. This time they had used the leftovers from the previous meal to make a hearty soup. 'Eat,' Garcia said, handing me a large bowl. 'It will warm you up.' It consisted of chunks of meat, flecked with what appeared to be pieces of intestines. When I asked what was in it, they laughed.

'Everything,' Garcia replied. 'Nothing goes to waste, and it's seasoned with mountain herbs.'

For all its dubious appearance, it was one of the most delicious soups I'd ever tasted.

'When this war's over, I'm going to be a chef,' he said.

'In that case you'd better give it a fancy name,' I replied.

The men teased him. 'Garcia's Mountain Soup — fit for a king,' someone said. He threw a dish of dirty water at them.

'Alright, what will *you* do after the war?' he asked the man sarcastically.
'Marry a rich, voluptuous woman, make love day and night, and die in my bed, a happy, contented man.' Everyone roared with laughter.

Another said he would learn German so that he could understand what the "Boche bastards" were talking about next time they attacked. That too caused howls of laughter.

A smaller man with wire-rimmed glasses said he would become a painter so that he could restore the paintings of the Madonna in churches that Franco had destroyed. That comment brought the laughter to an end. Dreams. It's what kept them going through the long days and nights in their mountain hideaways. When the soup was finished, the mood became sombre again as they checked their guns and rifles in readiness for the journey. At around nine thirty, we left the safety of the cave. Don Manuel divided his men into three small groups of six which left at twenty-minute intervals. Garcia Mendez's group went first. I was with don Manuel in the second group. The weather had worsened, with a freezing blizzard cutting our cheeks.

We skied downhill into the valley, crossed a fast-running river at a point where someone had constructed a rope bridge that swung dangerously over the rapids, and then headed upwards into the mountains. Don Manuel walked ahead, frequently looking back to check if I was alright. We passed through a couple of hamlets which at first appeared deserted. This proved not to be the case. Here and there packages containing food had been left on doorsteps where the owners had cleared away the snow, but there was no sign of the inhabitants, only a thin line of smoke from a chimney here and there.

Sometime later we stopped to eat their offerings, reserving some for later. I particularly enjoyed the aged semi-hard cheese wrapped in vine leaves. It was accompanied by bread made from mixed grains and was washed down with a cupful of red wine. Don Manuel asked if I was finding the going tough. I was, but could cope. My legs were already aching and my hands were frozen, even though I wore thick gloves. He laughed, knowing I was putting on a brave face.

The path meandered upwards in such a fashion that I became confused as to where we were. At this height, there was already thick snow and I wore snow shoes in order not to slip. Even with a full moon, it was hard to tell just how far the drop below was. It was best to concentrate, step by step, not looking far ahead. It made it easier and less daunting. Throughout this time, the men rarely spoke. At one point, we had to cross a waterfall thundering down from the rocks high above us. It was so cold that sections were frozen solid, icicles hung precariously overhead, and the ground around it glistened with ice. Don Manuel took my hand and guided me slowly across the rocks in such a way that we managed to cross behind the waterfall. I recall that the water resembled a glistening curtain of sheer glass in the moonlight — a spectacular sight, although I had never been so cold in my life. At dawn, the steep mountain gave way to a glorious alpine plateau, blindingly white in the morning sun. I was now in Spain, and surprisingly, had not encountered a French border guard or German anywhere. No wonder don Manuel took this route.

Garcia and his men were already waiting for us. With them was a local shepherd wearing dark purple corduroy clothes and beret, typical of the shepherds of this area. We shook hands. *'Bienvenida a españa, señorita,'* the man said. 'Welcome to Spain.'

Don Manuel and the shepherd conversed for a short while in a local dialect, little of which I could understand, and then told me this was where we parted company. 'This nimble ragamuffin will look after you now,' he said. It was a phrase I'd heard many times when describing these smugglers — nimble ragamuffins or picturesque rogues. 'In less than twenty-four hours you will reach your destination. When you return, I'll be waiting. *Buena suerte.'*

The shepherd took me to his farm, where I rested until the early evening when a diplomatic car arrived. I was surprised to find that the driver was actually a Scotsman working for the British Consulate. He checked my papers and gave me a pass which ensured that I was with someone who had diplomatic immunity, and told me to get in the car while he had a "little chat", as he called it, with the shepherd. The little chat consisted of him giving the shepherd an envelope, no doubt containing money, as the two could barely converse. The chauffeur's

French was better than his strange mixture of Spanish and Catalan, which was as difficult to understand as the shepherd's dialect. They shook hands and we drove away.

The chauffeur told me he'd escaped France himself soon after the debacle of Dunkirk. He didn't want to go back to Britain and was offered a job at the British Consulate in Barcelona and had been there ever since, picking people up and dropping them, here, there, and everywhere. He seemed quite a character — the sort of man who appeared to get a thrill out of covert operations and thumbing his nose at the authorities; a person who could get into trouble easily and yet get out of it just as quickly. He certainly knew the area very well and took us along all sorts of back roads to Barcelona, even though the car had diplomatic license plates. At one point we stopped at a restaurant and dined by a large log fire, taking in the view as if we were tourists. After a good meal accompanied by a bold Rioja, we continued to Barcelona, where he dropped me at a small hotel just off a wide boulevard near to the British Consulate.

He escorted me inside and informed the hotelier that as I was a guest of Winston Churchill and his Majesty the King, he must look after me well. Apparently, that was in case any *carabineros* came to check on new guests. I was shown to my room and told that I would be welcome to join the other guests of Señor Churchill in the bar. I was tired, but decided to see who else was seeking aid from the British Consulate. To my great surprise, I found the place full of British — men and women playing cards and drinking. I soon discovered that they too worked for the consulate. Someone offered me a glass of sherry and I sat with them, trying to take it all in. One of them told me I was lucky to be staying there as, usually, evaders and escapees were put into a smaller, less salubrious hotel down the road.

'In Madrid, they've even converted one of the garages at the Embassy for these people,' a woman said. 'The Spanish are a mixed bunch. Some feel sorry for us and others can't wait to get rid of us. Thankfully a few pesetas here and there can buy almost anyone these days.'

She told me I was lucky to have been picked up by the Scot as he knew that part of the Pyrenees well. I also discovered that hundreds of escapees had already safely made the crossing. Many had gone on to Portugal or Gibraltar and then to North Africa, England, or Palestine. Some had even gone to Cuba and South America. The French wanted to join de Gaulle. I was always worried whether the people we'd helped had made it or not, so this was heartening news. It made our work worthwhile.

In the morning I went to the consulate. Thankfully, the weather was much better than in the mountains and it felt good to wear a smart, lightweight suit rather than my winter hiking clothes. Two Spanish policemen at the gate asked to see my documents and emergency certificate. All was in order and they ushered me through. The consulate offices were on the second floor and although I had made a point of being early, the waiting room was already full. Most passed the time nervously, flicking through copies of *Town and Country*. An assortment of photographs of Winston Churchill and King George VII covered the walls, interspersed with the odd painting of the Scottish Highlands with a proud stag, and a serene English village with thatched-roofed cottages. There was also a photograph of Westminster and Big Ben. A secretary brought me a cup of tea while I waited. It was all very convivial — a slice of Britain in a place of uncertainty.

I didn't have to wait too long before being taken to an office where two men greeted me. One was the Consul-General, an elderly, genteel man, and the other was his aide, a younger man in his late thirties who smoked a pipe. Both were impeccably dressed in tailored suits that would have looked quite out of place in the villages of the Donezan.

The Consul-General began by saying that what was discussed in the room was private. 'You have our complete trust,' he said. 'You can begin by telling us your real name and all about yourself, including the network you work for.'

I had been warned by Cassou that when the time came, I would have to come clean about our operation and who I really was. This was the time, so I told them as much as I could: how we'd operated from the very beginning when the south was free, how far the network operated, and how difficult our work had become, especially since the occupation of the free zone and the introduction of the STO laws.

Where to begin? We had done so much. 'Many young men have fled into the countryside to join the maquis,' I said, 'but they have no experience with guns, and any attempt at sabotage will be limited and likely to see them rounded up. Thankfully, some of the Spanish maquis are better-trained.'

He told me he already knew this.

'We are in desperate need of money, sir,' I said. 'These helpers put their lives at risk. Many don't even do it for money, but they still need to feed people or bribe someone, and fake ration cards only go so far. The Spanish maquis that helped me come here would prefer arms rather than money though.' Spilling out the situation raised my pent-up emotions and brought tears to my eyes. I had tried so hard to be strong and felt embarrassed.

The aide told me that what we had done was extremely brave. 'We already know of your good work from those who have passed through here via your network. I congratulate you. Of course we will do everything in our power to help.' His words heartened me.

The Consul-General opened a file. 'Now, let's begin. This time we will go through it, point by point.'

Discussions began with the most pressing need — money. The aide was sent out of the room to discuss this with someone else in another office, while I went through Cassou's list with the Consul-General. 'We can certainly get someone to help train and equip you, but you understand this cannot be done overnight. These people will have to be parachuted into France and that can only happen around a full moon. It's too late for this full moon so that means it will be at least another month away — that is, if London approves the mission.'

He saw the look on my face. 'Surely they wouldn't say no?'

'I don't expect they will.' I could see he was doing his best to put my mind at rest. 'If all this goes ahead, have you thought where the agents will land?'

'As we cover a wide area with steep mountains between each group, our options are limited, but we've come up with a couple of places.'

He pulled out a large map of France, which covered his desk, and asked me to point to them. One of them was between Saint-Girons and Toulouse, and the other was in the Pays de Sault, not far from Razès, where the count and countess's villa was. It was the area favoured by Dr Berdu, whereas the first place suited Cassou better. I told him it was far too dangerous to parachute anyone near Mont-Saint-Jean because of the terrain. 'Further south of the village is a plateau.' I pointed to the area between Puyvalador and other towns in the Pyrénées-Orientales. 'These are part of the smugglers' routes, but the Germans have garrisons around here which make it too dangerous.'

'We will need the exact co-ordinates,' the Consul-General said. He was impressed that I already had them.

The next item on the agenda was to obtain a radio and operator. He told me I was in luck. There was a man in Barcelona who had lost contact with his network after they were betrayed. His contacts in London told him to lay low until they could get him into another network, but that too was compromised. That's when he fled to Spain. On the one hand, I was grateful there was someone who might be willing to help us, but on the other hand, it frightened me that two experienced networks had been broken. Most likely the Consul-General knew of more, but didn't want to alarm me.

'This radio operator — can you put me in touch with him?'

He wrote down an address on a piece of paper. 'His name is "Antonio". He will be at this address at eight o'clock.' I looked and saw that it was a bar in a hotel.

'Who does he work for?' I asked.

'I am restricted in what I can say. You will have to have this discussion with him yourself.' He closed his file and we started to talk about weapons and training. He didn't give much away, saying I'd have to discuss that with Antonio too. He did tell me one thing though — that the British preferred to work with the French maquis rather than the Spanish.

'Why?' I asked. 'We're all fighting for the same thing.'

'You may think that.' He adjusted his glasses and matter-of-factly told me it was a case of politics. 'The British are reluctant to cause trouble with Franco by arming Spanish Communists.'

I protested. 'That's preposterous. These men are helping *us*. They've helped the British flee France too. They're good fighters and reliable, so what does it matter if some are Communists?'

He nodded sympathetically. 'I'm afraid London view things differently, but I have a suggestion. There are Americans here in Barcelona too. Maybe you could put your case regarding the Spanish maquis to them. Antonio can advise you on this as well.'

It all sounded very murky and confusing.

The Consul-General leaned back in his chair. 'I must say, young lady, you impress me. Those you work for are lucky to have you.'

Praise was not something given lightly these days, and I certainly didn't feel like a hero at all. It was people like Robert who were to be praised. The aide returned. He gave a nod to the Consul-General which I took to mean they would give me money.

'Come and see me in two days' time,' he said. 'In the meantime, check Antonio out. He will know you as Marie-France.' He handed me his personal telephone number in case I got into difficulties. As soon as I left the room, another man with a worried look on his face was ushered in. It was 11:30 a.m. Judging by the number of people in the waiting room, they were having a busy day.

Outside the building, I took a look at the note again. It read *Antonio. 8:00 p.m. Bar del Rio, Hotel Mimosa.*

Antonio! He didn't sound at all like an English agent, but then, who could tell who was who they said they were? So many code names, so many agents, so many double-agents too. I had eight hours to wait and see.

At eight p.m. exactly, I entered the Bar del Rio at the Hotel Mimosa in a side street just off Barcelona's tree-lined pedestrian street known as la Rambla. Having crossed the Pyrenees with a light backpack, I had only one change of clothes — the same russet suit and cream silk shirt I'd worn to the consulate. Apart from a watch, the only jewellery I wore was a silver chain attached with a small cross which was given to me some years earlier by my parents. I considered it my good luck charm.

There were half a dozen people sitting around chatting and one man at the bar. When he saw me, he waved me over. 'Marie-France?'

'Antonio?'

'What will you have to drink?'

'The same as you.'

He asked the barman for another martini. 'Let's go and find somewhere more private,' he said. I followed him outside to a small bougainvillea-covered courtyard with a few outdoor tables and umbrellas.

'How did you know it was me?' I asked.

He grinned. 'You were the only one with a slightly lost look on your face.'

'Was it that obvious?'

'No, just kidding. The Consul-General described you well, although he didn't say how pretty you were.'

I ignored his flattery. Antonio was in his early thirties –a confidant man, slim with a tanned complexion, and he spoke French fluently.

'Antonio. That's a very Spanish name, but you don't strike me as being Spanish at all.'

'I'm not. I'm a Londoner, but my mother is French — from Marseille.'

'So Antonio is not your real name then?'

'He laughed. Is yours Marie-France? I suspect not.'

'*Touché.*'

'Now what can I do for you? I hear your network is looking for a radio operator, among other things.'

'That's right. I was told that's why you were in France, but apparently things didn't go as expected.' I asked if he would be prepared to come back to France and work for us. We talked about the network; I said as much as I could without giving too much away, and yet enough to assure him I was genuine.

'It sounds as if you've been doing an excellent job. Congratulations, especially since the Germans have infiltrated many networks.'

'We are always careful.'

Antonio sighed. 'So were some of those I worked for, but never underestimate a good spy. They infiltrate in many ways, and can be most disarming.'

'You're right. You could even be one yourself,' I replied.

'I could.' He smiled. 'So could you.'

'The Consul-General seems to believe me, so I hope you do.'

'Luckily for you, I do. I've met a couple of people you've helped, so I would be happy to assist you.'

From the way he spoke, I could tell he was desperate to get back into the field again. 'Who do you work for?' I asked.

'London. That's who I liaise with. Baker Street, but there are a couple of other organisations I liaise with too. They too are based in London.'

I already knew of the Special Operations Executive from Cassou, but had no idea of other organisations specifically set up for intelligence gathering or operating escape routes. I was to learn just how many different organisations there were.

'I told the Consul-General we needed weapons, medicine, and money — and someone to train our people in sabotage,' I said.

Antonio nodded. 'You don't have to explain. I know full well what you need. Do you have any idea where you want me to work from? I only take directions from a couple of people at the most. Safety and secrecy, you understand. Presumably, you would be one of these people?'

'I imagine so, especially as I've recruited you. We already have a good idea of where you will operate from. I can assure you that you'll be well looked after. There's something else I need to ask. Our friends in the Spanish maquis would prefer to be paid with guns. Not all of them, but they are excellent operators and we want to keep them happy. The Consul-General indicated that the British don't want to arm the Spanish if they intend to use these weapons to fight Franco. Is that right?'

'I try to keep out of politics,' he replied. 'We don't really know what's going on between those in power. There *are* American operatives here who work for OSS and they are more obliging than their British counterparts, who are suspicious of the Spaniards because they don't want to be seen to be fuelling problems with Franco. Besides, I think the fewer people we involve, the better, but I can liaise with a few chaps on the quiet. You'll have to trust me on that.'

I liked Antonio. My instincts told me he was just what we needed. He appeared to think on his feet like Cassou and Dr Berdu. I felt he could be of real service to us.

'Come back to France with me,' I said. 'I leave the day after tomorrow.'

'I must get the okay from London first. I'm sure they will agree. Don't worry, Marie-France, we will get you organized.' He gave me a little grin. '*And* your Spanish maquisards.'

It had been a long day, and finally, I believed my mission was bearing fruit. After Antonio gave his word, we spoke of other things — lighter subjects like music and the arts. He told me about Antoni Gaudí and asked if I would like to see some of the Art Nouveau buildings along la Rambla. I was amazed at their beauty and for a brief moment, I was able to forget the war. Afterwards, he dropped me off at my hotel and told me to meet him at the same time in the same place the next evening.

'I hope you will have good news for me,' I said, the anxiousness returning.

'Get some sleep,' he replied. 'You look as though you need it.'

The next day, Antonio did indeed give me the news I wanted to hear. Word of Cassou's network had already reached London and they agreed he could return to France, but they warned him to lie low as he was probably wanted by the Gestapo after the other two networks had been broken. The timing also suited them. By the next full moon, they expected him to have assessed the situation on the ground in the Ariège, in which case they would be ready to send over supplies and trained saboteurs. 'So,' he said with a cheeky smile, 'I'm all yours. My life is in your hands.'

I was elated and felt like throwing my arms around his neck. When I began the trip, I never thought I'd actually be returning with a radio operator *and* a radio. Instinctively, I kissed the crucifix around my neck. Dieu merci.

Antonio smiled. 'Are you religious?'

'I was brought up a good Catholic, but these days I think my faith has deserted me. I hope it returns. What about you?'

'Same here.'

I told him that I had to see the Consul-General the next day, and if all went well, we could leave that same night.

'Then that gives us one extra night for me to show you more of this beautiful city,' he replied. I was so happy, I looped my arm through his and we set off for another stroll along la Rambla. I fully intended to make the most of this moment of freedom.

The next day, the Consul-General and his aide introduced me to someone working in intelligence in London and he handed me a wad of money — far more than I'd hoped for.

'That should keep you going for a while,' he said. 'So don't get robbed.' His tone was serious. 'We don't hand over money lightly.' He shook my hand firmly and wished me good luck.

On behalf of the network, I thanked them all for their help. The meeting did not last more than twenty minutes and as I exited the office, I looked at the anxious faces of those in the waiting room and hoped they would be as lucky as I had been. That evening, the consular car arrived to pick me up at the hotel. Antonio was already in the back seat.

'Have you got it with you?' I asked, referring to the radio.

He patted the seat. 'I'm sitting on it.' Underneath the seat was a hidden compartment with his backpack. 'The thing is, do *you* have everything?'

'Of course!' I'd spent the last few hours sewing the money into the lining of my clothes.

After we left Barcelona, we were stopped twice by the carabineros, but allowed to continue without any problems. By midnight we arrived at the smuggler's house and after giving and receiving a coded message that all was well, were dropped off. The driver wished us a safe journey and returned to Barcelona.

'Are we crossing back into France tonight?' I asked the smuggler.

He shook his head. 'We have to wait another day. There's a problem.' Antonio and I looked at each other. 'What's happened?' I asked.

The man said he was not told why. The first thing that crossed our minds was that the network had been infiltrated and don Manuel's men were in trouble, and the idea that this was the third time something like this had happened to Antonio made him rethink his decision. He thought it was another set-up, but I assured him that wouldn't be the case, although I did wonder if I was assuring myself rather than him. My words sounded hollow but the smuggler seemed to take it all in his stride. 'These things happen,' he said with a shrug. Waiting another twenty-four hours felt like an eternity. Finally, at nine o'clock the next evening, we were told it was time to get going.

I had a good memory and realised we were taking a slightly different route, but I kept it to myself, all the time preparing myself for an ambush. Would my new-found self-defence skills stand me in good stead? I was sure Antonio was capable of looking after himself. I also worried about the radio strapped to his back. It was our lifeline.

CHAPTER 16

Unscrupulous Smugglers and Village Justice

THE PATHWAY LED into the scrub, past several large boulders perched against the edge of a ravine. At a certain point, the smuggler stopped and put his finger to his lips. 'Shush!' We waited for a few minutes, listening for any sign of movement. When he was sure all was fine, he gave a shrill whistle. From behind the rocks, we heard two whistles in return, and Garcia appeared. With him were two burly men who Justine recognised from her first crossing.

'Señorita Marie-France. Welcome back. I hope your trip was a success?' Antonio was introduced and told that he would be a lifeline for them all. 'Will you get us guns?' Garcia asked, reverting to French rather than Spanish and at the same time sizing Antonio up.

'I will do my best. You have my word,' Antonio replied.

'An Englishman who will not break his word. I hope so.' He smiled and made a swift gesture of slitting his own throat. 'Or else.' It was meant as a little joke, except that they all knew it was not a joke at all.

His job done, the smuggler departed. Justine asked Garcia why there'd been a delay.

'You'll find out soon enough. Let's get going.' Using their skis, they skirted between the rocks and spindly pines poking up from the undulating snow drifts until they approached a hamlet. A dog barked and another maquisard appeared, pointing a rifle at them. When he realised who it was, he waved them on. The scene Justine encountered both frightened and appalled her. In the centre of the hamlet was a square lit by lanterns that cast a soft, flickering light that highlighted the terrified looks on the villagers' faces. With them, standing next to

178

the village fountain, was don Manuel and his men, questioning two men who appeared to have been badly beaten. Garcia pulled Justine into the shadows and advised her and Antonio to stay hidden from view.

'What's going on?' she asked in a low voice.

'You'll see.'

The scene unfolding grew worse. In Catalan, don Manuel asked the bloodied men who had sent the evaders to them. Neither answered and they were beaten again with the butt of his rifle. One man passed out and a bucket of ice-cold water was thrown over him.

'If you don't tell us, you will meet the same fate as those you murdered,' don Manuel growled.

At the mention of the word murder, Justine and Antonio realised they were looking at the sort of men they had always feared — smugglers who robbed and left their victims for dead. Justine had been warned of such people, time and time again. These men had evidently not just robbed their victims and left them stranded, they had murdered them. How? Who were they?

A villager came forward and pointed his finger at the men, saying they had brought them into ill repute. He kicked and spat on them. 'You thought we wouldn't find out!' he screamed. 'Mouchards!'

'Where did you find the bodies?' don Manuel asked.

'At the bottom of the ravine. I never would have found them had I not noticed the vultures circling. They appeared to have been there for several days and I could tell wild animals had feasted on them. I was sick to my stomach.'

'How many bodies?'

'Four. They must have ranged from twenty to forty-five. Three men and a woman.'

'How did they die?'

'It was hard to tell, as there appeared to be no bullet or knife wounds, so at first I assumed they must have fallen from the cliff ledge while trying to cross the border. It's a sheer drop and if there's snow, you have no idea where you're walking.'

'What did you do then?'

179

'I searched for any documents, but there were none. That's when I had a bad feeling about it. Neither did they have any belongings — watches, jewellery, money, no backpack. Nothing. Just the clothes they were wearing at the time, which were in shreds when I found them. I came back and notified my neighbours straight away. We all went to see what had happened. It was pointless bringing them all the way here, so we buried them there, even though the ground was frozen.'

'And you didn't notify anyone — the gendarmes or border guards?'

'No. We thought they'd be suspicious of us. They snoop around anyway and we didn't want them to think this had anything to do with us.'

Don Manuel paced up and down while he listened to the man's story. 'Then how did you know it was these two?' He waved his finger towards the men. 'Two of your own.'

'My wife overheard them talking in the café in another village on market day. They were too busy drinking and celebrating to notice her.'

Don Manuel called the man's wife over. 'Tell us what you heard.' The villagers hung on to every word.

'That one,' — she pointed to the one who had passed out earlier — 'he was laughing. He said they'd got away with it and they'd sell their belongings in Prades. He had two watches with him. Apparently the woman had been wearing a necklace. They had that too — and money. The other one asked how much he thought they'd get for them.'

'Did you hear what they did with their victims' documents?'

'No.'

After much questioning, it appeared that the woman came back immediately and told her husband. He, in turn, told another villager and they waited until the men went out of the village again and then searched the house. There they found money from the sale of valuables in Prades, along with a receipt. The absence of the two men at the time coincided with these events. When the men were confronted, they finally admitted they had tried to help some evaders, but they accidentally slipped, despite being warned the pathway was narrow and dangerous. Knowing it was a clear case of treachery, that's when they decided to call on don Manuel and the maquis. They trusted them rather than the border guards or police.

The two men were given one last chance to explain themselves before justice was passed. One of them eventually confessed they did it to get money. They were poor people and saw an opportunity. They also said they destroyed the evaders' documents. Don Manuel walked away for a moment and conferred with some of his men and the headman of the village. There was a deathly silence in the square and Justine held her breath, knowing what was coming next.

Minutes later, don Manuel came back and executed the two men by shooting them in the back of the head with his pistol. A cheer went up from the villagers and they rushed forward to kick the dead bodies and spit on them. Even the village dogs started sniffing around the rivulets of blood, wagging their tails in excitement at the smell. The only two people who did not join in their jubilation were the two men's wives. They were told they were banished from the village and if they spoke about this to anyone, they too would suffer the same fate.

Justine slumped down on the ground, shaking like a leaf. 'That's what you call village justice,' Antonio whispered. 'Was it justifiable for the maquis to be judge and jury?'

Justine looked at him sadly. 'It may seem reprehensible, but we are at war — with our own people sometimes. Those two men did not deserve compassion. They've caused immense suffering through their greed, and the villagers must maintain their honour. Their death was swift and without remorse.' She rested her head on the stone wall and sighed. 'We are living in odious times. I don't like it any more than you do, but those poor people who died could have been us. Remember that.' In that moment, her words sounded hollow. What they'd witnessed had impacted them both.

'Well, let's hope France doesn't turn into one big bloodbath after it's all over,' Antonio replied.

Their conversation was cut short and don Manuel appeared. Even for Antonio, who'd witnessed fully trained soldiers in action, he appeared a larger-than-life figure. No one mentioned what had just taken place. He told Garcia to get going and he would catch up with them.

'No time to waste if you want to get back before daylight,' he said.

They set off again while don Manuel organised a few men to bury the bodies for the villagers. Within half an hour, he'd caught up with them. With each step, the image of the scene in the square receded a little and they spoke of other things. Don Manuel asked about Spain and Antonio was only too happy to answer.

Don Manuel slapped Antonio on the shoulder. 'One day soon, we will return. Franco will not die peacefully in his bed.'

They parted ways in the mountains and Garcia took her to le renard's house. From there, it took them two days of skiing and hiking over a tiring and circuitous route to Pablo and Mercedes's farmhouse. From the farm, they moved in an arc into the mountains, skirting past the German camp protecting the dam at Puyvalador, and on to the forester's cabin at La Madrès. It was deserted, so Justine located the key hidden under a few logs and opened the door. There was no sign that anyone had been there over the last few days. No scraps of food, no tobacco smells, and no smell from a log fire. It was as it should be when it was unused. No evidence of evaders.

The evening was cold and it was snowing again. Justine put a few logs in the fireplace and lit it while Antonio took out the transmitter from his backpack and began to prepare a message to let London know that all was well. She helped him arrange the flexible seventy-foot-long aerial around the room in order for him to get good reception. The transmitter was cumbersome and hefty and she marvelled that he'd carried it so far without it getting damaged. It was hard for radio operators to be inconspicuous, but somehow they managed it. Antonio told her the worst part was always staying one step away from the enemy and their radio vans. Justine had seen them in Toulouse — predators in search of their prey. When all was ready, he made connection with London. His message was straight to the point — ARRIVED SAFELY. Shortly after, he received a response.

'They are very happy,' he said, taking off his earphones and packing up the transmitter. 'This calls for a celebration.' He looked around the cabin. 'But I see you don't have a bar. What a welcome!'

Justine burst out laughing, more out of relief and exhaustion than his funny comment. She had been living on adrenalin and fear for the last couple of weeks and the enormity of what she'd done was only just starting to sink in.

'I'm going to leave you now,' she said. 'I will return tomorrow with someone else.' She pulled a few thick blankets from a cupboard. 'Lock the door and get some sleep.' She was almost out the door when she turned round to face him. 'Thank you,' she said. 'You have no idea what your presence means to us. Oh, and when I return, I will bring you something to celebrate with.'

Left alone, Antonio hid the transmitter in a safe place, lay down on the bed, and covered himself with the blanket. He thought how glad he was to be back in France and how courageous and strong-willed Marie-France was. He'd met a few like her, but unfortunately, not all had survived.

Colette and Armand were asleep when Justine entered their bedroom. She shook them gently. 'Maman, Papa, I'm back.'

Colette sat up and held her daughter tightly in her arms. 'Look, Armand, our little girl is home again.' Her mother tenderly stroked her daughter's face. 'You are thinner — and your face is drawn, but thank God, you're safe.'

Armand too looked relieved. 'How was it?' he asked.

'I achieved everything I set out to do, and more. A British radio operator came back with me with a working transmitter. London has agreed to him working with us. *And* I got money.'

Her mother got out of bed and slipped on her robe. 'Let's go downstairs. You must be starving.'

'That can wait, Maman. I just wanted to tell you I am safe.'

Colette put her finger to her lips. 'Shush. Not so loud.'

Justine lowered her voice to a whisper. 'Do you have another evader?' she asked.

Colette flashed a look at Armand. 'No. It's Jeanne. She's still here.'

'What!' Justine jumped up off the bed. 'Why?'

'Let's go downstairs,' her mother said. 'We can speak better there.'

Armand followed them and closed the kitchen door so Jeanne wouldn't hear them. 'Why is she still here, Papa?' Justine asked. This was all she needed after a long and tiring trip.

'She's not well,' Armand replied.

Justine felt like screaming. She couldn't believe it. 'Do you realise how much harder it is to make the crossing now? It was even difficult for me and the snow was not at its heaviest. Apart from this, the border guards are everywhere, and don Manuel tells me of ruthless smugglers. Pablo too. From what I was told, three smugglers were caught in the last few weeks alone.' She pressed her fingers to her temples. 'This woman will be our undoing. Can't you see that?'

Armand sat at the table, unable to look at either of them while Colette prepared them something to eat. An oppressive silence filled the room.

'What's wrong with her now?' Justine asked, irritably. 'She was getting much stronger.'

Armand said she was scared she wouldn't make it. 'She's decided she wants to hide out somewhere until the war is over. She knows the Germans are losing the war. She's also worried about her daughter.'

'Fine!' Justine replied. 'But why here of all places — putting us all at risk. It's selfish. Give her a new identity and send her to a safe house somewhere. What about the convent near Prades? They hide Jewish women there.'

Armand said they were looking into it.

Her father's answers were starting to anger her. 'What does Théo have to say? Can't he give her something to help her mental state?'

'It's in hand.' Armand became agitated and changed the subject. He asked about the trip. When she'd told him everything, he said he was proud of her. She declined to talk about what took place in the village with don Manuel's maquis. 'I look forward to meeting the new radio operator in the morning. Now, if you excuse me, I'll get another couple of hours sleep and then you can take me to him. You'd better get some sleep yourself.'

She gave him a peck on the cheek. 'Goodnight, Papa. I love you.'

After he'd gone, Justine waited a couple of minutes, giving him time to get back into bed, and then looked across the table at her mother. She too had lost weight and her complexion had taken on a grey pallor. Tears welled up in Colette's eyes.

'Oh, Maman,' Justine said. 'I know something's wrong. What is it? Please tell me.'

'I just worry, that's all.' Colette refused to say anything else.

Just after dawn, Justine and her father left Mont-Saint-Jean for the refuge in La Madrès. At this time of the day, the forest was cool, sultry, and secretive; the meandering footpath was soft and moist with the dew. Here and there, soft ferns peeking out of the snow brushed against their legs, springing back as soon as they passed, and the ever-present invigorating scent of pine, juniper, and ash, filled their nostrils. Justine started to talk about Jeanne again. 'Why is she so reluctant to leave?'

Her father shook his head, saying she was afraid she wouldn't make it. All he would say was that he and Théo were looking for a more permanent safe house for her until the war was over. He asked her not to bring it up again as they had other things to worry about at the moment. Justine had never seen her father so tense. When she asked what, he said that the Milice had more than doubled their presence in the area.

'Important Milice commanders reporting to Paris have requisitioned villas in the area,' he said. 'So now we have them to contend with too. One has taken residence in a beautiful villa between Formiguères and Mont-Louis, and is very friendly with Commissioner Rossignol. Others reside in Quillan and Foix. They often make unannounced visits to the villages, checking in at the local gendarmerie. They even visit the school, and we've seen them a few times at the hôtel. Claude calls by if he knows they are coming to the village, but often it's a surprise for him too.'

Justine thought about Claude, and how hesitant she'd been about him in the beginning. 'So Claude is proving to be a good man,' she said. 'Helpful to the network?'

Her father smiled. 'Théo and I like him. He has a talent for spotting something that's not quite right. Take Alice, for instance. She seems to have got it into her head that there's something going on between you two.'

Justine burst out laughing. 'That's not surprising. You should have seen how she looked at us when he walked me part of the way home.'

'Claude said she still pesters him — takes him packages of food for his lunch. He doesn't encourage her, but at the same time, he doesn't exactly discourage her. He doesn't trust her. To make matters worse, her parents have approached him with the idea that they get married.'

Justine laughed again. 'Poor Claude. What a handful she is.'

At the refuge, Justine introduced Armand to Antonio as "Alain" and not as her father. She also handed him a package of food her mother had prepared. 'And a bottle of wine to celebrate your arrival back to France and our network.'

Armand said he was pleased to have him join them and assured him he was in good hands.

"Marie-France" had already proved herself a formidable friend. It was at this point that Justine told Antonio that from here on, she would be known to him as "Jacqueline".

'After today, Alain will look after you and get you to your destination. I will be in contact with you once you've settled in.'

Armand got out a map and showed him where he would be located. 'Here in these woods. It's a safe house, a fine villa belonging to the Count and Countess de Crispin, so you will be very comfortable. Not far from there, the forest opens up onto a plateau and rolling hills, which makes it easier for your planes to drop supplies rather than near Toulouse. Count Pierre and his wife, Elsa, are fine hosts with excellent contacts throughout France.'

Antonio studied the map for a while to get a good idea of the surroundings. He asked about the situation in the area and was told it had deteriorated, which came as no surprise. While he tucked into breakfast, Armand informed him that he would be moving him later that night. They wanted to get him installed in his new home as quickly as possible. He asked how the Special Operations Executive worked and were they proving successful. What did the British think of de Gaulle?

Antonio told him that not all SOE agents in the field were aware of what was going on between networks. 'The only time we work together is if we receive directives from London,' he said. 'Otherwise we keep a low profile. I had two couriers before, but they were caught. When you hear things like this, you are wary of trusting anyone, even other agents. Survival of the fittest.'

Armand understood. 'We have been fortunate so far,' he replied.

'Let's hope your luck continues then.' He asked if "Marie-France" — "Jacqueline" — would be one of his couriers.

Justine said it depended on her situation when she returned to Toulouse. 'I must confer with my handler, but I imagine so.' She hoped that would be the case as she had taken quite a liking to him.

After a few more questions were answered to Antonio's satisfaction, Justine and Armand left the refuge. 'Good luck, Antonio. Have a safe journey,' Justine said, and gave him an affectionate hug, which didn't go unnoticed by her father.

Returning to Mont-Saint-Jean, her father warned her to be careful of becoming close to someone she hardly knew, and a foreign radio operator at that.

She laughed. 'I spent the last few days with him. I think I'm a good judge of character. And as for him being a foreign radio operator, he's hardly foreign. His mother is French. We're lucky to find him. He just might end up saving our lives.'

That night, Armand moved Antonio from the refuge, and together with "Bertrand" — Dr Berdu — took him to stay the night at Henri the engineer's safe house at Rouze, not far from the Usson power plant. Henri would take him the rest of the way to the villa. Dr Berdu thanked him for coming back to France and said he would meet up with him again soon. 'It can't have been an easy decision to return,' he said.

'It wasn't difficult at all,' Antonio replied. 'I am half-French. It's my duty to fight for my country.'

CHAPTER 17

Parachute Drops and Justine's Assignment to Esterri d'Àneu

THE OLD BUS taking Justine back to Toulouse from Mont-Saint-Jean skirted around the dangerous hairpin bends, following the River Aude through the Gorges de Saint-Georges until the road finally levelled out into rolling countryside. Here and there, vineyards dotted the fertile agricultural land, which lay waiting to be ploughed over when spring arrived and the ground was less hard. Justine felt homesick for the region where life still went on much as it had for centuries, yet if she wanted a good job, there was little she could do back at home. Plus, there was a war to be fought and she was needed in Toulouse. She had a two-hour wait for the bus in Quillan and went to a restaurant for a bite to eat. Since the Germans had moved into the southern zone, there was a noticeable change on the people's faces. The place was shrouded in fear. She sat in a corner and read the collaborationist newspaper, *Le Matin*, with its anti-Churchill rhetoric while she waited for her food. When the waiter brought it over, she saw he was distracted. 'Is everything alright?' she asked.

In a low voice he informed her that the Milice and Gestapo had just raided a small hôtel a block away. 'They are looking for Jews — evaders on their way to Spain.' Three black cars passed by the window heading in the direction of the hôtel. Five minutes later, the cars passed by again, this time heading in the opposite direction. With them was a tarpaulin-covered truck. When it turned into the main street, she saw at least a dozen people sitting in the back, guarded by two soldiers with machine guns. Suddenly she didn't feel hungry anymore.

'Where are they taking them?' Justine asked.

'Probably to an internment camp. From there, who knows?' He shrugged. 'I would guess Drancy, then Poland. It's a depressing sight — all too common these days. The worst is when you are in your bed at night and you hear the familiar rumble of trucks passing through the town. I've lost count of how many, but I know they are filled with unfortunate souls going to Paradise.' He asked where she was heading and she replied Toulouse. 'I heard the same thing is happening there too,' he said, and walked away to serve another couple who looked equally distressed.

She paid for her meal and left, but the conversation depressed her. No matter how many people they had tried to save, it was a drop in the ocean next to those who had been deported. The small lapping waves had become a tsunami. The trip to Toulouse seemed to take forever and the bus was stopped several times. Occasionally someone was ordered off the bus when their papers looked suspicious and the bus continued on without them, leaving the hapless people in the hands of the Feldgendarmerie, often with their belongings still on the bus. The second time, it was a woman in her mid-thirties sitting in the seat in front of Justine. She put up a fight when they tried to take her off the bus, yelling at them until a man smacked her hard across the face, knocking her to the ground. She was bundled into a car immediately. Every time the bus was hailed down, Justine felt her heart pound louder. She had valid papers, but those pulled aside might have thought they had valid papers too.

Toulouse seemed different, even though she had been away only a short time. There were fewer civilians on the street, and here and there, the Milice strolled the streets, their eyes on the lookout for someone to terrorize. She breathed a sigh of relief when she eventually reached her apartment. The concierge asked how her trip home had gone. Were her parents well? He was as nice as they came, but she knew he was often questioned about the occupants by the Vichy police, and more recently, plain-clothed men who worked for the Germans. He also knew she was keen on botany and asked if she'd discovered anything new. She said no but showed him her drawings, which he admired. Her little book of pressed flowers and watercolours went everywhere with her when she travelled throughout the countryside. She still used it as a ruse to sit in the meadows and observe the surroundings while painting. Such an innocent pastime — what harm could a slip of a girl with an interest in botany be to anyone?

On entering the offices of the Ariège Charcoal Company the following day, she received a warm welcome. Knowing that she worked long hours, everyone assumed she had gone on a long-deserved break to stay with her parents. She had barely put her bag on the floor and looked at a flood of papers on her desk when Cassou called her into his office.

'Well?' he said, indicating for her to take a seat. 'How did it go? I can tell you now that I've already heard from Dr Berdu, and our new radio operator has been installed safe and sound with the count and his wife.'

Justine went through everything in detail, including what took place in the village with don Manuel's men, and the obvious presence of the Milice in the area. She told him that although the incident distressed her, she was impressed with el intrépid. Justine also mentioned that Jeanne was still in Mont-Saint-Jean which came as huge shock to him. Although he wondered what was wrong with her, he agreed with her father that it might be better to hide her, rather than have her become a liability for other evaders. He didn't want to see her left behind, or worse still, shot and pushed off the mountain just because she threw a tantrum. 'As far as the incident in the village is concerned,' he said, 'while I don't approve of this kind of justice being meted out, I can understand it. The escape routes are not safe anywhere now. It's either the Gestapo planting spies into the group or smugglers like those you mentioned.'

He paused to light up a cigarette. 'I have some more bad news, I'm afraid.' Justine felt her facial muscles tighten. Bad news was everywhere these days. 'The orphanage was raided by the Gestapo. Most of the older children were sent to the camp at Le Vernet. They were only there a few days and then transported to the north and on to Auschwitz. Thanks to the intervention of the Swiss director and the mayor, the authorities immediately began organizing the escape of those who had managed to hide at the time of the raid. The older ones were to go over the Pyrenees to Spain, and the younger ones towards the Alps to Switzerland with their Swiss carers. At the same time, several children are being hidden with farmers in the region. Eight teenagers have joined the resistance and two teenagers were shot while trying to escape the transit train.'

'And Fleur?'

'The last I heard, she was on her way to the Swiss border. That's all I know.'

Justine stared at him in shock. 'Oh, God,' she said after the news sank in, 'we certainly can't tell Jeanne this?'

Cassou agreed. 'If it's any consolation, I feel just as bad as you.' It was no consolation at all, but they had work to do and had to be strong.

Justine returned to her work and opened the file Cassou had given her, fighting back the tears. All she could think of was Fleur and she felt guilty for being too hard on Jeanne.

At the end of March, Cassou arranged a meeting at a bistro near the river telling her there was something he wanted her to do. 'It's important,' he said. 'Don't be late.'

At seven thirty exactly, she arrived at the bar where Cassou had reserved a table near the exit. With him were Jacques, Mimi, and three other young men, who, like many in Cassou's network, worked for the "Rural Works" coverage of the intelligence services of the armistice army. While Justine had been away, Mimi and these men had been gathering intelligence and distributing anti-German propaganda, leaflets, and tracts. Now Cassou wanted them to expand their work. Mimi and Justine were assigned to collect six evaders from Saint-Girons and escort them to Esterri d'Àneu, just over the border in Spain, where they would be handed over to a smuggler who had contacts with the British Embassy in Madrid. It wasn't an area Justine knew well and she protested. Mimi hardly knew the area too, and although she was a fit girl, Justine wondered if she was capable of making it that far as she was not an experienced hiker. Cassou said he'd used the route many times and, providing they were careful, there was nothing to worry about. The meet-up in Saint-Girons was to take place in a week. Justine had hoped to meet up with Antonio and discuss the parachute drops, but this trip now made that unlikely.

'Can't you get someone else to go with Mimi?' she asked. 'It's been quite a few weeks now and I haven't had chance to catch up with our new radio man at the villa.'

Cassou's reply was that he would meet him himself. The subject was closed.

Several days later, Mimi and Justine, accompanied by a young man from Saint-Girons, found themselves waiting on the embankment just outside Saint-Girons town at the precise area where the railway lines curved, slowing the train down before it reached the bridge over the river towards the railway station. They had taken cover in the bushes. In the distance they heard a piecing whistle from the approaching train. 'It's here,' the man said. 'Get ready.'

The train slowed to almost five kilometres an hour when two carriage doors flew open. Suitcases were hurled out, followed by a handful of terrified evaders jumping from the train. People looked at them from the carriage windows, but no one seemed to bother. Within minutes, Mimi, Justine, and their associate from Saint-Girons had gathered their suitcases and helped the evaders scramble up the embankment, where they hid behind more bushes until the train had passed. German sentries with machine guns were posted at the rear of the train on the lookout for escapees but thankfully noticed nothing unusual. The group hurried to two waiting cars and were directed to a barn by their young accomplice, while Mimi and Justine continued into Saint-Girons by bicycle. In the early hours of the morning the group met again near the bridge in the centre of Saint-Girons and their long journey began. All of them were checked for appropriate walking shoes. It was the beginning of spring but there would still be snow on the mountains so espadrilles were out of the question. Sturdy walking boots were what was required.

By the end of the first day they reached the spa town of Aulus-les-Bains, located at the head of the Garbet River valley and beneath the Guzet-Neige ski resort, some thirty-five kilometres south-east of

Saint-Girons. It was near here that in January 1942, 686 foreign Jews were sent to stay. The Vichy government arrested 174 Polish Jews out of this group and in August took them to Le Vernet internment camp, where they were joined by a further hundred from elsewhere in the department. From there they were sent via Drancy to Auschwitz.

Spies were still a problem and the Germans were billeted everywhere, but Cassou was sure of his contacts. The evaders were exhausted and Justine was glad spring was around the corner. She allowed them to rest overnight and they set off again in the early morning. The climb was getting harder, the mountains more dramatic, and there were rivers to be crossed which could only be done by wading through the freezing water as the bridges were manned by German and French guards. As she had suspected, Mimi was finding it tough, but she persevered. By the end of the second day, they neared a refuge, now occupied by Germans. To the left was an unmanned area which they had to bypass in order to find shelter for another night. On the fourth evening, they met the smuggler, "Salvador", at Esterri d'Àneu. Seeing the evaders safely cross the frontier was a huge relief. Exhausted, Mimi collapsed onto the ground, staring up at the darkening sky. 'Mon Dieu! I knew it would be difficult, but this has given me a better appreciation of what our people go through.'

Justine massaged her calves. 'I'm convinced that the fear of what might happen if they stay behind gives the evaders added adrenalin.'

On the way back, they stopped in the spa town for an extra day and paid for a hôtel room in order to refresh their aching bodies in the hot thermal springs. In the evening they dined in the hôtel restaurant, pretending to be mere hikers and nature lovers, when in reality, they were checking out how many Germans and Vichy officials were there. They purposely put on lipstick and did their hair nicely in order to impress. It worked. Two Germans asked to join them. The girls pretended to be flattered. By playing innocent, dancing to a small band, eating and drinking with them, which was more of a case of the girls plying them with drink than the other way round, they learned of the German presence in the area and discovered that more smuggling routes had been broken due to spies infiltrating the networks. They realised they'd had a lucky escape. At dawn the next morning they left the hôtel, glad to be out of the place.

In Saint-Girons, Jacques was there to meet them in one of Cassou's charcoal trucks. No sooner had they returned to Toulouse when another meeting was arranged. Justine told Cassou about the information from the Germans concerning spies infiltrating groups. It meant that every evader had to be thoroughly vetted before they were accepted, even if it took more time. Then came another bombshell. She was no longer officially employed in the office as a secretary. Instead, she was to be a saleswoman for the company, which would give her a suitable excuse to move around the countryside.

'Do I get a car again?' Justine asked, half expecting him to say no.

'Yes, but it won't be like the one you used to have. This is an old Renault which runs on wood and charcoal — ideal for your new job, I think.' Justine grimaced. They were notorious for being unpredictable. 'Driving this on behalf of the company means you will be able to carry on your courier work *and* help organise the distribution of weapons. There are a lot of garage owners between here and Quillan who work with us, so it's vital work. Come into work tomorrow, pick up the car, and someone will show you how to use it. I will give you a list of our clients. It's a genuine list so you should be fine if you are stopped and searched. Then I want you to make your way to see Antonio at the villa to discuss the upcoming parachute drops.'

Justine was exhausted, but this news breathed new life in her. 'How long will I be away?' she asked.

'Until we know the mission has been carried out successfully.'

The following morning, she picked up her car and after a brief lesson to see if she could handle it, Cassou gave her the list. It was a combination of garages and small companies. 'Not all are working with us, so be aware of the ones marked with a full stop after them. They are the ones to whom, under no circumstances, must we divulge what we are doing. They are bona fide companies and we are their preferred supplier. Keep your conversation limited to the supply of charcoal only and don't hang around no matter how friendly they are. The others will identify themselves with a simple code. "How is your mother? I hope she had a good birthday." Your reply will be, "We baked a cake for her." Bear in mind that these people may not always have news for you, but at least you will get to know them. Is everything clear?'

He handed her some money and a new pass authorizing her to travel on behalf of the company. The money could also be used should she want to stay in a hôtel rather than with a member of the network. 'Some of this money is from the Consul-General. Use it as you see fit.' He took a deep breath. 'That's about everything. As this work is legal, you can reach me by telephone, but preferably from a call box. Just be careful though.'

This was a big responsibility for Justine, but she was excited to think of the resistance and maquis having access to weapons and more money. It would boost their morale. It took her three days to reach the count and countess's villa due to calling on clients, most of whom were struggling to afford to buy anything at all. One of the resistance members she stayed with was a garage owner in the town of Lavelanet. He and his family were constantly harassed and threatened by the Vichy police, as two of their sons were eligible for the STO and had fled to join the maquis. The parents were steadfast that they had no idea as to the whereabouts of their sons, but it was wearing them down as they left food parcels for them at certain places outside the town whenever they could. It was the same everywhere. Parents were threatened with deportation when their sons went missing. Justine noted all this as she duly wrote out orders for the company.

Under the de Crispins' care at Quercorbès, Antonio had settled back into French life well. Rather than use the house for transmitting to London, they had given him the small gardener's cottage at the edge of the property, not far from the lake where Jeanne had tried to drown herself. The cottage was also partially hidden by the forest, ideal for a quick escape should the need arise. He wasn't aware she was coming and was pleased to see her.

'How long are you staying?' he asked.

'Until after the next parachute drops. My boss needs to know everything is going according to plan.'

'Ah, Monsieur "X". He was here for a few days to check me out. I think I passed with flying colours.' He laughed. 'A very nice man — never would have picked him as the boss of a network. Far too much of a gentleman.'

'Well, it takes all sorts in this job, doesn't it? When are we expecting the drops to take place?'

'In three days' time. The places you pointed out are perfect. I've checked them out myself, and the weather reports are favourable. The RAF has been notified. Now all we have to do is wait for the broadcast.'

That evening, Antonio and Justine were treated to another one of the count and countess's hearty meals accompanied by Blanquette de Limoux from their hidden cellar. There were only two STO evaders staying with them and they belonged to the local maquis and had come to collect supplies. Count de Crispin was a good hunter and kept them supplied with rabbit, pheasants, venison, and wild boar from the estate. Occasionally they were given a few bottles of wine too. After dinner, the evaders left and the count and countess, Justine, and Antonio prepared to listen to the BBC. There were so many messages, one had to be really careful not to miss anything. When it came to the night of the drops, Justine was a nervous wreck, continuously pacing the room until Antonio told her to go into another room where she wouldn't distract him.

She refused and scolded him. 'I've been waiting for ages for this; surely you can understand my predicament?'

He apologised and she sat back down again. Five minutes later, he called out excitedly, 'That one was for us. "The chickens have hatched". Come on, let's get going.'

Justine almost burst out laughing when she heard the coded signal. How could something so insignificant mean so much? But it was not a laughing matter. Everyone was deadly serious. They hurriedly put on their coats and made their way to the drop zones. Count Pierre was to meet up with the maquis in the area of Razès, while Justine and Antonio went to another area, further west in the Pays de Sault. The third area was nearer to Saint-Girons, and Cassou would be in charge of that drop.

They parted ways at the house, agreeing to meet back as soon as it was over. Praying that the roads were all clear, Antonio got into Justine's car.

The night was perfect; there was a glorious full moon and Justine could see well enough to drive without lights. On the way, they called at the various meeting points for the maquis waiting to be called to action. Three hours later, three RAF planes flew over the allotted drop zones and unloaded their cargo. Twenty containers at each drop zone floated to the ground, plus two parachutists — their extra radio operators. Justine had never seen anything like it. Their silhouettes floating effortlessly past the large, silvery moon, was something she would never forget. Instinctively, she kissed her little crucifix and gave thanks to God.

'There you go again,' Antonio said, 'I knew you believed in God.'

Justine laughed. 'I am so happy, I could even kiss you.' She blushed and apologised, which made Antonio smile.

Within half an hour, all was cleared and accounted for and everyone went back into hiding. When they arrived at the villa, Count Pierre was already there, opening up the containers with some of the maquis. In all, there were enough weapons and sabotage equipment to make their groups extremely happy. The next night there was another drop, this time including more tins of food, chocolate, cigarettes, and whisky. With no sight of a German reception committee, Antonio congratulated Justine on finding such excellent drop zones. The weapons were hidden well away from the villa, in caves and in the forest. After welcoming the two new radio operators, complete with working radios, Justine slept like a baby.

The two new radio operators — "James" and "Martin" — had flown into France before on a previous mission and had a good idea of the area. The only problem was their accents. James spoke French with a Belgian accent, and Martin, an English one. They were warned to say very little when in public. None of them could afford another broken network, especially Antonio. The following day, Dr Berdu and three maquisards from Mont-Saint-Jean arrived to pick up their cache of weapons. James was going with them. For the time being, he would operate from an outbuilding next to the pharmacy where the Berdus lived. Dr Berdu assured Justine he would see to it that el intrépid — don Manuel — would get his share of the weapons as promised. In the meantime, Martin would make his way to a farmhouse between Saint-Girons and Toulouse with Justine and operate from there under the leadership of Cassou.

The radio operators were told that once they had established themselves, trained saboteurs sent by SOE would join them. The past few years had been a roller-coaster of emotions, but now Justine could finally see a light at the end of the tunnel. The Germans had been defeated in North Africa, the Soviets were advancing towards Germany, the Americans had landed in Italy, and there was talk that the Allies would land in France next. It couldn't go on for much longer.

Justine remained at the villa for another two days before continuing her work for Cassou. Before she left, she brought up the subject of Jeanne still being in France with Countess Elsa. Unsurprisingly, she already knew.

'Théo told me,' she said. 'I kept a close eye on her. We all did, but she was so unstable, we never knew what she would do next. I'm saddened to hear she has regressed. I gather they are moving her to another safe house until the war is over.'

'It's puzzling,' Justine said. 'Yes, she's unstable, but she *was* getting better. The problem is, she waited too long and it's now much more dangerous.'

Countess Elsa thought as Justine did, and agreed that Jeanne must be moved as soon as possible. 'It only takes one troublemaker and the Gestapo will be onto us.'

'My father assured me it's in hand so let's hope he finds somewhere for her soon.'

Justine left the villa with Martin as soon as his new ID was ready. He stayed with the family of the garage owner in Lavelanet and was picked up the next day by someone else working for Cassou. Throughout the next month, there were more parachute drops, all in new places to avoid detection. During the winter of 1943–44, conditions for the maquis had been exceptionally miserable and harsh, but at least they now had guns and were being trained, and more importantly, they had won over the hearts of villagers who continued to put their lives at risk by supplying them with food when they barely had enough themselves.

In Mont-Saint-Jean, access to a radio transmitter meant that Dr Berdu and Armand were able to keep in contact with both agents of the OSS and the Rural Works networks of Cerdagne and Capcir. Along with don Manuel, Pablo, and another emeritus smuggler of the Pyrénées-Orientales, a Communist and charismatic man of action called André Dabouzi, admired by all who knew him, the group was now one of the most daring and effective smuggling organisations along the border of the Pyrénées-Orientales. They made at least six successful missions to Barcelona and became friends with the most important pro–de Gaulle industrialists and Catholic priests in the Pyrénées-Orientales. A small, private chapel on one of the industrialist's estates in a town close to a border was often used for the common activities of the resistance groups.

At a time when networks were being infiltrated across France and resistants were being arrested, shot, or deported to Germany, Cassou's network was keeping its head down and doing well. By the spring of 1944, they had moved over a thousand people across the border and supplied the maquis groups with arms. Then several incidents took place which were to have repercussions far and wide.

CHAPTER 18

The Denunciation

UNBEKNOWN TO JUSTINE, who had been too busy to keep in touch with her parents due to her new assignments, the first sign that all was not well in the Donezan came at the beginning of November, shortly after she had returned to Toulouse. An agitated Claude turned up at the school one afternoon to see Armand carrying a briefcase. 'I have bad news. Commissioner Rossignol has received an anonymous letter that you have been hiding someone in your house. They are sending out a search party.'

Armand felt his heart thumping in his chest. 'Jeanne?'

Claude looked downcast. 'I am sorry to say, but I warned you to register her...'

'Alright, alright!'

'I am not here to chastise you, Monsieur Joubert, merely to help — all of us. I have taken the liberty of bringing papers with me so that we can rectify her presence immediately and show all is in order.'

Armand asked Maria to take over his class while they went to the headmaster's room.

'Is everything alright?' she asked.

'Nothing that can't be fixed, Madame Maria,' Claude assured her.

When they were alone, Claude placed the relevant documents in front of Armand. 'Please fill in the details. No time to waste.'

'Does your boss know you are here?' Armand asked.

'Luckily he is in Foix.'

Jeanne was duly registered as a second cousin of Colette and given a fictitious address in Paris, the same one she had been using on her fake

ID. Her husband was reported as being sent to Germany as a labourer. No children were recorded. 'They will want to see her travel pass from Paris too, so I have prepared one for you.'

Armand examined it. 'This is perfect. I can't thank you enough. Let's hope this will satisfy them.' He signed the documents, and Claude took out his rubber stamp from his briefcase and officially stamped them.

'I would advise you to go home now and prepare for a visit. *Bon chance.*'

By now, most of the villagers knew of Jeanne's existence, even though she rarely ventured into the village, yet no one said anything. The only place she went to was Dr Berdu's to look after little Marie when Babette was busy in the pharmacy. Armand got on his bicycle and pedalled home as fast as he could. He felt sick to the stomach and his heart was filled with self-loathing. How could he have put everyone in danger like this?

Jeanne was peeling turnips in the kitchen with Colette when he arrived. The women were surprised to see him. When he told them about the anonymous letter, they went pale and Colette reached for the chair to steady herself.

'Claude has registered papers for you to be here,' Armand said to Jeanne. 'Together with the IDs you have, you should be covered. He's backdated it to the time you arrived.'

She looked the papers over. Before they had time to discuss anything, a black car arrived and Commissioner Rossignol, accompanied by two Germans, strode towards the front door. Colette's throat went dry but she forced a smile and invited them in. Rossignol did not beat about the bush. He said he'd received word that the Jouberts were hiding a woman who was not registered. They wanted to know why.

Armand feigned surprise. 'I don't know where you got that from? Jeanne was registered the day after she arrived.'

'Your papers please, madame?' The Germans started to look around the house.

Jeanne nonchalantly took her papers out of the sideboard drawer and handed them over. Commissioner Rossignol examined them thoroughly.

After a few minutes, the Germans returned. They could find no trace of anything out of the ordinary. They asked to see the documents and queried her on the district where she lived in Paris, although neither knew anything about Paris. It was more of a formality. As they could find nothing out of the ordinary, they apologised for inconveniencing them and departed, leaving the Jouberts and Jeanne in utter shock.

Colette put her arms around Jeanne's trembling body and Armand reached for a bottle of wine. Jeanne burst into a flood of tears. 'I'm sorry I've brought you so much misery. Believe me, it was not intended. I want to leave here as soon as possible. You have both been far too good to me and don't deserve this worry.' In a moment of panic, she reached for the carving knife and almost stabbed herself. Luckily, Armand caught her hand in time. He pulled her to him and she sobbed like a child.

'Colette, go and get Théo — quickly.'

Colette threw on her coat and rushed out of the house. When they were alone, Armand caressed her cheek. 'Oh, my sweet one, this is my fault. I should have been stronger and done what was right. I took advantage of you. I fell in love with you and could not let you go.'

Jeanne called out, 'No! No! It wasn't planned. I wanted you, and I want you even now. Can't you see that? But I am torn. Colette is my friend — an angel. It kills me to think of what I have done.'

'*We*,' Armand said. '*We* — but we cannot undo what we have done. Oh, *mon amour, mon précieux.*'

'I must leave here immediately. Take me somewhere tomorrow. Anywhere.' She pulled away from him and stroked his lips with her fingertips. 'I beg you. I cannot stay in this house a moment longer.'

Reluctantly, Armand agreed. Théo was away in Mijanès treating a child with meningitis, but Babette came over and brought some strong sedatives. Jeanne took them and then excused herself to lie down.

'What are you going to do?' Babette asked.

'She wants to leave straight away. Théo and I discussed taking her to another safe house or a convent near Perpignan, but so many are full.'

'What about taking her to live with Mercedes and Pablo until something comes up? I know that Mercedes needs help with the dairy and cheese production. The Germans stationed at the dam in Puyvalador and Formiguères take almost everything she can produce. Her papers are in order so working with Mercedes is a good excuse. That is if she agrees, of course.'

Colette thought this an excellent idea, and Armand said he would pay them a visit to see what they thought. He left straight away.

When they were alone, Colette burst out crying in her friend's arms. 'Oh, Babette, what will become of her? She is so unstable. One minute she's fine, the next, she's down.'

'I know this might sound harsh, but she is not your problem,' Babette replied. 'Théo warned Armand to let her try and cross the border. *He* thought she was fit enough to make it, even if Armand didn't.'

'Why is he so protective, Babette? Goodness knows, she's not the first fragile woman we've helped. They're all scared.'

'Armand is a good man so for the moment we must be patient. My biggest concern is who wrote that anonymous letter? It's a worry.'

The weather was overcast and much of the mountains covered in snow, but Armand managed to pass through the German roadblocks at Puyvalador without any problems and reached Pablo's farm by early evening. Louis was leaving one of the sheds after feeding the goats when he spotted him. He ran to his mother. 'Monsieur Joubert is here. Is he going to give me a lesson?'

Mercedes looked surprised to see him. 'What brings you out at this time?' She looked at the darkening sky. 'It's going to snow again soon.'

Armand warmed himself in front of the fire. 'Where's Pablo?'

'Visiting a friend. He'll be back in two days' time.' It was a coded message telling him that he was escorting evaders across the frontier. Mercedes glanced at Louis and told him to go and continue feeding the animals. 'Make sure the barn is properly locked,' she shouted after him. 'We don't want that fox to take any more hens.'

'Mercedes, I have something important to ask. We need somewhere for Jeanne to stay until we can find her a place in a convent. Has Pablo mentioned anything about her?'

'Only that she is an evader who he was supposed to take into Spain but it was delayed.'

Armand shook his head. 'That's right. She's rather a vulnerable woman — prone to bouts of anxiety. Because of this she'd never make the crossing. That's why Dr Berdu and I are looking for an available space in a convent. So that she can hide until the war is over. In the meantime, can you keep her here until a place becomes available? She can help you with the farm.'

'Are her papers in order? The Germans are always calling here for cheese and milk. I don't want any trouble.'

'Yes. She's registered as a Christian and Colette's second cousin from Paris whose husband is in Germany. The papers look genuine.'

'Tell me, Armand, why doesn't she stay with you then?'

'It's too much for Colette. She's a worrier. It's not good for her heart. We also think Jeanne needs something to occupy her and helping on the farm could be beneficial for you both.' Armand was normally a calm, measured type of person and Mercedes couldn't help noticing how desperate and frightened he seemed. 'It appears someone has it in for us,' he said. 'An anonymous letter about her was sent to Commissioner Rossignol. He came round with the Germans but they found her papers were in order.'

Mercedes raised her eyebrows. 'Do you have any idea who it was?'

Armand shook his head. 'Unfortunately, no. The thing is, you know our work is too valuable to be compromised. We cannot afford to have the Gestapo breathing down our necks.'

'Nether can we,' Mercedes replied rather curtly. She stared into the embers of the fire for a while, thinking it over. Pablo wouldn't be too pleased to have someone staying here, but neither could she forget how hard it was for her before she met him. She couldn't sit back and let another woman suffer as she had. And she did need help with the farm.

With a deep sigh she agreed. 'Alright, bring her here. I will look after her.'

The next day, Jeanne, heavily clad in a thick woollen blanket to keep out the cold and damp, left Mont-Saint-Jean and was taken to Matemale by Lucien, who was transporting logs and a sack of beets and cabbages on a cart to the German barracks at Puyvalador. Colette and Armand watched the cart slowly rumble out of the village, its wheels churning up mud as it clattered over the old cobblestones. At the last turn, Jeanne turned and waved, the tears streaking down her cheeks. Colette was relieved, but Armand felt as if his heart had turned to stone.

With her papers in order, she was allowed through the German checkpoint and delivered safely to the farm. For his trouble, Mercedes gave Lucien a wheel of cheese.

That afternoon, Armand went back to the school and told Maria that someone was sending anonymous notes to the commissioner in Formiguères and that they must be on their guard. Maria was a trustworthy and sensible woman, an anti-Pétainist, and a staunch Communist, which she was careful to hide these days. As much as they tried, they couldn't think of anyone who would do such a thing. With all this going on, Armand kept his head down, viewing everyone with suspicion. Who had it in for them? Even though he was tempted, he did not go to see if Jeanne had settled down at the farm. That was left to Dr Berdu, who informed him that she had settled in well and was feeling useful by helping Mercedes with her cheese-making.

A few weeks later, Claude called at the house after returning from a meeting with Rossignol in Formiguères where he was told there had been more denunciations. This time, one of them mentioned Justine. She was denounced as an ardent Communist. Colette and Armand couldn't believe it

'Why Justine?' Colette asked. 'She doesn't even live here now.'

Claude threw his hands in the air. 'Rossignol has a folder full of denunciations. He was extremely angry and said that whoever made such accusations needed to sign their name — otherwise they would not get paid a single franc. I couldn't see what was written on the papers, but obviously some people *had* signed their names. Thankfully for Justine, he tore it up in front of my eyes and put it in the bin, making a comment that "Justine Joubert works for Monsieur Cassou of the Ariège Charcoal Company and, thank goodness, he is not a Communist. He would never employ one either. If he was known to be supporting

Communists, his company would have been seized before now." I am telling you this so that you can warn her about such people. We are living in dangerous times. If this occupation goes on for much longer, everyone will be turning on each other.'

Armand was so concerned by this latest news and vowed to be extra vigilant, but as Rossignol had not believed the story about Justine, he did not take Claude's advice as he knew this would only worry her and she had enough on her mind as it was. He did, however, let her know that Jeanne was now with Pablo and Mercedes until another place was found. As much as Justine was thankful she was out of Mont-Saint-Jean, it still bothered her that Jeanne's presence could bring them undone.

As it was, there was no time to dwell on it — the network was working flat out to move evaders across the border and train the maquis in saboteur work. Everything had been running smoothly, despite the Gestapo and Milice expanding their networks of collaborators. All through the harsh winter of 1943 to the spring of 1944 the smugglers continued to take people across the border. Thankfully, the dangerous escapes through waist-deep snow and along the icy ledges of granite cliffs were now behind them, but with the warmer weather the border guards and Germans escalated their searches. Against sound advice, some evaders refused to listen to the warnings of unscrupulous smugglers and decided to find their own. Such smugglers could be found in cafés and bars in most of the larger towns, offering to help the gullible and desperate and would do anything for gemstones, watches, trinkets, and money. This resulted in the mountainside being littered with dead bodies, most of whom had been robbed and left to die, pushed over mountain ledges, or simply shot. The spring thaw exposed many. The locals tried to bury them without attracting unwelcome visits from the border guards, but the posters in every village and newspapers promising rewards to those who came forward with information was just too good an opportunity to miss, especially when people were suffering hardships.

Every month SOE had ensured that the RAF made drops and all were picked up safely. Antonio had also been in contact with the Americans, who made sure one of their agents passed weapons to don Manuel's maquis. Things were looking good and there were even rumours of an Allied landing somewhere which was even more heartening.

Almost immediately after Jeanne moved, Armand made excuses to call at the farm to see if she was alright. Sometimes he went with Dr Berdu; at other times he went alone. Within no time at all, Mercedes had taught her the art of cheese-making and, in exchange, Jeanne did extra chores around the house or helped Louis with his homework. Armand knew when market day was in Formiguères, La Llagonne, and Mont-Louis and tried to time his visits before Mercedes returned. He simply could not stop seeing Jeanne. She occupied his thoughts day and night.

Jeanne had also taken to learning about the Catholic Church from Mercedes, and whenever she had time, took a short walk to the nearby Chapelle Notre Dame de Villeneuve. It was a small church built in the fourteenth century and badly in need of repair, but it housed many small important figurines of the Virgin who, it was said, helped those in need. Jeanne was only one of many in need these days. All around the walls were votive offerings left by previous generations of believers in the hope that God and the Virgin would protect them. At first, Jeanne felt awkward, but with Mercedes's guidance, soon learned the prayers by heart and whenever she prayed, she felt herself enveloped in a cloak of calmness and holiness. She never forgot her Jewish faith but it was as if the Virgin herself was wrapping her arms around her.

'Mary and Jesus were Jews, Jeanne,' Mercedes said. 'They know what it's like to be persecuted and they welcome you into their house.'

It was sometime before Christmas that Jeanne started feeling sick. Dr Berdu was called and informed her that she was pregnant. Mercedes had already recognised the signs, but no one wanted to believe it, least of all Jeanne. When pressured to say who the father was, she said that a German from Puyvalador had called by a few times for cheese when Mercedes was away and, knowing that she was alone and vulnerable, he raped her over the course of a couple of weeks. Dr Berdu and Mercedes wanted to see the commandant at the barracks, but Jeanne begged them not to. 'It will only make trouble for everyone,' she said.

Armand was in shock. Why had she not told him? He felt like killing himself. This was his fault. He was a selfish man who had taken advantage of her. How could he live with himself now?

Mercedes promised that she would take care of Jeanne, but Dr Berdu, not at all pleased at this news, was even more adamant that she must go to a convent and spend the rest of the war hidden away. Life was too dangerous for them all at the moment without this added worry. Reluctantly, everyone agreed. Throughout the next few months, Mercedes, sometimes accompanied by Jeanne, visited the church whenever she could. Every time Pablo quietly disappeared for days on end without saying a word, she knew he was helping evaders and prayed for his safe return. Their cheese was always in demand too, and rain or snow, Mercedes wrapped herself in warm clothes and took the cheese to market — if there was any left as the Germans usually had first pick. The child was growing in Jeanne's belly but now Armand did not visit as often as he had before. Jeanne grew used to this, knowing his heart was torn.

CHAPTER 19

Betrayal and Reprisals

SOMETIME IN THE spring of 1944 a group of resistants received permission from SOE to step up their attacks on the Gestapo and key infrastructure. Their explosives expert successfully put the national gunpowder factory near Toulouse out of action and later blew up a tank and aircraft equipment plant. Although it was a success and no one was given away, Paul Cassou, having specifically cautioned the resistance and maquis groups to delay any sabotage work until the Allies landed, was dismayed as the intense resistance activity of such groups attracted the attention of the Sipo-SD which sent out more undercover agents to Quillan and Carcassonne. Somehow, the Germans had heard a schoolmaster was at the centre of a resistance group, and thinking it was in Quillan, raided a high school there. They arrested the headmaster, who said he knew nothing about a resistance group, but it contributed to the momentary disorganization of the network in all other areas of the upper valley of the Aude.

With little to do but wait until the Allies landed, many maquisards hiding out in the woods and forests with little food were growing restless. It seemed a never-ending waiting game, and some wanted to take matters into their own hands, itching to attack the Germans and Pétainists, despite their commanders threatening to shoot them if they acted without orders. In the area of Villefranche-de-Conflent, don Manuel had already executed two men for robbing a store in the middle of the night. Such happenings were not uncommon, and the villagers, most of whom supported the maquisards, complained. Shootouts were happening at an all too alarming rate.

It was during this heightened period of unrest that Pablo was caught red-handed as he handed three evaders over to a Spanish smuggler. It happened in the morning, just after dawn, a mere one kilometre away from the actual border. He gave the signal, but instead of the Spanish smuggler appearing, the border guards, accompanied by the Germans, arrived. Pablo was outnumbered and reached for his gun in an attempt to kill himself before he could be taken prisoner, but a German sniper, still in hiding, shot it out of his hand. Pablo keeled over in agony. The bullet almost severed his thumb and index finger. The group were rounded up and taken to the barracks at Bourg-Madame.

Pablo was beaten up badly but refused to say who he worked for, repeating that he worked alone to get extra money to feed his family. He was adamant that he didn't belong to a network. The three evaders all turned out to be Jewish — a middle-aged couple who had been hiding out near Marseille since the occupation, and a university professor from Belgium. All they could tell the authorities were that they had met a man called "Yves" in Perpignan who had given them directions to Pablo, who they knew as "the shepherd." They didn't even know his name until the Germans discovered his identity papers.

The next day, the three evaders were sent by truck to the Rivesaltes camp to await deportation to Poland. The woman would not stop screaming when she heard the order and was beaten senseless until she collapsed in a bloodied heap. She was later dragged unconscious to the waiting truck and driven away. In the meantime, Pablo still maintained he worked alone, but from his papers, the Gestapo learned of his address and telephoned the German Kommandant at Mont-Louis to get him checked out. Rossignol was immediately alerted and, accompanied by several aides, drove to the farm at Matemale to visit Mercedes. She was in the dairy preparing cheese with Jeanne when they arrived. When told that Pablo was in custody, she put on a brave face and acted surprised. Jeanne, who was worried that she too would be dragged in for questioning, was astonished at Mercedes's composure.

'Stay here,' she said to Jeanne, and went into the farmhouse with the commissioner. He asked his men to stay outside while he questioned her. Rossignol wanted names. 'Who is sending him these evaders? Tell me what you know, madame, or I will have to take you into custody too.' He paused for a moment and then took a step closer, his face so close to hers that she could smell his foul breath reeking of garlic and drink. 'I have developed a fondness for you, and I would like to help you, so in turn you must help me. Tell me what you know, otherwise...'

Mercedes put on a haughty face. 'Commissioner Rossignol, look around you. Do you think we have money? We struggle like everyone else. My husband doesn't discuss what he does with me, but I can assure you that he does not work for anyone. It's possible he found the evaders wandering around and simply tried to help them. Too many people have died trying to make that crossing. Pablo is a religious man — a good man — he wouldn't want that. I beg you. Let him go.'

Rossignol paced the room. It was indeed sparse, with no sign of luxury whatsoever. He asked his men to search the place and they found nothing. Louis ran to his mother's side, clutching her skirt. 'What's happened to Papa?' He started to cry and Rossignol put his hand on his head. 'Nothing will happen to your father if your mother answers a few questions.' He leaned down and looked into the boy's eyes. 'Does your father have many friends here?'

Louis was terrified and clung even closer to his mother. He was an astute child who knew there were secrets to be kept and said nothing.

The commissioner gave a deep sigh. 'Alright, I have tried to help you, but you are making it hard for me. Get your coat, madame. You are coming with me.'

Mercedes took Louis in her arms and kissed him. 'Stay with Jeanne, my son. She will look after you. Don't fret. I will be back soon. Now be a good boy for me.' She picked up her coat and calmly got in the car with the commissioner. Louis ran to the shed and burst out crying. Jeanne's heart was thumping wildly as she thought she too would be taken. 'Don't worry,' she said, trying her best to comfort him. 'Your maman and papa will be back soon.'

By evening, there was still no sign of Mercedes and all Jeanne could do was to wait until someone called by. Sometime after dark, there was a knock on the door. It was Armand and Dr Berdu. Word of the situation had reached them within hours.

'It's not looking good,' Dr Berdu said. 'Pablo is being held at Bourg-Madame and in all likelihood will be transferred to the prison at Perpignan. I will go to see Rossignol and plead for his release. In the meantime, you must prepare yourself to leave. It's too dangerous to stay here now.'

Dr Berdu left for Formiguères, leaving Armand and Jeanne alone. She ran to him and sobbed. 'What is to become of me? Where will I go now?'

Armand held her close in a futile attempt to soothe her. He stroked her swollen belly gently. 'There is a convent near Perpignan. It's full, but we have managed to get you a place as the doctor helps them out. He is going to take you there himself. You will have the child there in safety. By then, it is hoped that the Allies will have landed in France and our troubles will be over.' He lifted her chin upwards and she could see he too had tears in his eyes. 'With things the way they are, I don't know when I will see you again — my Hélène — but rest assured we will be notified about your welfare. You may be far away, but you will not be forgotten.'

It was the first time Armand had called her by her real name. She kissed him passionately — a long lingering kiss that she wanted to remember for as long as possible. In her heart, she knew she might never see him again.

'This damn war,' she said. 'It's ruined all our lives.'

'It's also given us precious moments of happiness, however fleeting. Moments that don't come often in one's life: moments that no Occupation can take away.'

She smiled one of her beautiful smiles, a rarity these past months. Her eyes flashed with passion and sensitivity, but there was little to say. Nothing was going to right the wrong they had done. She left him to check on Louis and then sat by his side in front of the fire until Dr Berdu returned. He shook his head in despair.

'Rossignol refuses to listen to me and is transferring Mercedes to

Mont-Louis and then Perpignan. He said their silence puts his own life in jeopardy. His superiors wanted results. Therefore, he was left with no other choice.'

Dr Berdu asked if they'd discussed the convent and Jeanne said she was ready to go, but she was worried about Louis.

'We'll take him back with us. He can stay with Babette and I. As for yourself, be ready; I will come for you tomorrow.'

Jeanne hurried to pack a few items for the child. Louis was the son of a proud woman and had been taught to put on a brave face, but it was impossible for them to know exactly what was going through his mind. Jeanne kissed him goodbye and he drove away with Dr Berdu and Armand, leaving her alone to contemplate an uncertain future.

She looked around the room for a small photograph frame. There was one on the dresser — an oval one with a faded picture of a family. She slid the photograph out and exchanged it for one of her own, which she'd hidden in the lining of her handbag. It was a photograph taken with her husband, Fleur, and baby Albert in their garden in Paris. She also cut a lock of her dark hair, wound it into a neat coil, and slipped it into the frame together with the photograph. After making sure the frame was secure, she covered herself with her shawl and headed for Chapelle Notre Dame de Villeneuve. It was dark when she arrived. The door was open but there was no one inside. She lit a candle and sat on one of the chairs to pray for a while. When she'd finished, she took the frame, kissed it, and placed it on a ledge next to other votive offerings.

'Loving Virgin, I was born a Jew, but I am a human being without any malice for other races. These last few months, I have come to understand your religion and I have felt your presence. I know that in the eyes of God I have sinned, and for that I beg your forgiveness. I leave this treasure of my family in your hands.' She gave the sign of the cross and said a little prayer that she'd learnt by heart.

You who are the Virgin and Mother of Capcir, the flower of life, pray to Jesus, our Father, and watch over us with your love. Guide me along the path of righteousness and look after all those I love. Amen.

Feeling that cloak of protection once more, she blew out the candle and left.

The next day, Dr Berdu arrived to collect her. She took one last look around the farmhouse where she had been made to feel so welcome and got into the passenger seat. The convent was some five kilometres outside of Perpignan, surrounded by high walls and well-kept gardens. Dr Berdu rang the bell and the Mother Superior came to the door. They were led to the office where Jeanne's papers were inspected and her meagre possessions taken from her and locked away until the day came to leave. She was given a change of clothes and shown to a dormitory with other women, some of them also pregnant.

'You will be safe here, Jeanne, but please do not talk about your past. Silence and prayer will keep you safe.'

In thanks for the convent taking her, Dr Berdu gave the Mother Superior a bag of badly needed medical supplies and a large donation of money sent by SOE which was to be used as the convent thought fit. He left, assured that Jeanne was in good hands.

Meanwhile, the Germans could get nothing out of Pablo and Mercedes and ordered them to be incarcerated in the prison in Perpignan. They were told it was likely they would be shot or deported. Garcia Mendez reported this latest news from an informer in Mont-Louis citadel to don Manuel, who immediately organized an ambush on the road to Perpignan at a point where the hairpin bend could not be seen from the mountainside. Forty of his men ambushed the three trucks, which also carried other prisoners, and killed all the Germans except for a few who managed to scramble away and hide. The prisoners were released, but it was too late for Pablo. He was already dead from his wounds. Mercedes was in a terrible state, having been badly beaten. Several bones were broken and she had cuts and gashes to her body that would need urgent attention, but at least she was alive. Don Manuel personally carried her back into the mountains, where she would remain until she recovered. The rest of the men took all the weapons and blew up the trucks. A few hours later, lying propped up against a rock and too numb to shed a tear, Mercedes watched on stoically while Pablo was given a burial by el intrépid's maquis in the mountains to the chant of *Ay Carmela*. He had prospered in France, yet in his heart, he was always a staunch Republican and he would be very much missed.

It didn't take long before the Germans heard about the ambush. Now the reprisals began. The Kommandant of Mont-Louis ordered one hundred prisoners kept in incarceration in the nearby towns to be brought to the citadel. From there they were taken under heavy escort to the border town of Bourg-Madame and publicly executed. The townspeople and villagers were so scared they rarely ventured out, even to leave food out for the maquis.

CHAPTER 20

The Raid on the Villa

THE PARACHUTE DROPS had been going well, but sometime after Antonio had installed himself on the count and countess's estate, two Allied planes dropped their containers in the wrong place by mistake. The co-ordinates given were correct and it was a mystery as to why this happened as the night sky was clear. Thankfully, the containers were spotted by several young members of the fledgling Maquis de Picaussel, east of the hamlet of l'Escale near the town of Puivert. The drop consisted of three transmitters, fifty-four revolvers and twenty kilos of explosives.

This unexpected event meant that this maquis group in the locality of the Pays de Sault, not far from the count and countess's villa, was able to arm itself well. Between April and May two more drops of equipment were organized nearby. They quickly became a small but well-formed group, especially after taking in réfractaires from the area, but their good luck hung in the balance. It wasn't long before the maquisards in the area became aware that the Gestapo had decided to hunt them down. A command post was set up in a cave near the hamlet of l'Escale and while the Maquis de Picaussel waited, unknown to the network, the Gestapo received a tip-off about a villa in the area of Razès.

At the beginning of June the Gestapo decided to act. They prepared roadblocks along the main road and raided the villa. It was dark when they were spotted by a lookout who quickly notified the count and countess. Five evaders and Antonio were with them in the drawing room listening to Radio Londres when the lookout banged on the door to warn them. The evaders grabbed their belongings and fled into the woods, as did Antonio, while the maid removed any evidence of more than two people eating at the table. In the meantime, Countess Elsa changed the radio station to a local Vichy one, picked up her knitting, and pretended to be listening to music.

When the Gestapo arrived, they were greeted courteously at the front door by Count Pierre. Four men entered and the others proceeded to search the outside gardens. The evaders managed to get away and didn't stop running until the sound of barking dogs receded. Back in the villa, the Gestapo proclaimed their two reasons for being there. The first was that they had information that the couple had been aiding the Allies. The second reason was that the countess was a Jew and had broken the law by hiding it. She protested, saying that her mother had converted to Catholicism when she married her father and that she herself had been brought up a Catholic.

One of the men produced an official document. 'This states that your grandparents were Belgian Jews — Samuel and Rebecca Rosenberg, residents of Antwerp.'

Countess Elsa was shocked. 'I don't even know my grandparents. I never met them. All I know is that they didn't agree with my mother marrying a French Catholic.'

The Gestapo officer sighed. 'I am afraid this makes you a Jew, madame. As such, you are required to come with us immediately.' He turned to Count Pierre. 'As for you, Monsieur le Comte, you are an accomplice. Marrying a Jew is prohibited under French law. Get your coats.' The maid, who had been standing outside the room, heard all this and gasped aloud. The Gestapo officer heard her and sent someone to bring her into the room. 'Mademoiselle, you too will accompany us.' The maid burst out crying. The countess put her arm around her. 'It will be alright,' she whispered.

The three were driven away in the direction of Toulouse. Six Germans stayed behind to thoroughly search the house and grounds. They found no evidence of evaders but didn't miss an opportunity to steal some of the countess's jewels, silverware, and various priceless paintings and other objects. Stealing was prohibited and the perpetrators liable to severe punishment, but all knew each other well and would distribute the goods accordingly.

In Toulouse, they were first taken to Gestapo headquarters and interrogated. Several prisoners, including two Allied soldiers and one SOE agent who could barely stand from his beatings, were brought in to identity them, but said they didn't know them. The Gestapo spared the de Crispins no mercy. The situation changed when they began to interrogate the maid. She tried hard to be strong, but relented after they threatened to have her toenails and fingernails pulled out, telling them what they wanted to hear: that the count and countess had indeed helped evaders, but she had no idea where they came from, or where they went when they left. She did not reveal Antonio's whereabouts.

The Gestapo stopped the torture and sent her back to her cell to recover. The next day they brought her back again and showed her a folder of photographs. Did she recognise anyone? The maid looked carefully and each time she shook her head. 'No, I don't know him. Never seen her before.'

She was then shown a picture of Justine, who she knew as Jacqueline, and Dr Berdu, who she knew as Bertrand. The Gestapo officer was astute and noticed the flicker in her eyes. He put them to one side. When she'd gone through them all, he placed those two back in front of her.

'Think carefully, mademoiselle.' His voice was calm yet his tone threatening.

The maid was in a dilemma. Bertrand had saved many people who were wounded or ill. On the other hand, she barely knew Jacqueline. She knew she had to say something, but what? After a while, she declared that she didn't know the man but thought she might have seen the girl, although it was quite a while ago so she couldn't be sure.

'Are you telling me this girl went to the villa?' the man asked.

'I don't recall. I may even have seen her when I was in town. I can't tell you anything else.'

The officer indicated to a man standing at the side of the room to begin his work. Her wrists were tied to the chair, her shirt torn open and pulled down, and she was beaten with a whip which drew blood and formed huge welts. An electric wire was then attached to her arm and she was electrocuted. The pain was too agonizing to endure and she admitted the woman had been to the house and they knew her as "Jacqueline".

The officer offered her a glass of water. 'Thank you. That wasn't so difficult after all, was it?' The maid thought she may just have saved herself, but she was wrong. The officer ordered her to be taken back to the cell again to await sentencing. After she'd gone, he gave the photograph of Justine to a man who had been sitting at another desk typing the details of the maid's confession. 'I want a poster of this woman circulated everywhere. The reward leading to her arrest will be 500,000 francs.'

The fate of Count Pierre and his wife was swift. Countess Elsa's papers were stamped with a red J for Jew and she was sent to the internment camp at Gurs. From there she would be transferred to Drancy. Her final destination would be Auschwitz. Count Pierre was to be sent to Buchenwald Concentration Camp.

News about the fate of Count and Countess de Crispin soon reached members of the network and was met with dismay. They had been an important connection at the intersection of the escape routes. After several days in hiding, Antonio ventured back to the villa, which he found deserted and ransacked. Whatever the Gestapo could carry away, they had. He returned to his cottage, which had also been searched, pulled out the hidden transmitter, and sent an urgent message to London. They told him to lay low for a while, but Antonio knew that lives were at risk and everyone needed to be warned. He made a quick transmission to James in Mont-Saint-Jean and one to Martin in Saint-Girons. Cassou told him to make his way to the garage used as a safe house in Lavelanet. For the time being he could operate from there. The good news was that the impending Allied invasion would take place any day now.

Justine was desperate to see how he was, but Cassou refused to let her go. They had no idea how the Gestapo had a photo of her, but her face was now plastered on notice boards in villages and towns far and wide. She was a wanted woman.

'You are going to have to change your appearance and code name and make yourself scarce for a while until things cool down.' Mimi, who had become accustomed to changing people's appearances, including her own, was called in to help. Justine's hair was dyed blonde and she was renamed "Maxine". All identity papers had to be changed too. Worst of all, Cassou was forced to terminate her employment with the company. It was far too risky to keep her on. With no job, except courier work under her new name, Cassou promised to pay her rent and a weekly stipend so that she could live. Justine was used to a life in the shadows, but this was a new phase and she was terrified.

Thoroughly depressed, she rarely went out of her apartment except to get food. Whenever she passed the concierge, she wore a large headscarf to cover her hair, but he noticed blonde pieces peeking out.

'I thought I needed a change,' she said, putting on a cheerful face.

The concierge smiled. 'Ah, you want to look like Jean Harlow?'

Justine put her finger to her lips. 'Shush! If the Germans think I look like an American film star they will lock me up.' They both grinned. 'Well, *I* think she is rather sexy.' At that moment Justine felt anything but sexy.

Around this time, two members of a local maquis group kidnapped a former agent of the Deuxième Bureau now working for the German Intelligence Service, in broad daylight. The next day they attacked a Gestapo convoy on the road from Toulouse to Carcassonne that resulted in the execution of five enemy agents, including an important Obersturmführer. During this raid the maquis seized important documents which made it possible to warn several people threatened with arrest, but the successes came at a cost. Reprisals were swift, and prisoners, mostly Communists, were executed in the village squares as an example to others.

In the evening, Justine tuned her radio to the BBC. The coded messages became more frequent by the day. Like Antonio, she was sure the Allied landing was imminent. These days the BBC was playing more American music for the American soldiers, but they always began with the opening bars of Beethoven's Fifth Symphony. Its familiar opening bars represented the Morse code for the letter *V* — the symbol adopted to represent "Victory", and Justine loved it. It lifted her spirits. Lately, Radio Londres was playing more resistance songs too. It was heartening.

As the resistance prepared for sabotage and attacks throughout France, Cassou advised Justine she should leave Toulouse and go back to Mont-Saint-Jean. She was now fully trained in sabotage herself and could use a gun as well as any of her male colleagues. He felt she would be far more useful to her father and Dr Berdu as she knew the area well. Besides, her face was still plastered on the walls throughout the area. Cassou assured her that these posters must not have reached the Donezan or he would have heard by now. She begged to be allowed to stay but Cassou was worried.

'It's the safest option,' he said. 'You have become like a daughter to me and I don't want to see you go, but I'm doing what's best for you.'

That night the news came through that the Allies had landed in Normandy, and Justine quietly celebrated with her friends. Their jubilation was marred when they thought of Robert. How he would have loved to see this day.

Cassou met up with her one last time and told her it was time to leave. She could stay in Lavelanet for a few weeks and help Antonio, but she was warned to be careful as the Allied invasion would only serve to anger the Germans. She left the next day, travelling by bus and careful this time that the headscarf covered all her hair. The garage owner welcomed her and took her to an old disused building on the edge of the town where Antonio was now operating from. When she took off her scarf, Antonio gave a long wolf-whistle. She blushed, saying that he was not meant to recognise her with her new disguise. He laughed. 'After spending so many days and nights with you, I would recognise you anywhere.'

'You're not going to give me away and get the reward, are you?' It was a light-hearted joke, but he was worried for her.

'Be careful. People are astute, you know, especially when they're hungry and there's a price on your head.'

'Cassou assured me that the posters are not in Mont-Saint-Jean,' she replied. 'My parents would have let him know. They are more likely to be looking for me in the larger towns.'

'There *were* posters of you here, however. You can thank the garage owner for tearing them down before anyone had a chance to see them.'

She asked how he'd been and could tell he was as devastated as the rest of them about the Count and Countess de Crispin.

'The maid? What happened to her?' Antonio asked.

'They must have tricked her into giving information so she gave them something, thinking they would have let her go. Poor woman — makes me ill to think of it. I believe she was executed in Saint-Michel Prison. I don't know who else she gave away; she knew none of us by our real names anyway.'

Antonio brought out a bottle of wine and they toasted the Allied invasion. 'So you're going home to Mont-Saint-Jean?'

'Yes. I will carry on my courier work for them there.'

'Terrible news about the smuggler from Capcir,' he said.

Justine's eyes widened. Antonio realised that she had no idea what he was talking about. 'I thought you knew. I wouldn't have mentioned it otherwise. Didn't "X" tell you?'

'No, and I haven't been in touch with my family for months now. What's happened?'

'The Spaniard — Pablo — they caught him near the border. I heard about it from Bertrand and our radio operator there. Apparently, everyone's on edge thinking someone has infiltrated the group.'

'Where is he? Is he alright?' Justine prepared herself for the worst.

'I'm sorry to be the bearer of bad news. They tortured him so badly that he was already dead when one of the maquis groups tried to rescue him during a transfer.'

Justine held her hands over her face. 'God, no!' There was a silence for a few minutes while she took it in. 'And his wife?'

'I believe she was rescued and is in hiding.'

'Thank God for that at least.'

'I don't know any more. All I know is that it's not as quiet in the Donezan as it used to be, so be careful. If I was you, I would stay here for a few weeks until things blow over. Anyway, I can use you. You can help me find new places for parachute drops and courier a few messages. I'll let Cassou know.'

His warning had a caring tone and as much as she wanted to return to Mont-Saint-Jean, she took his advice. 'Alright, but only for a few weeks. My family will be worried about me.'

Antonio said he would message Mont-Saint-Jean immediately. A reply came back that, given the worsening situation, it was better for her to stay where she was. The few weeks that she was there, Justine once again proved to be valuable. She met members of the maquis and helped distribute guns and ammunition with the garage owner. In the evening, she cooked for Antonio. She had always hoped that their friendship might blossom into something stronger, but he told her one evening that he had a fiancée in England and that he missed her terribly. 'You and I have a special bond, Jacqueline,' he said. 'Let's not tarnish it.' She was saddened but knew he was right.

'I like to think I am a good judge of character,' she told him, 'and I was sure of you from the beginning. You are a good man. I wish you and your fiancée much happiness.'

In July, Justine left Lavelanet. Every time the bus passed through the villages of the Donezan, she looked out for Wanted posters of her. There were plenty of other posters, but not one for a "Jacqueline". She breathed a huge sigh of relief. The problem was, she now had blonde hair, though it was growing out. When she arrived home, her mother hardly recognised her. In addition to her new hair colour and glasses, she walked with a stoop, wore an old brown ill-fitting coat, and covered her head with a dowdy cotton scarf of the type the women in the village used when they did their communal laundry.

Colette was aghast. '*Ma pauvre chérie*, what on earth has happened to you?' When Justine took off her coat and scarf, she was even more shocked. 'You look terrible. You've lost weight too.' She stared at the blonde hair. 'What on earth made you do that? You had such beautiful hair.'

Justine told her what had happened. Colette too had changed. 'You've also lost weight, Maman. And your face has a grey pallor. Are you ill?'

223

Colette threw her hands in the air. 'How can I be well when I worry every single minute of the day? I cannot sleep and I'm a nervous wreck until your father comes home.'

Armand was away in Axat and Colette told her what had been taking place. Justine held her mother in her arms. She was so frail and had aged beyond her years over the past four years. One thing did please Justine though. Jeanne was no longer there.

'So, Jeanne escaped across the frontier, after all,' Justine said. 'I was beginning to wonder if she'd ever go.'

Her mother fought back the tears. 'I am afraid not. *Quelle catastrophe!* Things didn't go according to plan.'

'What happened? Please don't tell me she was caught.'

Colette shook her head. 'Because of the situation, we moved her to Pablo and Mercedes's farm. Mercedes was only too happy to have extra help. Then Jeanne became sick, vomiting every day. We guessed what the problem was — morning sickness. She'd missed her period.'

Justine froze. 'What!'

'Mercedes was the first to notice. Then she told me, and I told your father. We were all shocked. At first Théo said it was not unusual for stress to cause women to miss their periods, but when he examined her, that's when he told her she was pregnant.'

Justine's hand flew to her mouth. 'Oh no! How did it happen?'

'Something happened at the farm. She said she was raped by a German soldier stationed at the dam. It happened during the first week she was there, when Mercedes was out selling her cheese.' Justine had a hard time digesting this news. 'After the arrest of Pablo and Mercedes, she was moved to a convent near Perpignan to have the child there.' Colette became agitated. 'I beg of you, please don't bring this up with your father. He's got a lot on his mind at the moment.'

In the quiet of her room, Justine sat on her bed and thought about it. For months she had been consumed with her resistance work; now she was consumed with Jeanne again. She had sympathy for her, but the woman had always been a problem. *Pregnant*, Justine said to herself, over and over again. It was just too awful to contemplate.

The following morning, Justine found Babette waiting for her in the kitchen. After welcoming her back, she waved a bottle of brown hair dye in front of her. 'Your mother called me to help you dye your hair.' She took a good look at it and made a face. 'You were right, Colette. It looks dreadful.'

Justine had already realised she would stand out as a blond in the village and was going to do something about it, but the speed with which they'd acted took her by surprise. She felt like a child again, being bossed around.

'This is the last bottle,' Babette said. 'If only you knew how many people's hair I've dyed over the past couple of years — beards and moustaches too. So the next time the radio operator asks for something from the Allies, tell London we desperately need hair dye besides guns.' Justine saw that Babette was deadly serious. Too many evaders with a price on their head had to be disguised. Two hours later, Justine's hair was almost back to normal. 'There,' Colette said, handing her the hand mirror. 'Do you approve?'

'You did a good job, although I *was* beginning to like being a blonde.'

'Bah! In Toulouse maybe, but not here. We don't want everyone staring at you, do we?'

Her work done, Babette left to attend to the pharmacy. Justine saw her to the door. 'Your mother has missed you,' Babette said in a whisper. 'She's not well these days. Take care of her. Life — the war — we've all changed, my dear.' She cast her eyes over Justine. 'You, too, have changed. You are too thin. We'll have to fatten you up.'

'I want to ask you something,' Justine said, closing the door behind her. 'Maman told me about Jeanne. What happened? Has she had the baby?'

Colette's face stiffened. 'I gather from Théo that she has. I believe it was in the last few weeks. We were told the child was premature and stillborn. I think she is still at the convent.' She leaned closer. 'Théo doesn't like to talk about it so don't mention it to your parents.'

'I promise.' Justine was shocked. Why all this secrecy? Her instincts told her there was more to the situation than met the eye.

The next day, Armand returned. Another evader was in the forester's hut waiting to be moved on. He was noticeably upset when she told him about the Wanted posters.

'At least there are none here, Papa, so let me help you with your work. I can be just as useful to the network here as in Toulouse.'

She asked who had taken over Pablo and Mercedes's farm, the animals, and the cheese-making operation and was pleased to know it was a local elderly couple whose sympathies were with the resistance. 'They allow us to hide people there for a short time only. The farm is in good hands for the moment.'

'Tell, me, Papa. How did they find out about Pablo?'

'We don't know. It may have been bad luck. But it was Rossignol who came for Mercedes. When she wouldn't tell him what he wanted to know, he sent her away. Bastard!'

'He always had a soft spot for her. Revolting as it sounds, maybe if she had given herself to him, he would have left her alone.'

Armand didn't want to speculate. He said the Milice were out and about far more these days too. Even Rossignol was scared of them.

'And Claude? How has he been?'

'He's a good man. He supplies us with papers and informs us of things when he can, but even he doesn't always know what's going on. He asks after you, you know.'

Justine recognised the look in her parents' eyes. That you-make-a-good-couple look. She said she'd catch up with him, but as for anything else, she had no interest.

That night, as they listened to the radio, they realised the Allies were about to make a move in the South of France. Armand jotted down last minute notes on bridges, railway lines, and installations that the maquisards were to sabotage when the time came. When he'd finished, he hid it underneath the stairs as usual.

CHAPTER 21

The Beginning of the End

THE JUBILATION OF the Normandy landings in the Donezan was short-lived. The Germans and Milice sent patrols through the area to let them know the Allies in Normandy would soon be defeated and they were warned not to aid the maquis or they would be shot. The maquis were used to this kind of intimidation and anxious for the action. Armand and Dr Berdu knew just how hard it was for the chiefs to keep their men in check. Justine took an Allied soldier to Pablo and Mercedes's farm and stayed there overnight. In the middle of the night, Garcia Mendez and two of his men came to collect the man, who had been wounded in the leg. He would spend the rest of the war hiding in the caves with don Manuel's group until the south was liberated. Garcia was happy to see her. 'Señorita Marie-France! How good to see you again. What are you doing back here?' he asked.

'I'm trying to be useful. You know a woman can move about easier than a man. Adriana has told me she finds the cheese-making difficult, so I can help out here too.' She smiled. 'Keep my eyes and ears open — you know.'

Sylvain and Adriana were the elderly couple who now looked after the farm. Adriana had been the only trusted friend of Mercedes, especially after the way the locals had treated her following Louis's birth.

'Tell me, how is Mercedes?'

'She's fine. She misses her son, of course, but knows he's with good people and she will be back once the Germans have gone.' He winked at her. 'Don Manuel has a soft spot for her, you know. He treats her like a queen. You should see them dance the jota together. Wonderful!'

Justine laughed. 'From what I heard, don Manuel has a soft spot for many women.'

'Ah, that is true, but Mercedes is different. He calls her his Queen of the Mountains. She has tamed him. He no longer visits brothels in Prades and Perpignan, except to collect information about the Germans of course. We all love her. She cooks and cleans for us, tells us stories — did you know she was a good storyteller? Yes, she has us all under her spell.'

'Well, I'm glad she is well looked after. Give her my love.'

Rossignol's name was mentioned as Garcia was also aware he had taken a liking to Mercedes. 'It was common knowledge. He could have saved her if he wanted to. I would like to shoot that *bastardo* myself.'

'Don't endanger yourself. His time will come.'

'Not soon enough if you ask me.'

During the next few days, Justine saw Garcia again. Don Manuel sent his thanks for supplying them with arms. She also caught up with Claude, who told her that certain maquisards were taking matters into their own hands. Several high-profile Milice men had been abducted in broad daylight and executed. It was putting them all at risk as this prompted retaliation. In the nearby village of Mijanès, a detachment of Germans on their way to Carcassonne from the border decided to visit the village and look for escapees and resistants. They discovered a Jewish family lived there. Two young men, Simon and Alphonso, fled into the mountain to escape. The latter was killed and Simon taken prisoner. Their sister, Regine, seven months pregnant, went to meet with the soldiers to try and save her brother but was threatened with death. In an attempt to save his son, their father, Abraham, offered himself up in exchange, but they were taken away and deported to Auschwitz. It was a terrible blow for the villagers.

As a result of what took place, Rossignol pulled more hapless villagers in and threatened to send them to prison if they didn't collaborate. Without telling her parents, Justine went to the farm and asked Adriana if she could take a wheel of cheese to Rossignol as she'd heard it was his birthday.

Adriana was astonished. 'Are you mad? Why do you want to go there? Besides, he hates my cheese. He came here for it after Mercedes left and told me it was awful. "You are not a gifted cheese-maker," he told me with disdain.'

'I have my reasons and I will be careful.' Justine said. Adriana eyed her with suspicion and reluctantly agreed. 'Take as many as you like. Anything to placate him.'

Justine went into the cheese-making shed, found a good wheel, cleaned it up well, and then laid out a few vine leaves. Next, she took out her botanical sketchbook filled with pressed flowers from her bag, and searched for one in particular — *aconitum napellus*– purple monkshood. It was the only one protected by several layers of tissue paper. She took a pair of tweezers and, careful not to touch it, tore it into tiny pieces over the vine leaves. Using gloves, she rolled the cheese in the leaves and tied it in beautifully with twine. She took off her gloves and examined it. Just like Mercedes used to make, she thought to herself. She placed it in a basket, alongside four others, careful not to mistake it, and walked all the way to Formiguères, where it was market day. She set down the basket near the Hôtel de Ville where Rossignol worked and started to sell her wares.

'Excellent cheese from Matemale,' she called out. 'Only a few wheels left.'

As she'd hoped, Rossignol saw her from his window. A few minutes later he marched through the crowd towards her. 'If it isn't the woman with the fancy car,' he said disdainfully. 'I see you've left the big city and become a cheese-maker. Whatever next?'

Justine gave him a polite smile. 'I heard that the cheese Mercedes used to make is no longer what it was, so I decided to see if I could perfect it. I used to watch her.'

Rossignol stood with his legs apart, hands on his hip, and scoffed. 'Give me one, I'll soon tell you.'

'Certainly, Monsieur le Commissioner.' Justine reached in the basket and brought out a wheel. 'This is the best.'

'How much?' the commissioner asked.

'For you, monsieur, nothing. It's a gift.'

He threw her a few francs anyway and walked back into the building with the wheel of cheese under his arm. Seeing this, others wanted to buy the rest. She sold them all and left quickly. On the way back, she called in at the inn and asked for a glass of wine. She needed to steady her nerves. Within an hour, news started to circulate that Commissioner Rossignol was found slumped over his desk. Apparently, he had suffered a major heart attack. An ambulance drove by and the innkeeper poked his head out the door to find out what was happening. He was told they were taking him to Bourg-Madame to conduct an autopsy.

'Good riddance!' the innkeeper said. 'That's one less *mouchard* to deal with.'

Justine grinned and returned to the farm. By the time she reached Mont-Saint-Jean, everyone knew of Rossignol's death. Colette said that Théo was in that area and would let them know what transpired.

When Théo returned two days later, he informed them that the autopsy apparently showed signs of asphyxia. The doctors were perplexed as he had been a healthy man. He noticed Justine's huge grin. Théo knew about the plant, as it was he who told her about its poisonous properties when she first took an interest in botany. She knew it must have crossed his mind that she might have had something to do with the commissioner's death, but he didn't pursue it. They were all too happy to hear of Rossignol's demise to sully the occasion.

Soon after Justine returned, Armand, who was travelling through Capcir, was pulled over by the Milice and taken to their HQ in Bourg-Madame and held overnight, the excuse being that his travel pass was out of date. When asked why he was in the area anyway, he said he was giving private tutoring. Claude and Justine went the next day to sort it out, but knowing there were likely to be Wanted posters of her, she told him she would wait for him in a bar on the edge of town. The office of the Milice chief was grand, decked out with the Milice flag, the Vichy flag, and the swastika. Four portraits graced the entrance: Pétain; Prime Minister Pierre Laval; Secretary-General Joseph Darnand, the chief of operations and de facto leader of the police forces; and Adolf Hitler. It was like entering a temple dedicated to fascism.

After hours of waiting, Claude finally secured his release, taking the blame for his travel papers being out of date, but it was not easy. They had threatened to send him to Germany citing rumours that he had been aiding the resistance. Whether they would have done so was questionable as they could produce no evidence, but Claude had to fight hard on his behalf. 'Armand is a man of learning and literature,' he told them. 'He is well respected in the area and it is not in his nature to go against the state.' In the end, Armand was fetched from the cell and told to leave before they changed their minds. He thanked them but he was visibly shaken up.

As they left the building, they noticed a smartly dressed woman chatting with one of the local Milice. It was Alice. She blushed when she saw Claude and Armand.

'What are you doing here?' Claude asked. 'Can we give you a lift back to Mont-Saint-Jean?'

'Thank you, but I will make my own way back.' She lifted her face in a haughty manner and turned her back on them.

Justine was ecstatic to see her father and threw her arms around him. 'Dear Papa. You had us worried.'

'We have Claude to thank for my release,' Armand said. 'He's a good man.'

They told her about Alice. 'That girl is bad news,' Justine said. 'Fancy flirting with the Milice. She has no principles.'

'I think she enjoyed trying to make me jealous,' Claude replied. They spoke about it throughout the drive back, but when they arrived in Mont-Saint-Jean, there were bigger things to think about. Colette was waiting for them.

'Théo wants to see us straight away.'

They walked the short distance to Théo's house and Colette told them to go upstairs while she put the children to bed. Théo was waiting for them in the drawing room with James and Lucien. It was the first time she'd met James since his arrival and was glad to see he had been looked after well.

'Prepare yourselves for bad news,' James said. 'I've just received a message from Saint-Girons. It's about Paul Cassou.' A group from Le Parti Populaire Français raided his villa near Saint-Girons in the early hours of the morning and took him away.'

Justine felt as if her legs would give way. Cassou had long suspected he was on the wanted list, but he was a respected member of the community and it didn't seem possible. He'd always suspected it would be the Gestapo that would come for him, but this group — they were worse than the Milice.

'Apparently one of his neighbours, the local doctor heard the commotion and went to investigate. He too was taken away. Luckily his wife was away at the time.'

'Where is he?' Justine asked.

There was a terrible silence for a few minutes. 'Tell me!' Justine screamed.

'Their bodies were found in the surrounding countryside. By all accounts they were tortured and executed,' James said. 'The factory has been closed on orders of the Germans.'

Armand put his arm around his daughter, stroking her hair to calm her down. Her body shook with emotion and fear. She thought of Mimi and Jacques and everyone else in the network.

James looked despondent, as if it was his fault for being the bearer of bad news. 'As soon as we hear anything else, we'll let you know.'

Justine could not stop crying. The war was almost over. They had almost made it, and now this. She wanted to go to Toulouse but everyone agreed it was far too dangerous.

'I can't just stay here,' she replied.

'You can and you will,' Théo said sternly. 'Cassou would not want that. Besides, you are needed here.' He gave her two strong sedatives to calm her down.

Justine did not recall much after that and she slept until the next day. When she woke, she wanted to believe it was a bad dream, but that was impossible. With no more news, she became deeply depressed and did not leave the house for days at a time.

What she could not know was that certain resistance groups in the area around Saint-Girons made a list of suspected collaborators and started to kill them. The situation escalated and, in the rush to get even, mistakes were made. People started to denounce each other out of fear, and innocent people on both sides were taken away and executed. The Milice and Gestapo were rounding people up and putting them in jails and internment camps, executing them, or sending them north to Germany. The situation was made worse by maquis groups sabotaging infrastructure and Allied planes strafing the countryside in an attempt to stop the Germans heading towards Normandy. Communication was becoming extremely difficult or non-existent.

Lavelanet was surrounded by the Gestapo and Antonio escaped just in time. Alone, he returned to the cottage in the woods where he had first stayed. In the aftermath of the count and countess's capture, the villa was not only deserted, it had been pillaged again. The walls were bare and pockmarked with bullet holes, the chandeliers gone, doors hung on their hinges, windows were broken, and the drapes stolen or ripped to shreds. It was a desolate sight which made Antonio all the more determined not to get captured.

During this period, another calamity occurred. The Germans got wind of the danger posed by the Maquis de Picaussel. Because of the remoteness of the village and the difficult approach, the Germans had not wanted to venture into the area for fear of getting trapped, but when they understood the group was receiving frequent arms drops, they decided to eliminate them once and for all. After an intense fight between the two, the 11th Panzer Division was at first repelled at the Col de la Babourade, but they returned the next day with heavy armoured vehicles and tanks. The Maquis de Picaussel faced the Germans valiantly, but against such heavy weaponry, were unable to contain the attack and many maquisards were killed or injured.

Antonio got to hear of this and radioed James immediately. In the night, Dr Berdu, Armand, Lucien, and others from the maquis around Mont-Saint-Jean took off through the mountainous roads to bring the able-bodied men and their wounded back to the village. The school was converted into a field hospital where several local women — including Marie, the teacher, Colette, Babette, and Justine — attended to them. Most of the wounded were in need of operations and, under Dr Berdu's supervision, Babette, Armand, and Justine removed bullets and mended shattered bones. With the maquis defeated, the Germans returned to the area and burned and destroyed the village of l'Escale. Fearing the Germans would make more sweeping attacks, Antonio decided to go to Mont-Saint-Jean and work alongside James.

CHAPTER 22

Armand Joubert Remembers: Darkness over the Donezan

IT'S HARD TO recall those last few weeks of the Occupation. It still seems a blur. We were all in fear for our lives and lived in constant terror of reprisals. We knew the Germans were finished, but their own fear was palpable too, as was that of the Milice. I never cared about myself, but I worried about Colette; her health had deteriorated noticeably since the Occupation began. I was also worried about my daughter. She was headstrong and we had to take care that she didn't leave the village and return to Toulouse. We soon learnt that a German detachment had been deployed from Saint-Girons, and in a final blow to the village where Paul Cassou lived, systematically set fire to it. A few villagers escaped, but others were taken hostage and shot. At least one woman was raped. Somehow, a call was made to the maquis and Spanish *guerilleros*, but by then it was too late. The village lay in ruins.

I discussed this at length with Théo and we decided not to tell Justine. What good would it have done anyway? On the night of August 12 and 13, there was an ambush closer to home. Members of a maquis group ambushed a German column south of Formiguères and six Germans were killed. The Germans retaliated by taking hostages.

And then the unthinkable happened. We were at home late at night when we heard a noise outside. The house was surrounded by the Gestapo. They had come for Justine. Fear gripped us all. When we asked why, one of them showed us a copy of the Wanted poster. There was no mistaking who it was. Outwardly Justine tried to act calm, but I knew my daughter only too well. The colour drained from her face as she picked up her jacket and kissed us both, whispering in our ears that we were not to worry, she would be back soon. She walked down the garden path, two men on either side, with her head held high and got into their car.

Colette clutched at her heart, calling after her, but it was useless. Distraught, she collapsed in my arms. Théo and Babette came over immediately and stayed with Colette while I hurried to find Claude. He took me in the police car to Bourg-Madame, where she was being questioned, and pleaded for her release, stating mistaken identity. They didn't believe us. I begged to be allowed to see her and was refused. I was told that if I didn't go away, I too would be locked up, but thanks to the intervention of Claude, they allowed me to stay while they questioned her.

I had always possessed a calm demeanour — outwardly at least — yet now I was shaking like a leaf. The thought of them hurting my little girl was killing me. Claude asked what was happening and was told she was being questioned. The clock on the wall ticked loudly. Every minute seemed like an eternity. In that moment, my senses were heightened. The bright flags of Vichy France and the Third Reich; a vase of wilting bright yellow sunflowers on a desk that reminded me of Van Gogh; large posters of happy and healthy young men extolling the virtue of working in the Reich; and most of all the smell. It was the smell of fear. Only those who have been in such circumstances would know this smell — a sickly stench that pervades the very soul. After almost two hours of persistence by Claude, I was told I could see her. I was taken down a corridor to the interview room — a cramped and airless space with a window that had been boarded up. A bare light-bulb hung over the desk that separated me from my beloved child. Here, the stench of fear was even more palpable.

'You have five minutes,' the man said, in a matter of fact manner. He left us alone, making sure that the door was open and he could hear everything we said, and sat outside in the corridor smoking a cigarette.

I sat on the wooden chair and looked into my daughter's eyes. Her hands were tied behind her back and it was evident she had been struck across the face. Blood trickled from her mouth. There was so much I wanted to say but I was struck dumb. I tried to open my mouth, but the words stuck in my throat. Justine saw my dilemma and our roles were reversed. She took charge of the moment. 'I am fine, Papa,' she said. She leaned forward and continued in a whisper. 'I regret nothing, except for the pain I have brought you and Maman.'

I put my hand out to touch her but a stern voice from the corridor called out. 'No touching!'

I asked if there was anything I could do for her. The question sounded silly, and I felt ashamed. Me, a man of learning who studied words, could not find the words I wanted in our hour of need.

'Do you know what I would like now, Papa?' she said in a wistful voice. 'A crème catalane made by Maman. It reminds me of my childhood.'

We both managed a smile. How strange that such a simple thing could comfort one in an hour of need. I told her that she could eat as many as she wanted when she returned.

'I look forward to it.' A tear trickled down her cheek. 'Papa, you taught me how to live — you and Maman. For that I will always love you. Remember that. Take care of yourselves. If I know you are both well, it will keep me going.'

I wanted to ask her so many things, but all I could do was say we loved her. Everything else seemed so unimportant.

'Time's up,' the man said entering the room.

I moved to kiss her but he stopped me. I thought my heart would break into pieces. 'It's alright, Papa,' Justine said.

Another man escorted me back to the waiting room where Claude was pacing up and down like a caged animal. Upon seeing me, he put an arm around me. We were told to leave the premises straight away.

'I could not save my little girl,' I said despairingly when we were outside. 'What sort of father am I? They should have taken me, not her.'

Justine refused to give them what they wanted. Shackled and under heavy guard, she was transported to Gestapo HQ in Toulouse. After bringing in people to verify she really was "Jacqueline", she was immediately deported to Ravensbrück. It all happened so quickly that we couldn't take it in. All I know is that from that day on, we were in mourning. She had become so thin, we never expected her to survive.

The skirmishes and battles continued, and then on August 15, we heard the Allies had landed in Provence. The invasion secured the vital ports on the French Mediterranean coast and increased pressure on the German forces by opening another front. Dr Berdu was in the area collecting medicine when the US VI Corps landed on the beaches of the Côte d'Azur under the protection of a large naval task force followed by several divisions of the French Army B. The scattered German forces were hindered by Allied air supremacy and a large-scale uprising by the French Resistance and were soon defeated. They withdrew north through the Rhône valley with the aim of defending Dijon, but the Allies soon overtook them. While the Germans were retreating, the French captured the important ports of Marseille and Toulon.

Finally, the Germans ordered a complete withdrawal from southern France. Town after town was liberated and the fighting ultimately came to a stop at the Vosges Mountains. There the Allied units joined together, and despite strong resistance, ultimately pushed the Germans out of France. While inflicting heavy casualties on the German forces, in just four weeks, the captured French ports were put into operation again, enabling the Allies to bring in supplies. We were indeed buoyed that the French Allied Forces that helped liberate Toulon and Marseille consisted of large numbers of men from the Free French Colonial Infantry Division — Algerians, Malians, Mauritanians, and Senegalese *tirailleurs*. It was day of jubilation in a sea of despair.

During this time, Claude came to visit us and gave us the bad news that it was Alice who had given away Justine's identity. It seems that she had gone to Foix with her French Milice lover and recognised Justine's face on the Wanted poster. As retribution for Claude rejecting her advances, she informed the Gestapo. This fact was only discovered when a satchel containing the papers signed by hundreds of collaborators came to light at the Gestapo HQ at Bourg-Madame, which was taken over by the resistance. Alice had been paid handsomely for her information.

A meeting was held, attended by at least fifteen people of the resistance including don Manuel, on what to do about her. Most wanted her dead. The decision finally fell to me, as Justine was my daughter. I wanted her brought to justice. It was not to be. One week later, as she jauntily walked through the village square humming an Occitan folksong, a black car approached. It slowed down and someone wound down the window and called her name. When she turned to look, she was shot dead in a hail of bullets. No one knew who had done it. There were several suspects, but none were brought to account. In fear of their own lives, Alice's parents — who, it seems, had put her up to it — hastily left the village. They were spotted getting on a bus in Carcassonne, and shot in full view of the passengers. The perpetrators disappeared into the crowd.

By now, Colette was very ill. She had suffered a major stroke and lost the use of one side of her body. We had our freedom back, but at what cost? Throughout all this, Jeanne was always on my mind. Not a day passed when I didn't think about her. She had turned my world upside down. I wanted to visit her after she was taken to the convent, but Théo refused to take me. He told me it was no longer safe to travel. However, he did tell me when she gave birth. He said the child was stillborn. My heart dropped. I was so desperate to see her that I even thought of getting travel documents from Claude and going myself without anyone knowing, but that was not possible. The maquis knew me, and Théo would eventually find out. It would cause a rift in our friendship.

Due to the traumatic events taking place around us, I was forced to put her behind me. The maquis needed me. I prayed she was safe. News reached us that the Germans had blown up most of the installations before the arrival of the Allied landing in Provence. In Perpignan the ammunition dump was destroyed, taking with it warehouses and — to my horror — a convent. My heart sank. I rushed to see what Théo knew about it, but he had gone to the city the day before. I was desperate and raced upstairs, where James was hiding with his radio. 'Have you news about the convent?' I asked. He shook his head, saying the death toll was not yet known. I wanted to tear my hair out.

While I was there, I saw Claude running towards the pharmacy.

The Berdus were one of the few to still have a telephone, but the line was now disconnected. When Babette opened the door, I heard a loud scream and ran downstairs. Claude was in tears. Théo, my dear, beloved friend, was dead. He had stepped on a mine and died from his injuries hours later.

Babette leaned against the wall and slid to the floor in a state of shock. Little Marie ran crying to her mother's side as did Louis. He asked if his mother was dead too.

Claude stroked his soft black curls affectionately. 'No, child. She is well.'

Many more souls would perish the same way. Between 1943 and 1944, the Germans had mined nine thousand hectares of land. Théo's body was brought back to Mont-Saint-Jean. We had lost a hero, one of our finest, and the church was packed. People came from as far as Quillan and Foix in the north and from the border towns with Spain. I had lost my soul mate — the person who had made a man out of me.

Throughout the following months, life slowly went back to normal. The things that I once held dear — my work as a schoolteacher, literature, nature, the joy of life itself — had left me. I made three trips to Perpignan in search of Jeanne, but every time, I came back a mess. She had vanished. That part of my life was behind me and I concentrated on trying to get Colette well again. By the time the Germans finally surrendered, she was able to walk, albeit with a limp, but she never smiled again. Neither of us did. As the months unfolded and the Unconditional Surrender of the Third Reich was signed, we learned more of the terrible camps and atrocities in Germany and Poland. Working in the resistance, I was already aware of the conditions in these camps, but nothing prepared us for the inhumanity that took place.

Then one day, I was notified of several women returning to Toulouse from the German camps, including Ravensbrück. Claude offered to take me to Toulouse himself. We were there for a week as emaciated women resembling corpses were helped off the trains by nurses, but there was no sign of Justine. By now, the nurses and doctors of the Red Cross knew us. One evening, we were called into their temporary office at the end of the station and given the news. Justine had not made it. It was said that she perished of typhoid two weeks before the camp was finally liberated. The doctor pointed to her name and date of death on a long list. There she was, my darling daughter, a mere name and number, dead.

I felt numb. The voices around me seemed jumbled. It hadn't sunk in — and it never would. I knew that. I cried like a baby all the way back to the village. By the time the car rounded the corner near the cemetery and headed towards the square, the villagers were lined up in silence. Claude had telephoned the commissioner and they already knew. Their heads bowed, and the men with their caps in their hands; I could tell that my shock was their shock too. The car pulled up outside the house and I saw Colette sitting in her favourite chair staring out of the window. Babette was with her.

When I entered the house, it felt cold, devoid of emotion. Colette looked at me with such sadness that it broke my shattered heart even more. Babette left the room and Colette and I held each other in our arms.

'I am so proud of her,' she said after a while. 'At least she is at peace.'

A week later, Colette's heart finally gave out and she died peacefully in her sleep. On the bedside table was Justine's botany notebook tied in a red ribbon.

CHAPTER 23

Babette Berdu Remembers: The Last Meeting with Armand Joubert

I WILL NEVER forget the last time I saw Armand Joubert. It was in the cemetery at Mont-Saint-Jean. The cemetery is a place of solitude and I went there often, sometimes to sit and reflect, at other times to have a conversation with my beloved Théo and the ghosts of dead friends whose souls now rest in a patch of earth topped with a small wrought-iron cross, their names delicately inscribed on a cream porcelain inset. The position of Théo's grave at the corner of the cemetery has a particularly beautiful aspect and from the bench on which I sat, I could see across the pastoral lands to the mountains beyond. On the left side was the village itself, set around the brooding old château that had seen much bloodshed throughout history. I loved to view the changing seasons from here. It was particularly beautiful in early spring and summer when the gentle breeze carried with it the sweet fragrance of the flowers and blossoms.

Over the years the area has changed. The old ones have passed on, and many of the young have left, seeking better opportunities in the big cities, including my only daughter, Maria. Who can blame them? Life here used to be so hard. For much of the year, many of the houses remain empty, their occupants only returning during the holidays. The oxen and sheep no longer clog the narrow roads as they used to, and much of the agricultural land has reverted back to woodlands, forests, or orchards. I often wonder what the occupants of the château would make of it all now. Despite the hardships, we were a happy lot, meeting frequently at the various local fêtes or at church, but the war changed

242

everything. First the Great War, which left no family untouched, and then the second — the one we were sure would never happen.

I will stop my ramblings and digressions, a feature of my age, and concentrate on the story in hand. That week, I heard that the house of my good friends, Colette and Armand Joubert, was finally being sold. It had been on the market for a few years. After Colette died, Armand moved away and we never kept in touch. The day he left, he told me he wanted to forget the village and the war. It was too much for him. He was a fine-looking man when he was young, with a proud bearing — a man of learning whom the villagers looked up to. Then the war came. By the time it ended, he was as weary as the rest of us.

I'd already heard the house was being sold to an American couple, and Armand was coming back to settle the sale. The first night he arrived, I waited for a knock on my door. I was sure he would come to visit me. Nothing. I knew he was staying at the hôtel, but it was not my place to visit him there. In the morning when I was told he'd met with the buyers and would be leaving the next day, I realised he probably had no intention of contacting what few friends were still here, which was most disheartening as we had been so close. I bought a bunch of flowers and came to put them on Théo's grave. The grave next to it belonged to Colette, and I took a stem from the bunch and lay it at the base of her cross.

Afterwards, I sat on the bench under the ash tree as I normally did and said a prayer for them. That's when I spotted an old man with white hair walking towards the cemetery gates. He was carrying a bunch of roses and a plastic bag, and walked at a slow pace, as if he had difficulty with one leg. I peered through my glasses and realised it was Armand. He headed towards Colette's grave with his head down and didn't see me. He knelt down, noticed the fresh flower I had just put there, moved it away, took a bottle full of water from the bag, and poured it into the vase. Then he carefully placed the roses in it. I watched him silently, wondering whether to speak or not. I heard him mutter a prayer, kiss his fingertips, and touch Colette's name on the oval porcelain inset. When he told her he loved her, I could stand it no longer.

'Lord help us!' I cried out. 'It's too late for that. *You* killed her.'

Armand switched his gaze towards me. He looked confused. 'Babette! Is it really you? I didn't recognise you.'

'We've all changed, Armand. We've both grown old and grey, but some things remain as clear as if it was yesterday.' For the first time, I saw how drawn his face looked. I should have left well alone, but I couldn't stop myself.

'*You* killed her,' I said again. 'You destroyed her with your sordid little affair with the Parisian woman.' He looked bewildered at my tirade. 'Bah! Don't give me that look. It was evident in the way you devoured her with your eyes from the moment you brought her here. I knew it, Théo knew it, and Colette knew it. Even Justine suspected something was wrong. From the moment she entered your home, you forgot the woman who really loved you and wouldn't hear a bad word against you. Armand Joubert — the upstanding schoolmaster that everyone looked up to. Whatever were you thinking of? You risked a lifetime of pain for a moment of pleasure. Was it really worth it?'

Armand gasped for air. 'Stop! Stop! I beg you. You don't understand.' He tried to say more, but his voice faltered. It was evident his muddled brain couldn't accept that the secret he thought he alone knew had not been a secret at all.

I refused to stop. 'Yes, Colette was ill, but Théo's medicine could not cure such a sickness — or yours either. You had your head in the clouds. *She's fragile, Théo; she's too nervous, Théo; she'll never make the crossing*; *she needs more time* — always more time. Did you think we were fools?' I was shaking with anger.

'You don't understand,' Armand repeated. 'I didn't want that. I *loved* Colette — do you hear? I loved her.'

'Not enough to give *la Parisienne* up?'

Armand switched his gaze towards the mountains. 'At first, I fought against it, but there was something about her — fragility, like a beautiful, graceful swan — yet at the same time there was great passion. She was so different from most women in the villages whose lives had hardened them. She had the body and looks of a film star, and in many ways, she resembled the women I read about in my novels. Our love was a force of nature. She was my Nana, Anna Karenina, and Manon Lescaut, all rolled into one. The truth of it is that she made me feel alive and my heart soared in her presence. May God forgive me for my sin, but she gave me back what life the war was sucking out of me.'

'Don't blame the war. It's unbecoming from a man of your stature.'

'It's true. My love for Jeanne was intense — pleasurable beyond words — but it also caused me great pain, and I suffered because of it.' He paused. 'I am sorry if I disappointed you all. That only adds to my misery.'

'It'll end badly, I used to tell Théo.'

Armand struck his head with his fist. 'Enough!'

'Not until you know the truth — what really happened after she left for Perpignan.' He stared at me like a frightened rabbit caught in headlights.

'Théo knew you were the father of her child. He already suspected it and Mercedes confirmed it.'

'What are you talking about?'

'There never was any rape by a German. That was a lie.'

'How do you know? How could Mercedes say such a thing? She was away when it happened.'

'My dear Armand, you thought you were alone, but you forgot about Louis. That boy has always been smart. He was curious when you used to visit Jeanne in the milk shed and used to spy on you, so you were not as careful as you thought. He told his mother.' I could see Armand was having a hard time taking this in, but he needed to know the truth once and for all. 'It's true that Théo kept an eye on her in the convent whenever he went to Perpignan, but it's also true that she confessed to him about your relationship on the way there. That is why he would never let you go with him. She entered the convent as 'Jeanne', using her false identity papers, but the Mother Superior knew she was Jewish. When the child was born, it was advised that she give it up for adoption.'

'But...' stammered Armand. 'I thought the child was stillborn.'

'No. Théo told you that because he knew you would try and search for them. Jeanne knew that too.' Confused and distressed, Armand clutched his chest, gasping for air. 'Tell me, Armand, could you really have brought another woman's child into your home — into this village? No! You would have destroyed yourself, and your own family would have drowned in shame. No one in the village would have spoken to you again. It was not possible. What Théo did was for the best.'

By now, my anger had subsided and I felt sorry for him. I got up and walked over to him. 'The child was given to an orphanage to be adopted. One week later the convent was betrayed for hiding Jewish refugees and searched by the Vichy police and Gestapo. They pulled Jeanne aside and looked at her documents. From what I gather, after the loss of yet another child, she said she was tired of being a fugitive. She'd had enough and told them she was indeed a Jew. She and the others, including the Mother Superior, were taken away.'

I paused before I told him what finally happened to her. Even I found it hard. 'She was deported to Drancy and on to Auschwitz. Around that time, Théo also found out that Fleur had been captured after hiding out in the Jura. She too was deported from Drancy on July 31, 1944. It was the last train to leave for Auschwitz and held over three hundred children.'

Armand was crying like a baby. I wrapped an arm around his shoulders. He was so frail. 'The day Théo died, he was on his way to the orphanage to check on the child. He never made it. Sometime after the Germans left France, I went to Perpignan myself and found the orphanage, but the child had gone. I was told it had been adopted by an American lieutenant whose wife could not have children. I was assured it had gone to a good home.'

Armand looked at me with such sad eyes. 'It was what she would have wanted,' I said. 'It was the best thing for everyone. There's something else. Jeanne left a letter with the child when it went to the orphanage. It was only to be opened if the child was adopted. Théo was the only one to read it.'

'What... what did it say?'

'It gave Jeanne's real name — Hélène Weiss — and her former

246

address in Paris. It also stated that there were other siblings. The letter was short, but she did say that she was sorry not to have known her, and she wished her a blessed life, full of love. With it was a photograph of Jeanne together with her family in the garden in Paris.'

'Her — you said her.'

'Yes, Armand. She gave birth to a girl.'

My words threw him and he crossed himself. 'Lord have mercy on my soul.'

Armand's eyes filled with tears and he clutched his heart, barely able to breathe. I had never seen a man cry so much as in that moment. After giving him time to digest this news, which I knew had cut him like a knife, I told him the child was named Sarah. I felt his hand tighten.

He stared at me for a while, almost afraid to ask the next question. 'Tell me, Babette, what was the name of the family who adopted her?'

'Swartz,' I replied.

He looked confused. 'You mean... Surely not — it can't be.'

'Yes, Armand, Sarah is indeed the woman you know as Madame Goldman, the same woman who wants to buy your home. Surely you recognised the likeness? She's the image of her mother.'

Armand sat by Colette's grave as if made of stone. I prodded him. 'Armand! Speak to me. Say something.'

'Babette, will you come to my hôtel room tonight?' There was a tremor in his voice. 'Six thirty.'

'Of course. Now go and get some rest. I know this has been a terrible shock for you.'

I watched him slowly walk through the cemetery gates and up the hill. Occasionally, he steadied himself against the wall. That evening I went to the hôtel as requested. The Goldman family was just returning from a tour of the surrounding area. As I passed the mother, I felt as if I was seeing a ghost. She called out happily to her children, 'Come on, let's get ready for dinner.'

At the reception I asked to see Armand. The hôtelier rang his room. 'There's no reply.' He checked the guest letter boxes and the key was missing. 'Maybe he's sleeping.'

'He told me to meet him here at six thirty,' I said. 'Can you check again? That's not like him.'

The man gave a sigh and dialled the room again. 'I'm sorry. He's not answering.'

I was worried. This was not the Armand I knew. 'Can we check his room?' I asked.

I followed him along the red carpeted hallway and up the stairs to the first floor. The hôtelier knocked on the door. 'Monsieur Joubert! You have a visitor.'

When there was still no answer, I begged him to open the door. He was reluctant, but I was persistent. Armand was in his room lying on the bed.

'There, I told you he was sleeping,' the hôtelier said.

'Armand! Armand!' I shook him, but he was unresponsive. I felt his pulse and quickly realised he was dead.

The hôtelier ran out of the room to fetch a doctor.

It was then that I noticed a large envelope addressed to me propped up against the bedside lamp. Inside was a letter and a copy of his will.

Dear Babette,

I leave this will in your hands. After I left you, I went to see the solicitor in Mont-Saint-Jean to amend it. The estate agent was with me. It states that the house is to go to my next of kin. After what I learned today, that person is Sarah. You are the only person who can tell her the truth. She must know. I learned long ago that ignoring the truth is not good for the soul. I now realise that Théo was right in his actions. Telling me then would only have brought more unhappiness. He was a loyal friend to the very end.

A part of Sarah belongs in this village and I hope she will be as happy here as I was.

Lastly, I ask for her forgiveness. What I did, I did out of love, but it was a sin nevertheless, and for that I could never find peace.

Yours,

Armand.

An hour later, Armand's body was removed on a stretcher and put into the ambulance as the startled guests looked on. I overheard a small voice with an American accent. 'Look, Mama, it's the man whose house we were going to buy.'

Out of the corner of my eye, I saw Sarah's husband put his arm around her. 'I am sorry,' she said to him in a low voice. 'He seemed such a nice man.'

How was I ever going to tell them what happened? But I knew I must. Later that evening when they'd finished their dinner, I asked to see them alone. During the next few hours, I was able to tell Sarah about her mother, about Fleur and Albert, and about the intense love that her mother and Armand had for each other. Her shock was as great as Armand's, and through her tears, she thanked me for filling in the blanks that had haunted her.

'I will always mourn my mother's death and the fact that I never knew her,' Sarah said, 'but at least one thing is clear — I was conceived in love. That at least heartens me.'

I told them that despite what happened, Armand was a good man. What could I say? My heart was as heavy as theirs.

Michael Goldman said what a great shame it was that they never got to know Armand better. 'At least their love created something wonderful,' he said, holding his wife's hand. 'Without it, I would never have had my Sarah.'

'Can I show you something?' Sarah asked. She took a photograph out of her bag. 'This is the photo my mother left at the orphanage. Is this the woman you know as "Jeanne"?'

The past came flooding back like a tidal wave. 'Yes, my dear. That's "Jeanne".'

POSTSCRIPT

DURING THE SUMMER of 2022 I had the good fortune to spend several weeks in the Donezan, an exceptionally beautiful region of the Ariège department of the Pyrenees close to Spain and Andorra. Not only is this area a land of majestic mountains, lush alpine meadows, and mysterious Cathar castles, it was also a land of occupation and resistance during the war from 1939 to 1944. Thankfully, the area has managed to preserve its traditions and its authenticity, much of which I was able to draw upon, and a large part of its territory has been a Regional Natural Park since 2009.

Although this is a work of fiction, it is based on factual events. When I first arrived in the village of Quérigut, which for the purpose of the novel, I have called Mont-Saint-Jean, I was told that the Donezan was a relatively quiet area during the Occupation and "not much happened", yet the more I explored the region, the more I realised this was not the case. Because of its mountainous terrain, it was relatively quiet if one compares it to the larger towns and cities, but it was precisely this isolation that made it ideal as an escape route into Spain, and a perfect hideout for the maquis and evaders. Indeed, one of the most famous escape routes passed through here — the Pat Line, which operated from Paris via Toulouse, Beziers and Perpignan, and Marseille.

The Donezan is situated next to the Pyrénées-Orientales, and Quérigut is a mere forty-eight kilometres from Bourg-Madame and the border with Spain. As such, it retains a link with Catalan culture. To reach Bourg-Madame, one must travel through the forested Col des Hares towards the tiny village of Puyvalador (ten kilometres). It was here that the Germans were billeted because of the dam. This area, known as Capcir and Cerdagne, is on a high plateau, bordered by dramatic snow-capped mountain ranges. Three mountain massifs dominate the area: "Madrès" (2,479 metres), the peak of Carlit (2,921 metres), and the Canigó (2,784 metres), the latter being symbolic for the Catalans. Once one has toured this area, it is easy to see how important it was to the escape routes.

Much of the setting in the novel is based on the actual towns and villages I visited throughout this region. The entire border with Spain was regarded as a forbidden zone, and as such, was actively patrolled by Germans and French border guards who were able to travel in this plateau with ease.

The importance of the Spanish in this area is vital to understanding it. Many fled Spain at the end of the Spanish Civil War. They arrived in the thousands and were rounded up and put into inhuman internment camps, along the Mediterranean, near Perpignan, and elsewhere in France. When the Phoney War began, the Spanish were allowed to leave and many found work in agriculture or factories. As most already had fighting experience, they soon formed maquis groups. It cannot be underestimated how important the Spanish refugees were to the resistance. From the very beginning of the Phoney War, their places in the internment camps were filled with France's new "undesirables", namely Communists and foreign Jews, even though many of the latter had been in France when the Nazis came to power.

Visiting the internment camp and the new museum at Rivesaltes near Perpignan gave me a glimpse into the abject horrors of these camps, where many died before being deported. The MontCapel Hat Factory near Quillan housed almost six hundred women and children from February 8, 1939 to May 8, 1940, and the six toilets and "showers" — a mere concrete block in a tiny overgrown garden — are still there. It is a desolate and haunting reminder of the past.

During the Occupation and the roundup of all Jews, these camps filled even more. Shortly after, the deportations to the concentration and death camps in the north — Germany, Austria, and Poland — began. One thing is clear: although this region was in the non-occupied zone for a while, the German presence was intense, albeit they operated under Vichy laws. Therefore, people started to flee south beginning in

September 1939 and what began as fledgling escape operations grew into organized networks.

Knowing that these escape routes involved hundreds of helpers far and wide, I chose this story to show just how interconnected they were. My characters are composites of real-life people and how I perceived the villagers might be during this time. I was shown a video of Quérigut a year or so after the war, and this proved invaluable, allowing me to visualize the agricultural setting, the school, and life in general. It was because of this video that I decided to make Armand Joubert a schoolteacher. Being a man of learning gave him some standing in a small village. The character of Théo Berdu was greatly influenced by a doctor who moved to Quérigut with his wife during the Occupation. One doctor would serve all the villages in the Donezan and was allowed a travel pass to operate further away in places nearer to the border. Ideal for the resistance.

Although Théo is entirely fictional, the person who inspired his character was a local, Dr Marrot. Marc Penchenat's book, *Jean Marrot: VIVRE — LEBEN Quérigut 1943–45* proved invaluable as it portrays life during this period and leaves little doubt that Dr Marrot was extremely active in the resistance with both the Americans and the British, as were other villagers in the area. I was fortunate to meet with Marc, who is also from Quérigut, and over an enjoyable evening of wine, saucisson, and local cheese, he told me more fascinating tales about Dr Marrot. The incident at Mijanès is based on fact and a memorial plaque commemorating the members of the Goldblum family can be seen at the church. A stele marks the spot where their friend and fellow resistant, Alphonse Galy, was killed. It is testament to the bravery of the villagers that they kept quiet about a Jewish family living among them.

The character of Paul Cassou is loosely based on the story of Paul Laffont and the martyred village of Rimont in the Ariège, not far from Saint-Girons. I visited Rimont and its surroundings, as Saint-Girons was a starting point for escapees going to Spain from Toulouse. Laffont was a senator and president of the Ariège General Council. He supported the maquis of La Crouzette located near Rimont, and sent them large sums of money on several occasions. The Germans and collaborationists distrusted him and were aware of his importance in the community. As the maquis became more active, in 1944, the PPF (Collaborationist Action Group for Social Justice) in Saint-Girons decided to act. In mid-July 1944, Laffont was kidnapped by members of the group and taken away in the direction of Lescure. His mutilated body was discovered eight days later by a shepherd. At the time he was taken, his neighbour and friend, Dr Charles Labro heard noises and went to investigate. He too was taken and suffered the same fate.

The murderers were identified, but the Sipo-SD prevented their being arrested or interrogated by the French police. These two murders only made the resistance more defiant. On the morning of August 21, the people of Rimont hoisted the French flag, only to find that a detachment of Germans, including a fierce group of soldiers the locals referred to as "the Mongols" (largely Muslim Central Asians recruited in the Soviet Union) had left Saint-Girons, headed for Rimont. When they reached the village, they systematically set fire to it. It has since been rebuilt and one can walk down the main street and see photographs of the aftermath. Paul Laffont's house still exists. On the wall outside, a plaque reads: "Here lived Paul Laffont (1885–1944), deputy, senator, of Ariège, Minister of PPT under the Third Republic executed on July 13, 1944". The names of those killed in the subsequent attack appear on a nearby monument for the victims of the collaborationists and the Germans, alongside a stele mounted with a bust of Laffont which reads: "Paul Laffont. Deputy Senator of the PTT martyr of the Resistance". An avenue in Saint-Girons is also named after him. He was recognised as a resistant internee No. 1207.00889.

Today, it is possible to walk The Chemin de la Liberté in the footsteps of the escapees and smugglers. The route starts at the bridge in Saint-Girons and finishes in Esterri d'Àneu in Spain. Inaugurated on July 8, 1994, it received the label of the President of the Republic as part of the fiftieth anniversary of the landings and the liberation of France. Along this route, three stelae and thirteen plaques testify to past actions and ensure the memory of the Escapees of France. One of them is dedicated to Louis Barrau, a nineteen-year-old smuggler, shot by the Germans while trying to flee after the fire in a barn where he had found refuge. It shows how young and fearless some of the smugglers were.

The story of the Maquis de Picaussel is well-documented, and the events in the book did indeed take place. Due to the terrain, it was difficult for the Germans to attack them as the hairpin bends through the forested mountainside are ideal for ambushes. Nevertheless, they continued to pursue the maquis, and after a battle in which ten were killed and twenty-five injured, the village of l'Escale was burned in retaliation on August 9, 1944. I was fortunate to be taken by a friend to visit the small museum there — Maison du Maquis at l'Escale — where explanatory boards document the rise of the Maquis de Picaussel, the people involved, and the destruction of the village. Many of the wounded were taken to Quérigut and cared for in the schoolhouse. L'Escale is in the area of Razès and borders Quercorbès and the plateau of the Pays de Sault, a quiet place ideal for parachute drops, and a central point for networks operating between Toulouse, Saint-Girons, Foix, Carcassonne, Quillan, Narbonne, Perpignan, and Quérigut. It for this reason that I chose to set Count and Countess de Crispin's villa in this area.

The Chapelle Notre Dame de Villeneuve in Capcir does indeed exist, and is filled with a collection of votive offerings from the parishioners, some of which are well over a hundred years old.

Lastly, I would like to thank the villagers of Quérigut and La Pla for their generous hospitality in welcoming me into their homes, and for tirelessly showing me around the area and giving me snippets of information that have enriched the novel. Without them, this novel would not have been possible.

ALSO BY THE AUTHOR

The Song of the Partisans

The Viennese Dressmaker

The Secret of the Grand Hôtel du Lac

The Poseidon Network

Conspiracy of Lies

The Blue Dolphin

Code Name Camille (Novella)

The Embroiderer

The Carpet Weaver of Uşak

Seraphina's Song

Website:

www.kathryngauci.com

To sign up to my newsletter,
please visit my website and fill out the form.

255

AUTHOR BIOGRAPHY

Kathryn Gauci is a critically acclaimed international, bestselling, author who produces strong, colourful, characters and riveting storylines. She is the recipient of numerous major international awards for her works of historical fiction.

Kathryn was born in Leicestershire, England, and studied textile design at Loughborough College of Art and later at Kidderminster College of Art and Design where she specialised in carpet design and technology. After graduating, she spent a year in Vienna, Austria, before moving to Greece to work as carpet designer in Athens for six years. There followed another brief period in New Zealand before eventually settling in Melbourne, Australia.

Before turning to writing full-time, Kathryn ran her own textile design studio in Melbourne for over fifteen years, work which she enjoyed tremendously as it allowed her the luxury of travelling worldwide, often taking her off the beaten track and exploring other cultures. *The Embroiderer* is her first novel; a culmination of those wonderful years of design and travel, and especially of those glorious years in her youth living and working in Greece. It has since been followed by more novels set in both Greece and Turkey. *Seraphina's Song*, *The Carpet Weaver of Uşak*, *The Poseidon Network*, and *The Blue Dolphin: A WWII Novel.*

Code Name Camille, written as part of *The Darkest Hour Anthology: WWII Tales of Resistance*, became a **USA TODAY** Bestseller in the first week of publication.

The Secret of the Grand Hôtel du Lac became an Amazon Best Seller in both German Literature and French Literature.

Both *The Secret of the Grand Hôtel du Lac* and *The Blue Dolphin* received **The Hemingway Finalist Award 2021**

The Poseidon Network received The Hemingway Award 2020 – 1st Place Best in Category – Chanticleer International Book Awards (CIBA) 20th Century Wartime Fiction.

The Viennese Dressmaker received The Hemingway Award 2022 – 1st Place Best in Category – Chanticleer International Book Awards (CIBA) 20th Century Wartime Fiction and The Coffee Pot Book Club Book of the Year Award - Gold Medal 2022

The Song of the Partisans received the Readers' Favourite 2023 Gold Medal Award for Military Fiction.

Made in the USA
Las Vegas, NV
04 January 2024